TOBY POTTS

IN THE TEMPLE OF GLOOM

By David Osborne

To my dear friends Sue,
Charlie,
with Love,
David
Dec '06

This is a fictional work. The characters portrayed are either the product of the author's imagination or they are used entirely fictitiously. Any resemblance to persons, living or dead, is entirely coincidental.

David Osborne © Copyright 2006

British Library Cataloguing In Publication Data

A Record of this Publication is available from the British Library

ISBN 1846854830
978-1-84685-483-5

First Published 2006 by

Exposure Publishing, an imprint of Diggory Press,
Three Rivers, Minions, Liskeard, Cornwall, PL14 5LE, UK
WWW.DIGGORYPRESS.COM

To Sally

My Rock and My Inspiration

DAVID OSBORNE

David Osborne is a barrister, author, public performer and keynote speaker. In 1991 he hit the headlines nationwide and made legal history when he delivered his final speech to the jury entirely in verse. For this *tour de force* he was dubbed the Barrister Bard.

He followed this with the publication of a short humorous book on advocacy entitled **No Holds Barred** written under the pseudonym of **Ivor Bigg-Wigg QC.**

Since then he has appeared on television and radio, and has written a number of articles of topical legal interest for the national and regional press as well as various journals.

In the recent past, he has written and presented two legal revues, both to full houses.

The author is married with four children, and lives in Somerset.

www.david-osborne.com.

FOREWORD

By the Right Honourable Lord Derry Ayr of Langsyne

It was a brave and typically selfless act on my part to hand on the Seal of State to whatsisname, and those who might be tempted to suggest that I was asked to resign are the perpetrators of a gross calumny. Since leaving high office to spend more time with my pension, I have undertaken a number of charitable works (for a modest fee and expenses), whilst at the same time keeping abreast with all the latest developments in the criminal law, a subject about which I know absolutely nothing. This admission, however, is not for public consumption, as I pride myself on having an informed opinion on everything and anything.

With this in mind, the publishers of David Osborne's new book, fetchingly entitled **Toby Potts in the Temple of Gloom** have asked me to pen a short foreword in return for a substantial donation to my favourite good cause, which happens to be me, together with an anonymous interest free loan to Labour Party funds. After anxious consideration, I have agreed to do so. No doubt with the stamp of my imprimatur upon this shoddy tome, sales will rocket out of all proportion to its literary merits, but you have been warned.

I am old and wise enough to remember the good old days of Marshall-Hall and F.E. Smith, two of the great luminaries of the legal profession who had the privilege of numbering me amongst their closest friends. When they spoke, the earth shook. When they wove their magic spell, juries swooned and matronly ladies of indeterminate pedigree who should have known better unbuttoned their under garments and threw them at their feet. Heady days indeed, but where are today's legal luminaries amongst the dross who wash aimlessly around the courts in their crumpled off the peg suits and scuffed shoes, braying endless verbiage in their regional dialects and moaning constantly about the ever decreasing level of legal aid?

On any view, I have had a brilliant career, first as an advocate, then as Queen's Counsel, elevated to the Peerage, and not a day too soon, and finally as a selfless public servant, devoting myself in my quiet self-effacing way to affairs of state, dragging my less fortunate colleagues from the slough of despond to the bright uplands of intellectual enlightenment, advising one and all, and never counting the cost. And what thanks do I get? You may well ask.

The celebrations at the start of the new millennium, personally supervised by me, are now but a distant memory, but I will never forget the unalloyed pleasure of Her Majesty, who has the privilege of numbering me amongst her closest friends, as I guided her gently but firmly through the various tasteless exhibits and other distractions of numb crunching banality in a large tent somewhere downwind of the Palace of Westminster, and yes, the dome *was* a good thing, unless and until I revise my position, and the Prime Minister, who has the privilege of numbering me amongst his closest friends, has my unequivocal support in his bold decision to press ahead when the faint hearted counselled caution and a cold *douche* of economic reality.

But I digress, which I'm allowed to do because I'm tremendously important and will not tolerate any interruptions.

The task of penning a foreword has not been an easy one for a number of reasons. Firstly, what I have heard of David Osborne does not bode well, and from all accounts he sounds like a complete bounder. My staff have researched his voluminous file and have no hesitation in concurring with my initial appraisal as they do with all my initial appraisals. After all, that's why they continue to enjoy my munificence and patronage. Nobody marches out of step in my little army of advisers, spin doctors and sycophants.

Secondly, my researchers inform me that David Osborne is also the author of **No Holds Barred** written under the pseudonym of **Ivor Bigg-Wigg QC.** Very witty, I'm sure, but We are not amused. No wonder the Lord Chancellor of the day, and I forget his name, put it on his list of obscene publications. That poisonous little book on the art of advocacy, which I thumbed through the other day, is just the sort of nonsense designed to bring our noble profession into disrepute, and this is something up with which I will not put. The fact that I never once addressed a jury in all my years at the Bar does not disqualify me by as much as one jot from holding myself out as the leading authority on the subject, and I so rule. I mean, anybody who describes High Court judges as looking like grumpy pantomime dames needs a damn good thrashing, and my advisers are happy to oblige. Penelope from the typing pool comes highly recommended, although, I hasten to add, this is only hearsay.

But back to the plot, which is more than I can say for **Toby Potts.** In a word, it's complete drivel, and leaves me absolutely cold, an emotion totally out of character to my warm and generous nature, and, as I am fond of saying, to know me is to love me.

According to the two page summary in front of me, the book recounts the adventures of a journeyman barrister named Toby Potts, hence the title. I didn't get where I am today without spotting the obvious. By all accounts, Potts is a total moron, bumbling from one case to another and making a complete horlicks of the lot. My advice to him, and others of a similar persuasion, if you want to climb the greasy pole to fame and fortune, is to pucker up and kiss arse. It worked for me in my early days as an aspiring barrister, but then, I had a certain style and gravitas which set me apart from lesser mortals. The book also lays bare the arcane and archaic rights of passage at the Criminal Bar, but quite what Jo Public needs to know about them is beyond me, and positively dangerous. I have always subscribed to the belief that, when dealing with the *sans lavés*, ignorance is bliss. After all, it is the only reason why I put up with trial by jury.

If you are one of the many who browse in Waterstones or the book department of W.H. Smith, for goodness sake put this book back on the shelf and buy instead a copy of my autobiography, fetchingly entitled **A Law unto Myself.** A much better read. Buy one copy, and get the second one half price. An offer you can't refuse, as I have never knowingly sold myself short. I have no hesitation in recommending it to you, and who knows, if, *per ardua ad astra,* you make it to the top of the greasy pole, you may have the privilege of numbering me as one of your closest friends, and I say that in all sincerity. Who could ask for anything more?

Derry Ayr of Langsyne,
House of Lords.

CHAPTER ONE

TOBY COMES OF AGE

*All of us know there's no better way of exercising
the imagination than the study of law. No poet ever
interpreted nature as freely as a lawyer interprets the truth*

(Jean Giraudoux)

"I do hereby call you to the Bar and do publish you utter barrister."

The Master Treasurer of the Honourable Society of Gray's Inn took Toby's outstretched hand, shook it limply, and turned to the next student. Poor old buffer, thought Toby, not long for this world, as he made his way back to his seat, hot and uncomfortable in his white tie and tails, and looking for all the world like a tailor's dummy.

In spite of the heat and discomfort, Toby was barely able to contain his excitement. In those few short words, he had been transformed from chrysalis to butterfly. Question though, would it be cabbage white or red admiral? Only time would tell, but Toby had no doubts. The legal profession, one of the oldest and most revered in the civilised world, was about to be shaken to its very foundations. How he envied those whose good fortune it would be to instruct him in their cause, to fight the good fight and emerge triumphant or, *tant pis,* to be comforted in the knowledge that their life savings had been well spent.

Only dimly aware of the ritual unfolding around him, Toby's thoughts wandered back to that fateful day when he took his first hesitant steps on the long and tortuous path towards a career at the Bar. He was in the lower sixth at school when old 'tripod' Biddle, the Head of Physics, who also doubled as the Careers Master, organised a symposium in the Great Hall. Various stalls were set out to promote

11

suitable careers for the sons of gentlefolk, and Toby and his friends washed aimlessly around them in the best traditions of gormless adolescents without a single creative thought between them. It must have been a depressing sight for all those old boys who had taken the time and trouble to enlighten them in return for drinks and lunch with the Headmaster and Governors.

The sciences were conspicuous by their absence, as they were considered akin to trade and wholly unsuitable, all grubby white coats with rows of cheap ballpoint pens in the breast pocket, lined up according to colour and height. Banking was represented, but only just, by some grey little man in an equally grey suit, horn rimmed spectacles perched menacingly on the end of his aquiline nose, and looking for all the world as if he were about to refuse an overdraft, so he was studiously ignored.

Farming filled Toby with dread. Up with the sparrow's fart, humping huge bales of hay and being jolly to the peasants, was hardly his idea of a good time. He could just about handle the Range Rover and green wellies, but he wasn't ready for a life of pastoral torpor married to some hearty ruddy faced county gel with enormous fetlocks and a Princess Anne headscarf. Medicine and dentistry were quickly relegated to the back burner. The sight of blood made Toby sick, and the thought of looking into somebody else's mouth for the rest of his working life was a fate worse than death.

Toby was just about to wander off and resign himself to an agreeable life of debauchery when Old Biddle bounded over and took him gently by the arm.

"Hello, Potts," he chirped, "seen anything you fancy?"

"Frankly, sir, not a lot."

"Then take my advice. If you can't find a proper job, go into the law."

From little acorns, mighty oaks do grow, and the seed was sown.

During the holidays, Toby mentioned his nascent interest to his father.

"Splendid idea, my boy," he beamed indulgently, "a good solicitor is the pillar of the community and highly respected."

"Well, actually, I was thinking of becoming a barrister."

"Good God, whatever for? They're pompous upper class idiots in fancy dress, who talk the hind leg off a donkey and charge the earth for saying bugger all. What you need is a proper job," and that was his last word on the subject.

Toby's determination to qualify as a barrister surprised even him, and he was not to be deflected. Once at University, he joined Gray's Inn as a student member and threw himself enthusiastically into the ritual of dining in Hall.

He was never to forget his first dinner. He'd arrived early to soak up the atmosphere, and as he walked into South Square, he stood for a few moments gazing up in wonder at the Georgian facades, behind which he could imagine learned counsel poring over grave and weighty opinions as they prepared for their next High Court appearance. This was the stuff of which dreams were made, and he was soon to be a part of it.

As the Hall doors were open, he made his way inside, to be intercepted by the Under Butler who, judging from the expression on his face, took him for a tourist.

"May I help you, sir?"

"I'm here to dine," Toby replied, feeling rather grand.

"Not without a gown, sir." His manner was dismissive.

Following his directions, Toby made his way to the cloakroom, selected the first gown that came to hand and returned, chastened but unbowed, to join the queue that had formed in his absence. As he waited, the Head Butler, resplendent in a purple frockcoat trimmed with gold braid and important enough to be addressed in Capital Letters, caught his eye and walked smartly over.

"Kindly follow me, sir," he said, plucking him from relative obscurity as he began to escort him to the top table. Flattered as he was by the Head Butler's solicitude, Toby had a mounting sense of foreboding as two hundred pairs of eyes followed his progress the length of the Hall.

"May I enquire when you were called, sir?" he asked as they reached the top table. Toby felt the blood rushing to his cheeks.

"I think there's been some mistake," he stammered foolishly, "I'm a student member."

"A student member?!?" repeated the Head Butler, doing a passable impression of Lady Bracknell, "then pray tell me why you are wearing a barrister's gown?"

Toby was escorted back the length of Hall like some common criminal, hoping against hope that the ground would open and swallow him up. The cloakroom attendant, too little too late, helped him select an inferior student's gown, and he was eventually seated on the bottom table near the door where the Head Butler could keep an eye on him. He had already been branded a troublemaker, but there was worse to come.

Toby had barely recovered his composure when three loud bangs of the gavel brought the assembled multitude to their feet. A pair of ancient doors swung open behind the top table, and a parade of octogenarians filed slowly into Hall.

"Who are they?" whispered Toby in a spirit of enquiry.

"Benchers," replied the know-all to his right, "retired judges and barristers who've long since passed their sell-by-date and who sit around all day drinking port and waiting to die." Toby nodded appreciatively.

After grace, in Latin of course, everybody sat back down again and the meal was served. As ill luck would have it, Toby found himself seated as head of his Mess. Each Mess consisted of four students, and in front of him was placed a sheet of paper. On this he was required to list the names of the other three students who formed his Mess, as well as the names of the four students above him forming the Upper Mess, and the names of the four students below him who formed the Lower Mess. At an appropriate moment, somewhere between the brown Windsor soup and the lamb cutlet, Toby had to ask permission of the Head of the Upper Mess to toast their Mess, each and everyone by name, but not before each and everyone had toasted each and everyone else in his Mess, and then repeat the performance with the Lower Mess. The Upper and Lower Messes would then toast each other and then Toby's Mess in return, and in this way each and everyone drank a lot of wine and ate precious little of the rapidly congealing cutlet. The upward learning curve was almost vertical, but Toby got there in the end.

After dinner, there was to be a debate in Hall, and once the octogenarians had tottered out to their decanters of port and cigars, Toby sat back exhausted to await the evening's entertainment. The President of the Debating Society introduced the speakers and then turned to the motion.

"The motion for tonight's debate," he announced over the hubbub of conversation, "is that this House deplores sexual discrimination at the Bar, and I now call upon Clarissa McCarthy to speak in favour of the motion."

A big girl with pursed lips and hair in a tight bun rose heavily to her feet.

"Gerr 'em off!" bellowed some lout at the back to roars of approval from his male companions, and the debate rapidly degenerated into farce. So much for the cut and thrust of rapier like wit. Toby stuck it out to the bitter end and then, just before ten, the Under Butler mercifully brought the proceedings to an end by turning off the lights. It was a memorable introduction to the arcane ceremony of dining in Hall.

The gavel shook Toby out of his reverie as two hundred newly called barristers rose noisily to their feet. "Members of Hall," intoned the Master Treasurer, "the toast is Domus." This was the first of many toasts that had one and all up and down like a pair of tart's knickers. They toasted each other, Gray's Inn and Good Queen Bess, got drunk on port, sang songs and did silly things as they rung down the curtain on their student years. Tomorrow was another day, and the beginning of a voyage into uncharted waters.

CHAPTER TWO

TOBY AND PUPILLAGE

God doth not need
Either man's work or his own gifts, who best
Bear his mild yoke, they serve Him best, his state
is kingly. Thousands at his bidding speed
and post o'er land and ocean without rest;
they also serve who only stand and wait.

[John Milton]

After an agreeably long summer vacation, too long by several weeks for his father's liking, Toby began the search for pupillage. He boasted no legal background or connections, so he had to start from scratch. His father was an accountant, good enough to earn a reasonable living in a solid rather than spectacular way, but then, as Toby surmised, accountants by definition were like that, not given to peaks and troughs except when they got the decimal point in the wrong place.

His mother was a sensitive and rather delicate flower, very much an orchid in a nettle bed, marrying her first true love and settling down comfortably to a life of domestic bliss. She had seen little of the world before making the ultimate sacrifice, but with few regrets. Toby was her only child, a decision she made after a difficult birth, and one accepted with equanimity by her husband. Her real passion in life was collecting Toby jugs, and what more natural than to indulge her passion when naming her first born. The fact that her son and heir had protruding ears was incidental to her choice of name and nothing more than an unfortunate coincidence. At least she didn't name him Jeremy, and for that Toby was exceedingly grateful.

Gray's Inn, forward thinking as ever, had appointed a Master of Students, whose task it was to place newly qualified members with suitable pupil masters. The Bencher who had drawn the short straw had had a distinguished career at the Chancery Bar, and was now seeing out his twilight years on the High Court Bench, so he was right at the cutting edge of youth culture. Toby made an appointment to see the great man.

"And have you chosen your field of specialisation?" he asked with no visible sign of enthusiasm, as he peered through his half moon spectacles at Toby's application form.

"Yes, Master, I'd like to specialise in crime."

"Good God, whatever for?" His expression was one of disbelief.

"I rather fancy the cut and thrust of advocacy," Toby replied brightly, "defending the innocent, the down trodden, the oppressed, holding high the sword of…….."

"Yes, yes, quite so," he interrupted rather testily, "although in my experience, they're all as guilty as sin. I'll do what I can, but frankly, I don't know any criminal barristers." Toby got up to go. "You're not a socialist by any chance, are you?" he asked as Toby was leaving. Not an auspicious start.

Toby's name was duly entered on the Register, and a fortnight later, he received a letter inviting him to meet one Lionel Berger in his Chambers in the Temple, promptly at nine in the forenoon, with a view to a possible pupillage. He arrived with ten minutes to spare, found Hare Court after a number of false starts, and marched purposefully up the stairs to the clerks' room.

Hare Court, unlike many parts of the Temple, had been spared the worst excesses of the Blitz, and remained as a lasting testament to late Georgian early Victorian architecture - functional without being ostentatious. Stone floors and stairs, off white tiles and cast iron balustrades were as they were when Hare Court opened for business all

those years ago. It looked and smelled like a converted public
lavatory.

There were four clerks serving the best interests of eighteen barristers,
seated in a cold and cheerless room at desks which mirrored their
seniority and importance. After establishing his credentials, Toby
wedged himself between two antediluvian filing cabinets to await his
prospective pupil master's pleasure.

At a quarter past nine, the senior clerk interrupted his call to his
bookmaker and glanced towards Toby. "Mr.Berger will see you now.
Jason will show you to his room."

Jason was a sixteen year old youth with tea stained hands who had his
foot on the first rung of the ladder to fame and fortune, and whilst
waiting for the call to come on up, had to content himself with the role
of Chambers gopher. Every chambers had one, they were like
mascots, some luckier than others. Toby followed the boy along a
gloomy corridor to a back room, which Berger shared with two others.

Seated behind a tiny desk was a grey haired man of advancing years
and diminutive stature with pink, well scrubbed features and a large
pair of gold-rimmed spectacles. Judging from the substantial deposits,
dandruff was a major social problem, which, with commendable
fortitude, he had chosen to ignore. He was dressed in pinstripe
trousers, worn permanently at half-mast, black waistcoat and jacket, a
somewhat Dickensian figure with overtones of Uriah Heap. Toby had
to admit that his first impressions of Berger and his Chambers fell far
short of what he'd imagined, and the pervading air of seediness was a
serious depressant. But then, as this was the first criminal barrister
he'd ever met, perhaps they were all like that.

"Thank you, Jason," said Berger in a high-pitched voice as the youth
retired. "You must be Potts," he continued, sharp as a sausage, "and
you're looking for a pupillage in crime."

Toby's first inclination was to deny any such ambition and return, cap
in hand, to the Master of Students for an in-depth reappraisal, but that

would have been defeatist, and pupil masters, good, bad or indifferent, were hard to come by.

"Yes, indeed," Toby replied with as much enthusiasm as he could muster in the circumstances.

"Good, good," he nodded, clasping his small, chubby hands over his stomach, "if you'd like to start on Monday, phone the clerks and they'll tell you where to find me." He stood up and consulted his watch, rather like the White Rabbit in Alice in Wonderland. "Now I must be on my way or I'll be late for court," and so saying, he gathered his wits and papers, not necessarily in that order, before scurrying off.

The interview was over, and in those few short minutes, Toby had wed himself to a complete stranger for the next six months.

In reflective mood, Toby made his way slowly up Chancery Lane to Ede & Ravenscroft, Robemakers to the profession since 1683. Like a Matador donning his Suit of Lights, he was transformed from head to toe by an unctuous assistant smelling strongly of mothballs. The list of apparel, like the bill, was enormous. Two pairs of pinstriped trousers, two black jackets with matching waistcoats, six white collarless shirts, six white starched day collars, six white starched wing collars for court, six white pairs of bands, two sets of collar studs, one barrister's gown and finally, one snowy white wig with personalised box which had to be specially ordered and would take at least three weeks.

One last stop before returning home to prepare his father for the shock was Butterworth's Law Bookshop in Bell Yard, where Toby purchased the latest edition of Archbold, the criminal practitioner's bible and an indispensable tool for the successful advocate. Booted, kitted and spurred, he was ready to do battle with the best of them.

CHAPTER THREE

TOBY AT THE BAILEY

Here stands one who meant well,
tried a little, and failed much:
surely that may be his epitaph

[after Robert Louis Stevenson]

In breathless anticipation, Toby phoned Berger's Chambers.

"Mr. Berger will be at the Bailey on Monday," mouthed the senior clerk in between mouthfuls of tea and ginger nut crunchies, "so if you care to meet him in Chambers at nine o'clock sharp, he'll walk down with you."

Toby put down the phone with a frisson of excitement as he contemplated his first day in pupillage, and at the Bailey no less. The Bailey, or more precisely, the Old Bailey, was the highest criminal court in the land, and had been since 1673, where murderers, rapists, felons and petty criminals were prosecuted, convicted and then taken to a place of execution to be hanged by the neck until dead, and may God have mercy on their souls. The guilty and innocent alike, man, woman and child, were charged, condemned and dispatched to their Maker by Judges, cast in the mould of Pontius Pilate, who had only a passing acquaintance with the law, and who went about the more pleasurable business of eating and drinking and fornicating without a moment's reflection on the plight of those less fortunate than themselves. Juries were threatened, cajoled and suborned into returning guilty verdicts regardless of the evidence, and those who had the temerity to kick against the prick were kept without food, or drink, or heat, or any creature comfort, until they saw the error of their ways.

Toby was as nervous as a kitten all weekend, and greatly relieved when the great day dawned. He was awake to greet it, which was just as well. It took him over an hour to strap himself into the starched white collar, which was as stiff as a board and totally unyielding. Once locked into place, Toby found it impossible to turn his head independently of his body, attracting a number of very strange looks and a helping hand across the road from an elderly lady as he made his way to the Underground. Hot and bothered, he alighted at the Temple and hurried along to Hare Court. Berger was there to greet him, and after the briefest of polite exchanges, they set off down Fleet Street to walk the short distance to the Bailey.

The security in these parlous times was impressive, if somewhat heavy handed. After all, Toby was a fully qualified barrister, but that cut no ice at all, as he was searched, x-rayed and patted down before being allowed into the main building. From there they made their way to the fourth floor and the relative sanctuary of the robing room.

This was the moment Toby had been dreading all morning. He had to release himself from the starched white day collar and replace it with an equally starched wing collar and bands. To avoid attracting attention to himself, he kept moving around the room as if deep in thought. His very smart Gray's Inn tie was the first obstacle. In his efforts to remove it from the vice like grip of the collar, it became firmly knotted around his neck and the loop was not quite wide enough to lift it over his head, as Toby discovered when he attempted the manoeuvre. It looked to the innocent bystander, a rare commodity at the Bailey, as if he'd decided to end it all. Next came the problem of trying to separate the collar from its restraining stud. The two were locked together in mortal combat, and it took all his strength to prise them apart. Toby's composure was slipping by the minute, but fortunately Berger had shuffled off to the lavatory and was not witness to his pupil's discomfort. At last, with numb and aching fingers, the offending restraint, like a medieval garrotte, was torn from his neck and he collapsed, exhausted, into a chair.

The reverse performance with the wing collar had barely begun when Berger, refreshed and ready for the day's drama to unfold, poked his head round the corner.

"I'll go ahead," he whined in that high pitched whine of his, "we have a clear start in Court One, and I want to check if all our witnesses are here." Toby nodded with difficulty. "Don't be late."

Easier said than done, as Toby returned to the uneven struggle.

"Having trouble?" Toby turned round to see a tall, distinguished man with a friendly face smiling indulgently in his direction.

"I'm afraid so. I can't seem to get the hang of this collar."

"Let me help," and his saviour, with years of practice, soon had Toby battened down and laced up. "You must be a pupil," he continued, standing back to admire his handiwork.

"First day," Toby confessed.

"Never mind," he replied, "it can only get worse. Who's your pupil master?"

"Lionel Berger."

He chuckled. "Known affectionately in the profession as Ham Berger, but don't tell him I said so. He's not renowned for his sense of humour." He glanced up at the clock. "You'd better get going, it's nearly half past ten. Good luck," he added, and with that, he swept majestically out of the robing room.

Donning his snowy white wig and black, well pressed gown, Toby made his way purposefully and with as much expedition as the dignity of his profession would allow to the ground floor and thence, after helpful directions from a passing usher, to Court One. Opening the door as quietly as possible, he tiptoed in and glanced around for Ham, who was nowhere to be seen. To his left were rows of seats occupied by members of the public, and to his right, more seats, fortuitously unoccupied, and as Toby was beginning to feel conspicuous, they seemed as good a place as any to sit and observe the trial process. Barely had he sat down when a loud bang of the gavel announced the arrival of the judge.

"All rise," intoned the judge's clerk, as the judge emerged from behind the impressive solid oak throne to take his seat in the place of judgment. As Toby was later to discover, this was no less a personage than the Honourable Mr. Justice Boniface, known to one and all as Old Sour Puss, and one of Her Majesty's High Court Judges. He wore a robe of scarlet red, fetchingly trimmed with ermine, and clutching a pair of white gloves. A small wig perched precariously on his bald pate, which nearly slipped off as he bowed to the court. Pink, fleshy and bejowled features glared out at the assembled multitude, only breaking into a fleeting and wintry smile as he acknowledged defence counsel.

The court clerk rose, as did the Defendant. "Are you Sir Adrian Browne?" he asked in a loud and pompous voice.

"I am," came the reply. Toby glanced over at the dock to see the former Director of Public Prosecutions and the object of intense press and media speculation, a dignified man with greying hair, standing composed with head held high, staring straight ahead as the gentlemen of the Press began scribbling feverishly. This was very exciting indeed.

"Sit down." Mr. Justice Boniface glowered at Ham "Is this to be a trial, Mr…" he glanced down at the slip of paper containing the names of counsel, "Berger?"

"It is indeed, my lord," replied Ham confidently.

"So be it," he said, with no discernable enthusiasm, "then summon the jury panel."

It took a good ten minutes for the jury panel to assemble in court, brought as they were from the catacombs of the building usually reserved for filing cabinets, refuse disposal and miscellaneous. As they stood, blinking in the cold light of the court, and totally disorientated, Mr. Justice Boniface glanced over to Toby, and then back to Berger.

"Mr. Berger," the Judge's voice was dripping with sarcasm, "whilst the Secretary of State for Constitutional Affairs, in his infinite wisdom, has seen fit to include members of the Bar on the jury panel, I know of no regulation requiring them to appear fully robed."

Ham leapt to his feet, shot a glance over to Toby, coloured visibly, and started to jerk his head uncontrollably in his direction. Defence Counsel rose slowly to his feet, bowed, and turned towards Toby. To Toby's amazement and relief, it was the same tall, distinguished and friendly face from the robing room, who leant down towards him and whispered "Don't worry, old chap, but you're sitting in the jury box. Why don't you go and sit behind Berger?"

It was the worst day of his life, or so he thought at the time, as Toby clambered out of the jury box, all eyes upon him, and made his way down into the well of the court. Ham, for his part, was apologising profusely, which, in the circumstances, was the least he could do.

"Mr. Potts is my pupil, my lord," he whined, "and this is his first day in court. He is obviously unfamiliar with our ways."

"A self evident observation, Mr. Berger," snapped his lordship, "and precisely why pupils have pupil masters, to show them the ropes." Ham looked uncomfortable, and glowered at Toby. "Now shall we get on?"

"Quite so, my lord," Berger stammered, shuffling through his papers, "the Defendant stands charged with the grave offence of persistently importuning in a public place for immoral purposes, and on arraignment, pleaded not guilty."

"The gravity of the offence is for me to decide, Mr. Berger, not you or the jury as well you know. But now that you mention it, I have in my years on the Bench tried many grave offences, and when the law allowed, sent better men than you to the gallows," Ham smiled weakly. "However, I can state without fear of contradiction that I have never been called upon to try a case as grave as this. So I ask, in a spirit of enquiry, why me, and why is this case here?"

Was it Toby's imagination, or had the judge taken against him?

"My lord," Berger was at his most unctuous, "as your lordship will recall, the murder trial listed before your lordship this morning has been vacated to enable the defence to instruct their own forensic expert, so by hap chance, this trial was allocated to your lordship at very short notice. The case is here because, as your lordship may know, this offence was committed within the bailiwick of the Bailey, which is the only court having jurisdiction to try it."

"Very droll, I'm sure." There was the faintest of smiles playing around the judge's mouth.

"I'm sorry, my lord?"

"Within the bailiwick of the Bailey, very droll, Mr. Berger." Berger stood open mouthed, the fleeting moment of unintended wit going right over his head. "Never mind, never mind, get on." His lordship sat back and closed his eyes.

The jury duly empanelled, Ham rose to his feet to open the case for the prosecution. "Mem' jury," he began, "I appear on behalf of the prosecution in this case, and my learned friend Sir Archibald Scott-Malden QC appears for the Defendant." Toby drew in his breath sharply. His saviour and the distinguished man with the friendly face was none other than the former Attorney-General who, after the last General Election, had stood down to return to private practice. This was history in the making, and Toby was there to witness it. Whatever else, Berger was hopelessly outgunned. A distinguished Defendant, an even more distinguished defence counsel, and a hostile judge. An irresistible combination. Good luck, Ham, Toby muttered to himself, you're going to need it.

"At approximately nineteen thirty six hours…"

His lordship threw down his pen and pushed back in his chair. "What is this gibberish, Mr. Berger? He snapped irritably, "nineteen thirty six hours? The purpose of an opening address by prosecution counsel is to

26

illuminate, not obfuscate. The jury and I are totally bemused, and I dare say, so is your abandoned pupil."

"My lord," Ham was going down for the second time, and was still a long way from the shore. With grim determination, he plunged on. "At approximately seven thirty six in the evening, the defendant was seen in a notorious red light district of London, driving his motor car slowly along the street. You will hear evidence that he stopped his motor car and was approached by a lady of easy virtue. There was a brief conversation, and the defendant drove on. The Crown say that he was importuning for an immoral purpose." Ham had now broken into a gallop, such was his anxiety to conclude his opening speech without further interruption, and was babbling like a baboon. "At approximately nineteen....I mean seven forty four, he stopped for a second time, was again approached, and before he could agree terms, was arrested. With your lordship's leave," he panted triumphantly, "I will call my first witness. Miss Dolores Del Fabro."

There was an audible stir of anticipation in the court as Dolores entered, followed by a thick impenetrable cloud of Gala Passion. Toby's eyes began to water with the sheer intoxication of it as she swayed seductively past him on her way to the witness box. Dolores, otherwise known as Madge Dorkins, was a dyed bright redheaded woman on the wrong side of forty, plump, with a painted face worthy of Toulose Lautrec. Mutton dressed as lamb, thought Toby uncharitably, as she minced her way to the witness box in a provocative polka dot mini dress which was only just decent by anybody's standards. His lordship's eyes lit up, and his welcoming smile had an almost lascivious edge to it. Deep down in the jungle something was stirring, and he was beginning to enjoy himself.

Dolores took the oath in a quiet, demure voice, gave the judge an engaging smile and then sat down.

"Please state your name and address," said Ham, totally unmoved by this vision of loveliness.

"Dolores del Fabro, Miss," she added for good measure, "of 24 Eaton Square, London. Do you want my phone number as well?" she giggled, displaying a row of pearly white teeth.

"I think not," replied Ham, colouring visibly.

"Eaton Square?" asked the judge. Dolores nodded. "What a coincidence," he continued, smiling warmly, "we're near neighbours."

"I thought your lordship looked familiar."

There was an audible chuckle from the public gallery as the judge cleared his throat and regained his composure. "You were saying, Mr. Berger?"

"Madam," he began, putting both feet right in it. Even Toby could see that one coming.

Dolores immediately burst into tears. "Madam?!" she exploded through hysterical sobs, "just who do you think you are, calling me Madam?! I didn't come here to be insulted by an ignorant little moron like you!"

His lordship rushed to her side, metaphorically speaking of course. "Please calm yourself, Miss del Fabro, no slight on your character was intended, I'm sure. The ignorant little moron is prosecution counsel who is duty bound to ask you questions, and we must all bear with him, for the time being at least." The judge stared icily at Berger. "Shall we try again, Mr. Berger, and this time with a little sensitivity?"

"As your lordship pleases," Ham whined, and turned back to Dolores. "Were you in Argyle Square on the night of the eleventh of November?"

"No, my lord," said Sir Archibald, rising from his seat, "that, as my learned friend should know, is a leading question, and is not permitted under the rules of evidence."

His lordship nodded. "Quite right, Sir Archibald. Mr. Berger, it is a basic rule of evidence that you cannot lead your own witness. Even your pupil knows that." Toby winced. "Rephrase your question."

"I apologise, my lord." Back to Dolores. "Where were you on the night of the eleventh of November last?"

"That's nearly a year ago, how can I possibly remember? I'm a very busy girl."

"Busy at what?" snapped Berger, beginning to lose his composure.

"That's none of your business," Dolores snapped back.

"Yes it is."

"No it isn't."

"Really, Mr. Berger," interrupted the judge as Sir Archibald was on the way up again, "this is getting us nowhere. I suggest you try another approach."

Ham smiled thinly. "Very well, my lord." Taking a deep breath, he plunged on. "Do you know the defendant Sir Adrian Browne?" he asked, pointing to the dock.

This time Sir Archibald was up like a jackrabbit. "Again, my lord, and with respect to my learned friend, a dock identification is not permitted. Identity is in issue, and there has been no formal identification in this case."

"Is that right, Mr. Berger?" His lordship was not amused.

"Well…er," Ham was going down for the third time, "Sir Adrian Browne is a well known public figure, arrested in Argyle Square whilst persistently importuning for sexual favours…."

"Yes, yes, that, as you explained in your opening address, is your case." Sour Puss was losing patience. "The question, however, for the jury, is can you prove it on admissible evidence? The jury are not remotely interested in what you say, it doesn't amount to a row of beans."

There was a long pause, the silence broken only by the ticking of the court clock, as Berger took stock of his hopeless situation.

"But, but.." Ham whined.

"But, but, will not do, Mr. Berger. Have you any admissible evidence connecting the Defendant with Miss del Fabro, and, more to the point, any evidence that Miss del Fabro was even there on the night in question?"

Ham was not going down without a fight. He pictured his prosecution practice sinking without trace, and taking him down with it. There was now an irritable note to his whine. "My lord, had Miss del Fabro come up to proof and given evidence consistent with her witness statement, the question of identity would not have arisen. She is obviously a recalcitrant witness, and I apply to treat her as hostile."

The judge's eyebrows shot up. "Do you agree, Sir Archibald?" he asked.

"No, my lord, I do not," came the reply as Sir Archibald rose from his seat.

"And neither do I, and I rule against you. So where does that leave you?"

One last headlong rush into the Valley of Death. "I have another prostitute to call...."

Dolores was about to explode as Sour Puss waved her down. "Mr. Berger, this is intolerable. You have not proved that Miss del Fabro is a prostitute, as you somewhat crudely put it, so even if your next witness surmounts that particular hurdle, do you have any admissible evidence of a formal identification? I thought not," continued the judge before Berger could reply. "And besides, where is your evidence that the defendant was persistently importuning for immoral purposes? 'Persistently', in my vocabulary at least, suggests more than once. Am I right, Sir Archibald?"

Sir Archibald rose with all the dignity that his high office and professional esteem could muster. "Your lordship is, as ever, a Solomon come to judgment," he purred. Game, set and match.

Sour Puss turned to the totally bemused jury. "There you have it, members of the jury. On the admissible evidence called before you, the Crown haven't even begun to establish a case for this defendant to answer, and I direct you to return a verdict of not guilty. The defendant may leave the dock without a stain on his character. I shall rise."

Toby accompanied Ham back to the robing room for the briefest of post mortems. Toby had to hand it to him, Ham had a skin as thick as a rhinoceros, and seemed completely unfazed by the mauling he'd just received. "Well," he whined, "now you've seen the cut and thrust of advocacy at its highest level, has it whetted your appetite for a life of crime?" Frankly, Toby couldn't think of anything to say in reply. "I'm going back to Chambers," he continued, "I've brought my own sandwiches," no expense spared, "so I'll see you later," and with that, he was gone.

Toby wanted to discuss the case and learn something from what went wrong, but he judged now was not the time, so after the starched collar ordeal in reverse, he made his way up to the Bar Mess, the dining room set aside for barristers. Over by the window sat Sir Archibald with the great and the good and assorted acolytes, deep in animated conversation. Seeing no familiar faces from his year of call, he selected the **plat du jour** and sponge pudding with custard and sat down on his own, trying not to draw attention to himself. He had just finished when, to his trepidation, he saw Sir Archibald making his way over. Toby immediately stood up.

"Please sit down, young man. Do you mind if I join you?"

"I..I..I ."

"I didn't quite catch your name when we met earlier," said Sir Archibald, sitting down opposite.

"Toby, sir, Toby Potts."

"Please call me Archie," he continued, smiling kindly, "and where is your pupil master?"

"Gone back to Chambers to eat his sandwiches," Toby blurted out, immediately feeling disloyal.

"Ah, that's Berger for you, not one for socialising. Still, it takes all sorts. So, what did you make of this morning's high drama?" he continued.

"Totally confused, to be honest," replied Toby. "I don't pretend to understand all the rules of evidence, but the case seemed to fall apart with the first witness. The prosecution made certain assumptions about her evidence they were clearly unable to prove."

Sir Archibald chuckled. "A very perspicacious observation."

"I mean," Toby went on, "I hadn't read the papers or discussed the case with Berger before going into court," Sir Archibald raised his eyebrows, "but from his opening, it seemed an open and shut case."

"On the face of the papers, you are right. We all know Miss del Fabro earns her living staring up at the ceiling, but knowing it and proving it are not always one and the same thing. My advice to you, Toby, starting out on what I hope is an illustrious career at the Bar, is that you can never over prepare. Never assume some fact or other will prove itself, always be ready to prove it, just in case your star witness loses the plot."

"So should Sir Adrian have been acquitted?"

"Under our system of justice, yes. The prosecution must prove the guilt of the accused to a very high standard, and even if the guilty are acquitted from time to time, you don't throw the baby out with the bath water. To coin Winston Churchill, it ain't perfect, but it's the best we've got. God help us, if our lords and masters get their way and abolish trial by jury. Although it worked for the defendant today, can you imagine anything worse than being tried by Old Sour Puss?" Toby smiled, he hoped deferentially. "And as for Sir Adrian, whatever else, he behaved foolishly, his career is in ruins, and he'll never rise to high office again. That is his punishment, so justice of sorts has been done." Sir Archibald paused to light a cigar right under a prominent

'No Smoking' sign, but nobody saw fit to admonish him. "So, your first day with Lionel Berger? Can't say I know him well, an honest journeyman rather than a shooting star. Should make it to the Circuit Bench in a few years' time."

"Really?" The surprise in Toby's voice didn't go unnoticed. "Is he that good?"

"Being a good or able advocate is no longer an essential prerequisite to judicial advancement, and more's the pity. If you keep your nose clean, don't upset anybody on the way up, and toe the party line, you've got as good a chance as the next man. Not so long ago it was different," he continued, sending clouds of smoke into the air. "Judges were appointed on ability and usually after a distinguished career at the Bar. They had a feel for it, and the Bench was the richer for it. Nowadays all sorts of ignorant little morons are getting appointed," Toby laughed and wished he hadn't, "they get their idiot guides printed for them by the Department of Constitutional Affairs, whatever that is, and their specimen directions, and their hours of sitting, and some, I'm told, even bring their laptops into court and tap away, noses buried, hearing but not seeing. You can't get a feel for the case if you don't observe human nature. It's not what a witness says, it's the way he says it, the body language, that can make the difference between truth and lies, conviction or acquittal."

Toby sat transfixed as Sir Archibald glanced down at his watch. Should he ask him for his autograph, or perhaps a photo opportunity for posterity? What a story to tell his friends and parents, 'this one is of me and my good chum Archie, you know Archie, the former Attorney-General?' If only....

Sir Archibald stood up to go. "It's been a pleasure chatting to you, Toby, but I've detained you long enough. Let me leave you with one final piece of advice - never settle for second best. Why be ordinary if you have it in you to be extraordinary. Good luck," and with that he was gone.

CHAPTER FOUR

TOBY'S FIRST OUTING

Experience is the name everyone
Gives to their mistakes.
Whether they learn from them is a different matter entirely

[after Oscar Wilde]

Horseferry Road Magistrates Court. Within chiming distance of Big Ben, and a stone's throw from Smith Square and Lord North Street in the heart of Westminster Village, where the real business of government is done behind closed doors and heavily draped curtains, where dutiful wives, dripping in Versace and Chanel, attend to their masters' every wishes as the good, the bad and the ugly wheel and deal into the small hours and put the world to rights, whilst their mistresses, also dripping in Versace and Chanel, await their return and a snatched moment of carnal pleasure before they return to the fray. There are a lot of drips in politics.

Toby had other things on his mind as he travelled to court, clutching his first ever brief. He had duly completed his first six months with Berger, not a conspicuous success, even by Berger's modest standards, and they seemed to drag on forever. Sadly for Toby, Berger's big day out at the Bailey was the high point in an otherwise undistinguished and mundane practice, fed as it was on an unremitting diet of low grade crime, always prosecuting, always whining, winning some and losing some more, keeping his nose clean and waiting for the call to come on up onto the Circuit Bench. An ideal candidate, if Sir Archibald were to be believed. How depressing.

Toby couldn't move fast enough to wave Berger goodbye, and with luck on his side, found a second pupillage in Brick Court, another converted Victorian lavatory. His new pupil master, Nick Ridley, was cut from a different cloth altogether, dynamic, upwardly mobile, with a good solid practice in serious crime and tipped, by many, for elevation to the ranks of Queen's Counsel.

After a week or three of getting to know each other and bonding, Toby found himself passing the clerks' room one evening, just before close of play, when the senior clerk called him in.

"I'd like you to help me out, Sir." Toby didn't know what to expect, and was rooted to the spot. For the senior clerk to address him at all was privilege indeed. "Chambers solicitor can't make it to court tomorrow, so I've agreed to cover it. It's plea before venue at Horseferry Road Magistrates Court, client charged with making off without payment. Straightforward case, you'll be on your own, but I'm sure you can handle it. Here's the brief. Meet the client at court," and so saying, in that seminal moment when the Heavens conjoin, the brief was ceremonially handed over to Toby in much the same way as Jehovah handed down the Ten Commandments to Moses. All that was missing was the burning bush and the deep yet manly voice of Charlton Heston.

Toby's hands trembled as he took possession of the backsheet, fondly enclosing two pages of instructions, and lovingly tied together with pink ribbon. He smiled weakly, and like a dog with a favourite bone, scurried off to worry over it and digest the enormity of the task ahead. He could picture it all. The short and pithy statement on the steps of the court to the waiting press and Sky News, announcing to the world and his dog that his client was innocent of the heinous charge levelled against him, that justice would prevail and that his client would leave court without a blemish on his impeccable character. What a glorious start to a glorious career!

That night, as he burned the midnight oil, Toby poured over the brief, reading and rereading his instructions, commendable for their brevity if nothing else. In précis form they described how the defendant, one Anthony Hercules Smith, had disgorged himself from a taxi owing ten pounds and sixty pence on the meter and, to put it crudely, had legged it, followed in hot pursuit by the irate driver. Rounding the corner in full flight, the hapless Smith had barrelled straight into PC. Plod.

35

After a moment to take stock of the situation, Plod had nicked, cuffed and spanked the defendant in short order, dumping him unceremoniously into the back of a passing police van, and thence into custody. In the fullness of time, Smith had been charged with making off without payment, and bailed to appear at Horseferry Road Magistrates Court to await the full majesty of the law. Enter Toby stage right.

Incessantly picking up the brief and putting it back down, almost reverentially, Toby thumbed through Archbold and made detailed notes about plea before venue, something to do with the Defendant's right to elect trial by jury if, of course, the offence was triable either way, and what did that mean, and was it? Why couldn't the editors of Archbold write in plain English?

After a lengthy trawl, he found the relevant section of the Theft Act 1978, section 4, and read to his horror that on conviction (an unlikely event with Toby's firm hand on the tiller, but one that had to be countenanced in case of an incompetent tribunal or a perverse jury), a person (presumably his client) shall be liable, for an offence under section 1 or section 2 of this Act, (what's this got to do with anything?) to imprisonment for up to 5 years (What!!) and for an offence under section 3 of this Act, to imprisonment for up to 2 years (that's better, but not a lot). He read on, more in hope than enlightenment, to discover that this section (whatever) is printed as amended by the Magistrates Court Act 1980 section 154(1) and Schedule 7 paragraph 170. For section 32 of the 1980 Act, see *ante* § 1 - 30. Finally, to add to his misery, Toby discovered that section 5(3) was repealed by the *Extradition Act* 1989 section 37(1) and Schedule 2. Section 5(4), to be ignored at his peril, included offences under the Act (which Act?) in the schedule to the *Visiting Forces Act* 1952, which defines for England and Wales "offence against property" for purposes of exclusion in certain cases of the jurisdiction of the United Kingdom courts (there's a load off!). Was this complete gibberish, or had he lost the plot? He should have followed his father and become an accountant. Too late now for regrets.

Toby began to panic. His instructions told him nothing about Smith's status in this our sceptred isle. Smith was a common enough English name, but not conclusive. Perhaps Smith was an alias. After all, what right-minded Anglo-Saxon parent names their son Hercules? Was Toby's Smith an illegal alien? That might explain his sudden dash for freedom. If so, was he liable to extradition? Was he part of the visiting forces, and if so, who's visiting forces, and where was he visiting from? Did the court have jurisdiction, and was legging it without paying the fare an "offence against property?" At first blush, Toby thought not, but remembering Sir Archibald's words of wisdom about being prepared for every eventuality, he plunged back into Archbold, and in the Table of Statutes, wedged between Visiting Forces (British Commonwealth) Act 1933, and the Wages Act 1986, were at least a dozen further references to the Visiting Forces Act 1952.

It was past two in the morning when Toby finally got to bed. He slept fitfully, waking each hour on the hour, and forcing himself back to sleep. By six he abandoned the uneven struggle and prepared himself for his date with destiny.

As it was the Magistrates Court, he was not required to robe, so he dressed in his best dark suit with the subtle pinstripe, white shirt with double cuffs and a sober, quasi-regimental tie. Kicking around his small apartment off Earls Court Road, he forced down a bowl of Wheetie Bangs, buttered toast with marmite and a cup of tea, and then, fortified for the task ahead, he gathered up the brief, counsel's notebook and his copy of Archbold, and, bracing himself, took one last look in the mirror:

I see you stand like greyhounds in the slips,
Straining upon the start. The game's afoot,
Follow your spirit; and upon this charge
Cry 'God help me! England and St. George!'

As ill-luck would have it, a points failure down the line had him sitting, powerless and frustrated, for a good fifteen minutes before disgorging him at Westminster Underground Station. His carefully laid plans had been shot to pieces. It was now twenty to ten, and with the court sitting promptly at ten, there was no time to lose. The illegal alien would be pacing the court precincts, glancing anxiously at his watch, waiting for his Armageddon and no sign of his saviour. Toby walked as fast as he could, almost trotting but not quite, conscious as he was of the dignity of his profession and determined to arrive with his Gravitas intact. A damp shirt and beads of perspiration starting out from his forehead was hardly the image he was hoping to cultivate, and not good for client confidence. He was only dimly aware of the roar of traffic past the Mother of Parliaments and the House of Lords where, one day, in the not too distant future, he might be appearing in the highest court in the land, a pleasure in store for their lordships as he charmed them with his brilliant and incisive advocacy. All that and more as he turned into Horseferry Road and up the steps to the court. Ten minutes to spare.

As he emerged into the waiting area, it was bun fight at the OK Corral. It seemed as if all the flotsam and jetsam of humanity were washing aimlessly around the assembly area, with screaming kids running amok, disinterested mothers staring vacantly into the middle distance, and defendants, friends, relatives and solicitors all milling about. It was like a Hogarth cartoon. Matronly ladies from the Women's Royal Volunteer Service were manning large trolleys, from which they dispensed beverages, snacks, sandwiches and confectionary to all comers, innocent and guilty alike. It was gumboot territory only as the recipients of this largesse waded in and out, relieving the ever-increasing tension of not knowing whether their loved ones would be coming home with them.

Toby glanced anxiously around. How was he to identify Mr. Smith from all these likely candidates? After a moment's reflection, he thought it best to find the court and work his way back. Easier said than done. There were four courts sitting that day, and the list of defendants of biblical proportions was posted on a board between Courts Two and Three. The scrum around the board made easy access impossible as Toby peered over countless shoulders, hoping to catch a glimpse of his client's name. No sooner had he managed to jostle his way to the front, when the court tannoy crackled into life:

"The case of Smith will now be heard in Court Two."

A combination of blind panic and rising nausea gripped him, his mouth went dry, and for a moment, he felt he might lose his composure. It was his worst nightmare. Taking a deep breath, he hurried to Court Two, almost stumbling through the double doors and into court.

Seated on the dais at the far end in an imposing chair embossed with the royal coat of arms was the District Judge, who, from his countenance, was in no mood to brook any nonsense. In his early fifties, he cut an imposing figure, his pallid complexion, thinning hair and aquiline nose on which were perched half moon spectacles gave him the look of a bird of prey as he glowered at the file of papers handed up to him by the court clerk. His bristling moustache and regimental tie gave him the appearance of a military man, used to doing everything by numbers. In front of him, on the advocates' benches, sat an array of solicitors and acolytes, shuffling papers, conferring with colleagues in hushed whispers and ready to snap to attention when their case was called on. At the back of the court was the dock, encased in bullet-proof glass, with well worn steps leading down to the cells.

As Toby stood, wondering what to do next, there was a loud clanging of keys, the door at the back of the dock opened, and in walked the defendant flanked by two dock officers. On any view, he was not the sort of man to meet in a dark alley late at night. His short sleeved shirt revealed arms the size of hams, both heavily decorated with assorted tattoos proclaiming love and hate in equal measure, with serpents locked in mortal combat around Satan and his hordes from Hell. With no sign of a neck, his shaved head sat brutishly on his massive shoulders, gold studs adorned his small, pink ears, and his mouth, snapped permanently open, displayed a set of uneven and discoloured teeth.

Toby had to do something, anything, to redeem the situation, so he sidled over to the dock, hoping he wouldn't be noticed, and pressed his lips between the cracks in the glass.

"Mr. Smith?" he whispered.

"Yer."

"My name's Toby Potts. I'm Counsel, and I'm here to represent you. Sorry I couldn't speak to you earlier, but leave it to me, and we'll have a chat afterwards. Alright?"

Mr. Smith stared blankly back. Clearly several sandwiches short of a picnic, but Toby didn't have the time to dawdle, and, making his way to the front of the court, squeezed himself onto the end of the advocates' bench. All the other advocates had to shuffle along as the District Judge glowered at Toby and this unforgivable interruption to the smooth running of Her Majesty's business.

The court clerk addressed the defendant. "You are charged that on divers days between the thirteenth and fifteenth of May you did murder one Sharon Jane Kershaw. You may sit down."

Toby was awed and appalled in equal measure. Not only was his client a fare dodging illegal alien, he was also a murderer most foul. He was wholly unprepared for this dramatic turn of events, and the thought of flicking through Archbold 'on the hoof' whilst at the same time wading well out of his depth was an unattractive option. There was nothing else for it but to confess and avoid, as they say in the profession, so he rose to his feet at the same time as the learned prosecutor down the far end of the bench. Toby was not to be outranked as he waved his colleague back down. The District Judge stared at them both, seeing but not believing.

"What on earth is going on?" he snapped, addressing himself to Toby, "and who and what are you?"

"I apologise for interrupting my learned friend, Sir," Toby began with as much composure as he could muster under difficult circumstances, "I am learned counsel and I appear here today to represent this defendant. This new and very grave charge has taken me and my client totally by surprise. We are here to face a charge of making off without payment, yet without any prior warning or notice, a charge of murder has been added to the indictment which, I would respectfully submit, is a denial of natural justice and contrary to the defendant's rights under the European Convention on Human Rights." A nice touch, thought Toby, it always impresses the punters. "In the circumstances, I have no option but to ask for an adjournment, so that I can see my client in conference and take instructions."

There followed a crashing silence as the District Judge absorbed the enormity of Toby's application. He glanced down at the list of advocates in front of him, and then looked up. "Mr. Throgmorton, do you have anything to add?"

Mr. Throgmorton, a local and respected solicitor well known to the court, rose slowly to his feet. "My learned friend's application takes me by surprise, sir," he began, obviously bemused. "I have certainly not instructed him in this case, nor would I contemplate doing so. If my learned friend can be persuaded to withdraw his application, we are ready to proceed without further delay."

"This is intolerable. You are?" he looked hard at Toby.

"Potts, sir, Toby Potts of counsel."

"And you believe that you are instructed to represent this defendant, Brian George Smith, on a charge of making off without payment?"

"I....I...I...." Dawn's early light was beginning to break through the mists of obfuscation as Toby flapped helplessly. If only he could rewind the tape and start all over again. He picked up the brief, studied the name on the backsheet, which he knew off by heart anyway, and looked up. "There may have been some mistake, sir," Toby stammered, "my client's name is Anthony Hercules Smith. It hadn't occurred to me until now, but perhaps there is another Mr. Smith appearing at court today."

"An understandable mistake," the Judge sighed heavily. "Mister Clerk?"

The court clerk took out the list of cases for the day, and found that Anthony Hercules Smith, charged with making off without payment, was listed to appear in Court Three. "Well, there we are, Mr. Potts, out of chaos comes forth order. Don't let me detain you any longer."

"I am so sorry, sir." Toby bowed reverentially, and made to leave.

"Blues and Royals?" asked the Judge, fingering his regimental tie.

"Er, actually, no sir. Marks and Spencers."

The Judge threw his head back in disgust as Toby the poseur withdrew. He was about to leave court when the defendant stirred from his seat in the dock.

"'ang on a minute," he grunted, "where's me brief off to?"

Toby quickly made his way to Court Three. Although he didn't know it at the time, as he walked in, walking out past him was Anthony Hercules Smith who, in spite of assurances given to him by his solicitor the previous day, had appeared unrepresented and unloved to face the serious charge of making off without payment. Without Toby's guiding hand, he had pleaded guilty, was fined £250 with costs and compensation, and warned as to his future conduct.

Sad to relate, Toby never received another brief from that solicitor, but in the fullness of time, and to his surprise and delight, he was rewarded for his *tour de force* with a brief from Mr. Throgmorton. Even the worst day has its compensations.

CHAPTER FIVE

TOBY AND THE PARROTS

Come fill the cup, and in the Fire of Spring
The Winter Garment of Repentance fling;
The Bird of Time has but a little way to fly
And lo! The Bird is on the wing

[Omar Khayyàm]

Fortunately for Toby, his initial shaky start didn't turn out to be career threatening, and time is a great healer. After a few days in purdah and quiet reflection, he was soon back in the saddle and whetting his appetite on several mentions, applications and even one plea in mitigation. Confidence returned, and he was beginning to feel ready for the big time. In this positive spirit of upward mobility came the case of the Crown versus John Gray, a perfectly respectable man charged with the death of two Amazonian Blue parrots. Not that Toby knew much about birds. His Great Aunt Maud once had a canary, very briefly, which she christened Chirpy, if for no other reason because it chirped a lot. Birds have a habit of doing that a lot, whether they're happy or miserable.

The dear woman was a bit batty, and didn't realise that if you let a bird of any description out of its cage, it was the devil's own job getting it back in again, and the more it flew around the room, in a heightened state of agitation, the looser became its bowels. If nothing else, Great Aunt Maud was very house proud, in fact, living on her own and with little else to do, being proud of her house was a full time obsession, so Chirpy's bowel problems became a significant issue in the great disorder of things. Chirpy's habit of emptying the bottom of its cage onto Great Aunt Maud's best Persian rug at the drop of a beak was an additional source of irritation.

After mature consideration, she decided Chirpy should do its poos outside in the garden, where all well trained birds perform, and that was the last she saw of it. For days after, at all hours of the day and night, and much to the annoyance of her neighbours, Great Aunt Maud would stand outside her garden door, calling Chirpy's name. Great Aunt Maud had a particularly shrill voice. But Toby was soon to discover that Chirpy, and its little peckadilloes, was as nought compared to the Amazonian Blue.

As parrots go, the Amazonian Blue is a wondrous bird indeed. Its gaily-coloured plumage, predominantly blue, hence the name, marks it out for special note in the great pecking order of things. Sadly, it's also becoming an increasingly rare species as it flits from one treetop to another in search of what motivates man and bird alike, an acceptable partner for friendship, common interests and a fulfilling relationship.

But given the nature of the Amazonian rain forest, acceptable partners are hard to come by. If the truth be told, the Amazonian rain forest is not exactly your average woodland glade, so the notion that scores of amorous Blues are on the wing and spoilt for choice is sadly misplaced.

To combat the dearth of acceptable partners, the male has developed a particularly ear piercing screech to touch first base. Not to be outdone, the female returns the male's screech with a particularly ear piercing screech of her own. In this way, contact is established, names and addresses exchanged and the rest, as they say, is history.

Paul and Marion Grundy were bird fanciers, but not your common all garden variety. They aimed their sights much higher, and digging deep into their savings, they acquired a pair of mating Blues, or that's what they were told by the local pet shop. With healthy chicks selling for up to a thousand pounds a time, they couldn't go wrong, or so they thought.

The Grundys did nothing by half measures, and nothing was too good for their newly acquired money machines. In anticipation of their arrival, the rear garden of Number 26 Acacia Avenue was transformed into a veritable bird paradise, with a stately pleasure dome of epic proportions replacing the purple spouting broccoli in the former vegetable patch. Fully climate controlled, the dome was equipped with everything an Amazonian Blue's heart could desire, including 'his' and 'her' perches, walkways, the ubiquitous bell and mirror, foliage to remind them of happier days in the wild, and a nesting box with all the creature comforts.

John and Liz Gray, with an 'A', had bought Number 28 Acacia Avenue some eight years previously, intending it to see out their retirement years. They were not exactly unsociable, but preferred their own company and kept themselves to themselves. They acknowledged the Grundys on the chance encounter, such as the car washing ritual and the stroll to the Newsagents on a Sunday morning, but that was about the height of it.

John Gray had risen to the rank of regional sales manager of a well known double glazing firm, had lived frugally, invested wisely, and retired relatively comfortably. As a leaving present after all those years in service, John's firm had replaced all the windows at Number 28 with their end-of-line Georgian effect double glazed condensation proof PVC windows, a handsome gift by any standards, which Liz had decorated with matching net curtains. John had added a conservatory and decking in the rear south-facing garden, which, according to the estate agent, caught all available sun, and, come rain or shine, it became their second home. A patio set of all-weather furniture and a gas-fired, top of the range, barbeque completed their Shangri-La.

The arrival of Pride and Joy, for this is what the Grundys had christened their Blues, was an eagerly awaited affair and very much a red-letter day in the Grundy calendar. Once installed, out came the digital camera, and a brand new photo album in pristine condition was unwrapped, ready to record all those memorable moments to treasure in the years to come.

One problem not immediately appreciated by the Grundys was that Amazonian Blues are creatures of habit, and habits acquired over the centuries flying free in the forest die hard. Being creatures of habit, Amazonian Blues, indeed, all birds worth their tail feathers, wake up and greet dawn's early light. Now we're not talking here about a discreet tweet or chirp as uttered by your average hedge sparrow or chaffinch, we're talking about the sort of screech that can shatter a glass goblet at fifty paces. And to add insult to injury, in the summer months, dawn's early light usually arrives in Acacia Avenue between four and four thirty in the morning when most God fearing folk, including the Grays, are asleep in bed and would like it to keep it that way until at least nine o'clock before enjoying a leisurely breakfast on the patio.

But if that were not bad enough, once awake, Amazonian Blues continue to screech all day long. The fact that, in the case of Pride and Joy, they were perched right next to each other and within easy screeching distance, was of no consequence whatsoever to the decibel rating.

Amazingly the Grundys took all this screeching in their stride, a sign perhaps that their investment was bearing fruit. Not so the Grays. Relationships, never warm at the best of times, rapidly became arctic. In the way of all things English, words were not immediately exchanged, which simply added to the tension that was finally to explode.

John Gray took to keeping a log, with duplicate copies dated and countersigned by Liz for presentation in due course to the Environmental Health department of their local council.

As the summer wore on, other irritants besides the screeching were added to the log. To achieve some semblance of sleep, the Grays had to spend the nights with their end-of-line Georgian effect double glazed condensation proof PVC windows hermetically sealed, which simply added to their discomfort. When the wind was in the west, and it invariably was, the overpowering smell of bird droppings stung their nostrils as they sat, grim faced, on their patio, glowering at the laplock fence dividing their two gardens.

Eventually the Grays mounted a deputation of two and presented themselves at the Grundys' front door. It was not a happy encounter, and whilst there ensued a full and frank exchange of views, including doubts cast upon their respective progenies, nothing was achieved to the satisfaction of the Grays. John concluded the lively exchange by announcing that they hadn't heard the last of this, and Paul telling John to f*** off. Not a man to mince his words was our Paul.

Marion, who hadn't had an intelligent conversation with Paul for as long as she could remember, took to chatting to Pride and Joy at every opportunity, and her persistence was soon rewarded. She discovered that Amazonian Blues, in common with most parrots and even the humble budgerigar, were excellent mimics, and by dint of constant repetition, one of her strong suits, the three of them were screeching away in no time.

The laplock fence, unlike the end-of-line Georgian effect double glazed condensation proof PVC windows, provided no effective sound barrier to this constant chattering. It wasn't as if it could be remotely described as interesting or informative, the sort of conversation worth overhearing and repeating when the right moment presented itself. It started predictably, with Marion asking, "Who's a pretty boy?" and "Who's a pretty girl?" directed, it has to be said, in a somewhat random fashion at whichever bird looked remotely interested in this gibberish. No fault of Marion's, as the sexing of Amazonian Blues is notoriously difficult even to the tutored eye. It progressed, inevitably, down the etymological scale to "give us a kiss," distant memories of her courting days with the monosyllabic Paul, and Marion's all-time favourite "birdy birdy num-nums."

The Grays had tried the neighbourly approach to no avail. Now it was time for action. Armed, as John believed, with sufficient ammunition, he made a formal complaint. If the truth be told, Environmental Health were not as sympathetic as the Grays would have wished, but their persistence was eventually rewarded with a visit from a callow youth sporting an identification label around his neck and a clipboard tucked under his arm, demonstrably bored and obviously poorly informed. Unfortunately for the Grays, Murphy's Law prevailed. The callow youth dutifully accompanied the Grays into their rear garden where, moments before, Pride and Joy had been screeching away, only to be met with a wall of deafening silence. After what seemed like an eternity, the youth gave John a long hard 'troublemaker' look and turned to go. But John, with his captive audience, was having none of it, as he jumped up and down on his side of the laplock fence, screaming at his tormentors and hurling abuse. The youth made some notes on his clipboard and left, never to be seen again. He was barely in his car before Pride and Joy started up again, but it was too late.

The straw that finally broke the camel's back came when Marion, aided and abetted by Paul no doubt, decided to add to Pride and Joy's vocabulary. The Grays could hardly believe their ears as the unmistakeable squawk of "F*** off John" stabbed the air and turned it blue. Not just once or twice, but repeated over and over again. It was more than a man could bear.

And so it was, on that fateful evening in late August, with one Sangria too many and one "F*** off John" too many, that John rose slowly from his patio chair. Something inside him snapped as he ran headlong at the laplock fence, flattening it and the Grundys' fine display of Dahlias in the same motion, and without breaking stride, on he ran towards the pleasure dome, all those months of pent-up anger finally released in a surge of uncontrollable violence. Flinging the cage door open, and undaunted by Pride's, or Joy's fearsome beak, he grabbed his tormentor by the neck and with one twist, despatched it to its maker. Paul, alerted by the commotion, leapt from his chair, hurtled down the garden and cannoned into John who now had Joy's, or Pride's, life in his hands. The three of them went down in a heap of feathers and droppings as the stately pleasure dome collapsed around their ears. Sad to report that Joy, or Pride, died shortly afterwards of shock.

And so it was that John found himself summonsed to appear before the local Magistrates Court, charged with the criminal damage of two rare Amazonian Blue parrots, which the local press dubbed 'Pollycide'. He was also charged with criminal damage to the stately pleasure dome, now nothing better than matchwood, and using threatening words and behaviour.

Into this hot house of fur and feathers flew one Toby Potts Esquire, learned counsel, instructed to make bricks without straw. A conference was arranged in Chambers ahead of the hearing, listed before the Justices at Surbiton Magistrates Court.

By convention, conferences were arranged at four thirty in the afternoon, on the assumption that able counsel would be fully occupied in court during the day, and this was the earliest opportunity to see the client. The fact that Toby had no court commitments, indeed no commitments whatsoever, that day, cut no ice with the clerks, so four thirty it was when the Grays, together with their solicitor, arrived in chambers ready for a full and frank exchange of views.

Once again, and thanks to Archbold, Toby had researched the law and procedure relating to criminal damage. He had discovered, to his chagrin, that where the value of property damaged or destroyed fell below the benchmark of £5000, the offence was summary only, by virtue of section 22 of the Magistrates Court Act and Schedule 2. As the value of the two Pollies and the incredibly naff pleasure dome were a derisory £3000, summary trial was the order of the day. Never mind, at least Toby could reassure Mr. Gray that in the event of conviction, and at first blush he couldn't spot the defence, the sentence was limited to a maximum of three months imprisonment, instead of ten years available to the sentencing judge after trial by jury. However, as Toby was soon to find out, conviction was the last thing on Mr. Gray's mind.

Toby read on. Property, he discovered, means property of a tangible nature, whether real or personal, pretty obvious really, including wild creatures which have been tamed or are ordinarily kept in captivity if, but only if, they have been reduced into possession which has not been lost or abandoned, whatever that might mean. But wait! Toby paused in his reading as he espied a faint glimmer of light at the end of the tunnel. The two Pollies were obviously kept in captivity, but not, he mused, ordinarily, and had the Grundys left open the pleasure dome door, they would almost certainly have flown the coop. This was interesting and a possible line of defence. Furthermore, as he could hear himself submitting to the court with compelling logic, had they actually been tamed? Just because they could screech obscenities was far from conclusive.

Self-induced intoxication was no defence. More's the pity for the sangria soaked defendant; he'd be home and dry if it were. Toby concluded his researches by reading a convoluted definition of 'lawful excuse', which made no sense whatsoever, hammering on as it did about proprietary rights and interests and consent and reasonableness, so he decided to put it on the back burner and return to it if necessary.

Promptly at four thirty, Mr. Gray, accompanied by the fragrant Liz, was shown into the conference room, together with Debbie, their solicitor's junior clerk, there to take notes and report back. Drawing on his experiences in pupillage, Toby decided, after the usual pleasantries, to allow Mr. Gray to open the proceedings by speaking his mind, so that he could see which way the wind was blowing so to speak, before asserting himself and proposing the way forward, firmly but fairly. No point in exciting the punter's expectations if there was nothing to get excited about.

Gray was a stubborn and self-opinionated man, born of years of persuading home owners to buy replacement windows they didn't want and never taking 'No' for an answer, a man whose body language and attitude would brook no contradiction. Liz turned out to be his echo. Everything he said, she repeated, an irritating habit reminding Toby of the two dead parrots. By the end of their opening remarks, Toby was ready to tell them both to F*** off! But he didn't. After all, the punters were always right, particularly those paying coin of the realm for legal services rendered.

"So you see, Mr. Potter," Gray concluded, "I'd tried everything else…"

"You'd tried everything else, hadn't you dear?" Liz repeated.

"And no jury in the land is going to convict me, unless, of course, we get twelve bird fanciers."

"Well," Toby interjected before Liz could repeat, "I'm afraid you can't elect trial by jury. It has to be tried in the Magistrates Court."

"Poppycock!" An unfortunate word in the circumstances. "I know my rights, young man, and it's my inalienable right to be tried by a jury of my peers. It's guaranteed under the Magna Carta!"

"It's your right, isn't it, dear?"

"The law has moved on since the Magna Carta, Mr. Gray," it was time for Toby to assert himself, "and I can assure you there is no right to trial by jury."

"What do you say, young lady?" Gray snapped at Debbie, who blushed and smiled weakly.

Toby rode quickly to her rescue. "There's no need to involve Debbie at this stage, Mr. Gray."

"Why not! I'm paying for legal advice, you're giving me the wrong advice and she's giving me no advice at all. Why buy a dog and bark yourself, that's what I want to know!"

"That's what you want to know, isn't it dear?"

Toby felt an enormous groundswell of sympathy for the Grundys welling up inside, but with an agreed fee of £100 plus VAT, already spent, he wasn't about to kiss it goodbye, not yet anyway, so he decided to try another tack.

"How are things between you and the Grundys now? I wonder if there's any room for compromise?" Wrong tack, as Gray's face went a brighter shade of puce.

"Compromise!! You must be joking! My only regret is I didn't wring Grundy's scrawny neck along with his f***ing parrots!!"

"I have every sympathy with your predicament," Toby lied, trying to calm the situation, "but as I see it, you can't enter your neighbour's garden and throttle his parrots without lawful excuse." As soon as he'd said it, Toby wished he hadn't.

Gray's dark mood suddenly lifted like the early morning mist as he slammed his fist down on the desk. "That's it!" he bellowed triumphantly, "You've got it in one. Why didn't you say so first off? Well done, Mr. Potter, we'll go with lawful excuse!"

"That's right, dear, lawful excuse," Liz chimed in without the faintest idea what she was talking about.

She was not alone, as Toby stared back, with a fixed grin and a mounting sense of panic. A quick glance at Debbie, who was keeping her head well below the parapet. He couldn't now start flicking through Archbold to bone up on 'lawful excuse', with the punter sat opposite and his £100 hanging in the balance, so if in doubt, cut and run.

"Well," he said, with as much authority as he could command, "we've had a full and frank exchange, and unless you have any more questions," Dear Lord, please, no more questions! "I suggest we adjourn and I'll see you at court."

Two days later, on a warm afternoon in the leafy suburbs of Surbiton, the warring parties assembled in the foyer of the court, ready to do battle. Debbie was there, keeping her distance, as was Paul Grundy, who turned up wearing an orthopaedic collar, a pained expression and a black armband. You could cut the atmosphere with a knife.

By now Toby had boned up on 'lawful excuse', and as he suspected, it didn't apply. He had also considered, and rejected, all other defences, so it fell to him to break the news to Gray.

The client was far from amused. "You told me I had a defence!" he glared at Toby.

This was going to be difficult. "Actually, all I said was that 'lawful excuse' was a defence. I didn't say it was a defence in your case." It sounded as lame as it was, and Toby knew it.

"So what's your advice now?!"

There was no alternative as Toby plunged in. "I'm afraid you have no defence to killing the parrots, so I must advise you to plead guilty."

"Over my dead body!" bellowed Gray.

"That can be arranged!" Paul Grundy bellowed back, and it was only the timely intervention of the court staff that prevented another ugly incident.

Gray's inclination was to fight each and every charge to the last breath in his body, all the way to the House of Lords and beyond if necessary, such was his sense of grievance, but wiser counsel eventually prevailed, and after protracted consultations between Toby and the prosecutor, Gray pleaded guilty to Pollycide, and the remaining charges were dropped. At Gray's insistence, Toby by way of mitigation played the tapes of Pride and Joy in happier times and in full "F*** off" screech, but this fell on deaf ears. The injustice of it all! Gray was fined £500 and ordered to pay £2000 compensation. He left court muttering darkly about incompetent lawyers, but at least he was comforted in the knowledge that peace and tranquillity would now fall like a warm blanket over Number 28 Acacia Avenue.

Some weeks later, after the fine and compensation had been paid, Gray was out in the garden attending to those little chores in anticipation of spring fever when his attention was drawn to the sound of hammering in the garden at Number 26. Standing on an upturned plant pot and peering cautiously over the recently repaired laplock fence, he saw to his horror the odious Grundy putting the finishing touches to a brand new stately pleasure dome which had risen, Phoenix like, from the ashes of its predecessor.

Oh dear, oh dear oh dear! Here we go again!

CHAPTER SIX

TOBY AT THE SCRUBS

I never saw a man who looked
With such a wistful eye
Upon that little tent of blue
Which prisoners call the sky

[Oscar Wilde]

"Mr. Gazzard will see you tomorrow at two o'clock sharp," and so saying, Fred, the senior clerk returned to the business of the day.

For Toby, it was high noon, or two o'clock to be precise, when he would find out if he were to be offered a tenancy in Brick Court, or cast adrift on a sea of troubles. It was make or break time. A tenancy would secure his future at the Bar for the rest of his professional life, an invitation to join the club as a fulltime member and to begin the climb, ***per ardua ad astra.***

He had completed his second six months in pupillage and, by all accounts, had done as well as could be expected. Chambers solicitors had, for the most part, spoken warmly of him, he'd kept his nose clean, his shoes shined and his mind focussed on the task in hand.

Fortunately for Toby, Nick Ridley, his pupil master, supported his application, and had put in a good word for him with other senior members. Toby was confident, but not over-confident, about his chances, but Nigel Gazzard, the Head of Chambers, had a reputation for being eccentric and unpredictable, and if he didn't like what he saw, there was no chance.

"One thing to bear in mind, Toby," said Nick when he heard the news, "nobody gets into these Chambers unless they can recite by heart the case of Palmer against Camley Borough Council. You may remember it from your lectures on Tort." Toby nodded, and wished he did. "Bone up on it, and you should be alright."

Off went Toby like the wind to the library and found the case, locked into a dusty law report from the early fifties. Mr. Palmer, a grumpy old man in the twilight of his years, was walking down the street in Camley, glaring at one and all, as was his wont, when he fell into an open manhole and injured himself, as one does when falling into an open manhole. Step forward one Nigel Gazzard, son of Nigel Gazzard, Queen's Counsel, and grandson of Nigel Gazzard, Queen's Counsel, who founded Brick Court Chambers. Not much originality of thought went into naming the male line in the Gazzard family. Gazzard's father had made shed loads of money advising large corporations on how to spend their employees' pension funds and get away with it, was burnt out by fifty and dropped dead three weeks short of his fifty first birthday. Toby's Gazzard was not cut in the same mould, but carried an illustrious name, which helped, and over the years carved out a solid if unspectacular practice in general common law. Enter the grumpy Mr. Palmer, Gazzard's salvation and role model and, as it turned out, his only claim to fame. Acting on counsel's advice, Mr. Palmer sued Camley for negligence. Gazzard was nothing if not tenacious, as he lost in the High Court and the Court of Appeal. Their lordships took the view that if grumpy old men were stupid enough to be wandering down the street, not looking where they were going, they had only themselves to blame. Gazzard, stubbornly undeterred, took Mr. Palmer's case to the House of Lords. Happily for Gazzard and Mr. Palmer, the court was composed of grumpy old men who spent every waking moment glaring at one and all, so they allowed the appeal and awarded modest damages and costs.

Gazzard never looked back. Sadly, he never looked forward either, and after innumerable applications to the Lord Chancellor, was eventually rewarded for his persistence and appointed Queen's Counsel. The shock was almost too much to bear. He went into semi-retirement, became a grumpy old man, and saw out the remainder of his days living comfortably off his father's shed loads of money, bossing the snot out of his long suffering wife Mildred and discharging his duties as Head of Chambers when the mood took him.

The next afternoon, promptly at two, Toby presented himself for inspection.

"So," Gazzard began, "you want to join chambers."

Toby nodded enthusiastically. "One of the best sets in the Temple."

"**The** best set in the Temple, young man," Gazzard snapped back, glaring at him.

"Yes, yes, absolutely."

There was a long pause. "I gather from Ridley you want to specialise in crime. Poppycock! All this nonsense about bamboozling the jury into acquitting the guilty, and what do they do? They go out and do it again! I can't be doing with it!" This was not going at all well, and not what Toby was expecting. "A solid common law practitioner is what these chambers need. It did me no harm," he continued, looking into the middle distance with a misty eye.

Another long pause. "I suppose you've heard of the case of Palmer against Camley Borough Council?"

Toby was on firm ground, having memorised it down to the last detail. "Yes indeed," he began, "one of the leading cases on public liability negligence…"

"**The** leading case, young man!" Gazzard snapped back.

"Yes, yes," Toby hurried on, "and a ground breaking case, if you'll forgive the pun."

Gazzard didn't, and as soon as he's said it, Toby wished he hadn't. Gazzard was not amused, as he glared at Toby in the way of a diner studying a foreign body floating in his soup.

"Very well," he said at last, "I shall consult senior members of chambers and let you have my decision in due course." Toby got up to go. "A word of advice, young man." Toby turned back. "Don't try and be clever, it doesn't become you. There's no room in these chambers for clever people."

Toby retired to Ridley's room to lick his wounds. The interview had been disastrous, and he knew it. If only, but too late for regrets. To while away the time, Toby flicked listlessly through the Chambers Vacancies section in Counsel magazine as his mood of depression deepened. Just as the clock moved towards six and close of play, Ridley walked in, clutching a bottle of champagne and two glasses.

"A toast to the new member of chambers," he beamed, "congratulations!" Toby didn't know whether to laugh or cry, so he did both as Ridley slapped him warmly on the back. "And the icing on the cake," he continued, "and awaiting you in the clerks' room, is your first jury trial brief, a fine start to a glorious career, I'm sure of it. Cheers."

Toby couldn't stop shaking, so he sat down to compose himself. "I can't begin to thank you enough, Nick," he stammered.

"No need, dear boy. Now, when you've finished your champagne, I suggest you collect your brief and we'll have an early supper at my club. Tonight's for celebrating, tomorrow's another day."

And indeed it was, as Toby unfolded the brief and peered bleary eyed and hung over at the case of Darren 'Tosser' Willis who, together with Matt 'The Knife' Lucas, Luke 'Puker' May and John 'Jo-Jo' Radcliff, was charged with affray. After a night on the piss, the four amigos were pitch forked out of the Cock and Bull public house into the cold night air, well lashed and spoiling for a fight. They trod the well-worn path to Dellers Nightclub, the local hot spot for spare Totty and lashings of vodka and Red Bull.

Tosser had only just finished a six-month ban from the club for previous misunderstandings, so the bouncers were keeping a close eye on him. True to form, as he lolled semi-comatose on the bar, somebody jogged his drinking arm, and the rest, as they say, is history. Chairs, glasses, skin and hair flew in all directions as the bouncers ran around like headless chickens, trying to bring forth order out of chaos. They failed miserably, so they called in the cavalry, and the next thing Tosser remembered was the friendly face of the duty solicitor peering at him out of the gloom of a police cell. Not feeling his best, he elected to say nothing when interviewed, an invariable practice cultivated over years in police custody, so he was duly charged and remanded to appear next morning at the local Magistrates Court. Their Worships took one look at his record, refused him bail, and committed his case for trial to the Crown Court, together with the three Apostles.

There was closed circuit television footage taken of the incident from the club's in-house camera. A tape had been produced, which Toby loaded into the chambers video recorder. It was like watching the moon landing, one giant step for mankind, only worse, as silent blurred images flitted across the screen in lapsed time, and as he had no idea what Tosser looked like, it told him nothing. So far, so good. Tosser's defence, courtesy of the duty solicitor who'd drawn the short straw and wished he hadn't, was ambivalent to say the least. He wasn't there, and if he was, he didn't do it.

The conference had been arranged that very afternoon, at four thirty sharp, in the depths of Her Majesty's Prison at Wormwood Scrubs.

Wormwood Scrubs lived up to its name. A Victorian creation on the outer margins of west London, where decent folk feared to tread, it had been built to house four hundred and eighty of the Good Queen's less fortunate subjects but, with the advance of a more civilised society, was now home to over eleven hundred, all crammed together in small, unhygienic cells like a German holiday camp in the Canaries. In spite of later additions and some updating, the prison still retained its original and rather grand crenulated façade, totally out of keeping with the squalid mass of squirming humanity behind its high walls.. A slate grey sky and a biting wind simply confirmed Toby's first impressions, this was hell on earth, and the sooner he was out of it, the better.

Entry to the Scrubs was a performance in itself, proving, if proof were needed, that getting out was a good deal easier than getting in. Toby produced his driving licence and letter of authority at the gate, and after careful scrutiny, he was escorted across the yard, together with twenty or more of the inmates' nearest and dearest, all clutching their visitors' vouchers, to a sort of holding pen. Toby's first and lasting memory was the overpowering smell of body odour and strong disinfectant as they all shuffled forward to be searched. When it came to Toby's turn, he was confronted by a female prison officer, it was the skirt that gave her away, built like a brick barn, smelling like a dog's bottom and sporting an incipient moustache. As she'd clearly had her sense of humour surgically removed when she took the job, you stepped across her shadow at your peril. After he had removed every metal object he could think of, Toby walked through the electronic gate, which of course bleeped. To the accompaniment of a groundswell of hostile mutterings behind him, back he went, and short of walking through stark naked, everything he had to his name was deposited into a plastic dish and pored over like the droppings of a sacred cow. After what seemed like an eternity, he was given a clean bill of health and moved on to the final hurdle, the conference admissions officer.

"I have a conference booked with Darren Willis." Toby was at his most charming. No point upsetting the natives, although his patience was being tested to its limits. "I am his counsel."

"Are you indeed?" The admissions officer, unimpressed, picked up his clipboard and ran his finger down the list. "Willis, you say?"

"That's right, W-I-L-L-I-S."

The admissions officer gave Toby an old-fashioned look, and returned to the clipboard. "Sorry, but I've no record of a conference booked with W-I-L-L-I-S."

This was not going well. He was about to snap, when the admissions officer's supernumerary detached the enormous mug of tea from his lips and offered his two bit's worth.

"'ang on a minute, George," thus spake the Oracle, "ain't that DS. Farmer's collar? You know, Tosser?"

George's brow furrowed as the thought processes cranked into gear. Back to the clipboard and the descending finger. Eureka! Got it at last! "Tosser, why didn't you say so? Room Seventeen. Mr. Farmer's with him, 'as been for the last twenty minutes." George looked up. "You're late, Squire."

Toby was about to say something, thought better of it, and hurried down the corridor to Room Seventeen.

DS. 'Bootsy' Farmer was a big man with gnarled features and a disposition to match. Now retired, and acting as gamekeeper turned poacher, he'd spent the best years of his life in the Met, kicking the proverbial out of villains who had the temerity to stray onto his patch. One kick too many had forced the Commissioner to part with his services, with full pension and benefits of course, and 'Bootsy' found himself out on the street with nothing to do. After mature reflection, 'Bootsy' decided to keep his finger in the pie and offer his services to solicitors as their outdoor clerk. Some, with personal experience of 'Bootsy' from the good old days, found the pill too bitter to swallow, but a doughty band from the twilight zone provided him with enough work and more to top up his pension and keep him ticking over. It was not particularly onerous work. 'Bootsy' was delegated to sit in on interviews with suspects during unsocial hours at the local police station, attend conferences with counsel and sit in court, taking notes and reporting back. Taking accurate notes had never been his forté. When he was in the Met he used to make them up as he went along, but no matter, he was better than nothing, which wasn't saying much.

Bootsy and Tosser were in animated conversation as Toby walked in. He had the feeling he was interrupting a private conversation. Both were smoking, in spite of prominent No Smoking signs on the walls, Bootsy dragging on a disgusting Panatella that smelled like old socks, and Tosser about to roll his third smoke from his stash of Old Holborn shag. Toby's eyes began to water as he sat down and opened his Counsel's notebook, containing as it did various bullet points, flow charts and diagrams, all designed to put flesh on Tosser's paper-thin defence.

"I'm sorry I'm late," Toby began tentatively, "but the security is something to be believed."

"That's strange," said Bootsy, "I didn't have any problems."

Toby ignored the slight and pressed on. Directing his remarks to Tosser, he continued. "My name is Potts, Toby Potts, and I'm counsel instructed to represent you at your forthcoming trial." Tosser stared back vacantly. Twenty-eight years old, with more convictions than you could shake a stick at, he was an unedifying spectacle. Scrawny, with a sunken, sallow complexion, a grade two haircut exaggerating his protruding, studded, ears, uneven, tobacco stained teeth, and tattoos crawling all over his body and reaching up to his neck, as if to throttle him. Born head down in the dustbin of life, he'd never looked up.

"Now," said Toby, trying to concentrate, "there are a number of matters we need to discuss if we're to fine tune your defence."

"Look, Tobe," Tosser interrupted, the note of familiarity jarring with Toby's sense of his own self-importance, "me and Mr. Farmer 'ere 'ave been 'aving a little chat, d'yer know what I mean," Toby didn't. "Now me and Mr. Farmer go back a long way, d'yer know what I mean, 'e first felt me collar when I was no more than seventeen," Bootsy nodded knowingly, "'e was an 'ard bastard, d'yer know what I mean," Bootsy stopped nodding and blew a cloud of noxious smoke over the cheeky little sod, but Tosser was on a roll and nothing was going to stop him now, "but a fair bastard, and when Mr. Farmer tells me to cop a plea, then I cop a plea, simple as that, d'yer know what I mean?"

There followed an awkward silence as Toby absorbed the enormity of Tosser's peroration. What should he do?

The silence was broken by Bootsy, who leaned forward and, placing his massive forearms on the table, stared intently at Toby. "The way we see it, Mr. Potts," he said, warming to his theme, "is that Tosser doesn't have a prayer, not even with you representing him." A nice touch, wholly lacking in sincerity. "So if Tosser cops a plea, with credit and time spent on remand, he'll do twelve months tops and be out before he knows it. After all," he continued, waxing lyrical, "as Churchill once said, you can fool some of the people all of the time, but you can't fool all of the people all of the time, d'yer know what I mean?"

"Actually, it was Abraham Lincoln, not Churchill," and as it turned out, that was Toby's only significant contribution to the conference.

"Yeah, yeah, whatever, you're the scholar, Mr. Potts," a backhanded compliment if ever there was, "I could see that the moment I clapped eyes on you, but Tosser and me, we're streetwise, ain't we Tosser? And there are times when that counts for everything."

And that was it. Toby thought about asserting his authority as learned counsel, but as he had none, there seemed little point. And besides, with the oxygen supply dipping dangerously low, and a rising tide of nausea welling up from the pit of his stomach, he couldn't get out fast enough.

After a clammy handshake, Tosser sloped off and Bootsy gave Toby a friendly slap on the back. "See you at court, then, Mr. Potts." Over my dead body, Toby muttered, smiling weakly. Bootsy accepted the offer of an enormous mug of hot sweet tea with the admissions officers, leaving Toby to make his own way out. As fast as he could, he went back through security and eventually, gasping for breath, out into the cold light of day.

He took one last, lingering look at the Scrubs, shuddered, counted his blessings, and hurried back to the Temple.

Never mind, he thought, win some, lose some. Now was it General Custer who said that?

CHAPTER SEVEN

TOBY AT THE ASYLUM

The Judge, without knowing how or why,
Made still a blund'ring kind of melody;
Spurred boldly on, and dashed through thick and thin,
Through sense and nonsense, never out nor in;
Free from all meaning, whether good or bad,
And in one word, heroically mad.

[after John Dryden]

Snaresbrook Crown Court, the last outpost of the Empire, was buried at the outer margins of civilisation and close to Epping Forest, where more than squirrel nuts had been buried over the centuries. For some, it hadn't been buried deep enough, such was its reputation. It was where most of the human detritus of the East end of London got deposited, and where the lament of tortured souls seeking vengeance could be heard when the moon was full. For a while, it became Toby's second home in those early days of cutting his professional teeth on unpalatable fare.

In the middle of the nineteenth century, not long after Good Queen Victoria had eased her firm but ample posterior onto the Throne of Great Britain, Ireland and the burgeoning Empire, soon to be Queen of all she surveyed from the length and breadth of Africa to the shores of Araby, through the known and unknown world to the very edge of civilisation and beyond, on the road to Mandalay where the flying fishes played and where not even Christopher Columbus had dared to venture, a colonisation of a different kind was taking place.

The lesser gentry and the ***nouveau riche*** bourgeoisie, tired of the cut and thrust of the Metropolis and yearning for pastures new, began a slow but steady exodus to the leafy suburbs, where nothing is heard but the song of a bird, and the skies are not cloudy all day.

One such object of their attention was Epping Forest, barely a day's gentle trot from Pall Mall yet in the heart of the countryside, a veritable oasis and, with some radical pruning, a potential Garden of Eden.

However, to the irritation of the ***Belle Monde***, Epping Forest had more than its fair share of the great unwashed. Footpads, beggars, miscreants, creatures of the night and the just plain bonkers were to be found behind every tree, so something had to give, and give quickly, in this demi-paradise. Meetings were organised, Members of Parliament lobbied, and as the great unwashed had no say in the great scheme of things, the colonists had their way.

It was decreed that a magnificent edifice be constructed, using only the finest materials and paid from the public purse, ostensibly to house the less fortunate of society, but in reality to lock them up out of harm's way. After all, out of sight is out of mind, and in the fullness of time, Snaresbrook Lunatic Asylum was formally opened by the Mayor, accompanied by his good lady wife the Lady Mayoress and the Aldermen of the Borough. By all accounts, and with the obvious exception of the inmates, a splendid day was had by all. The same architect who had designed Wormwood Scrubs was engaged to display his genius, so plenty of crenulated walls, and fetching little turrets rising majestically into the perpetual grey sky.

One hundred and thirty years later, lunatics of all persuasions, having become the mentally disorientated and no longer social pariahs, were eased back into the community from whence they came, and life turned full circle. With that inspired lateral thinking which only governments can lay claim to, it was decided that the now vacant building should become the new Snaresbrook Crown Court. A case, if ever there was, of the lunatics taking over the asylum.

The new court was not exactly the jewel in the Crown Court hierarchy, and finding a resident judge to hold sway and bring much-needed gravitas to the post proved almost a bridge too far. However, more by luck than good judgment, word reached the Mandarins in the Lord Chancellor's department that His Honour Judge 'Bonkers' Clarke, recently separated from his wife following unfounded revelations in the tabloid press, had been advised to look for a change of scene well away from his usual watering hole if he were ever to enjoy his index linked pension. Such advice from the Lord Chancellor was not to be lightly discarded, so after a suitable period in retreat, he was duly installed. The fact that he was known by one and all as 'Bonkers' from his earliest days on the Bench made the appointment almost apocryphal.

Bonkers was nothing if not fully committed to his resident status, throwing himself energetically into every aspect of court life. Arriving each morning at the crack of dawn, and sporting an old knitted cardigan, he was regularly to be seen patrolling the corridors, noting down broken light bulbs and unemptied bins, bringing his own brand of order out of chaos. He was accompanied, as always, by Max, his faithful black Labrador, with a wet and inquisitive nose as many a court usher would attest. An irresistible combination.

After ten years of unstinting labour at the coalface, he modestly accepted the Honorary Recordership of Epping Forest, bestowed upon him by the grateful burghers. On the appointed day, assembled in Court One were all the judges, barristers, staff and assorted acolytes, together with the Mayor and his good lady wife the Lady Mayoress and Aldermen of the Borough, all there to pay tribute to His Honour Judge 'Bonkers' Clarke. Hardly a dry eye in the court, and after speeches, they adjourned, briefly, for sandwiches and coffee, before Bonkers and Max returned to Her Majesty's business. After all, time is money.

The Crown Prosecution Service used counsel from time to time when it suited their convenience and when their Higher Courts Advocates were otherwise engaged. And so it was that one evening Toby was summoned into the clerks' room and handed his first prosecution brief.

"Nothing special," observed the senior clerk, "but the CPS are short staffed and I've agreed to help out. Besides," he added, "if you pull this one off, there'll be more to come."

Toby nodded gratefully, and went off to his room to study the brief. The backsheet looked like a map of Ireland, with Tippex erasing the names of his predecessors in title who had picked up the brief, run with it and then dropped it. No matter, it was his now, and a chance to prove himself as the Hammer of the Ungodly.

His instructions were light on the facts, directing him as they did to the case summary, and heavy on the law. There were pro-forma pages about human rights and the advocate's duty to the court, sentencing procedures and, most important of all, the advocate's duty to apply for costs. Finally, **in bold type,** were strictures against the advocate making any decisions of his own. All decisions had to be referred to the reviewing lawyer, Paul Newman...., Surely not? No, it can't be, whose telephone number was appended, again **in bold type.** So much for the independent Bar.

The case summary described the defendant, Wayne Pedder, as a serial shoplifter who, on the day in question, helped himself to a DVD player courtesy of his local one-stop shop and made a dash for the exit. Sadly for him, the automatic doors failed to respond to his fleet of foot, as he barrelled straight into them and bounced straight back into the arms of the security staff. He was charged with theft and attempted criminal damage to a pair of automatic doors. Fair enough, thought Toby, an open and shut case. Even the reviewing lawyer seemed to agree, as a guilty plea had been indicated.

Toby arrived early, and after a brisk walk from the station, decided on a stroll around the extensive and well-manicured grounds. Although it was winter, there was a watery sun reflecting off the enormous lake, the squirrels were busy collecting nuts, and a large flock of Canada geese were paddling along the shore. It was an idyllic scene totally out of keeping with the past and present occupants.

Toby's reverie was rudely interrupted by a loud bellow. Looking up, he saw a strange figure, dressed in an old knitted cardigan, standing on one of the crenulated parapets of the court. Toby cupped his hands to his ears.

"Get off the grass," bellowed the strange figure.

One of the inmates, thought Toby, obviously overlooked when the asylum was vacated. Poor old fool, better humour him. Toby gave him a cheery wave and strolled towards the main entrance.

Having found the robing room, small and crowded, Toby was about to be exposed to some old-fashioned sandbagging, although he didn't know it at the time.

"Are you Potts?" Toby turned round to be confronted by a short, wiry man in his early forties, greying hair, with pursed lips and an aggressive demeanour. "I defend Pedder," he continued before Toby could answer, "and I'm led to believe that you prosecute."

"Yes, that's right."

"My name's Cantwell." Toby nodded. "Now, the defendant will accept a bind over if you offer no evidence. Done and dusted, and we can be on our way by eleven. After all, some of us have better things to do than fart around here all day. So what do you say?"

"I'm afraid it's not my decision," Toby replied, remembering his instructions, "but if it were, I'd say the defendant was as guilty as sin. Haven't you seen the CCTV?" he added mischievously, knowing full well that the assistant manager had forgotten to put in a cassette that morning when he arrived for work, thus sparing Toby the ordeal of viewing the unviewable.

Cantwell was not to be wrong-footed, especially by some callow youth in the first flush of advocacy. "Good try, Potts, but you know as well as I do that there was no CCTV footage of the incident. I didn't ride into town on the head of a cabbage, you know."

Touché. Toby tried a different tack. "What about his previous convictions?" he continued, "your client's a prolific offender."

"And just how do you intend getting that into evidence? You haven't served a BC1. Anyway, I can see we're wasting each other's time. We'll let the jury decide where the truth lies," and with that, he flounced out of the robing room in high dudgeon.

A BC1? It sounded very old. Why hadn't Toby heard of it before? So much to learn, so little time.

Cantwell was almost a permanent fixture at Snaresbrook. He lived locally, so it suited him. He had two golden rules - never prosecute, and never plead guilty, so he got regular work from local defence solicitors whom he kept on a very tight rein. He had a third golden rule, which he followed without exception - never fraternise with the prosecution, they were the enemy, to be tolerated as a necessary evil, but never to be humoured.

As Toby made his way to Court Thirteen, he contemplated the prospect of his first jury trial with obvious trepidation. He was hardly prepared for the task ahead, but no fault of his. Even the reviewing lawyer had expected a plea of guilty. Some review, some lawyer! And to cap it all, Cantwell as his opponent, with the bit between his teeth. He'd have to be at his sharpest to win the shining hour, but then, the evidence was overwhelming.

With five minutes to go, no sign of the CPS law clerk, who was supposed to hold his hand and steer him effortlessly through the stormy waters. As he was contemplating his next move, the usher popped her head around the door. Addressing nobody in particular, "the case of Pedder will be heard in Court One," she bellowed like a fishwife shouting the odds. Bellowing was almost endemic at Snaresbrook Crown Court.

After a clutch of applications, mentions and reviews lasting most of the morning, the case of Pedder was called on. Toby shuffled into court with Cantwell barging his way forward and studiously ignoring him, all the time under the watchful gaze of His Honour Judge 'Bonkers' Clarke.

Toby was about to take his seat when Bonkers addressed him. "Now, Mr...er...Potts," he began, glancing down at the names of the advocates on the sheet of paper in front of him, "I don't think much of this indictment. How do you justify the count of attempted criminal damage to an automatic door?"

"I agree, your Honour," smarmed Cantwell, rising from his seat. Cantwell reminded Toby of that ditty:

Oozing charm from every pore,
He oiled his way across the floor.

"Not yet, Mr.Cantwell, you'll have your turn, I'm sure of it. Who was the idiot who drafted that particular count, Mr. Potts?"

Toby turned to the law clerk, Tracey by name, as he was subsequently to discover. She might as well do something. After all, this was supposed to be a team effort. "Who was the idiot who drafted that particular count?" he whispered. "Can you help?"

"That'll be our Mr. Newman," she whispered back, and took out a form, ominously headed 'Advocate's Evaluation'.

So be it, thought Toby, if you can't stand and fight, better cut and run. "I am instructed that it was our Mr. Newman, the reviewing lawyer. If your Honour will rise for five minutes, I can take instructions." Tracey was not amused, and made a note to that effect on the form - 'found wanting under fire'.

"Bunkum," Bonkers was even less amused, "I shall enter a verdict of not guilty on that count." Could he do that? Toby wondered, plunging into his Archbold.

"You can close that book now, Mr. Potts. I am the law in this court!" There was no answer to that. Bonkers paused, peering intently over his spectacles. "Have we met before, Mr. Potts?"

Toby peered back, and the vision of the strange figure on the parapet loomed large. "I don't think so, your Honour, this is my first appearance at Snaresbrook."

There was a long pause. "Very well," he said at last, "let's hope it's a memorable one. Now, Mr. Cantwell, what's the defence to the charge of theft? The defendant was caught red-handed."

Cantwell oiled his way to his feet. "The defence will be placed fairly and squarely before the jury in the course of the trial…"

"Yes, yes, I have no doubt, but what is it?"

"Your Honour presses me."

"I do."

"Very well, the defendant will say that whilst on a legitimate shopping expedition in the One-Stop Shop to buy a DVD for his severely disabled son, he was suddenly caught short following a particularly powerful Vindaloo curry the night before, and in his anxiety not to disgrace himself, he made a dash to the nearest evacuation point, forgetting he still had the DVD player under his arm. His progress was thwarted by the malfunctioning automatic doors, with the result that, after the inevitable acquittal of this spurious charge, he has engaged my services to sue the store for negligence and the replacement cost of a pair of soiled trousers. Your Honour will be familiar with the case of Palmer and Camley Borough Council?"

In all his years on the Bench, Bonkers thought he'd heard it all, but this was the best by far. He raised his eyes to the ceiling in total disbelief. "And what about the confession he made when he was arrested?" Bonkers looked down at the case papers. "It's fair cop, guv. What does the defendant say about that?"

Cantwell was equal to the task. "He didn't say it, your Honour, but if he did, he was referring to the shop, not cop."

"What! He said 'it's a fair shop, guv'! Is that what you're telling me!"

"Your Honour has it in one," smarmed Cantwell, totally unfazed by the absurdity of his instructions. "But, pausing there," he continued,

70

"do I detect a certain scepticism about the defence in your Honour's remarks?"

"You do indeed, Mr. Cantwell. It's a complete waste of public time and money."

"Then may I remind your Honour, with the greatest of respect, of course," Cantwell was positively dripping, "that the defendant is entitled to a fair trial in front of an independent tribunal, regardless of the merits or otherwise of the defence...."

"Don't lecture me on the law, Mr. Cantwell, I am perfectly well aware of the defendant's rights, and as for merits, as you so delicately put it, there are none. That said," he continued with a full head of steam, "I have no intention whatsoever of wasting my time trying this case." He glanced down at his court list. "I shall release it back to Court Thirteen and Mr. Recorder Twigg," and so saying, he slammed the file shut and threw it at the court clerk. "Don't let me detain you," he glowered. "Call on the next case."

Mr. Recorder Twigg was in the full blush of youth and barely old enough to shave. With a substantial Chancery practice, and making more money in a week than most journeymen barristers make in a year, he was climbing the greasy pole at a rate of knots. He knew nothing whatsoever about the criminal law, so, in the eyes of the Lord Chancellor, he was an ideal candidate to preside over the cut and thrust of life at the coalface. Equipped as he was with a large red folder fetchingly entitled 'An idiot's guide to the criminal law - Judge's copy', he felt equal to the task. To add lustre to his judicial role, he had brought his laptop, plugged in and powered up, ready to roll.

On any view, Toby's first jury trial was a disappointment. The jury, to a man, looked catatonic and positively hostile. The evidence went as predicted. After his opening speech, he called the security person as his star witness, who looked, for all the world, like a character from a Gilbert and Sullivan operetta. His uniform was straight from The Pirates of Penzance, the very model of a modern Major General, with epaulettes and tassels and lanyards and badges fit to burst.

Fortunately for Toby, Mr. Security was a seasoned campaigner. He'd seen it all before, so immediately after the event, he'd made a witness statement, which he'd memorised by heart before giving evidence. If it was in the statement, it had happened. If it wasn't, it hadn't, or if it had, he couldn't remember. He was not going to give an inch.

The defendant's evidence, as trailed by Cantwell, was true to form, as he trotted out the Vindaloo defence. Toby's incisive cross-examination, a model of its kind if he were to say so himself, was commendable for its brevity if nothing else. A tissue of lies, he heard himself suggesting. The defendant disagreed, and Toby sat down with a flourish as Twigg tapped away on his laptop. Never once did he look up, to get a feel for the case or to study human nature in the raw. For him it was nothing more than a forensic exercise, so he kept well out of the evidential arena. It was antiseptic justice with a capital 'A', devoid of all emotion, but, with the help of his Idiot Guide, unobjectionable down to the last comma and full stop.

The jury were out for a full twelve minutes before returning to find the defendant not guilty as charged. Another notch on Cantwell's belt as Tracey scribbled furiously on the 'Advocate's Evaluation' sheet. So much for his prosecution practice as he returned, crestfallen, to the Temple. What had he done wrong?

On the train back, Toby was joined by an older and wiser colleague who'd seen it all before.

"Don't blame yourself. It's an impossible nut to crack. The CPS have an indifferent bottle of *vin mousseau,* which they keep in their vaults, to be opened when any defendant is convicted of an offence of dishonesty. It isn't going to happen."

"I don't understand. I mean, the law is the law."

"Not in Epping Forest it isn't. At least, not our idea of the law. Think about it. Years ago, we locked them away, for no good reason, simply because they blighted the landscape and bruised the sensibilities of middle class suburbia. Then we let them all out again, and expect them to behave like model citizens. Old habits die hard, so when they're not out thieving and wheeling and dealing and getting nicked, they're sitting on juries. Whatever else, there's honour amongst thieves, so is it any wonder they stick together?"

A sobering thought, but how was Toby going to sell that to Paul Newman and the senior clerk? Even now, Tracey's moving finger writes, and having writ, moves on. The Advocate's Evaluation form was set in stone. Oh well, too late for regrets, and besides, tomorrow's another day.

CHAPTER EIGHT

TOBY TAIRLEH HEAU

'Twas the sound of his horn called me from my bed,
And the cry of his hounds has me oft-times led;
For Peel's view-hollo would waken the dead,
Or a fox from his lair in the morning.

[John Woodcock Graves]

Toby's dismal failure to secure a conviction at Snaresbrook left him in *mal odeur* with the CPS. They briefed counsel on results, not good looks or advocacy, and those who fell at the first hurdle were deemed unworthy to wield the hammer of the ungodly. To add insult to injury, Paul Newman, the reviewing lawyer, was singularly unimpressed with the Advocate's Evaluation form, duly completed and filed by our Tracey. Words like 'dismissive', and 'discourteous' jumped out from our Tracey's copybook handwriting, always a pleasure to read. A period in the sin bin was called for, and Toby found himself out of favour and relegated to less demanding work, like applications, mentions and the occasional committal for sentence.

In the meantime, as he waited in the wings for his next call to centre stage, life went on much as before, the world continued turning, and it was business as usual at Brick Court. But there was trouble brewing down in the Sticks, and soon to present Toby with his greatest challenge.

Charles Marjoribanks Dalziel Cholmondeley Fitzherbert, twenty-third Earl of Brockenhurst, known affectionately to his small but eclectic circle of friends as Buffy, could trace his ancestry back to the Norman Conquest. For services rendered to the usurping King William, his

forebears were granted lands in Hampshire, which stretched as far as
the eye could see and beyond. Over the centuries, and with judicious
unions arranged on the nuptial couch or in the stables, whatever, the
Brockenhursts added to their lands and possessions in equal measure,
and thanks to fee tails and entails, held in trust for successive
generations, their power and influence remained undiminished. At the
last count, the Brockenhursts were the third greatest landowners in the
country, after HM of course, and the Cavendish boy.

Sandle Manor was the family seat, situated in magnificent parkland at
the end of a long tree-lined drive. The house itself was mainly Tudor,
built at much the same time as the ill-fated Cardinal Wolsey was
building Hampton Court. History relates that Good Queen Bess, not
this one, that one, spent a night at Sandle Manor during one of her
whirlwind tours. It was the time of papist plots and social unrest, so
she was testing the goodwill, loyalty and hospitality of her courtesans.
As the Brockenhursts were one of the premier Catholic families in the
country, a visit was inevitable. Having been shown to her apartments
for a wash and brush up before dinner, she observed, in idle chit-chat,
how much better the view from her window would be without so many
trees. As soon as she had retired for the night, hundreds of estate
workers were dragooned into felling an equal number of mighty oaks.
They laboured ceaselessly all night, groping their way from tree to
tree, trying to keep the sound of chopping and the crashing of newly
hewn timber down to a dull roar, interspersed with the occasional oath,
and by dawn's early light, an avenue of sorts had been created for Her
Majesty's pleasure. The Good Queen breakfasted lightly on pheasant,
swan, pigeon and quail, washed down with champagne, but she was in
poor spirits and a pale shadow of her former self, having spent a
restless night to the accompaniment of chopping, crashing and cursing,
which she found most aggravating. History does not relate what
comment, if any, she made about the newly created avenue, or even if
she noticed it, but Sandle Manor was well-stocked with firewood for
the next two hundred years. The earl's ancestor kept his head and his
estates, and mercifully for both parties, the Queen never visited again.

On his twenty-second birthday, Charles's father called him into the
study and announced he was to marry. A suitable bride had been
chosen for him from the society pages of Country Life, a handsome

filly with good bone structure and impeccable antecedents and, most important of all, not yet broken to the harness.

And so it was that Camilla Fortescue-Woodcock married Charles in a fitting ceremony at St. Paul's Cathedral, and after a honeymoon on the Fitzherbert estates in Scotland, they settled down to married bliss. Ensuring the blood line of the Fitzherberts began slowly, but once Charles had got the hang of it, there was no stopping him, and five or six children were born of their union.

The family had weathered many storms as the social and political climate changed, and then changed back again. Governments of varying hues had attempted to divest them and their ilk of their rank, privilege and wealth, and had failed. All had been seen off, in one form or another, until New Labour burst onto the political landscape. Suddenly, the benches of the House of Commons were packed with spotty youths from working class backgrounds, braying incessantly in their regional accents, and hell-bent on making a thorough nuisance of themselves. The Devil makes work for idle minds. As Charles was fond of saying, it's often the way when you give head to a stupid animal, it's the devil's own job to rein it in.

Not that Charles had anything against the working classes. On the contrary, he employed more than his fair share. Butlers, maids, gardeners, chauffeurs, stable lads, all had their part to play. And he treated them fairly, make no mistake. At Christmas time and on his birthday, they had the whole day off, with cider and beer and hot oatcakes provided, at no little expense, for their enjoyment. If nothing else, Charles was a munificent employer.

And then came the ban on fox-hunting, brought in by the same spotty youths who wouldn't know a fox if they fell over one. Whilst Oscar Wilde may have declaimed it as "the unspeakable in pursuit of the uneatable," he was a girlie fop with long hair, who had never saddled a horse in his entire life, and who should have stuck to what he did best, which was writing mediocre plays and fooling around with young men half his age.

To Charles, it was an attack on the very fabric of society. There had been fox-hunting at Sandle Manor for as long as there'd been foxes, and no poxy ban was going to interfere with that. Charles had become Master of the Sandle Manor Hunt upon the death of his father, and it was one of the finest in the land, patronised by Royalty no less.

On the first Saturday after the ban came into force, word went out on the bush telegraph that the Hunt would be meeting as usual. Indeed, Charles made no secret of the fact. It was his Hunt, his land and his right to do as he pleased. A small but noisy demonstration was held at one of the main gates, kept back by the local constabulary. Banners were unfurled, horns and whistles blown, together with some good-natured chanting. But with the main house some two miles away up the avenue dedicated to the memory of Good Queen Bess, it had little impact.

In any crowd, there were always the occasional hotheads, determined to cause mischief, and even though the estate was surrounded by high walls, a small band of protestors, no doubt related to the spotty youths in Westminster, managed to clamber over and into the grounds.

Later that afternoon, a formal complaint was lodged at the local police station by one Steve Gardner, part time lecturer at one of the new universities and full time hunt saboteur, that, whilst attempting to make a citizen's arrest, he had been viciously assaulted by his lordship and had the marks to show for it. And he had. Two livid red welts across his back bore testimony to his earlier confrontation. When asked what he was doing on private land, he claimed it was his duty as a law-abiding citizen to prevent the commission of a criminal act, and besides, he added testily, "you lot weren't doing anything about it, were you?"

The Duty Sergeant's first inclination was to send the odious Gardner packing with a flea in his ear, and was about to do so, when the phone rang. It was the newshound from the local paper, and before sunset it would be all over the national press. Against his better judgment, the Sergeant decided Gardner must have his day, so in the fullness of time his lordship was charged with assault occasioning actual bodily harm and hunting with dogs, and respectfully requested to appear at Little

Hampton Magistrates Court on a day to be appointed, at his lordship's convenience, of course, to answer the charges.

To Toby's surprise and trepidation, the brief to represent the Earl of Brockenhurst came into chambers, in Toby's name no less, and marked with two hundred guineas. He was at a complete loss to know why he'd been chosen, ***primus inter partes,*** so he phoned the Earl's solicitor, Peter Simkins.

"Ah, yes, Mr. Potts, you come highly recommended."

"I don't understand."

"Then let me explain. His lordship had a chat about the case with his old friend Sir Archibald Scott-Malden QC. I believe the two of you are acquainted?" Toby didn't know what to say, but immediately stood up. This was not the sort of phone call to be taken sitting down. "Anyway, Sir Archibald felt unable to take the case personally due to a conflict of interests. They were at Eton together, don't you know, and have remained firm friends ever since. Added to which, Sir Archibald has ridden regularly with the Hunt whilst staying as a weekend guest at Sandle Manor." Toby was in awe as Mr. Simkins continued. "Sir Archibald felt this was a case where we should keep as low a profile as possible. No offence intended, Mr. Potts," he added hastily.

"And none taken, Mr. Simkins, I assure you."

"Splendid, splendid, I knew you'd understand. The Press will have a field day, whatever happens, and if Sir Archibald were there as well," he paused, "Well, I'm sure you get the picture."

"Of course." Toby felt a little deflated, but it quickly passed.

"Splendid, splendid. Now, we have a conference booked with you tomorrow morning at eleven thirty in your chambers. His lordship is staying at his London house even as we speak, so it will suit his convenience, and he is greatly looking forward to meeting you, as am I."

Chambers was already abuzz with the news, and for the first time since joining chambers, Fred, the senior clerk was almost deferential.

"All is ready for the conference, Mr. Potts," he was positively drooling. "I shall sit in, of course, to take notes and ensure everything goes like clockwork. Chambers best china is being washed and polished by Paul even as we speak, fresh coffee and a selection of biscuits will be available. You'll use Mr. Gazzard's room, of course, and Paul will give it a good hoovering and dusting before he goes home tonight, won't you, Paul?" Paul, the chambers gopher, grunted. "Now, if there's nothing else…."

Just then the phone rang, answered by the first junior clerk. As he listened, the colour drained from his face and he started shaking.

"Who is it, Mike?"

"It's…it's Sir Archibald Scott-Malden, and he wants to speak to Mr. Potts."

There was a deathly hush as the clerks' room absorbed the enormity of that statement. Toby turned to Fred, who was gaping like a fish out of water. "Do you mind if I take it in here?"

"Not at all, Sir." What a signal honour. Toby walked over and took the receiver. "Is that you, Archie?" He couldn't resist it. "Thank you so much for recommending me to his lordship." He listened for a minute. "Yes, of course, I shall pass on your best wishes, and I look forward to thanking you in person when we next meet."

Toby's star never shone so bright as he replaced the receiver and smiled graciously at one and all. "Until tomorrow then," as he swept majestically out of the room. It was a moment to savour.

Toby had no particular axe to grind in either camp when it came to hunting, shooting and fishing. For his part, he couldn't see the point of big, sweaty horses, with big sweaty riders, galloping around the countryside in pursuit of the uneatable. He was inclined to agree with the poet William Shenstone, who remarked that 'the world may be divided into people that read, people that write, people that think, and fox-hunters'.

Toby had tried riding, briefly, in his student days, when he was anxious to impress a very comely girlfriend who was devoted to riding and her big white horse Cascade. He bought all the gear, at considerable expense, including riding boots that took him over an hour to remove, and enrolled at his local riding stable. He was allocated an enormous brown horse called Bertie, which farted a lot, and was as stupid as they come. The nag had the unnerving habit of walking backwards, which was scary, and had no interest whatsoever in Toby's wish to bond. Each ride out consisted of Bertie, with his nose up the lead horse's bottom, and oblivious to Toby's commands, going at a snail's pace, until the command from the riding mistress to return to stables. Up went Bertie's ears, and off he went at a full gallop, farting all the way back, with Toby holding on for dear life. After six lessons, Toby, Bertie and the girlfriend parted company.

Whatever else, and despite his reservations, Toby was determined to be supportive, as the twenty-third Earl of Brockenhurst arrived promptly at eleven thirty, decanted onto the steps of Brick Court from a magnificent Rolls-Royce Phantom VI. The car park attendants had been forewarned, so there was a lot of running around and tugging of forelocks as his lordship smiled graciously and was ushered inside by Fred, in a frock coat no less. The only thing missing was a trumpet fanfare.

Toby stood up to greet his lordship, accompanied as he was by Mr. Simkins, and the earl's personal secretary, delegated to attend to his lordship's every wish.

The Earl cut an impressive figure. Tall, well-built, silver haired, yet fit looking for his sixty three years, his tanned complexion suggesting many hours in the saddle or on the moor. He was immaculately dressed in a tweed, three-piece suit, and he held himself in the manner of a man who brooked no nonsense.

"So you're the young chairp who's going to see orf this pack of mongrels baying for me blood." He paused, fixing Toby with piercing blue eyes. "Splendid, splendid," and he beamed at Simkins. "Now, what's our line of attack?"

"I assume your lordship is familiar with the case and the charges you have to answer?" Toby began, trembling slightly and trying to sound confident.

"'Earce, of course."

For the next half hour, Toby went through the evidence and the law, with his lordship grunting occasionally, and Fred scribbling furiously. Although he was as nervous as a kitten, Toby tried to sound confident and composed, and hoped he was succeeding. Paul arrived to lighten the mood, bearing the best chambers china with coffee and biscuits.

At last, with the conference over, his lordship glanced over at Simkins. "The court clerk has been in touch, tedder-blinnice of him, don't yer know, wishing to fix a date for my convenience.....and yours, of course, Mr. Potts," he added, almost as an after thought.

Fred immediately interjected. "Mr. Potts will make himself available at your lordship's convenience," he grovelled, "I shall see to it personally."

"That's kind of you, but I know how busy Mr. Potts must be, as a successful criminal practitioner." Toby smiled winningly at Fred, who averted his gaze. "Johnson." The Earl's secretary slid effortlessly to his master's side and produced a large, leather bound book, embossed with the Brockenhurst Coat of Arms. His lordship flicked through. "Fortunately we are ite of season," he continued, "harver, I have a week's shootin pencilled in at Sandringham after Christmas." Fred almost fell to his knees. "Then a cupla week zorf in Injure with the Dollamores," he looked up, "me old bones need a spell of winter sunshine to relieve the monotony of this dreadful climate," he chuckled, as did one and all. "So I suggest Thursday the seventeenth of Febray at two in the afternoon. Does that suit?"

Toby turned to Fred. "Do you have my diary available, Fred?" Toby was loving every minute of his new found fame.

"That will be fine, your lordship," replied Fred, "and I shall mark it in the diary forthwith."

"Splendid, splendid, then let battle commence." His lordship passed the book back to Johnson and stood up, as did one and all. "You'll come on dine and stay at the hice the night before, Mr. Potts, I insist on it," Toby wasn't about to refuse, "when we can have another liddle chairt and fine tune our plan of campaign. Idd'll prob'leh be priddeh chaotic, so take us as you find us. Until then."

As Fred escorted the Earl down the stairs, Toby felt a frisson of excitement and a dull, aching, feeling in the pit of his stomach. Regardless of the outcome, to the Earl this was, at most, a minor irritant, and life would go on as it had for centuries. For Toby however, with the national press and the media crammed into the courtroom, it was make or break time, and it terrified him. But the thought of a night at Sandle Manor, where Royalty and the highest born in the land had set foot, was a moment to savour. Strolling along the south terrace, with one of the Earl's daughters on his arm, muttering sweet nothings, and a lingering kiss beneath a moonlit sky. The fact that it would be darkest February was of no consequence, after all, true love knows no bounds, and as his mother was fond of saying, time to find a nice girl and settle down.

Toby's reveries were interrupted by Fred's return. He was at his most effusive, trembling with excitement. "What a gentleman, the noble earl, such quality, and what an honour and privilege for you and chambers as a whole. What a feather in your cap if you pull it off!" He paused, and his expression changed. "My Gawd, what happens if you don't?"

Little Hampton Court was surprisingly quiet, almost deserted, as Toby arrived with Mr. Simkins at a quarter to two and introduced himself to the usher. The plan, hatched the night before, was for the Earl to arrive after them, promptly at two, to avoid the media scrum.

In truth, the night before had been something of an anti-climax. Lady Camilla and her children were abroad, skiing, so his lordship and Toby dined informally and alone in the small green dining room. So much for the budding romance, nipped in the bud. There were roaring fires in the dining room and the drawing room, but the rest of the house was as cold as charity. With the ordeal of the day ahead uppermost in his mind, and with his host and client at his elbow, this was not the time to get lashed, or even slightly tipsy, so Toby held back on the wine and brandy, and had very little of both. Fortunately, the small sip of brandy saved him from hypothermia in the night. There was frost actually on the inside of his bedroom windows when he retired, and the bed was no warmer. He was all in favour of crisp white sheets, but this was ridiculous.

At least he was rewarded with a full English breakfast the next morning, and by eleven had sufficiently thawed out to take a turn around the house. Two hours later, and not a sign of his lordship, Toby set off for court.

As they stood in the assembly area, waiting for his lordship, Toby turned to Simkins. "It's very quiet. I wonder if we've got the right day."

Mr. Simkins smiled. "We have, they haven't. His lordship is very astute, as you will have observed, so we put it about that the hearing had been postponed to another date to put the papparatpack off the scent. It looks as if our little subterfuge has worked a treat."

Toby was disappointed to say the least. How could he have his hour of fame if there was nobody there to record it for posterity? Still, all was not lost as he spotted the cub reporter from the local paper, ready to report grave and weighty misdemeanours such as excess speeding through the village and the growing litter problem outside the Post Office.

Promptly at two, his lordship alighted from Johnson's Fiat Panda and strode into court. The case was to be heard by a Lay Bench of Magistrates, consisting of three local worthies, imbued with a smattering of the law, and assisted by a qualified clerk. The Chairman, ruddy-faced, quite jovial looking, obviously liked a pint, and from his appearance, Toby guessed he was a local Yeoman farmer. To his left, and with a new, light blue perm for the occasion, sat a woman of indeterminate years who looked as if she sucked lemons for a living. A difficult nut to crack. To the Chairman's right sat a youngish, nervous man who fidgeted a lot, possibly a trainee bank manager. Toby put him down as a floating voter, he could go either way.

At the request of the court clerk, his lordship rose regally from his seat.

"Are you Charles Marjoribanks Dalziel Cholmondeley Fitzherbert?" he intoned.

"Well, axshleh, yes and no," replied the Earl.

The court clerk stared back incomprehensively. "What do you mean?"

"I mean, my good man," snapped his lordship irritably, "that my names are Marshbanks, Dee -Ell and Chumley. You got the Charles and Fitzherbert right, I'll give you that."

"That's not what it says here," the court clerk snapped back, equally irritated.

"Perhaps I can help," Toby intervened, now steeped in the ways of the aristocracy. "The spelling is correct, only the pronunciation leaves something to be desired."

Like thunder rolling over the hills, this could rumble on and on, so the court clerk, chastened but unenlightened, decided to call it a day, and advised the Bench that the hearing could now commence.

After the formalities, the case for the prosecution was opened by Gordon Bennett of the Crown Prosecution Service, based at Eastleigh and an aspiring Higher Courts Advocate. He took himself very seriously indeed. After a short but pithy rehearsal of the facts, with Lemon Face sucking away, he called his star witness.

Steve Gardner had scrubbed up for the occasion. Gone were the greasy hair, jeans, open-tocd sandals and the T-shirt proclaiming the right to life for all God's creatures. He was wearing a jacket and tie, and the pained expression of a martyr who had suffered much for the cause and was ready to suffer again.

Bennett took him through his evidence, competently delivered, if at times somewhat emotive. He came up to proof, and there was a case to answer. Then it was Toby's turn to cross-examine.

He rose slowly and placed his notebook onto Gazzard's lectern, which he had 'borrowed' to give himself extra courtroom presence.

"Now, Mr. Gardner," he began, trying to sound wise beyond his years, "you are a seasoned campaigner against blood sports, are you not?"

"I am," replied Gardner smugly, directing his answer to the Bench.

"And in furtherance of your campaigns, you attend many Hunts, do you not?"

"Yes I do. The law is the law and must be upheld. Just because somebody thinks he's God Almighty doesn't give him the right to do as he pleases." He glared at his lordship.

"Quite so." Toby was at his most charming, the velvet glove. "And would you describe yourself as a law abiding citizen?"

Gardner's eyes narrowed, but it was too late for turning back. "Yes I would."

"And yet, according to this document," Toby held it up, doing a passable impression of Neville Chamberlain returning from Munich, "you have seven previous convictions recorded against you over the past four years."

Bennett was up like a jackrabbit. "Where did you get that document?" he snapped, "who gave it to you?"

"Is Mr. Bennett suggesting that Mr. Gardner's previous convictions should not have been disclosed to the defence? If so, I know of no authority for that proposition. Justice has to be transparent." Toby smiled at the Bench, and even the Lemon Sucker nodded in agreement.

"Well…well…I….I…"

"Thank you, Mr. Bennett." Toby turned back to Gardner, looking increasingly uncomfortable. "These convictions show that, in the course of your campaigning against blood sports, you have been found guilty of assaulting a constable, wilful obstruction, and using threatening words and behaviour, is that not right?"

Gardner was on the defensive, and it showed. "There are times when a law-abiding citizen has to stand up and be counted for what he believes. If that's a crime, then I'm guilty and proud of it!"

"So you have no hesitation in breaking the law when it suits you, is that what you're saying?" Gardner was about to reply, but thought better of it.

"Turning now to the day in question, are you familiar with the law of trespass?" Again no answer. "Do you accept that when you climbed over his lordship's wall, you were trespassing?"

"Of course, I'm not an idiot."

"So you say, Mr. Gardner."

"But there are times when the means justify the end, if you know what I mean."

"You claim that when you trespassed on Lord Brockenhurst's estate, it was to prevent him and his companions from fox-hunting, is that right?"

"Yes."

"And when you approached Lord Brockenhurst, was he in fact fox-hunting?"

Gardner paused for a moment, sensing a trap, then blundered on. "Well, no, but he was about to, wasn't he?"

"About to? Mr. Gardner, about to? Is that your answer?" The iron fist.

"Yeah, that's right."

"And it was your intention to effect a citizen's arrest on Lord Brockenhurst, is that correct?"

"Correct. He had it coming."

"But when you approached Lord Brockenhurst, he had committed no offence whatsoever, do you agree?"

"So what?"

"So what?! Mr. Gardner? Is that all you have to say? Surely as a seasoned campaigner, you know that as a private citizen, you have no power of arrest unless an offence has actually been committed? Even Mr. Bennett will agree with me there, won't you, Mr. Bennett?" Bennett was keeping his head well below the parapet, and feeling increasingly uncomfortable. No prosecution briefs from Eastleigh winging their way, but, in the words of Gardner, the law is the law.

Toby pressed his advantage. "At the time when Lord Brockenhurst struck you across your back with his riding crop, you were assaulting him, were you not?"

"I was making a citizen's arrest."

"We've dealt with that. Do you admit that you had hold of Lord Brockenhurst and were attempting to pull him from the saddle?"

"I do, and I'd do it again." Gardner was at his most belligerent.

"I have no doubt you would." Onto the last lap. "After the incident with Lord Brockenhurst, he and his party rode off. Did you follow?"

"No I did not. I was too badly injured."

"So how can you say they were fox-hunting?"

"It's pretty obvious, isn't it? They didn't get all dolled up for a gentle canter round the estate, did they?"

"How do you know?"

"Well, you don't need rocket science to work that one out, do you?"

"Exercising horse and hound is not yet, mercifully, a criminal offence. Thank you, Mr. Gardner." Toby turned to the Bench as Gardner slunk off to lick his wounds. "I submit there is no case to answer, and I invite you to dismiss the charges."

Toby felt he had done enough as he waited impatiently for the Bench to return from their deliberations. He exchanged a few pleasantries with Lord Brockenhurst and Mr. Simkins, both speaking fulsomely of Toby's forensic skills. His lordship in particular seemed remarkably unconcerned about the outcome, almost too confident.

Happily his confidence was not misplaced as the Bench returned and dismissed both charges, together with two hundred guineas awarded to his lordship, to be paid by the CPS.

It was a great victory, and Toby felt elated. The cub reporter faithfully recorded the proceedings, and the case was taken up by a select few of the national dailies as one of their bi-lines. His lordship took his leave, Johnson handed over the cheque for services rendered, and Toby prepared for the long journey home. That was the last Toby saw of Lord Brockenhurst.

What Toby didn't know at the time was that the Chairman of the Bench was one of his lordship's tenant farmers, and you don't bite the hand that feeds you. What his lordship and Mr. Simkins didn't know was that Sir Archibald had sent Toby, in confidence, a copy of Gardner's previous convictions, together with a list of questions which might win the day. The Old Boy network was alive and well, in spite of New Labour. Thank God Almighty for friends in high places. Right verdicts, wrong reasons. Now who said that?

CHAPTER NINE

TOBY IN THE TEMPLE OF GLOOM

Through me is the way to the sorrowful city.
Through me is the way to eternal suffering.
Through me is the way to join the lost people.
Abandon all hope, you who enter here.

[Dante Alighieri]

Beware of clerks who say "Just a short application, straight in and out, no problems, and you'll be back in Chambers by eleven," as Toby was to discover to his cost.

He had just celebrated his first twelve months as a member of Brick Court, and it had gone passably well. There had been highs and lows, as with any barrister feeling his way, but that was to be expected as he climbed the greasy pole. He wasn't in the 'fat cat' club as yet, and his modest earnings seemed to dissipate at an alarming rate. There was value added tax to be paid at the end of each quarter, expenses to include his tuna salad sandwich and Kit Kat at lunchtime, travel to and from court, chambers rent, clerks' commission and then, of course, the dreaded income tax, all of which left him perilously short at the end of each month. Still, he thought, it was only a matter of time.

The euphoria surrounding his modest day of fame in Little Hampton Magistrates Court, rubbing shoulders with the Great and the Good, was but a distant memory. No invitations were forthcoming to join the Earl and his party at Henley, or Ascot, or the glorious twelfth on the extensive Fitzherbert estates in bonny Scotland, in fact, not even a postcard for old times' sake, so the wedding plans to the fragrant Lady Lucinda, or whoever, had to be put on hold.

Sad to report, in spite of effusive promises after the case, no work either from Mr. Simkins. All that heady praise about a star in the making and a glittering career were nothing more than puffs of wind. It was a strange old world, Toby mused in his cups, and there was nothing stranger than solicitors. One minute they were all over you like a cheap suit, the next minute they were but a distant memory.

Toby was shaken out of his dark mood by a knock at the door, and before he had time to answer, in sloped Paul the gopher, bearing a brief, which he plonked down unceremoniously on Toby's desk.

"Brief for tomorrow," he grunted, "short application, straight in and out, back in Chambers by eleven," and before Toby could reply, Paul sloped back out again. What a charmer!

The head note on the backsheet was enough to stiffen his sinews, and more, as he read, seeing but not believing. "In the Court of Appeal, Criminal Division." This can't be right. Nobody appears in the Court of Appeal Criminal Division, or any Division, for that matter, without months of painstaking preparation and a new set of brown trousers, specially purchased for the occasion. After all, for most practitioners, the Court of Appeal was the highest court in the land. Yes, of course, there was the House of Lords, but few indeed, with the obvious exception of Gazzard, sought fit to jolt the old fossils out of their bucolic torpor. The Court of Appeal was the business end of the law in action, where the buck stopped, and usually with a full stop.

Toby read on. The defendant had been charged with murder most foul and had pleaded guilty to manslaughter on the grounds of provocation. The plea had been accepted by the prosecution, no doubt after referring the matter to the reviewing lawyer, and he had been sentenced to seven years' imprisonment. On the advice of leading counsel, Queen's Counsel no less, the defendant had sought leave to appeal against this sentence. His application had been considered by a single High Court Judge, and refused, so he was exercising his right to renew his application before the full court. Queen's Counsel, having been paid handsomely for his input, had long since moved on to his next forensic triumph, leaving his hapless junior to pick up the pieces.

An addendum psychiatric report had been requested by the defence, but would not be available for at least another four weeks, so Toby was instructed to apply for the application to be adjourned until such time as the addendum psychiatric report was available, when the application would be renewed.

Fair enough, thought Toby. Up on his feet, application to adjourn the application, application granted, sit back down again, and back in chambers by eleven. A doddle.

The Royal Courts of Justice clung precariously to the outer rim of London Town by a whisker, situated as they were at the very end of the Strand and on the cusp of the City of London, where wheelers and dealers and movers and shakers played around with billions like monopoly money and put the world to rights.

Queen Victoria, who bestrode the nineteenth century like a Colossus, presided over the building of many fine edifices, one of which was the Royal Courts of Justice. When completed, it bore more than a passing resemblance to Wormwood Scrubs and Snaresbrook Crown Court, formerly the lunatic asylum, and there was much tittle-tattle at the time about the choice of architect. Whoever he was, he was to architecture what Gladstone and Disraeli were to politics - ubiquitous. Malicious gossip had it that the goodly architect had more to show Her Majesty than a set of over embellished drawings, and she was, after all, in mourning for the best part of thirty years, and besides, what better way to while away those long, cold, winter nights in Balmoral? Come to think of it, Balmoral bore more than a passing resemblance…………

It was no more than a stone's throw from the Temple to the Royal Courts, as Toby crossed the Strand, through the neo-gothic portals and into the impressive main hall. He eventually found the robing room, presided over by Whistling Jack, the attendant who spent every day listening to the radio and whistling along with the better known tunes. He seemed to do nothing else.

Toby checked the court lists, found his application third on in Court Seven, and went off in search of the cells. A few words of introduction and explanation wouldn't come amiss, especially as legal aid didn't extend to the defendant's solicitor. After what seemed like an eternity, bolts and keys rattled in the original studded door, the hatch window opened and a close relative of the Gauleiter from Wormwood Scrubs peered out at him. He smiled winningly, the hatch was slammed shut, more rattling, and then the door was opened.

"I'm Counsel representing Mr. Smith, listed in Court Seven. Is he here?"

Without saying a word, the Gauleiter moved slowly and deliberately over to her list, ran her finger down, found the name, and requested Toby to sign in. Actually, it was more like an order, but Toby wasn't about to argue.

He sat in the small interview room, waiting patiently for the defendant's arrival, and flicking idly through his papers. Suddenly the room darkened as a ghost from the past stood, menacingly, at the doorway. Toby stared, Brian George Smith stared back, and then, almost simultaneously, the penny dropped.

Smith spoke first, his face creasing into a smile of recognition. "Gawd 'elp us, as I live and breathe, me brief from 'orseferry!" There was a bone-crunching handshake as he clattered into a chair. "Where've yer bin? Yer pushed off like a rat up a drainpipe! But yer 'ere now, and that's what counts."

Toby didn't know what to say, and he wasn't about to relive that particular nightmare. It would take too long, and now wasn't the time.

Patiently he explained what was going to happen, and that trial counsel would be available when the case was listed for the renewed application. Smith was disappointed, but if that's what Mr. Potts advised, then it was good enough for him.

Toby shuffled into court and took his seat just as their lordships entered. He decided to sit in on the first two appeals, to gauge the mood and see which way the wind was blowing. By all accounts, it was blowing from the Arctic.

By convention, there were three appeal judges, with a Lord Justice of Appeal presiding. Today it was Lord Justice Thorne, who rose to the High Court on the back of a successful libel practice, representing the likes of Egyptian shopkeepers and second division politicians. He had the added advantage of a large château in France, which he made available to friends in high places, not, of course, that this made any difference to his appointment, made wholly on merit. The bookends were Mr. Justice Hare, a relative newcomer from the Chancery Bar, and keen to impress, and Mr. Justice Burke. That said, there was nothing more to say.

The first appeal, even though presented eloquently by experienced counsel, was blown out of the water in pretty short order. Their lordships were scathing about the merits of the appeal, and made it plain from the outset. They didn't even consider it necessary to retire after hearing submissions. They simply huddled together for a minute or two, conferring, like the three witches in Macbeth:

When shall we three meet again
In Thunder, lightning or in rain?
When the hurly-burly's done,
When the battle's lost and won,
Fair is foul, and foul is fair;
Hover through the fog and filthy air.

Just as the second appeal was being called on, the usher came up to Toby. "Their lordships were wondering if you'd received a copy of this," she whispered, handing him a four-page document. "It came by fax last night. You may need it."

Toby glanced down at the document headed 'Addendum Psychiatric Report'. His mouth went dry, and he broke into a cold sweat. Quickly he flicked through it. In essence, the trick cyclist had nothing further to add to his first report, prepared for the original sentencing hearing, and took four pages to say so.

What to do? He found himself between a rock and a hard place. Smith, for reasons only he knew, thought Toby was the bee's knees, so he couldn't withdraw on that account. The brief contained all the information required to advance the application, including the judge's sentencing remarks, together with the original psychiatric report. The only two variables in the equation were the absence of trial counsel and Toby's manifest inexperience. He sat, rooted to the spot, as the second appeal went the way of the first, and before he knew it, the clerk was on his feet.

"The application of Brian George Smith."

Smith was brought into the dock, where he stood for a moment, blinking, as he took in the unfamiliar surroundings. He spotted Toby, smiled, gave him the 'thumbs up', and sat down.

"Yes, Mr. Potts?" Lord Justice Thorne addressed Toby as he rose to his feet.

"May it please your lordship," Toby began, more in hope than expectation, "I am instructed to apply for an adjournment of the defendant's application to renew his application for leave to appeal against sentence."

"Why so, Mr. Potts?"

"Well, my lord," no point beating about the bush, "the basis of the application was to await the addendum psychiatric report, so that trial counsel could address you on the merits."

"And you were not trial counsel, is that it?"

"Quite so, my lord." A shaft of light at the end of the tunnel, but it was fleeting.

"Have you now received a copy of the addendum report?"

"I have, my lord."

"And it adds nothing to our store of information, do you agree?"

"Well, no, my lord," Toby was down but not out, "that may be so, but I'm not sure if I can do justice to this application." Better to be up front, whatever the consequences.

Lord Justice Thorne glanced at the bookends, and then turned back to Toby. "You have all the information you require, so the only question remaining is whether you have the confidence of your lay client, the defendant?"

Smith stood up, unprompted. "Yeah, 'e's me brief, is Mr. Potts!"

Lord Justice Thorne smiled. "Well, there you have it, Mr. Potts, kindly proceed."

Toby took a deep breath as he tried to marshal his thoughts. What price now for Sir Archibald's advice about the need to be prepared for every eventuality? It was 'seat of pants' time, and Toby knew it.

"My lord, I apply for leave to appeal against sentence on the ground that it was manifestly excessive."

So far, so good, but not for Mr. Justice Burke. "How can you say that? The sentencing judge applied the guidelines to cases such as this."

"Well, my lord," Toby stammered, "guidelines are only guidelines, and they don't always take into account compelling mitigation."

"And what is your compelling mitigation, Mr. Potts?" Lord Justice Thorne interjected.

From his body language, Mr. Justice Hare had decided to sit this one out, and was doodling on his notebook, reminiscing no doubt about the glory days when he was earning six times his present salary and not having to listen to some 'wet behind the ears' callow youth chuntering on about this, that and the other. Mr. Justice Burke, however, remained ever vigilant, ready to jump in with some withering remark.

"My lord," Toby began slowly, "the defendant pleaded guilty at the first opportunity to the manslaughter of his common law wife. I submit that the learned judge did not give sufficient weight to the circumstances surrounding the events of that fateful day."

"The defendant killed his wife, Mr. Potts," snapped Mr. Justice Burke, "that's the reality, so how can you say he didn't deserve every day of the sentence passed?"

"If your lordship will allow me," Toby wasn't going to be browbeaten, "here was a thoroughly decent, hard working man, the father of three children, who worked every hour God sent him to provide a good life for them all. He was a long-distance lorry driver, taking him away from home for days on end. On that fateful day, he arrived home unexpectedly to find his wife in bed with another man. I doubt, my lord," Toby added, addressing Mr. Justice Burke directly, "if any man, let alone the defendant, could not fail to be affected by that sight." Burke was about to say something, but a glance from Lord Justice Thorne silenced him. Toby, taking advantage of the moral high ground, pressed on. "In a fit of blind fury, he lashed out, struck his wife a blow, sent her reeling, and she banged her head against the wall. As your lordships will have seen from the papers, she died nine days later in hospital, never regaining consciousness."

Their lordships were strangely silent. Was that a good sign or not?

"So," Toby continued, "he has lost everything, the wife he loved and adored, the children he loved and adored, and who are now in care, and his life is in ruins. Nobody regrets more than the defendant what he did that day, no punishment can bring his wife back. But your lordships can ease the pain by tempering justice with mercy. After all, justice without mercy is no justice at all." He'd heard Nick Ridley use that line before and had squirreled it away for just such a moment. "Those are my submissions." Toby sat down.

"Thank you, Mr. Potts," said Lord Justice Thorne, and the three went into a huddle. After a few minutes of whispered discussion, they stood up. "We will retire to consider your submissions."

Toby sat and waited. Had he done enough, or had their lordships merely slipped out for coffee and biscuits? He glanced over at Smith in the dock, and gave him a reassuring smile. It was like one of those hospital dramas, 'Your life in their hands'; such was the weight of responsibility on Toby's slender and inexperienced shoulders. If only that wretched addendum report hadn't been faxed through, if only trial counsel had made himself available, if only…

There was a loud knock on the door behind the Bench, everybody rose, and their lordships filed back into court.

Lord Justice Thorne spoke. "We have decided to grant the defendant's application, and will treat this hearing as the full appeal. I shall ask Mr. Justice Burke to deliver the judgment of the court."

Toby's heart sank. It was doomsday, and no going back.

"We have listened carefully to the able submissions made on behalf of the defendant by Mr. Potts. He has submitted that the sentence of seven years imprisonment was manifestly excessive, given all the circumstances of the case and what Mr. Potts has described as compelling mitigation. The sentencing judge had before him the original psychiatric report and, no doubt, the same compelling mitigation submitted to him by eminent Queen's Counsel, appearing for the defendant at the time. Mr. Potts did not appear in the court below, so he comes fresh to the task set him in different and difficult circumstances. The sentencing judge applied the guidelines handed down by this court in cases similar to this, and we cannot fault his reasoning or the sentence he passed." Oh well, thought Toby, at least he tried, but he was bitterly disappointed. Smith deserved a kinder fate. "However, there are cases which, in exceptional circumstances, fall outside the guidelines, and we are persuaded that this is one. We are further persuaded that the sentencing judge did not give sufficient credit for the compelling mitigation placed before us by Mr. Potts. A single blow in extreme provocation led to disastrous and tragic consequences, which could not have been contemplated by the defendant when he acted as he did." A glimmer of hope against all adversity. Toby listened, spellbound. "Therefore, as an act of compassion, tempering justice with mercy," Mr. Justice Burke allowed himself a wintry smile as he looked down at Toby, "we shall allow this appeal and reduce the sentence to one of three years imprisonment."

Toby wanted to throw his papers in the air, such was his relief and elation. As the next appeal was called on, Toby bowed low to their lordships, Lord Justice Thorne gave him an encouraging nod, and after a minute or two to catch his breath outside court, made his way back down to the cells.

Brian George Smith stood for a moment in the doorway, and then walked over to Toby and embraced him in a large, sweaty, bear hug. As he held him, Smith sobbed quietly and uncontrollably on Toby's shoulder. There was no need for words. Then, breaking away, he touched Toby lightly on the cheek, and was gone. It was all Toby could do to keep his composure.

Back in chambers, Fred looked up. "Everything went well, I hope?" he enquired.

"Yes thanks, Fred, very well indeed."

"Good. Now tomorrow, I've got you down for a custody time limits application for the CPS at Snaresbrook. Doesn't pay much, but we've got to get you back onside. Here's the brief, ten sharp in front of Bonkers."

Toby sat staring out of the window in reflective mood. Brian George Smith would be out in less than a year, with time served and good behaviour, to rake over the ashes and get on with what remained of his broken life. As for Toby, life also moved on, to the next challenge and the next mountain to climb.

And what of the future? To the likes of Mr. Justice Hare, as he sat doodling and counting his millions, the Criminal Bar was an irrelevance and the first repository of the intellectually challenged. He had never met the likes of Brian George Smith, with his big sweaty hands and his tattoos, and had no wish to do so. To him the Bar was a money machine, and if you couldn't afford him, then you couldn't have him.

But there had to be more to it than that. To Toby, it was all about real people, with their weaknesses and hardships, their sweat and tattoos, their poverty and sheer hopelessness. Even with the constant struggle over legal aid, inadequate payment, arguing over the pennies, if that was what it was all about, if the next case was just another meal ticket, then it wasn't worth the candle. You might as well give it all up and become a lorry driver. Now there's a thought!

Brian George Smith made it all seem worthwhile. The memory of that bear hug would remain with Toby for the rest of his life. He had done something good, noble, and he had given hope to a man who had lost it all.

CHAPTER TEN

TOBY GOES TO POT

I could be the catalyst that sparks the revolution,
I could be a player in a major institution,
I could lean to wild extremes, I could do or die,
But I'd rather yawn and be withdrawn and watch them gallop by.
What a waste, what a waste, what a waste.

[After Ian Dury]

Toby had never been into drugs, not even at university, where they were freely available. Well, to be strictly accurate, he'd been offered a spliff at a party once, but like all those people in high places who set such a good example for lesser mortals to follow, he hadn't actually inhaled, which, according to his friends in the know, defeated the object of the exercise. But in his professional capacity, drink and drugs formed a sizeable part of his practice, from yobs in town centres drinking themselves senseless, assuming they had any sense in the first place, and charged with being drunk and disorderly, to low life on dark street corners offering coke, and brown, and hash, and speed, and E's and anything else that took your fancy. It was very depressing, as it was to the Bobbies on the beat who found themselves in the front line, night after night. In their constant war against the drug dealers, many different tactics were employed, including the use of undercover officers.

Linda Black and Clare White were inseparable, even at school. They played together, pulled together, got drunk together, left together, and joined the police together. They'd sat together through one of those career mornings in their last year, presented by some poor Plod who'd drawn the short straw and had been delegated to persuade the local kids that it was better to uphold the law than to break it. For the most part, it was stony ground, with lots of snide comments from the back row about "If pigs could fly, New Scotland Yard would be an airport." Not original, but hurtful nonetheless. Each year, more in hope than expectation, the Plods of this world went through the motions, smiling through gritted teeth and making a mental note of the troublemakers. Their time would come. It was all part of building rapport with the wider community, before giving the cheeky little buggers the cuffing they richly deserved.

But every now and then, like a beacon in the night, somebody stood up to be counted, and so it was, in that memorable year, that Linda and Clare took the forms together, enrolled together, trained together and passed out together, before being posted together to Hackney Police Station, that jewel in the armpit of south London.

Their first two years as fully-fledged police officers were uneventful. They were spat on, had lager poured over them, were assaulted in the street, mainly by drunks and addicts, were sexually harassed and generally abused, in keeping with their new found status. All part of a day's work, but they persevered, and eventually their perseverance was rewarded.

Chief Inspector Derek 'Hot Hands' Spinks, their Station commander, so named because no female bottom or bosom was safe from his persistent groping, had risen through the ranks, more by devotion to duty than by conspicuous talent, and had his eye on the main chance and a well-turned ankle. When he wasn't form filling and sifting through statistics and meeting targets, he was dreaming of becoming Commander Spinks, or even, Commissioner Spinks. Why not? After all, if the present incumbent, a complete plonker, could reach the top of the greasy pole, there was hope for them all. Imagine the honour and the glory - Commissioner Sir 'Hot Hands' Spinks, a trip to the Palace, his photo in all the tabloids spouting utter garbage about law and order and his vision of making the streets of London safe for decent law abiding citizens to walk at night, and attending Gala dinners with the frightful Lady Hot Hands in close attendance. Better still, leave her at home, and invite Madonna or Britney Spears, or some other gorgeous arm candy almost as eye-catching as his array of service medals.

And so it was that 'Hot Hands' devised a force initiative, to grab the headlines and thrust himself into the limelight, where he would modestly take all the credit for a job well done. The peddling of drugs was reaching epidemic proportions on his patch, and it was time to act decisively. He summoned Linda and Clare into his office. He motioned them to sit down.

"Now, girls," he began, momentarily distracted as they both crossed their legs together, "you've done very well in your first two years with us, and reports from the station sergeant are most encouraging."

"Thank you, sir," they replied together, giving him a winning smile.

"So I've decided it's time to give you a leg up, so to speak, a chance to show what you're made of and to display your obvious talents." Linda and Clare exchanged nervous glances. "I'm going to recommend you both for some undercover work." Linda and Clare exchanged even more nervous glances. 'Hot Hands', as they both knew, was not averse to a bit of undercover work himself.

"We don't quite understand, sir." Linda spoke for them both.

"Of course you don't," he snapped, "but if you'll stop interrupting, I'll explain." The momentary scowl quickly gave way to a munificent smile, almost a leer. "I'm setting up a task force to target drug dealers on my patch. It's becoming a scandal, and I want it stamped out." He slammed his fist on the desk to underline his determination. "Now, as you know, as soon as the uniformed branch approach the dealers, they scuttle for cover like rats up a drainpipe, and the few collars we feel don't amount to a row of beans. I want the big time dealers caught and put behind bars. We're going to hit 'em," his voice rising to a crescendo, "and hit 'em hard."

As 'Hot Hands' leaned back in his executive, simulated leather, fully rotating, chair, he could almost taste the press conference on the steps of the town hall, with that dreadful little Scrote from the Hackney

Evening Herald scribbling something positive for a change. "And that's where you girls come in." They sat there, breathless with anticipation. "I want you to go undercover, find the dealers, and collar the lot of them. Are you up for it?" he asked rhetorically.

"Yes sir," replied the girls together, both springing to their feet.

"Good. I knew I could rely on you, and who knows, if you pull it off," an unfortunate turn of phrase in the circumstances, "there might be a promotion in it for the two of you. Now report to Sergeant Major, and good luck."

Len Major was the long serving and long suffering station sergeant who, since his promotion several years ago, had resigned himself to what passed for witticisms about his name and rank. But he had broad shoulders and a stoical disposition, and he'd been called worse in his time, so he took it in his stride, as he did most things that happened on his daily tour of duty. Very little ruffled Sergeant Major.

The girls were clearly excited about the challenge that lay ahead as they reported for briefing.

"Right, girls, settle down and listen carefully. This could be a dangerous assignment, so keep your wits about you at all times. You'll be playing the part of ladies of easy virtue looking to score, so you'll have to dress appropriately." Linda and Clare were even more excited. It would be like their last year at school all over again - vertigo inducing platform shoes, short skirts, and low-cut blouses, "the lower, the better," advised Sergeant Major, "as it distracts the dealers and catches them off guard. As they say," he added somewhat crudely, "if you've got them, flaunt them." The girls giggled together, and of course, lashings of makeup and cheap perfume. If the low-cut blouses didn't overwhelm the dealers, then the cheap perfume should do the trick.

"Last but not least, you'll each carry a handbag, but not just any old handbag. These bags," he continued, producing a specimen from under the counter, "are state of the art Hi-Tec with a concealed mini-recorder and camera." He paused whilst the girls absorbed the enormity of this statement. "All your dealings with the low life need to be filmed and recorded, so you've got it on tape. Otherwise, with some poncy overpaid barrister arguing the toss with the jury, it's your word against theirs, and that may not be enough." The girls nodded together. "You simply press this button on the clasp, here, to start recording, and press again to stop. It's as simple as that." Famous last words.

The next evening, promptly at six, the girls tottered into the station, looking every inch a pair of slappers out on the game. Dressed like that, they were bound to score, drugs or no drugs. Sergeant Major took a long drink of cold water, put them through their paces, handed over the handbags containing marked bank notes, and off they went into the gathering gloom.

Wandering up Mare Street in the general direction of Clapton, they spotted a creature from the dark side of the moon selling copies of Big Issue. He was certainly dressed for the part - matted, greasy hair, a three day stubble clinging precariously to his receding chin, wearing a filthy old anorak and faded jeans. If he wasn't on drugs, then he should be. A good place to start. He was accompanied by his ever faithful hound, the mangy Biggles, specially trained to sniff out Plod, and who growled menacingly as the girls approached.

"Quiet, Biggles," said Scruff Bag, smiling winningly at the girls with a full set of black teeth as they approached him. "Can I interest yer in a copy of Big Issue? This week it's all abart police brutality and corruption in 'igh places."

Cheeky bugger. "Yeah, OK," said Linda. Might as well start somewhere.

"You girls looking for business?"

"What sort of business?" asked Clare, not yet into the part.

"Well, sweetheart, looking like that, 'ow many businesses are y'in?" He gave her a nudge and a wink.

"Maybe later, mate," replied Clare, blushing to her roots, "but what we need now is a little smack. Can you help?"

"'appy to oblige both of you," said Scruff Bag, thinking Christmas had come early by several months, "you drop 'em, and I'll smack 'em. Best offer I've 'ad all day."

"That's not what she meant," said Linda, glowering at Clare, as she tried to redeem the situation. "We're after a score."

Scruff Bag's yellow eyes narrowed as he looked them up and down, and then glanced around. "Don't use the stuff meself," he lied, "disgusting 'abit." He paused, and from his expression, was obviously performing mental gymnastics within a very limited repertoire. "Alright," he said at last, with his beady eyes fixed on the girls' ample software, "but what's in it for me?"

Linda looked at Clare, who nodded. "Maybe a deal, depends on the quality."

"Yer on. Follow me."

Scruff Bag ducked down a side street, all the time looking around him, and led the girls to a seedy block of flats on the Trelawney Estate. He pushed a button on the grimy intercom, and after several minutes, it crackled into life.

"What yer want?" came a disembowelled voice.

"Dave, it's Mick. I've got a couple of slappers want a bit of brown. Are yer dealing?"

"For fuck's sake, Mick, keep yer fuckin' voice down! Why don't yer shout it from the fucking roof tops!"

"Sorry, Dave."

There was a long pause. "Can yer vouch for 'em?"

"The real thing, Dave, and play yer cards right, they might give yer a freebie."

"You can cut that out right now," said Linda. Freebies were definitively not in the job description.

"Alright, come on up."

With the lift long since broken, they climbed the stairs to the seventh floor, pausing on each landing for Scruff Bag to catch his breath. As they approached Dave's door, Linda signalled to Clare to press the recording buttons on their handbags. Immediately there was a perceptible whirring noise from the depths within, fortunately masked by Scruff Bag's heavy panting. He rang the bell, which didn't work, so he knocked loudly. Within a few seconds the door was opened, and there stood Dave 'Dogface' Brown - Brown's the name, Brown's the game, was his motto, glaring at the three of them.

"Shut the fuck up, Mick!" he snapped. "Sometimes yer a real pain." He studied the girls for a moment, then motioned them inside. Putting his hand across Scruff Bag's chest, he added, "Thanks for the business, Mick, see yer around," and with that, shut the door in his face.

Dogface was a child of the sixties, flower power, Woodstock, make love not war and all that, who used to get stoned on Jefferson Airplane and had never moved on. Now in his middle fifties, with a face like a bloodhound and habits to match, Dave had never grown up, and what he couldn't smoke himself, he sold to others. By all accounts he was doing well. His flat was nicely furnished, in a tasteless sort of way, with an expensive plasma wrap around television system and a stereo that would knock your socks off at thirty paces. Dave liked his gadgets. Fortunately for the girls and their long-lost virginity, Dave had just been chilling out to White Rabbit by the one and only JA, and was feeling cool. The only fly in the ointment to disturb his Karma was this incessant whirring sound. Was it the onset of tinnitis or was the stereo on the blink?

"'aven't seen you girls on me patch before. Yer new?"

Linda and Clare looked at each other. Who said it was going to be easy?

"Yeah," replied Linda, taking the initiative, "we've moved down from Kings Cross, change of scene, change of air. More politicians and judges to swing a cat at, cruising around, so the Filth are crawling all over the place, looking to make a name for themselves. I mean, respectable girls like us can hardly make a living no more. We don't need the hassle."

Dave chuckled. "Don't blame yer." He stretched back in his armchair. "You'll get no 'assle in this part of town. The Plod are a dozy bunch of buggers, don't know their arses from their elbows, and the doziest bugger of them all is the station gaffer, 'ot 'ands Spinks they call 'im, too busy groping the new recruits to bother with the likes of me."

Linda and Clare exchanged knowing glances. "Yeah, we've heard he's a randy old git."

So 'ow much yer want?"

"Two twenty bags and a ten bag for Mick."

"Good old Mick, never knowingly paid for 'is fix in all the years I've known 'im. Let's see the colour of yer money, then."

Linda extracted the marked bank notes, handed them over, and Dave left the room, returning a minute later with three wraps. "Enjoy, girls, it's the best shit sarf of the river."

"Thanks, Dave," said Linda. She paused. "Are you the main dealer in these parts?"

Dave's expression changed. "'oo wants to know?" he asked. There was menace in his voice.

"It's just if we want another bag, do we come to you?" The girls were beginning to feel threatened, so they got up to leave.

"Speak to Mick, 'ee knows the score. Now, on yer bikes, girls, I've got things to do."

Linda and Clare didn't need a second invitation as they clattered back down the stairs and out into the street. It wasn't until they were well away that they stopped and hugged each other, both shaking uncontrollably.

Mick, standing in the shadows on the other side of the road, saw the girls hurrying past and was about to call out, but there was something about the way Biggles growled that made him stop. Linda and Clare were so excited about their first undercover assignment, they'd completely forgotten about Mick, and never gave him a second thought. They didn't see him following them back to the station, or watching them from the doorway as Linda punched in the security code to the inner door, on their way to report personally to 'Hot Hands'.

Fortunately for the girls, Sergeant Major, vigilant as ever at the front counter, spotted Mick through the glass pane just as Mick moved out of sight. The phone rang.

"Sergeant," it was Hot Hands, "bring in the video recorder and let's see what we've got."

In his office, as Len entered with the recorder, Hot Hands was leaning forward, almost as excited as the girls as they recounted their exploits, but for different reasons. The low cut blouses were bringing him out in a hot flush.

"If Dave's not the main dealer on the patch, then he's certainly one of them," Linda was bubbling on, "and now we know where he lives, we can go back any time."

"That's right," Clare nodded, not wishing to be left out.

The peep show as evidence against Dave was a disappointment. As ill luck would have it, Linda had her handbag pointing backwards, giving the viewer a close up of two of Clare's most prominent features. It was a video that Hot Hands would watch many times over in the privacy of his office, for training purposes only of course. Clare, for the most part, filmed Linda's bottom, with only the occasional glimpses of Dave relaxing in his armchair.

The sound recording was no better, as little could be heard over the incessant whirring noise. Only snatched pieces of conversation could be heard, something about the Filth looking to make a name for themselves, and politicians and judges on the prowl for a bit of Totty.

Hot Hands was disappointed and made no bones about it. "Incompetent, that's what it is. It's virtually unusable." He glowered at Sergeant Major. "I blame you for this, sergeant, they should have had a dummy run." Len was unmoved. After all, he'd heard it all before. When things went right, Hot Hands took all the credit, but when they went wrong, it was everybody's fault except his. So it is privilege of rank.

Hot Hands leaned back and stared at the ceiling. "Still, all is not lost. We've got the drugs, this Dave has got our marked notes, we know where he deals from, so all we need now is his supplier."

"Sunning himself on the Costa del Sol, I shouldn't wonder," said the sergeant, "you'll not lay a finger on him."

"Don't be so negative, sergeant. With the girls on the team, it's only a matter of time." He beamed expansively as the girls nodded in agreement.

"Just as a matter of interest," Len continued, "how did you girls find Dave so easily?"

"A stroke of luck, really," replied Clare. "We saw this bloke selling the Big Issue, and we took it from there."

"What? Mick Rafferty? The druggie in Mare Street? With a dog called Biggles?"

"Yeah," replied Clare, "how did you know?"

There was a deafening silence. "What's the problem, sergeant?" asked Hot Hands.

"I saw Mick Rafferty in the doorway, not ten minutes ago. What was he doing there?"

Linda and Clare stared at each other, seeing but not believing. Then it dawned on them. "Oh shit," said Clare, "we promised him a ten bag, but in all the excitement we forgot about him. He must've followed us back."

The colour drained from Hot Hand's face. Suddenly he was on his feet, foaming at the mouth. "You incompetent idiots, you've blown your cover! You want excitement?! I'll give you excitement! You'll be directing traffic for the rest of your miserable lives!"

"It's too late for recriminations, sir," said Len, trying to salvage something from the wreckage. "We need a squad round there now."

"So what are you waiting for, sergeant? Let's go, go!"

With the girls showing them the way, and Spinks in the lead car spearheading the raid, they were outside Dave's flat in a matter of minutes. But thanks to the miracles of technology, Mick had already phoned Dave on his mobile, and as the boys in blue burst in, the flat was as clean as a whistle.

Hot Hands, having caught his breath after the exhausting climb, took immediate charge. "Right, I want this flat searched from top to bottom, starting now, and as for you, sunshine, you're nicked."

"Nicked? What for?" asked Dave in all innocence. "And besides, where's yer warrant? I know me rights."

"The only rights you need to know, sunshine, is that you're bangs to rights. Now get him out of here!"

Hot Hands accompanied Dave back to the station, confident of a strong case, and he wanted to be in at the kill, to claim the credit and the headlines. "Right, Sergeant, book him in, and then I want a full strip search."

Ten minutes later, one of the searching officers emerged from the cell with a brown lump in a tamper proof bag. Hot Hands was almost triumphant as he inspected the offending article from a safe distance.

"Where did you find this, constable?" he asked.

"In the suspect's back passage, sir."

"And what, pray tell me, is it?" he asked Dave, now standing at the cell door in the regulation force issue paper suit.

Dave peered at the object. "Looks like a turd to me."

Len and the constable just managed to stifle a laugh, but Hot Hands was not amused.

"A turd, wrapped in cling film? Don't play the joker with me, sunshine. I didn't ride into town on the head of a cabbage."

"That's not what I 'eard, Inspector," replied Dave, enjoying the moment.

The brown substance was duly sent off for analysis, and in the fullness of time came back as a lump of cannabis resin. As for Dave, he was interviewed under caution, elected to make no comment throughout, as was his right, and was charged with supplying a controlled drug of Class A to another and possession of a small quantity of cannabis resin.

The search of the flat revealed nothing, and worse still, no sign whatsoever of the marked bank notes. Unbeknown to Hot Hands and his team, Dave also rented the flat next door, where he kept the bulk of his stash, money and drugs paraphernalia. Mick was hauled in and given a verbal spanking, but he denied ever meeting the girls, and was released without charge. Not a wise decision, but as far as Hot Hands was concerned, it kept down on the paperwork and they had a strong enough case without him.

Toby arrived early at Southwark Crown Court, to see Dave in conference and prepare for trial. Counsel originally instructed was detained elsewhere, as his trial had overrun, so Toby had inherited the brief the night before. He'd long since reconciled himself to second or third choice in the pecking order, but work was work, and with two years experience at the coalface, he was growing in confidence and getting his fair share of the pickings.

Southwark Crown Court had been purpose-built barely ten years earlier, just south of Blackfriars Bridge, wedged between anonymous office blocks, and decked out with chrome and neon and garish carpets. A truly forgettable building, but justice was justice wherever it was administered, and at least there was a decent wine bar just around the corner.

Once robed, Toby presented himself at Reception on the ground floor. The tannoy crackled into life.

"Would the legal representative of David Brown please report to reception."

To his horror, and bearing down on him from the other side of the foyer, loomed the formidable figure of Bootsy Farmer, smiling broadly with his hand extended.

"What a pleasure, Mr. Potts. We meet again, and another lost cause if I may say so. Still, as Churchill used to say, we also serve who only strut and fret our hour upon the stage."

Very droll I'm sure, muttered Toby under his breath. Poor Churchill, poor Shakespeare, and more to the point, poor Dogface at the sight of Bootsy the Bard bearing down on him, ready to put the boot in and get him to plead guilty. Worse still, had Bootsy already seen him and carved a deal? The instructions, on this point at least, were clear. Dave was to plead not guilty to supply, and guilty to possession. Fair enough, thought Toby. A lump of cannabis resin found where the sun never shines, wrapped in cling film, didn't just get there on its own, and as Hot Hands would put it, had him bang to rights.

112

Toby was determined to assert himself from the outset and not play second fiddle again. "Good morning, Mr. Farmer, how nice to see you again," he lied. "Have you seen the defendant yet?"

"'Fraid not, Mr. Potts. I got here early for that specific purpose, but the prison van was late, and he's only just arrived. Shall we go and pay our respects?" What a blessed relief.

Toby walked purposefully ahead towards the Custody Suite as it was called, determined not to be lobbied by Bootsy on the way. Dave was brought into the interview room, and after the usual niceties, the conference began.

"The Crown will be calling the two girls, now calling themselves Karen and Sharon. Not their real names, you understand, to protect their undercover status." Dave chuckled. "They've also been given permission by the judge to give their evidence from behind screens, which means the judge, counsel and the jury will see them, but not you."

Dave chuckled again. "The whole Manor knows 'oo they are, so it doesn't matter a tinker's toss! Nice girls, big tits, been transferred to Islington, last I 'eard. Won't see 'em again for a while, more's the pity." Whatever else, Dave wasn't a violent man, make love not war and all that.

"So how are you coping with prison?" asked Toby in his 'getting to know you' mode, to put Dave at his ease.

"Not bad, thanks man, but the shit was awful when I first got remanded. As soon as I'd arranged me own supply, no problem, if yer know what I mean." Dave sniffed loudly and wiped his nose on the back of his hand. A pinch of brown before leaving that morning was working wonders, and he was cool, if yer know what I mean.

Toby was horrified but decided not to press the matter, especially as Bootsy was making a careful note. "Needless to say, anything discussed here in conference is subject to client confidentiality," he looked pointedly at Bootsy, "so you can speak freely. Now, turning to the evidence, I've got your signed proof, and for the most part it'll be their word against yours. Just out of interest," he continued, "didn't you suspect they might be police officers? Flat feet, 'ello, 'ello, 'ello and all that. Short of them taking out their pocket books and pencils and making notes as they went along, I would have thought it was pretty obvious." Toby's stereotypes of such a fine body of men and women irritated Bootsy intensely. He was about to say something, but thought better of it, wholly out of character for Bootsy.

"Hey man, they were cool chicks," Dave replied, "and besides, I was stoned, know what I mean? A line of brown brings on a kaleidoscope of colours and inner peace, and brings out the best in me." A rare treat, thought Toby, for those privileged enough to witness it.

Court Ten, on the fourth floor, was like second home to His Honour Bertrand Trubshawe, known affectionately as Bertie Trubsnore for his endearing habit of falling asleep when not actively involved in the proceedings. As he was seldom actively involved in the proceedings, he fell asleep a lot. In a strange sort of way, it seemed to help rather than hinder the trial process, and was to be commended to his more interventionist colleagues.

He was not exactly cast in the mould of the new breed of judges so favoured by the Lord Chancellor's Department, all work and no play and doing everything by numbers, but he didn't visit brothels, or download child pornography from the Internet, or have a mistress, or get falling down drunk at judicial functions, in short, he led a blameless life, so he was tolerated, even humoured. The bonus for the LCD was that his cases were hardly ever referred to the Court of Appeal, as a somnolent judge can't really cock it up.

Toby's opponent was the Prosecutor in Residence, William Boyo Williams from Lamb Buildings, with his roots firmly planted in the Welsh foothills. He did nothing but prosecute, Grade Three, and by dint of careful personnel management and regular visits with police officers and members of the CPS to the wine bar round the corner, he avoided the fate of other lesser mortals who came and went like the seasons. In his early fifties, with dark, wavy hair, bushy eyebrows and a very pink face, coloured over the years by too many large glasses of

Sauvignon Blanc, he had a loud, mellifluous voice, as if about to burst into song at any moment with a rendition of 'There'll be a welcome in the Valleys'.

With the court assembled, Toby glanced over to Boyo. Sitting behind him was the prosecution team. Hot Hands was there, not as a witness but an interested spectator, the officer in the case, DC. Munro, and the fragrant CPS law clerk, ready to take notes, fill in forms and report back to the reviewing lawyer. All Toby had on offer was the truculent Bootsy Farmer, still smarting from the conference and Toby's determination to keep him firmly in check.

With the jury empanelled, Boyo opened the case for the prosecution. It was a fair summary, if a tad too long, and just as Trubsnore's head was beginning to droop, he called Linda, or Karen as she was to be known, to give evidence.

With Hot Hands smiling encouragement, and Dave semi-supine in the dock and right out of it, Linda gave her evidence well enough, and then it was Toby's turn to cross examine. This was the signal for Trubsnore to push his notebook away and settle down for the first of his daily naps.

"This was entrapment by any other name, wasn't it?" Start high, that's what Nick Ridley had taught him, grab the jury's attention and hold it.

"Well," replied Karen, or Linda, "nobody forced the defendant to sell us drugs."

"That wasn't my question."

Karen, or Linda paused, hesitating. "Well, yes, I suppose it was, but it's not against the law, is it?" She looked over to Hot Hands, who shook his head.

"You were dressed that night for what purpose?"

"We were undercover."

"Yes, I appreciate that, but how were you dressed?"

"In plain clothes," replied Karen, or Linda.

"A low cut, revealing blouse, a mini skirt that would make a face flannel look like a horse blanket, fishnet stockings and platform shoes, is that right?"

Karen, or Linda, paused, clearly embarrassed by the description. "Something like that," she replied.

"In short, you and your colleague were dressed like prostitutes, or slappers to use the common parlance. That's right, isn't it?"

Karen, or Linda, was on the defensive. "We were just playing a part."

"And you were chosen for this undercover assignment, not for your experience but for your obvious female attractions?"

"In part, I suppose."

"Which part do you suppose?"

Boyo rose to his feet. "Really, your Honour, are these sexual innuendos appropriate?"

"Moving on," Toby continued, ignoring Boyo, "you told the defendant you had come south of the river to escape the clutches of politicians and judges hassling you for sex in King's Cross?"

Trubsnore jerked himself into life. "What's that you say? Judges hassling you for sex?"

"It was only an act, your Honour. We were playing a role."

"I should hope so too," Trubsnore was not amused. "The very idea! Members of the jury, I direct you to disregard such a disgraceful suggestion! Proceed, Mr. Potts."

"Thank you, Your Honour. What brought you to the defendant's flat?"

116

"We were taken there by Mick Rafferty, a well-known local junkie." Replied Karen, or Linda, regaining her confidence.

"That's inadmissible, Your Honour, as opinion evidence."

"Quite so, Mr. Potts." Trubsnore stifled a yawn. "Do get on."

"Mick Rafferty is not being called as a witness in this case, is he?"

"That's right. He was arrested but.."

Toby interrupted quickly before any further damage could be done. "You and your colleague had never been to the flats before that night, had you?"

"That's right."

"And you had never met the defendant before that night, had you?"

"No, we hadn't."

So far, so good, thought Toby, but was he making any real progress? Time to find out.

"These flats are notorious in the area?"

"What do you mean?"

Well, for a start, they're a regular stamping ground for prostitutes plying their trade, aren't they?"

"I wouldn't know," replied Karen, or Linda.

"Really? And yet you are your colleague had been stationed barely half a mile away for the best part of two years?"

"Well, yes, but we weren't involved in prostitution."

"I should hope not," replied Toby to a few titters from the jury.

"That's not what I meant."

"It comes down to this, doesn't it? You went to the flats dressed as prostitutes, you were invited into the defendant's flat dressed as prostitutes, and you actually told the defendant you were prostitutes from Kings Cross?"

"Yes, but I've already explained that."

"And he asked how much did you want?"

"That's right."

"For sex."

"That's not true."

"You said twenty pounds each for a quickie, he said it was too much and showed you to the door, that's right, isn't it?"

Trubsnore opened one eye. "Twenty pounds for a quickie, Mr. Potts? What does that mean?"

"Your Honour, it means sexual intercourse lasting less than five minutes."

Trubsnore chuckled. "Not much for your money, then? No wonder the defendant declined the offer."

Boyo was up on his feet. "Your Honour, the witness does not accept my learned friend's suggestion, so your Honour's speculation is irrelevant."

"Kindly allow me to decide what is relevant or irrelevant, Mr. Williams." One in the eye for Boyo, thought Toby. I wonder what that's called. "Please continue Mr. Potts, but I hope there's a point to all this, as the jury and I are in danger of losing the plot."

"Of course, your Honour." Turning back to Karen, or Linda. "I suggest you were there offering sex."

"No we were not. We were there to buy drugs. Sex didn't come into it. We handed over fifty pounds…"

Trubsnore was taking an unusually active part in the proceedings, even if he was on the wrong tack. "So if twenty pounds buys you a quickie, what does fifty pounds buy?"

Boyo thought about objecting, but changed his mind half way up.

"Can you help his Honour?" Toby asked mischievously.

"No I can't," she snapped back. "You're deliberately trying to confuse me. The fifty pounds was for drugs, we handed over fifty pounds and the defendant gave us the drugs. How many more times do I have to say it?"

Trubsnore, still awake, rebuked Karen, or Linda. "Just answer counsel's questions, and leave the comments to me."

"I'm sorry, your Honour."

"Very well. Continue Mr. Potts, but let brevity be your watchword."

"Thank you, your Honour. You say the defendant sold you the drugs, but are there any fingerprints to support your allegation?"
"No."

"His flat was searched from top to bottom. Was anything found?"

"No, but…."

"So these drugs could have come from anywhere?"

"Yes, but…"

2222222222

"Other than your word for it, there is no independent evidence to connect these drugs with the defendant, isn't that right?"

"No, but…"

"Thank you, no further questions."

Boyo did his best to shore up the sinking ship in re-examination. Sharon, or Clare, fared no better, and then the searching officer was called to give evidence. Trubsnore had fallen back into a fitful doze, only to wake up as Boyo was waving the sealed tamper proof bag in front of the jury.

"What have you got there, Mr. Williams?" he asked in a spirit of enquiry.

"A lump of cannabis resin, your Honour."

"Really? Pass it up." Feigning a passing interest, Trubsnore removed it from the bag, smelled it, licked it, and then replaced it into the bag. "And remind me where exactly was it found, Mr. Williams?" he asked in all innocence.

Boyo paused. "Does your Honour *really* want to know the answer to that question?"

Trubsnore paused, looked at the offending article, then back at Boyo, then, with an agility that belied his years, leapt up from the Bench and headed for the door.

"All rise," intoned the usher at the judge's departing back.

Ten minutes later, and with the colour drained from his face, Trubsnore returned to court and the trial resumed. Dave declined to give evidence, whether sitting or standing up, just as he'd declined to answer questions when arrested. It wasn't cool, and besides, he'd rather yawn, and be withdrawn, and watch them gallop by.

Toby's efforts to persuade the jury that Dave was not a drug dealer were undermined in large measure by the sight of his client, slumped in the dock, spaced out, eyes glazed, head snapped back and humming a selection from The Greatest Hits of Jefferson Airplane quietly to himself.

The jury were out for nearly three hours before returning a verdict of guilty by a majority of ten to two. Dave was sentenced to three years imprisonment, and having spent twelve months on remand, would be out in no time at all.

It was a victory of sorts for everyone. Mick was minding the store in Dave's absence, and business was brisk. Dave had extended his client list by several dozen amongst his newfound friends, and Mick was pushed to keep up with demand.

Hot Hands had his five minutes of glory on the steps of the court, and the girls got their promotion. Bootsy greeted the verdict with smug satisfaction. He may be gamekeeper turned poacher, but his heart was still in the Met, with the best bunch of lads you'd never wish to meet. You crossed them at your peril. As for Smart Alec lawyers, they're all the same, all mouth and no trousers, and not worth spit! As Churchill once said, a policeman's lot is not an 'appy one, and he was right. Give credit where credit's due, that was his motto, and if you can't stand the heat, get out of the kitchen.

Boyo, in full song, was in the wine bar, clutching a bottle of Sauvignon Blanc and tomorrow's brief and making merry with the officers in the case and the law clerk from the CPS.

And as for Toby, his time would come, he was sure of it. As he made his way back to Chambers, he reflected on his time at the Bar and what the future might hold for him. As Dave 'Dogface' Brown would put it, the answer, my friend, is blowin' in the wind. Problem was, though, he'd forgotten the question.

CHAPTER ELEVEN

TOBY IN LOVE

If I could write the beauty of thine eyes,
And in fresh numbers number all thy graces,
The age to come would say "This Poet lies,
Such heavenly touches ne'er touched earthly faces."

[William Shakespeare]

It was a memorable week in Toby' life as the pace quickened. He had been instructed to represent an eighteen-year-old youth charged with mugging a group of schoolboys and relieving them of their pocket money and a BMX bike. Without Bootsy's firm hand on the tiller, the youth had decided to chance his arm with the jury, and it was an uphill struggle. Toby was pushed to make a fist of it, especially as the school kids all knew the defendant from earlier encounters in the playground, and the BMX was found in his auntie's shed. But the best evidence came from a veritable vision of loveliness, Camilla Foster-James, who was on her way to a modelling assignment in her Audi TT and witnessed the whole incident. Unlike many who would simply drive on, she stopped to comfort the kids and left her name and address with Plod.

From the moment she swayed into court, the defendant's fate was sealed. Whatever else the jury were going to make of the school kids, they were totally captivated by the fragrant Camilla and every word she uttered. The defendant went crashing down in record time.

To refresh his spirits after such a depressing ordeal, Toby popped into a nearby wine bar. Seeing Camilla, eating alone at a corner table, his heart skipped a beat, and taking a deep breath, went over and introduced himself. Camilla didn't seem hugely impressed, but nodded to the chair opposite and Toby sat down.

As the wine loosened his natural reserve, they chatted easily about this and that and, mercifully, very little about the case. Fortunately Camilla was in forgiving mood, after Toby had attacked her evidence as a tissue of lies. Not quite so crudely, but that was the thrust of it. In fact, she found the whole experience amusing and light relief from earning shed loads of money on the catwalk. Toby was smitten, not just by her natural beauty, but also by her confident and relaxed manner. Was it love at first sight? Toby thought so, but did he have the courage to ask her out?

At first blush, Camilla was way up there out of Toby's league, but then, stranger things had happened, and he'd watched Four Weddings and a Funeral several times, where Andie McDowell, the fashion model in the big hat, had fallen for Hugh Grant, albeit by a very circuitous route. And what did Hugh Grant have that Toby didn't?

He could see it all, Camilla and Toby snapped secretly by the paparazzi whilst cavorting on the beach in Barbados, or coming out of Stringfellows, or, better still, Annabel's.

As she got up to leave, it was now or never. Offering to pay for her meal was a big mistake, and she made that very clear. She was rich, independent and only willing to be indulged on her own terms. But his gesture obviously struck a chord, and his invitation to dinner was not dismissed totally out of hand.

"Look," she said casually, "I'm having a few friends round for supper tomorrow night. Why don't you come along, that's if you've got nothing better to do?"

Toby could hardly believe his ears. "Thanks, that would be great."

Camilla gave him her address. "See you about nine," and with that she was gone.

Fortunately for Toby, he was out of court the next day and able to concentrate on the evening ahead. A gesture of some sort was *de rigueur.* Perhaps a bottle of Chateau Plonk, wine you never dreamed of drinking yourself but which was passed on round the drinks party set like an unexploded bomb until eventually, with the off-licences and pubs closed, some unlucky sod actually uncorked the noxious liquid and passed out from the aroma. A safer bet would be flowers and chocolates, not very imaginative, but less likely to cause offence. But a moment's reflection exposed the folly of that idea. You don't give chocolates to a model. What would Hugh Grant take, besides his enormous sex drive and smarmy ways? As Toby had neither, that was of no help at all.

Shortly after nine that evening, and clutching an expensive and elaborately presented corsage, Toby rang the doorbell to a delightful mews house just off the Portobello Road where the supper party for a few friends was in full swing. Not what he'd expected at all. Somebody he had never seen before opened the door, and leaving it open, walked back inside without a word. Toby followed her into the living room, jam-packed with forty or fifty beautiful people straight from the pages of OK and Hello magazines, screaming at each other over the primordial beat of Ozzy Osbourne and Black Sabbath.

Glancing round the room, Toby spotted Camilla, draped across a sofa and being nuzzled by, oh My God, it can't be! It is! Hugh Grant himself!

Camilla waved and beckoned him over. "So glad you made it. You know Hugh of course. Hugh, this is Toby, that absolute darling of a barrister I was telling you about. Very good and very grand. Had me quivering like a jelly!"

"Now that, my darling," purred Hugh, batting his eyelids, "is something I wouldn't have missed for the world," and he gave them both his million dollar smile. "Good to meet you, Toby," he lied. "Now, Millie, I must love you and leave you. Got things to do. See you next time around," and with a long, lingering, parting kiss, he sloped out.

With the departure of his main rival, Toby, feeling conspicuous in his suit and tie but trying to blend in, handed over the corsage.

"Oh Toby," said Camilla, "how absolutely divine! You shouldn't have. Now, there's lasagne and salad in the kitchen. Help yourself, and there's champers all over the place. Then I'll introduce you around."

It was one of those parties where you bellowed at the person standing right in front of you, they bellowed back, and you couldn't hear a word each other said. Still, Toby went through the motions and smiled and nodded a lot.

It was past two in the morning before the party began to disperse, and Toby, exhausted, decided it was time to go. But Camilla was having none of it. "Don't be so wet, Toby. Stay the night."

It was an invitation no red blooded male could resist.

"Are you sure?" he asked, "won't that be a frightful inconvenience?"

Camilla smiled indulgently. "Have another glass of champers, and I'll get rid of the stragglers."

An hour later, Camilla led him upstairs to the master bedroom.

"I'm going to have a shower. There are condoms in the bedside drawer, all sizes and flavours, so help yourself. See you in five." Her dress fell lightly from her exquisite shoulders and, as she was about to close the bathroom door, she turned and added seductively. "I prefer raspberry."

Not at all what Toby had expected. He wasn't a complete novice, and had had his fair share of flings at university. Well, two, actually, but he was a shy and sensitive boy, he got that from his mother, so it usually took him weeks, if not months, of courting, before the moment was right. And now, confronted with the most beautiful girl he'd ever met, would he be up to it?

Toby opened the drawer to find three packs of condoms, labelled small, medium and large, all in assorted flavours. He found himself on the horns of a dilemma. Which size to choose? He couldn't help but notice the pack of large condoms nearly empty, speaking volumes for Camilla's previous conquests. The small pack was unopened, so if he took one, he'd be the laughing stock of Notting Hill and never live it down. Safer to choose the medium size, mercifully already opened, so long as it didn't cramp his style.

He had just slipped it on and was getting into bed when Camilla appeared, completely naked and ready for action. "Right, Toby," she said, jumping on the bed and pulling back the covers, "let's see what you're made of." She grabbed hold of his manhood and wiggled it about. "I hope you can do better than that."

Toby felt the onset of brewer's droop in the face of her rebuke, but he was not to be beaten before he'd even reached the starting line. "Let's have a kiss and a cuddle, darling, to get us in the mood."

"Ok," and within a few minutes she felt him stiffening. "Good, now let's see what you're made of! You start on top, and then we'll swap. Go easy on the nipples and the breasts. I've got a topless shoot later on today. And don't come too soon, I take a while to climax. I'll give you a twenty second warning, so you can come at the same time." How thoughtful.

It was like a military campaign, planned down to the last detail only with smaller equipment, but where was the romance?

Toby climbed on top and slid effortlessly in.

Camilla was hot and ready. "Come on, Toby, come on in," she groaned.

"I *am* in, for Chrissake!" he muttered back.

"Then what are you waiting for? Go, go!" and off he went.

She grabbed hold of his protruding ears as he thrust in and out. "God, how I love these ears!" she squealed in delight, "better than bugger grips!"

Toby began to feel excited, in spite of having the lifeblood squeezed out of his ears, but he was a long way from the finishing line. He started to think of icebergs off Newfoundland to cool his ardour, which rather defeated the purpose of the exercise, but he was determined to please the love of his life. Eat your heart out, Hugh!

The sweat was now pouring off his back when Camilla signalled time for the changeover. Now it was her turn to pump up and down as Toby lay back and waited for the countdown. It was like Cape Canaveral. Eventually, and after what seemed like an eternity, they climaxed together.

Well pleased with his performance, they showered together, and as Toby dried her lovingly, she kissed him and whispered, "blackcurrant this time, I think."

Fortunately for Toby, he just managed to keep his end up during another torrid encounter, and then fell back, exhausted, into a deep sleep.

He awoke to find Camilla putting the finishing touches to her makeup, ready for the day's shoot.

"Help yourself to toast and coffee," she said, standing up and checking her dress for creases in the full-length mirror. "If you're really hungry, there's cold lasagne and warm champers," she giggled. "Mrs. Do-For-Me will be here at nine, so if you leave before she arrives, slam the door behind you, there's a darling."

Toby propped himself up on one arm and gazed at her sleepily. "What a wonderful party," he smiled lovingly, "and what a wonderful night." He paused. "So when do I see you again?"

Camilla smiled back, tossing her hair. "Easy, big fella!" she replied. "Let's not rush into anything we can't handle."

"But I'm hopelessly in love with you," said Toby, surprising even himself, "and I can't live without you."

"And I love you too," she replied, bending over the bed and kissing him lightly on the forehead to avoid smudging her lipstick. "Now I must get going or I'll be late."

"It's my birthday on Friday. I'm having a party, nothing as grand as yours, but it should be fun. Will you come?"

"Sure, it sounds great."

Toby was excited. "Gray's Inn, starting about seven thirty. Shall I pick you up?"

"No need, I'll find it, don't worry. Now I really must be going. See you Friday."

Toby had planned to celebrate his twenty-fifth birthday in style. Several chums were to assemble in Gray's Inn Common Room to kick start the evening's activities, then on to Henekey's Wine Bar on High Holborn for champagne and oysters, and then, well refreshed, to the Mille Pini Italian Restaurant just off Theobalds Road, where the basement had been reserved for food, wine and laddish behaviour.

Toby had bragged to his inner circle about Camilla, how they were hopelessly in love and, as they would see for themselves, she was the most beautiful girl on earth. He was greatly looking forward to showing her off, and watching their envious glances as they wined and dined and cavorted the night away. And then, to round off a memorable night, back to her place, or his, for another bout of passionate lovemaking. He'd even bought his own supply of condoms in Camilla's favourite flavours, ribbed and electronically tested for maximum satisfaction. He could hardly wait.

No sign of Camilla at Gray's Inn, but then, he reasoned, not easy to find, tucked away as it was behind a small arched entrance off High Holborn. Leaving a message with the barman in case she showed up late, they moved on to Henekeys, but still no show. Toby, hoping against hope she would come breezing through the door at any moment, considered the various options. Perhaps she'd been detained on a late shoot, yes, that was it, and as she didn't have his number, there was no way of letting him know. Never mind, perhaps she'll catch up with him at the Mille Pini. After all, the night was yet young, and she was very much a party animal.

The Mille Pini Restaurant, or Thousand Pines for the linguistically challenged, may have called itself an Italian Restaurant, but there the similarity ended. The waiters were all Cockney to a man, but to maintain the Italian theme, had been rechristened, so Paul became Paulo, Fred Frederico, John José and so on, with Bill the owner, a lateral thinker, calling himself Manuel. They had also been schooled to speak Italian, which consisted of adding the letter 'A' after almost every English word they uttered. So when taking the order, Paulo, or Frederico or José, whichever, would say: "Wadda you wanna eata?" and wave their hands around. You could almost smell Naples.

The chef, Jock Romsey, was Scottish, with flaming red hair and a temper to match, who swore like a trooper and threw knives around, mostly in the direction of the long-suffering kitchen staff. But he made a Spaghetti alla Vongole to die for, his cannelloni was always fresh and, best of all, by London standards it was cheap and cheerful.

And so Toby and his friends dined, and drank, and sang badly, and danced the conga round the tables and into the small hours and, eventually, into bed, with only his unused condoms for company. Still, there'd be other times, he was sure of it.

Toby had promised to spend what remained of the weekend with his parents, and, if all had gone to plan, to take Camilla with him. Next weekend, perhaps.

Home for Toby's parents was in the village of Prestwood, a leafy suburb just outside Great Missenden in the rolling hills of Buckinghamshire. The late Clement Atlee had made it his retirement home, and took the title Earl of Prestwood, as former Prime Ministers did in those days. He was once described by Churchill as a modest man, with much to be modest about. One for Bootsy should their paths ever cross again.

His mother had promised Toby a quiet family dinner to celebrate his birthday in more genteel surroundings. To the accompaniment of a few well-spun homilies from his father, he would open his presents whilst she put the finishing touches to his favourite meal, boiled ham and carrots with parsley sauce, and apple charlotte with custard for pudding. Then, if his mother had anything to do with it, early to bed with a cup of cocoa and a good night's sleep before returning to London and another week defending all those dreadful criminals.

Toby arrived on the six o'clock train and decided to walk the mile up the hill. It was a pleasant early summer evening, and he needed the exercise to loosen the hangover and expel the overpowering taste of garlic still clinging remorselessly to his breath.

After kisses and hugs and the usual comments from his mother about how thin and tired he looked, Toby went upstairs to shower, clean his teeth and dress for dinner. Smart casual was the order of the evening as he joined his father in the drawing room.

"So, my boy, how's it going? Still glad you joined the Bar? I know a good solicitor, member of Rotary, who may have an opening if you want me to put in a good word."

Toby smiled, remembering his father's dismissive description of barristers as pompous upper class idiots in fancy dress, and nothing he'd seen or heard over the past two years had persuaded him to change his opinion.

"Thanks, Pa, I'll bear it in mind, but for the time being I'm enjoying my work. Can't say I'm winning many cases, but it's only a matter of time," or so he hoped.

"Well," replied his father, "you can't make bricks without straw. If it's really what you want," he added, "then stick to it. Your mother and I are very proud of you, you know that."

"I do, and thanks, Pa, for everything." Toby took a sip of champagne and glanced through to the dining room. "I see the table's laid for six. Is that ominous?"

"Didn't your mother tell you? She's invited the Sandwells."

"Oh no, don't tell me, Susie Sandwell on parade, yet again."

His father smiled. "You can't blame your mother for trying. She thinks it's time you met a nice girl and settled down. And besides, you have a lot in common."

"Actually, Pa, I have a girlfriend," replied Toby, his chest swelling, "she's a top model, absolutely stunning, name's Camilla Foster-James, you may have heard of her?" His father shook his head. "I'd hoped to bring her down for the weekend, but she was unavoidably detained at the last minute. You know what life can be like for a top model, on call twenty-four hours a day. Still, you and mother will meet her soon enough."

Just then the doorbell rang, and Toby's mother hurried through from the kitchen to greet the Sandwells. George Sandwell, now in his late fifties, was also in accountancy and a fellow Rotarian. The two families had known each other for as long as Toby could remember, and like Toby, Susie was an only child. She was also the same age as Toby, so they had spent many days together in their respective gardens, splashing happily in the paddling pool, running naked round the lawn, and, of course, their first kiss, aged four, lovingly captured on celluloid for posterity by Toby's proud mother and now enjoying pride of place in the family album.

As they grew up, Toby remembered Susie as a rather gawky teenager, not unattractive but not sufficiently stunning to arouse any serious interest when he was exploring his sexuality, and her straightened teeth clamped into position with unsightly braces was a real turn off. They went away to different schools, and different universities, so they saw little of each other as they ploughed their respective furrows. Susie had spent the last year in Botswana, comforting the less fortunate and rubbing shoulders with royalty, and had only just returned.

"Evening, George," said Sandwell, walking into the drawing room, "are you well?"

"Yes, thanks, George," replied Toby's father. For years, when he was growing up, Toby had believed that all accountants were called George. It seemed to go with the territory. Next came Mrs. Sandwell, and bringing up the rear, Susie, under the close supervision of Toby's mother, clutching hold of her in the manner of a trainer leading his horse around the saddling enclosure before the three thirty at Kempton Park. That was uncharitable, Toby had to admit, as Susie looked stunning. Not in Camilla's class, but then, who was? She was tall and slim, lightly tanned from her time abroad, with shining light brown hair and hazel eyes. She had a beautiful smile, which lit up her whole face. The braces had obviously worked wonders.

After the obligatory Mwah Mwah all round, the champagne was poured, all the usual pleasantries exchanged and presents opened. Susie gave Toby an African wood carving of a warrior with a huge erection, which had the ladies blushing and the men folk roaring with laughter. It was a very agreeable evening, helped enormously by Susie's charm and easy manner. Susie described her time in Botswana, and meeting Prince Harry, and Toby was prevailed upon to recount some of his more interesting cases. That didn't take long.

"What I want to know, Toby," said George Sandwell as the cheese board was passed around, "is how can you defend all these ghastly criminals when you know they're guilty?"

If Toby had a pound for every time he'd been asked that question, he'd be thinking of early retirement. "Not my decision, Mr. Sandwell," he replied rather pompously. "That's why we have trial by jury. They decide where the truth lies, and for the most part, it seems to work. The prosecution bring the case, they have to prove it beyond a reasonable doubt, and it's the defendant's right to be acquitted if there's a reasonable doubt. That's the system, warts and all."

"I was called to jury service once," mused Mrs. Sandwell.

"And did you enjoy it?" asked Toby.

"Well, I got through two of Jilly Cooper's books, cover to cover, during my two weeks, and met some delightful people, but we did have one trial."

132

"Oh yes? And what was that about?"

"It was a policeman charged with dangerous driving. We were told he was going ninety in a thirty mile an hour speed limit. Apparently all to do with familiarising himself with a new car."

"And did you find him guilty?"

"Oh no, he was such a nice man, and you've got to support the police, haven't you? Besides, the black recording box, you know, the box that records the speed of the car, had mysteriously gone missing, and nobody could find it. All rather curious."

"So you don't think the missing box had anything to do with police corruption?" Toby was wearing his defence counsel's wig.

Mrs. Sandwell was horrified at the suggestion, and said so, but Toby was on a roll.

"And what would have happened if a pedestrian had stepped off the pavement just as the policeman was speeding by?"

Toby's father had had enough. It was getting too confrontational. He shot Toby a glance. "Well, I don't know anything about these legal niceties, but you've just told us the prosecution bring the case and must prove it. So if they couldn't prove what speed the police officer was going, he was entitled to be acquitted. Well done, Molly," he beamed encouragingly at Mrs. Sandwell. Before Toby could come back, he rose from his chair. "Coffee in the drawing room."

"What a good idea," said Toby's mother. "Toby, will you look after Susie, and I know Molly will help me in the kitchen."

Toby had been a bore, and he knew it. It was one of Nick Ridley's golden rules; when you leave chambers, take off your wig and gown.

The mood lightened with the arrival of the coffee, and the two Georges helped themselves to large brandies. Toby chatted idly with Susie, but his thoughts were elsewhere. When would he see Camilla again?

133

Should he wait for her to contact him? After all, she knew his name and could look him up in the Bar Directory. Or should he give it a couple of days and call round to her house, on the pretext he was passing and thought he'd just drop in?

When it was time for the Sandwells to leave, Toby exchanged the usual platitudes with Susie, about how lovely it was to see her again, and how they must keep in touch, but they lacked sincerity and it showed.

He slept fitfully, awoke early, and decided on a brisk walk round the village to clear his head. On the way back, he bought a selection of the Sunday papers, and planned a leisurely browse after one of his mother's full English breakfasts. He was feeling better already.

The thunderbolt that hit him right between the eyes, and cut him to the quick, was to be found lurking in the Atticus column of the Sunday Times. Toby stared, seeing but not believing, at the photo of Camilla and Hugh Grant, emerging from Annabel's in the early hours of the morning. With trepidation he read the short report. The top model and Britain's favourite film star had spent an intimate evening at Annabel's, and were seen leaving at about the same time as Toby was flopping into bed with his unused condoms. He was devastated. He should've taken the last large condom when he had the chance, just to spite Super Stud.

It finally, and painfully, dawned on him. He was nothing more than a one night stand, and once he'd served his purpose, to be tossed aside like a used whatever!

Toby's first reaction was one of blind anger. He wanted to go round to her house, bang on her door and give her a piece of his mind, the ungrateful girl! But then, when he'd calmed down, he analysed the situation. Camilla had made no promises, and besides, could they ever be happy together? She led a fast track life, modelling, and jumping into bed, and jetting here and there with the jet set, and the idea of settling down to domestic bliss and kids would be anathema to her. It would destroy her, and anyway, she'd want to call the kids Apple, or Tiger Lily, or, worst of all, Hugh!

134

He'd get over it and move on with the rest of his life. No point dwelling on the past, count your blessings, as his mother was fond of saying. And so he did. He had a loving family, he was a member of the best set of chambers in the Temple, he smiled as he remembered Gazzard's comment, and he was climbing the greasy pole at a steady pace, or so he believed.

"Come on, Toby," he hadn't seen his father come into the room, "time for a pint at the Polecat whilst your mother's cooking lunch. I always feel I'm under her feet if I don't go out." He winked.

The pub was busy, as it always was before Sunday lunch, with husbands and fathers getting out from under feet. Whilst supping their first pints, Toby's father nudged him and indicated a corner table. Toby looked over to see Susie, relaxed and laughing with a Hugh Grant look-alike and in animated conversation. God! The man was everywhere. Susie looked up, saw Toby and gave him a smile.

"Go over and say hello," said his father.

"But she's with someone."

"I can see that, but it's rude to ignore her."

At his father's insistence, Toby went over.

"You've met Rupert, haven't you?" Susie asked. "He's my first cousin, and down for the weekend."

What a relief. Now why did Toby feel that?

"Good to meet you," said Rupert, standing up. "I promised to help Aunt Molly lay the table, so I'd better get going. See you later."

Toby stood there for a moment, feeling awkward. "Can I buy you a drink?"

Toby brought the drinks over and sat down. "I wanted to apologise for my behaviour last night," he began, "and especially to your mother. I was being pompous and rude. I just got carried away."

135

"That's alright, Toby. Mummy thought you were charming," Susie put her hand on his, "and so did I."

After lunch, and feeling more relaxed than he'd felt for a long time, Toby tossed the Sunday Times into the waste bin and looked over to his mother. "Do you mind if I come down again next weekend?"

"Not at all, dear, it's always a pleasure to see you. Any special reason?"

"Er, I've invited Susie out for dinner next Saturday, and she's accepted."

CHAPTER TWELVE

TOBY AND THE SILK

For men may come,
And men may go,
But he goes on for ever.

[Alfred, Lord Tennyson]

At ten thirty six on the night of November the fifth, the sergeant on duty at Wood Green Police Station received a telephone call.

"I think I've killed my mother," and the line went dead.

The call was traced, police and ambulance dispatched, and when they broke in, they found Andrew Stubbs sitting in a chair, staring vacantly at the badly injured and motionless body of his mother, and nursing an empty two litre bottle of cider. The unfortunate woman was taken to hospital, where she never regained consciousness and died nine days later. Andrew was charged with her murder and remanded in custody. After the usual preliminary hearings, trial was set at Wood Green Crown Court in front of the newly appointed Mr. Justice Greengross, better known as the Grocer, and as dry as a sea biscuit.

Life for Toby couldn't have been better. Camilla was but a distant memory, and romance with Susie was definitely blossoming. Her pace suited him, long walks in the woods holding hands, romantic dinners when finances allowed, a stolen kiss and a cuddle, whispering sweet nothings in her ear. It was all his dreams come true. He loved just holding her, stroking her hair, smelling her wonderful freshness, never wanting to let go.

But let go he must, at least during the week, as there were battles to fight and dragons to slay. That Wednesday evening, just as he was preparing to leave chambers, Fred beckoned him into the clerks room.

"Got an interesting case for you, Mr. Potts," he said, pointing to a large volume of papers in front of him. "I'm returning your brief for tomorrow at Barnet Magistrates Court. One of the pupils can cover it for you. This is much more important, and who knows, could do you the power of good. Murder," Toby felt weak at the knees, "fixed for trial on Monday," my God, so little time, and was he ready for the ultimate challenge? He thought so, and with his incisive cross-examination and impassioned final speech to the jury, who could say? "And you're being led by Sir James Bingham of Queen's Counsel no less." Toby felt a little deflated at not taking centre stage, but then, even junior counsel have their part to play, and holding the hand of such an eminent silk would be a challenge in itself. A quiet word here, a suggestion there, earning the approbation of the great man, he could see it all, possibly even a bi-line in the press and media: 'Sir James Bingham QC, ably assisted by Mr. Toby Potts, the rising star of the profession, secured a glorious acquittal in the teeth of the evidence'. That would do nicely. He couldn't wait to get home to Prestwood and break the news to Susie.

"His junior had to drop out at the last minute," Fred continued, bringing Toby back down to earth with a bump, "so his bad luck is your good fortune. Consultation with leader has been booked for tomorrow at four thirty in his chambers," and with that, Paul handed over the papers. Toby studied the four lever arch files. Forget about that drink at Henekeys, it was going to be a long night.

Sir James 'Jumbo' Bingham QC was a legend in the profession, and larger than life in every sense of the word. Six foot three in his red stocking feet, and weighing in at twenty-four stone, he strode the stage like a colossus, and his courtroom triumphs were the talk of the profession. Now in his early seventies, but still a formidable adversary, he was generally regarded as one of the finest advocates in silk, but he had a fearsome temper and didn't suffer fools gladly, whether on the Bench or at the Bar.

Toby, clutching his files, was shown into the great man's room promptly at four thirty. Sir James peered at him over several double chins, and smiled.

"So you're Potts?" nodding towards a chair, "sorry to have landed you with this brief so near to trial. Wretched juniors, don't know where their priorities lie, too busy making money!" He paused, taking a long hard look at his new junior. "So, are you up to speed, Potts? Got it boxed?"

"I think so, Sir James," Toby started tentatively, "I've been through the papers twice."

"Good, good," he boomed, "now let's see what we're up against. Our client Stubbs is a very troubled young man, and according to the reports from the trick cyclists who've prodded and poked him for the past six months, everybody has an opinion to offer whilst saying nothing relevant at all." He scrabbled amongst his papers and found what he was looking for. "The list of possibilities is endless. His father died when he was twelve, his mother was over-protective, he was bullied at school, he was awkward with girls, he has low self-esteem and, hardly surprising, unemployable. A total recluse by all accounts." Sir James read on. "His only pleasures in life seem to be drinking White Lightning cider to excess, smoking the occasional joint and listening to Wagner. Wagner!" he snorted. "Enough to depress anyone! Huge, leaden breasted women with horns coming out of their ears staggering around the stage and belting out cacophonous arias and being chased by booming men with spears, and all the while competing for air space with the orchestra hell-bent on drowning them out! And to cap it all, the whole thing's sung in Kraut!" He paused to regain his breath. "I was taken to the Ring Cycle once, some years ago, by a failed politician," he continued in reflective mood, "damned if I can remember his name, but made my excuses and managed to slip out before the half-time whistle. Worst night of my life!" and he bellowed with laughter. Drying his eyes with an enormous spotted red handkerchief, he looked warily at Toby. "You're not a buff, are you by any chance?"

"No, no Sir James, definitely not," replied Toby.

"Good, good, wouldn't want to tread on junior toes so soon in our professional relationship. To my way of thinking, the only natural language of opera is Italian, don't you agree? The most tuneful language on earth, it's divine. No wonder Rome is the centre of the Christian universe. But I digress. Back to the plot." Sir James flicked through more papers. "I've been to see the lad in Brixton Prison, totally pointless exercise. Since his arrest he hasn't uttered a word, so no help there. Bit like that chap found wandering on a beach in Kent, you know the one, it was in all the papers, never spoke a word but played the piano like Rubenstein. Fortunately for those listening, he didn't include Wagner in his repertoire, thank the Lord!" Again the bellow of laughter and the spotted red handkerchief. "But there the similarity ends. As far as I know, our punter doesn't play the piano, in fact he doesn't do anything except stare at the wall, poor blighter."

"So his defence is insanity?" suggested Toby, trying to be helpful and appear up to speed.

Not helpful at all, as Sir James made abundantly clear. His smile vanished in an instant. He had an idiot for a junior. "Insanity?! What on earth are you prattling on about? There's no such defence to a charge of murder, as you should know all too well. Didn't they teach you anything at Law School?" He glowered at Toby and then composed himself. "If, however, you mean diminished responsibility, and if you had bothered to read the reports from the trick cyclists, they are unable to form any opinion as to the defendant's mental state, and who can blame them? After all, how can you certify somebody as suffering from abnormality of the mind when he remains as silent as the grave, a virtue in some, which I suggest you follow."

Oh dear, thought Toby, feeling thoroughly depressed and humiliated, bang goes the bi-line.

"You have much to do before Monday, so let me detain you no longer. Now, we shall meet, promptly at ten thirty, when we can reappraise the situation and take it from there."

"I'm sorry to interrupt, Sir James, but the trial is listed to start at ten thirty."

140

"The trial, Potts, will start when I am ready." Sir James leaned back in his chair. "For reasons that wholly escape me, the trial is listed at Wood Green Crown Court. Until I accepted instructions in this case, I have to confess I'd never heard of it. Do you know it?"

"I've been there twice, Sir James, but not long enough to make a lasting impression."

Jumbo's cold manner changed, and he chuckled. "Bad as that, is it?" Toby nodded. "I blame this new Lord Chancellor, complete jackass if you ask me. He wants to make us 'user friendly', all singing from the same song sheet. Can't be doing with the man! I was at the Bailey last week, and do you know, I saw a notice on the board headed 'Do you have a complaint about the judge?' My dear boy, I didn't know where to begin!" Another bellow, and out came the red spotted handkerchief again. "And the Bar Council is no better, bunch of chancers waiting to climb aboard the judicial bandwagon. Whatever happened to the independent Bar?" He threw down his pen in disgust. "Anyway, I'm too old a dog to teach new tricks. Now, to more important matters, what about the scoff?"

Toby smiled. "I've never been there long enough to explore the culinary delights, Sir James, but I'm not hopeful."

"Nonsense, Potts, you give up too easily. I am delegating to you the supremely important task of seeking out the best watering hole within hailing distance of this ghastly court. Do not fail me, on pain of death, or worse! And no foreign muck that looks like something you tread in during a country ramble. English, French at a pinch, or better still, la Bella Italia. You have your orders. Now off you go, and I'll see you on Monday."

Sadly for Toby, preparing for trial to meet Sir James' exacting demands meant spending his weekend in London and away from his beloved Susie. She was very understanding, of course, and thrilled at the news of the awesome responsibility falling on his slender shoulders. "They must think you're very good, Toby. How exciting!"

Needless to say, Toby had been somewhat economical when describing his role in the trial, but no need to bother Susie with trivial details. Fortunately for him, the law library at Gray's Inn was open over the weekend, so he plunged into Black's Medical Dictionary and made copious notes of all the medical terminology. Why couldn't doctors use plain English? It was just showing off to use all these Latin words and totally unnecessary, and besides, Latin was a dead language. Quite witty, thought Toby to himself, as he pored over the post mortem.

The prosecution pathologist was having a field day with the poor woman's fractured tibia, haematomas around the parietal region of the cranium, extensive comminuted fracturing over the body including the left ulna and right clavicle, and grazing over the left patella. He concluded that death occurred as a result of a subdural haematoma, which, according to Dr. Black, was bleeding from the brain into the cavity of the skull, causing massive brain damage. The subdural haematoma was the result of blunt trauma, such as a blow or blows with a fist or a foot. The defence pathologist agreed.

Sir James was right, of course. In the face of the defendant's silence, the trick cyclists were unable to offer a positive opinion, but could find nothing to suggest he was unfit to plead or stand his trial. So be it, let battle commence!

Wood Green might have been a leafy suburb once upon a time, but was now conspicuous by the absence of any wood or any green. Rows upon rows of artisan terraced houses, crowded together and fighting for space, were the hallmark of this unattractive part of north London, wedged between Muswell Hill and Tottenham, home to the eponymous football club, which, like the area from which it took its name, had seen better days. There was the now obligatory shopping arcade, fetchingly named the Arndale Centre, with stores selling goods nobody needed and still fewer could afford, the occasional corner shop scratching a living, and dozens of ethnic restaurants and fast food outlets from every corner of the globe.

The Crown Court was originally built in Victorian times as an orphanage, and before the Lord Chancellor's Department had discovered the chrome and neon and purpose built button for the construction of new crown courts, had been converted at much the same time as the lunatic asylum in Snaresbrook. Indeed, the outward manifestations of the two buildings bore an uncanny resemblance to each other, as they did to Wormwood Scrubs, the Royal Courts of Justice, and Balmoral. The hand of Queen Victoria's favourite architect was there for all to see. But unlike Snaresbrook, which had a lake and well-manicured gardens to soften it, Wood Green Crown Court had nothing to lift it above the depressingly mundane.

Toby had taken the task set for him very seriously indeed, and was determined to impress Sir James with the results of his researches if nothing else. For the most part, the various authorities he'd consulted confirmed what he'd suspected all along, that Wood Green was a gastronomic desert. English food was confined to a handful of pubs dotted here and there, but he couldn't quite see Sir James leaning on the bar and munching his way through last week's shepherd's pie, or the plat du jour with chips. The French had absented themselves altogether, and who could blame them? But there was one possible nugget in the wash pan that might just fit the bill, an Italian restaurant named La Bella Notte. Toby arrived early, very early, to reconnoitre the terrain, and found it situated in a small precinct of shops, travel agents and building societies. It was closed, of course, at nine in the morning, but from the outside looked clean and respectable, with a varied menu boasting authentic Italian cuisine. To his great relief, it also met two essential requirements: it was open at lunchtime, and was within ten minutes walking distance from the court, taken at a leisurely pace.

Whilst waiting for Sir James to arrive, Toby discovered that prosecution counsel was Giles Warburton QC, and a new kid on the block. In his late forties, of average height and build, in fact the word 'average' had been invented to describe him, with fair hair swept aggressively back, and an aquiline nose with nostrils that flared when he was under pressure. As he was cutting his teeth on steady CPS fare, he took himself very seriously indeed, not a natural bedfellow for Sir James. By ten fifteen Warburton, nostrils flared, was fussing around like the school prefect, clicking his teeth and clearly agitated.

"I really think this is most discourteous of your leader," he kept saying, turning on Toby. "There's so much to discuss before the trial, and Mr. Justice Greengross will want to start promptly at ten thirty." Warburton paced up and down the hallway with his junior, the infamous Paul Newman from the CPS who had obtained the Higher Courts Advocacy Certificate and had decided to instruct himself. Not a good idea as it transpired. As the saying goes, the advocate who instructs himself has a fool for a client, but the CPS were slow learners. As the hour approached, Warburton and his junior were joined by his lordship's clerk and the court usher, and together the four of them paced up and down, glancing frantically at the main door. It was like a scene from a Gilbert and Sullivan operetta.

Promptly at ten thirty, Sir James arrived and made his way magisterially through the main door, accompanied by the senior partner of the defendant's solicitors. Toby rushed forward to greet him and carry his bags as Warburton and his posse closed in.

"Sir James," Warburton smiled thinly, "or may I call you Jumbo?"

"No, you most certainly may not!" replied the great man, "and who the blazes are you?"

"I am Giles Warburton, QC," he added, still getting used to the idea, "and leading counsel for the Crown. I was hoping to discuss the shape of the trial with you before we begin."

"All in good time, my dear fellow. First things first. I shall robe. Then a cup of strong coffee whilst my junior goes to see the defendant in the cells. If he deigns to say anything, which I doubt, I shall be informed immediately. As to the shape of the trial, as you rather quaintly put it, I suggest you call such evidence as you believe will prove the guilt of the defendant, and I shall rebut it. Isn't that the way it's usually done?" That said, Sir James made his way to the third floor and the robing room, leaving the posse speechless.

The court usher was the first to break the silence. "What shall we tell his lordship? He told me he wanted to start at ten thirty sharp."

This was Toby's first encounter with the defendant, and it shook him. There sat opposite him Andrew Stubbs, a twenty-sex year old man, totally traumatised, with lifeless, sunken, eyes set in a cadaverous white face, staring vacantly at the wall. His hands trembled visibly as Toby explained what was about to happen, and how he was represented by the best silk in the country, and if he had any questions now or at any time during the trial, he had only to ask. Nothing. As Toby got up to go, he touched Andrew's hand and smiled reassuringly. To his surprise, the hand stopped trembling for just a moment, there was a flicker of understanding in his eyes and the faintest trace of a smile, and then he was gone again.

The court assembled at five past eleven, and the Grocer was not best pleased. He almost sprinted into court, and began by addressing counsel in a high-pitched voice with a querulous and irritating edge to it. "This trial was listed to begin promptly at ten thirty, and it is now five minutes past eleven. Whatever the reason for the delay, I propose starting each morning from now on promptly at ten. Is that clear?"

Sir James eased himself to his feet. "Your lordship displays a commendable devotion to duty and an example to us all. However," he paused for dramatic effect, "if your lordship is determined to sit each morning at ten, then you will do so without me." The Grocer's mouth snapped open as Sir James continued at his most urbane. "That being so, I doubt if the Court of Appeal would look favourably on a conviction secured, in part, during my absence." The Grocer was about to say something, but Sir James cut him short. "Unlike your lordship, who is accommodated in agreeable and, I hope, comfortable, lodgings nearby, we lesser mortals must rely on the vagaries of public transport. In addition, as head of chambers, I have many duties to perform, both before and after the court sitting, and these cannot be abandoned on a whim." Toby was loving every minute of it. The Grocer was not.

"So what do you propose, Sir James?" he asked testily.

"My clerk informs me that the most convenient train with first class facilities leaves Kings Cross Station at five past nine, arriving at Wood Green at five minutes past ten. After a ten minute journey by car to court, I then need time to consult with my lay client, in the unlikely event that he should choose to speak to me, and with my learned junior. Let me assure your lordship that with goodwill on all sides, the trial can resume each morning at ten forty-five."

The Grocer sat, grim-faced, knuckles white, absorbing the enormity of Sir James's statement and the man who'd just made it. "Very well, Sir James, but I shall insist on no more than an hour for the short adjournment."

That was worse than questioning Sir James's progeny, and you did so at your peril.

"No, my lord," he replied, "that will not be possible," and he smiled graciously. "Whilst your lordship will avail yourself of the judicial dining room, we lesser mortals must find sustenance elsewhere. I am confident that if we rise promptly at one, we should be able to resume the afternoon sitting at two thirty."

The Grocer was onto a hiding to nothing, but still he blundered on. "In that case, Sir James, I propose making up the time lost by sitting until four thirty."

"No, my lord, that will not be possible. With the good offices of my instructing solicitor, if we rise promptly at four, and no later," he added with emphasis, "then I should be able to catch the four twenty train back to the Temple. I am obliged for your lordship's indulgence, and unless there are any other matters, I suggest we delay the trial no further and empanel the jury." Game, set and match! Sir James sat down, signalling the end of the discussion. It was pure theatre, and a real *tour de force.*

The Grocer, put firmly back in his box, chose discretion as the better part of valour, nodded towards the jury bailiff and the trial began.

Warburton opened the case for the prosecution in meticulous detail, no doubt wishing to impress those who sat behind him with his command of the case and all its complexities. It was boring but clinically efficient. Sir James occupied the time by doodling, whilst Toby took a

146

careful note. With the court clock nudging twelve, and Warburton still in full flow, Sir James turned round to Toby. Toby was all ears, as his mother was fond of saying, and leaned forward, expecting some incisive comment about the law or the evidence.

"What about the scoff, Potts? Have you got it sorted?" he asked in a stage whisper. All eyes in the jury box turned to Sir James as Warburton hesitated, stumbled and then waited, expecting an objection to something he'd said.

"I think I've found a reasonable Italian restaurant about ten minutes' walk away," Toby whispered back.

"Good boy," he beamed expansively. "Have you booked a table?"

"Not yet, Sir James."

"Then get to it."

"What? Now?"

"Yes, now."

Toby, conscious he was now the centre of attention, and avoiding his lordship's withering gaze, rose, bowed, and sidled out of court.

Warburton, put out, turned to the Grocer for moral support. "I pause, my lord, in case my learned friend wishes to raise an objection."

"Do you, Sir James?" asked the Grocer in that high-pitched voice of his.

"No, thank you, my lord. Objections will almost certainly be taken when my learned friend calls his evidence, but as his opening speech is not evidence in the case, I see no point whatsoever. However," he added ominously, "the jury and I will remain vigilant."

With the clock at one, and with Warburton in mid-sentence, Sir James rose. "Is this a convenient moment, my lord?"

The Grocer looked up. "Very well, Sir James. We will resume at two thirty."

In no time at all, Sir James was ready for the off. "Right, Potts, lead on," he boomed, and striding out at a formidable pace, they reached La Bella Notte in six minutes flat. Toby had forewarned the restaurant of the impending arrival of the great man, and as luck would have it, they had the place to themselves.

Sir James entered with a mighty flourish. "Buon Giorno, Signore," he enthused, "lei è il padrone?"

The owner, Mario, was in awe of this great English baronet, an honour and a privilege, and after all, great men in Wood Green were as rare as hen's teeth. "Si, è vero, milord. Mi piace ad accogliervi al mio ristorante."

"Piace. Di dove Lei?"

"Di Verona, milord."

"Ah, Verona, la città di sogni con l'opera piu bellissima in tutta l'Italia."

"Lei é stato in Verona, milord?"

"Tanto volte, ed ogni volta era meglio." Sir James embraced Mario in his massive arms. "Adesso, padrone, parliamo di affari importanti. Vorremo due bottiglie del suo Barolo ed un grande antipasto. Poi, vorrei il cannelloni, e dopo, la bistecca alla Milanese. Non abbiamo molto tempo, dunque, vogliamo mangiare subito, grazie."

"Subito, milord," replied Mario, bowing low as Sir James and Toby sat down. The meal was superb, and the wine exquisite, although Toby's appetite was no match for Sir James's.

"I wasn't sure if you wanted me to invite your solicitor, Sir James," said Toby, in between mouthfuls of cannelloni, "so I didn't. I hope I did the right thing."

"Absolutely, my boy," Sir James replied, refilling his glass. "Henry Paige has been instructing me for the past thirty years, he's an excellent solicitor and a first rate colleague. But we have different roles to play, and we respect the professional boundaries during the trial. I've watched their erosion over the years, and today, I'm informed, it's not uncommon for barristers with indifferent practices to actually tout for business, taking solicitors out for lunch or dinner, inviting them to their homes, and, for all I know, letting them sleep with their partners, as they're now known in common parlance." He snorted in disgust. "The Warbler's a case in point, and even as I speak, no doubt eating in the works canteen with that self-important twerp from the CPS. Might get him his next brief, but if he stops kissing arse, that's the end of him. A dangerous and demeaning game. Sadly, there's too many mice chasing the same piece of cheese, too many who shouldn't be in the profession at all. Don't go down that road, my boy, that's my advice. If a solicitor won't brief you unless you fawn all over him, he's not worth the candle. Padrone," he bellowed, pushing the empty plate away from him, "il dulce per favore."

After café expresso dople and a large Vecchia Romagna, it was time to return to the fray. True to his word, Sir James entered court at exactly two thirty, and the trial resumed.

Warburton, or the Warbler as Sir James had christened him, was ready to put the final touches to his speech and was checking and cross-referencing his notes.

"Had a good lunch, old boy?" enquired Sir James, feeling in expansive mood.

"More of a working lunch, Sir James," he replied, "no time to leave court, so my junior and I had lunch in the Bar Mess." Sir James winked at Toby, who was already fighting to stay awake.

Warburton concluded his opening speech and then called the evidence. The rest of the afternoon was taken up with the preliminaries, finding the body, the arrest of the defendant, lurid photographs and a plan of the room showing the exact position of the body when it was found.

Sir James asked a few perfunctory questions, nothing incisive, simply showing the flag.

At five minutes to four, the Warbler rose to call his next witness.

"My lord," said Sir James, rising slowly from his seat, "this witness may take a little time, and as we've made such splendid progress, may I suggest we adjourn until the morning? The jury have had enough for one day." Nice touch, thought Toby.

"Very well, Sir James."

Tuesday was the day of medical evidence, starting with the psychiatrists, or trick cyclists, as Sir James was fond of calling them. As there was broad agreement, only two of the four were called, both sporting bow ties and looking as mad as hatters. The defendant's mental state was dissected down to the last nodule, with lofty statements about dysfunctional atrophy and amnesiac related memory loss associated with high anxiety paranoia. It was all complete gibberish to Toby, but they confirmed that the defendant was fit to plead and fit to stand trial. Sir James asked a few questions, just to get the sympathy vote, but no more. As far as the trick cyclists were concerned, not one suggested a disposal under the Mental Health Act in the event of a conviction.

Next came the medical evidence, starting with the paramedics who attended the scene. Sir James showed some interest in their findings and treatment, and in particular, their patient's comatose state. He highlighted this particular aspect of their evidence, Toby didn't know why, but assumed it must be important. The Warbler asked no questions in re-examination, so like Toby, hadn't seen its relevance.

Back to the ever welcoming Mario and more excellent Italian scoff, and then more of the same in the afternoon. The Warbler called the doctors who treated Mrs. Stubbs on arrival and who admitted her to the intensive care unit. As senior housemen newly qualified, they trotted out all the Latin jargon, word perfect, which the Grocer, after searching inquiry, translated for the jury. This part of the evidence held no terrors for Toby, and he was itching to chime in and show off the fruits of his labours. They had also prepared diagrams, copies available for the jury, one between two, showing the extent and severity of the assault.

After the court adjourned for the day, and with Sir James departing for the station, Toby reviewed the evidence on his own, and was deeply troubled. Using the same forensic skills he thought Sir James would apply, he simply couldn't spot the defence. The prosecution could prove beyond a shadow of a doubt that Mrs. Stubbs was seriously assaulted by the defendant and had died, nine days later, without regaining consciousness. Cause of death was a brain haemorrhage. The statements of all the medical witnesses, and there were many, indicated she had received constant and expert attention during those nine days, and that the damage inflicted by the defendant was simply irreversible. In the absence of a defence of insanity, and Toby wasn't going to revisit that particular low point, there was no defence to the charge of murder. But he couldn't believe Sir James was simply going through the motions. That would achieve nothing, and certainly wasn't in the defendant's interests. Toby was missing something, but what? Perhaps manslaughter? Time to go back to chambers and consider the possibility, just in case Sir James wanted Toby's input.

That momentous Wednesday began when Warburton called as his first witness the consultant in overall charge of the intensive care unit. His evidence confirmed the medical evidence already given and simply drew the strings together. He also confirmed the cause of death. Then Sir James got up to cross-examine.

"Mr. Rowbotham," he began, "when the deceased was admitted to the intensive care unit, she was, and remained, deeply unconscious, did she not?"

"That's correct."

"We can agree, can we not, that the other injuries to her body, about which we have already heard detailed evidence, were not life threatening?"

"Correct."

"So for the purposes of my cross-examination into the cause of death, we can concentrate on the head injuries?"

"I agree."

"Very well." He paused, looking down at his notes. "Now your considerable experience will tell you that in most cases, even after a severe beating, the patient normally regains consciousness within a relatively short period of time, possibly within ten to fifteen minutes of the assault. Do you agree?"

"In general terms, yes, but…"

"Good. So the fact that the deceased was deeply unconsciousness on admission suggests two things, does it not? Firstly, that she had sustained an injury to the brain, certainly a subdural haematoma, or, worse still, an extradural haematoma? And secondly, you would agree, these haematomas build up after a head injury of this sort over a period of hours, anywhere between two to three hours, sometimes much longer?"

"In broad terms, I would agree with your analysis, and that coincides with our clinical findings. Shortly after her admission, we conducted a brain scan and found a subdural haematoma."

"Explain that for the benefit of the jury and," he added with heavy irony, "for his lordship."

"Well, a subdural haematoma arises as a result of damage to the membrane between the brain and the skull, which manifests itself in bleeding. As the skull is fixed, and the brain is not, the bleeding as it accumulates presses down onto the brain, and in severe cases forces the brain down towards the base of the skull and the spine."

"And without surgical intervention can prove fatal?"

"Yes, but as you know, there was surgical intervention within four hours of admission. We drilled into the skull and the accumulation of blood was evacuated, thereby relieving the pressure on the brain. This is standard procedure in these cases."

"Excellent, Mr. Rowbotham, I was not going to suggest otherwise." Sir James smiled reassuringly. "And in the vast majority of such cases, with the pressure relieved and the bleeding stemmed, the patient will make a full, albeit slow, recovery, do you agree?"

"That's correct."

"And in the case of the deceased, following the operation, she remained critical but stable, correct?"

"So pausing there for a moment, there was every expectation that the operation had been a success?"

"I agree."

"And yet, sadly, the deceased died nine days later as a result of the very same subdural haematoma we've been discussing?"

Rowbotham was on the defensive. "If you're suggesting…"

"I'm not suggesting anything, Mr. Rowbotham, I'm simply stating a fact and inviting you to accept it."

He paused, sensing a trap but not seeing it coming. "Put like that," he answered cautiously, "I have to agree."

"Thank you. So what the jury need to do now, with your help of course, is to resolve the apparent contradiction between a successful operation to relieve and stabilise her condition, and the deceased's subsequent death from the self same haematoma?"

"Well," Rowbotham was now firmly on the back foot, "there could be any number of explanations…"

"With respect, Mr. Rowbotham, there could be only two reasonable explanations for death. Either the operation was not the success you claim it to be, or something happened during the deceased's time on the intensive care unit."

Rowbotham's eyes narrowed as he envisaged a medical negligence action against his hospital and all the adverse publicity. "The deceased received the best possible medical attention, and I resent any implication to the contrary."

Sir James was having none of it. "I am not here to defend the good name of your Hospital, Mr. Rowbotham, but to get to the truth, so bear with me." Back to his notes. "After the operation, the deceased showed every sign of making a slow and steady recovery, that's right?"

"Yes."

"So on the face of it, the operation was a success?"

"I have no doubt about that."

"Excellent, so in your opinion, the jury can ignore inadequate or incompetent surgical intervention?"

"Absolutely."

"Then let us turn to the second explanation for death. Something happened between operation and death."

"Such as?"

Sir James held up three sets of papers. "Usher, give these to the witness, and copies for his lordship and my learned friend for the Crown. Taking a moment to digest them, Mr. Rowbotham," he continued, "kindly confirm they are the hospital records of the deceased."

Rowbotham flicked through the pages. "That would appear to be so."

"Is that a yes?"

"Yes."

"Good. Now for the benefit of the jury, each time an event occurs with a patient, indeed, each time the patient is visited, a note is made to this effect, is it not?"

"Correct."

"So these notes provide a running narrative of the patient's stay?" Rowbotham nodded in agreement. "And they are hand written by the nurse or doctor visiting the patient and at the time of the visit?" Again, Rowbotham nodded. "Some of these notes are difficult to decipher," Sir James smiled at the jury, "not unknown in the medical profession," Rowbotham wore the pained expression of a man who'd heard that one many times before, "but if I can draw your attention to twenty three twenty on day seven," he paused, "do you have it?"

"Yes."

"Can you read it out for us?"

Rowbotham peered at the entry. "Patient on floor, returned to bed, still unconscious."

Toby made a careful note. This was dynamite, although he wasn't sure why. Rowbotham looked visibly shaken.

"Have you seen that entry before?"

"I must confess I haven't, but then, I was never asked," he added lamely.

"Never asked!?" Sir James retorted, staring at the Warbler. "The prosecution never once asked you to read these notes!? Extraordinary!"

The Warbler rose. "That was a comment, my lord," he whined.

"And a well aimed one, Mr. Warburton," replied the Grocer. Good for you, thought Toby, warming briefly to the man.

"So if you have never seen this entry before, can I assume that it was never brought to your attention at the time?"

"Well, yes, but…"

"Your hospital beds are two and a half feet from the ground, are they not?"

"I haven't the faintest idea."

"We've had them measured, my lord," Sir James glanced at the Bench, "so perhaps you will take it from me?"

"If you say so."

"I do say so, Mr. Rowbotham, and furthermore, the floor in the intensive care unit is linoleum with a concrete base, do you agree?"

"So I believe."

"So what we have here, I suggest, is a patient making a slow but steady recovery, who falls from the bed, bangs her head on the hard concrete floor, thus starting a fresh bleeding into the skull, which, if not spotted in time, could be fatal . That's right, isn't it?"

Rowbotham had the air of a defeated man. "It's one possibility," he replied in almost a whisper.

"It's more than that," Sir James was at his most scathing, "it's a probability! Take your time, but you will see from the notes there was no further surgical intervention from the time of the operation shortly after the deceased's admission to her untimely death. And there wouldn't have been, as nobody had sought fit to bring this significant event to the attention of the doctors, correct?"

"No, but…"

"And looking at the notes after her fall from bed, her condition, from slow but steady recovery, worsens dramatically, and she died at three in the morning of the ninth day. Yes, thank you, Mr. Rowbotham, no further questions."

Toby wanted to leap to his feet and applaud his learned leader. It was a wonderful display of forensic cross-examination. Of course he'd spotted his obvious line of defence, but was too modest to take the credit.

A cathedral silence fell over the court as Warburton got to his feet. "I have no questions in re-examination," he said, "does your lordship have any questions?"

"No I do not. The witness may leave the court." The Grocer turned to the jury. "There are matters of law to discuss, members of the jury, so please leave, and I'll call you back when we are ready to continue."

The Grocer was brief and to the point. "Unless you seek to persuade me to the contrary, Mr. Warburton, I shall direct the jury to find the defendant not guilty of murder."

The Warbler was not going to throw in the towel without a fight. "I do indeed seek to persuade your lordship to the contrary. The hospital records are public documents, and examined by both parties, so the fall from bed takes nobody by surprise. There are two possibilities for the jury to consider, the first that the deceased died as a result of the injuries sustained by her at the hands and feet of the defendant, the other is ***novus actus interveniens.*** It is a matter for the jury."

The Grocer, elevated to the High Court on the back of a thriving intellectual property practice, had had enough of tibias, tabias and flatulas to last a lifetime, and the thought of grinding through that lot in his summing up appalled him. Sir James had thrown him a lifeline, and he grabbed it. "No, Mr. Warburton, I am against you. It cannot be right to leave two equally consistent causes of death to the jury." He turned to Jumbo. "Sir James, can you resist a verdict of inflicting grievous bodily harm, contrary to section 20 of the Offences against the Person Act 1861?"

"No, my lord, I cannot. This is a tragic case where the defendant has lost the only person who ever really loved him, and made the more tragic by the regrettable and avoidable events in hospital."

"Tragic, indeed. I shall be making a report for the consideration of the Director of Public Prosecutions, and no doubt there will be a full inquiry. Turning to the defendant, and given the fact that a conviction to section 20, at the very least, was inevitable, I have in mind a sentence of three years imprisonment."

The jury were called back into court and duly returned their verdicts as directed. Then, after the formalities, it was off to La Bella Notte.

"Potts," Sir James roared across the robing room, "now the trial's over, go and find Henry and invite him to join us." Just then, Warburton came in. "We're off for a spot of scoff, dear boy, come along and drown your sorrows."

Warburton's face lit up. "That's very kind of you, Sir James, if you're sure it's not too much of an imposition?"

"Not at all, a pleasure." Sir James hesitated. "What about your junior, Mr.Newboy?"

"He's gone back to the office to file a report."

"Well there's a blessed relief. Each one to his own."

Mario excelled himself, and to Toby's delight and surprise, Warburton turned out to be a very agreeable companion, particularly after the third bottle of Barolo. It was nearly four when they left to go their separate ways.

For Toby it was the experience of a lifetime, and one he'd never forget. Sir James moved on to the next case, the next triumph, and Warburton, after a period out in the cold, also moved on. Newman reviewed himself favourably, of course, but determined never to sit behind counsel again. Next time he'd do it himself! Why buy a dog if you can bark yourself?

And as for Andrew Stubbs, he remained as silent as the grave into which he consigned himself three weeks after the trial, when his lifeless body was found hanging from the bars of his prison cell. In the words of the Grocer, there would have to be a full inquiry, but for Stubbs, it was too little, too late.

CHAPTER THIRTEEN

TOBY GOES TO SCHOOL

We don't need no education,
We don't need no thought control,
No dark sarcasm in the classroom,
Hey, teacher, leave us kids alone,
All in all you're just another brick in the wall

[Pink Floyd]

It was one of the great anomalies of the English Establishment. If you wanted a good education, and the best possible start in life, and assuming your parents could afford it, the lucky seven per cent of children went to private schools, curiously referred to as public schools, from the very grand, like Eton, Winchester and Harrow, to the very ordinary, hanging on by their finger tips and surviving by the seat of their scholastic pants. For the remaining ninety three per cent, they went to state schools, otherwise known as bog standard comprehensives.

Toby had been one of the fortunate few, and whilst Rougemont College for the sons and daughters of gentlefolk was not exactly at the cutting edge of private education, it provided Toby with the necessary tools and a kick start into the big, wide, world. For others, comprehensive education provided the ultimate challenge.

Joseph, call me Jack, Masters, had always wanted to be a teacher, and not just because of his name. He'd had all the advantages of an affluent upbringing, a happy family life, a good education at a well-respected public school, and then straight into a teacher training college. His parents had hoped for better, perhaps something in the

City, but a child who actually knew what he wanted to do in life from an early age was a rare commodity, so they bit their tongues, put on a brave face and smiled encouragingly.

Jack was also a man with a mission. His parents blamed their son's English teacher for all that nonsense, a remarkable man with an obvious gift for communication and a great motivator. He brought alive the classics, from Shakespeare, Dickens and Hardy through to Marx, not many laughs there, Virginia Wolfe, Kurt Vonnegut and the hugely boring James Joyce. In their book, anybody who could bring alive the works of James Joyce deserved a medal.

Jack's parents boasted no particular literary pretensions. If they were to read at all, it was during their annual two-week pilgrimage to that delightful little village in Provence, populated by quaint little Froggies wearing striped jerseys and berets and reeking of garlic and body odour. Some grave and weighty tome such as Jilly Cooper was more their cup of tea, or even Jeff Archer before his fall from grace. And besides, when at home, they watched Newsnight and Panorama, which were the same as heavy literature without the effort of turning the pages.

But Jack was cut from a different cloth altogether. His mission in life was to bring enlightenment where there was darkness and ignorance, so he eschewed the easy life of private education, with polite, well-mannered children calling him 'Sir', listening attentively in class, doing their homework on time and moving effortlessly towards good grades in their exams, and opted instead for the state sector. To add spice to this otherwise unleavened fare, and a rod for his back, he applied for a teaching post at a bog-standard comprehensive school in Cowley, within striking distance of the dreaming spires of Oxford and the meadows of Christ Church College.

As far as his parents were concerned, it added insult to injury, but then, it wasn't their decision, so they smiled encouragingly, hoped this would get it out of his system and he'd find a decent job in the profession with real career prospects. After all, their son as an Oxford don would be something they could brag about at one of their endless dinner parties, a real feather in their social cap.

Jack had seen the film Dead Poet's Society at least three times, with the hirsute Robin Williams, a good character actor and, by all accounts, an equally good singer, firing up his class of adolescents by marching them out of step across desktops and getting them to think for themselves, not to accept the shibboleths of conformity but to express themselves in their own way and on their own terms. The fact that Robin Williams got the heave-ho at the end of the film was irrelevant to Jack's way of thinking. Williams never compromised his standards, that's what Jack most admired, and nor would he.

St. Jude's Comprehensive School had as part of its catchment area the less salubrious quarters of Cowley, and in particular, the notorious Blackbird Leys estate. Quite what St. Jude had done to suffer this second martyrdom, when he should be enjoying eternal redemption and a well-earned rest, was never fully explained by the local education authority, but then, such are the vagaries of sainthood.

In the good old days, Cowley was the centre of the motor industry, and the flagship of Austin Morris, the biggest car making plant in the country. There was full employment, with jobs for life, and a strong, vibrant and stable community. But then came the sixties, with a weak and ineffectual Labour Government pandering to every whim of greedy and self-interested trade unions, rampant inflation, devaluation of the pound, and ludicrous wage demands. It was only a matter of time before Austin Morris went bankrupt, and it did, leaving thousands out of work where there was no other work to be found. It was a classic case of biting the hand that feeds you, but try telling that to the unions. They blamed the bosses, the bosses blamed the Government, and so it went on, in a vicious, self-perpetuating circle. Nobody was a winner. And not content with ruining the economy, the self-same Government set about ruining the educational system, which had worked very well for decades. From the ashes of their misguided policies arose the comprehensive system, one size fits all, and doomed to failure.

Cowley became an industrial wasteland, and with it, the collapse of the strong, vibrant and stable community. Some of the men folk moved away in search of jobs, others simply loafed around, hoping against hope that something better would turn up, but it didn't. Families fell apart, and without the discipline of a secure home environment and a structured educational system, respect for authority and law and order began to crumble. Gangs of teenagers hung around the estate and street corners, with nothing to do, and it wasn't long before the drug pushers moved in to exploit these easy targets. First soft drugs, then crack cocaine and heroin, and alcohol, usually stolen from the local convenience stores, followed by petty crime and mindless acts of vandalism. It was a depressing state of affairs.

Vicky Bollard's mum Kylie was no different from scores of other young mums on the estate. Her dad had left home when she was a babe in arms, off to look for work, or so he said, and never returned. Kylie was only sixteen when she gave birth, and a slap on the bottom from the midwife was probably the most affectionate gesture Vicky was to experience in her short and troubled life. The lucky father could have been any one of four during the weekend of conception, but not one stepped forward to claim the prize, and besides, Kylie wasn't fussed. They were all complete deadbeats and only after one thing which, needless to say, they got in full measure.

But unprotected sex had its compensations. No sooner had Vicky been born than the caring agencies gathered in force. Housing benefit, income support, child allowance and special needs payments ensured her financial security, and health visitors and the social services did the rest. It was an offer too good to pass up, and Kylie quickly added three more to her brood until the caring agencies persuaded her to call it a day and shut up shop.

Vicky grew up in her mother's image, and by the time she enrolled at St. Jude's, aged twelve, she was already street-wise. At primary school, she'd excelled at the practical side of her education, like hurling abuse at the teachers, throwing her Jamie Oliver highly nutritional dinner onto the floor in favour of a large bag of salt and vinegar chips, and chasing the other kids around the playground. Sad to report, her vocabulary hardly advanced beyond the four letter word, so academic progress was slow.

By the time Vicky celebrated her fifteenth birthday, she'd reached the high water mark in her formal education. The three Rs were firmly on the back burner, where they were to remain, but if the sixty seven positions during the sexual act were ever to become part of the GCSE syllabus, she was predicted an A grade with distinction.

The Governors of St. Jude's, in consultation with the Head Teacher, decreed that mixed ability classes should be actively encouraged. After all, this was the very ethos of the comprehensive system, with the dullards benefiting from exposure to the more gifted pupils and inspiring them to reach beyond their natural intellectual vacuity. Quite what the more gifted pupils were to derive from this social engineering was never satisfactorily explained.

And so it was that Vicky and some of her soul mates found themselves at the back of Jack's class, and, on any view, it was a bridge too far. Jack was in his second year at St. Jude's, and despite a first year marked more by failure than success, he was determined to persevere. After all, he kept telling himself, Rome wasn't built in a day. Getting his pupils to march out of step across desktops was the easy part, but getting them to think for themselves, or even to think at all, was the real challenge, and there was still much work to be done.

The Head Teacher, eager to curry favour with the Governors and promote St. Jude's as a progressive school without equal in the county, accepted Jack's suggestion that his class should study the works of Nietzsche as their specialist subject, with particular emphasis on the great man's philosophical need to understand the infinite chaos underlying primitive life if we are to understand the future of our evolution. Not that he knew anything about the bloke at all, and could barely spell his name. He'd heard of him, of course, just as he'd heard of Proust and all that humbug about rediscovering lost time. It was all foreign gibberish to him, and eminently forgettable, along with Goethe and Sartre and that lot, but it looked good on the Curriculum Scholae, so he gave Jack's idea his qualified blessing and turned to the main business of the day, trying to bring forth order out of the infinite chaos underlying primitive life and prevent Ms. Baxter from being goosed, yet again, during playground duty. To his mind, these were self-inflicted wounds, as Ms. Baxter's ample posterior was barely hidden beneath a skirt far too short for her age and build, but in these politically correct times, there was nothing he dare say without a sexual discrimination suit hitting the fan.

Jack's first two lessons were dominated by attempts, largely unsuccessful, to spell Nietzsche's name correctly. Once inscribed in large capital letters on the blackboard, three of the class of forty-six got it right first time, with the others coming on side in dribs and drabs. It was a mistake, as Jack had to admit in hindsight, to offer the phonetic spelling Neetsher to help those at the back of the class, and once the seed was sown, it was the devil's own job to uproot it. The great man's nickname Fritz was easier to remember, as it coincided with the British stereotype of all things German, but Jack's attempts to move the class onto a higher intellectual plain met with deep-seated resistance and apathy. The first two weeks of study could best be summarised in one sentence: "Fritz Neetsher woz a Krawt." A poor return indeed on Jack's investment.

It went from bad to worse, and by the end of the third week, Jack could barely make himself heard above the general mayhem. Other teachers began to complain that the noise was disrupting their classes, which was nonsense, as they needed no help in that regard. But Jack was an easy target, as he tried to reason with the unreasonable, still clinging to the mistaken belief that his passion for literature and philosophy was infectious. It wasn't.

Vicky, who hadn't even mastered the spelling of Nietzsche in its phonetic form, was bored rigid, and her idle mind turned to more important matters, like boys, and sex, and chips, not necessarily in that order. Those were her priorities in life, and Jack wasn't one of them.

That particular morning, Jack's class started where it had left off the day before, with a few bright sparks at the front showing interest, a grey area in the middle showing total indifference, and the back two rows showing the usual overt hostility, with Vicky, as ever, the ringleader. Finally, something snapped. Jack marched the length of the classroom, and placing his hand firmly behind Vicky's neck, propelled her out into the corridor before her feet could touch the ground. There was a stunned and sullen silence from the remaining forty-five pupils as he returned to the uneven struggle. For a few minutes at least, he had earned the respect of the class, but it wasn't to last.

Vicky didn't turn up the next day, which was ominous, and Jack's reaction was one of apprehension mixed with relief. Still, he told himself, he'd done nothing wrong, and following his firm handling, class discipline improved overnight. It was almost a pleasure to be teaching again, rather than wasting so much time on crowd control. It was like waking from a nightmare, but, unbeknown to Jack, his nightmare was just beginning.

At the end of the second day of Vicky's continuing absence, Jack was summoned to the Head Teacher's office.

"Bad news, I'm afraid. Vicky Bollard's made a complaint against you, and her mother has reported the matter to the police."

"What!?" Jack couldn't believe his ears. "I put her out of my class because she was disruptive, as always. I should have done it sooner," he added. "So what's the problem?"

"She's going to be formally interviewed tomorrow, but from what I gather, she claims you assaulted her when removing her from your class, and once out in the corridor, you indecently assaulted her by fondling her breast."

Jack was horrified. "I can't believe this is happening."

"I'm sorry, Jack, but you know the school rules. I have no choice but to suspend you with immediate effect until the matter is sorted out. Ms. Baxter will cover for you in your absence, but I doubt if Neetsher will survive the ordeal. By all accounts, she knows less about him than Vicky, which isn't saying much. If only she'd wear more appropriate attire," he mused, "those short skirts and meaty thighs are most distracting." He paused to mop his brow. "Still, that's the least of my worries. If this drags on, I'll have to get in a supply teacher."

Acting on Vicky's complaint, Jack was duly charged, and the case sent to Oxford Crown Court for trial by jury.

166

Basil Wheatcroft had been at the same Oxford College as Nick Ridley, Toby's former pupil master, had qualified as a solicitor the year before Nick was called to the Bar, and they'd remained good friends ever since. When Jack turned to Basil for help, Nick was tied up in a long fraud trial, so the brief was returned to Toby. It was a high-risk strategy, given Toby's inexperience in such a serious case, but Basil was persuaded.

Toby was understandably nervous as he arrived at court that Monday morning, with the Press buzzing around like flies and totally ignoring him. The trial was listed before the Recorder of Oxford, His Honour Judge Francis Coker QC, nicknamed 'Chuckles' because of his inability to laugh at anything, least of all himself. Tall and distinguished, with silver hair framing a pink, fleshy countenance fixed into a permanent scowl, he was an interventionist by inclination, frequently interrupting counsel and witnesses alike to make telling points in favour of the prosecution, all, of course, in the interests of justice and steering the jury in the right direction. He came from the old school who believed that the police didn't arrest and charge the innocent, and if a defendant had the temerity to plead not guilty and waste his time and public money, then let him suffer the consequences. By all accounts, Toby and Jack were in for a rough ride.

The court convened promptly at ten thirty. Chuckles sat down and glowered at Toby. "So what's the defence, Mr. Potts?" he snapped, knowing full well.

"Does your Honour have a copy of the Defence Statement, where the defence is clearly set out?"

"I never read the Defence Statement, Mr. Potts, it's invariably humbug and a waste of my time."

"In that case, the defendant admits using minimum but necessary force to remove the complainant from his class, as she was being disruptive, but totally denies indecently assaulting her."

"So how does he account for the finger marks on the girl's left breast when she was examined by the police surgeon?"

167

"They are not his finger marks, your Honour?"

"Then who's, pray, are they?"

"According to my instructions, your Honour, any one of half a dozen candidates, but as the prosecution are not adducing expert evidence, the owner of the fingers in question remains a mystery."

"Don't get clever with me, Mr. Potts. It ill behoves you or your client." Chuckles flicked through his papers. "Has the defendant been advised of a reduction in sentence if he pleads guilty, and the real risk he runs of a substantial sentence of imprisonment if he is convicted by the jury?"

Toby was beginning to feel punch drunk, and the trial hadn't even begun. "He has, your Honour, and he's also been advised that as he hasn't committed the offences charged, he should plead not guilty, confident in the knowledge that he'll receive a fair trial in your Honour's court."

There was a long pause. "Very well, be it on his own head. Now, is the defendant on bail?"

"He is, your Honour, and I ask that bail continue until further order."

"You may ask, Mr. Potts, that is your prerogative. Whether I accede to your request is a different matter. These are serious allegations…"

"Not yet proved, your Honour."

"Yes, yes, I know that." Another long pause. "What is known about the defendant? Do you have his antecedents?" Toby handed them up. "A man of good character with no convictions recorded against him. That remains to be seen," he added ominously as he continued to read. "Educated Highgate School London." Chuckles looked up and studied the defendant intently. Very slowly, almost imperceptibly, his countenance softened. "Is that Highgate Public School?" he asked.

"It is, your Honour," Toby replied.

"I'm not addressing you, Mr. Potts. Do sit down and stop interrupting." Toby did as he was told. "Highgate, eh?" Chuckles continued, reliving the happiest days of his life. "We used to play you at soccer, Mr. Masters."

Jack was still in a state of shock, but quickly recovered his composure. "Which school was that, your Honour?"

"Shrewsbury."

"The Salopian fixture was the highlight of the soccer calendar, your Honour, and always keenly contested." Good man, thought Toby, lay it on with a trowel, we need all the help we can get.

"I can imagine. You played, no doubt?"

Toby offered up a silent prayer.

"I did indeed, your Honour. I had the distinction of captaining the school first eleven in my last year." Who said prayers are never answered?

"I trust we thrashed you," said Chuckles with a gleam in his eye.

Another silent prayer.

"An honourable draw, your Honour, but a memorable match." Hallelujah! Praise the Lord!

In a ground-breaking moment of seismic proportions, Chuckles actually chuckled. "I see you were teaching a course on Friedrich Nietzsche, Mr. Masters. One of my favourite philosophers." This is getting better by the minute, thought Toby. "I particularly like his treatise in *Also Sprach Zarathustra*."

"A seminal work, your Honour, but my favourite must be *Die Götzendämmerung*, a thought provoking criticism of the Greek tradition's overemphasis on reason."

169

"Thought provoking indeed, and in different circumstances, we could debate for hours. But sadly, we must return to the business in hand." Chuckles addressed Toby.

"Of course Mr. Masters may have unconditional bail, Mr. Potts, and if at any time your client needs a break, he has only to ask. Now, if you're ready, I suggest we empanel the jury."

The prosecution chose to call first the battle-weary Head Teacher to set the scene, after which, it was Toby's turn to cross-examine.

"Dealing first with the allegation of common assault," he began, "this arises because the defendant put his hand behind Vicky's neck to remove her from his class. Is that right?"

"As I understand it, yes."

"And do you accept she was being disruptive?"

"As I understand it, yes."

"She had been repeatedly asked to behave. She was constantly interrupting, and at one stage, when asked by Mr. Masters to stop talking, she told him to f*** off?"

"As I understand it, yes."

"She was asked to leave the class, and when she refused, Mr. Masters used minimum and necessary force to remove her, do you agree?"

"Well...er...no."

Chuckles was out of the traps like a greyhound. "What do you mean, no?"

"Well, your Honour, the school rules are quite specific about physical contact between staff and pupils. There is to be no physical contact whatsoever. It's Department of Education policy, as set out in their policy document entitled 'Memorandum for Teachers - Forward

Together', and provided free of charge to each new member of staff. It is mandatory reading, needless to say. I have a copy with me if you're interested," and with that, HT, as he was known to one and all, produced a three hundred and twelve page manual from his battered briefcase, covering every aspect of school life, how, when, where and what to do in any given situation.

"I am not remotely interested, but of greater interest to the jury is the answer to a very simple question. If Mr. Masters is forbidden to touch the recalcitrant pupil, and she refuses to leave his class, what is he supposed to do?" Chuckles glowered at the unfortunate HT.

"The rules are quite specific. He is to bring the class to an end and refer the matter to me. By the authority vested in me and the Governors by the local education authority, and acting on behalf of the Department of Education, I shall then decide the appropriate response."

"Which is what?" snapped Chuckles, who was losing patience.

"Well, your Honour, there are a number of responses, starting at page two hundred and forty three, paragraph seven."

Chuckles opened the manual. "Have you received a copy of this document, Mr. Potts?" he asked.

"I have, your Honour."

"Looking at page two hundred and forty four, paragraph two, it deals with physical contact between staff and pupils in the playground. Is that the section you wish to draw to my attention?"

"Well, actually no, but it deals comprehensively with all aspects of physical contact between teachers and pupils. If I can refer you back…"

"Before you do so, this section clearly states that if a pupil falls over and injures herself, the teacher on duty must not touch the pupil, but must summon the designated first-aider, whatever that might mean."

"Every school has a designated first-aider, your Honour, trained in first aid," HT added helpfully.

"But what happens if the pupil has cut herself on broken glass and has severed an artery, and what if the designated first-aider is taking the day off, suffering no doubt from post traumatic stress disorder, a common complaint, I gather, in the state sector of education," he added waspishly, "is the pupil left to bleed to death?"

"There is no broken glass in **my** school playground, I can assure you of that."

Chuckles was having none of it. "We are losing the plot, whatever the state of your playground. Mr. Masters is accused of assaulting Vicky Bollard. You're telling this jury that if a teacher gives the recalcitrant and abusive pupil a well-deserved clip around the ear, he'll be suspended and finish up in a court of law?! How can you possibly defend such an asinine policy?"

"I don't devise the policy, your Honour," replied HT lamely, "I simply implement it."

"The same response given by thousands of Nazis after the Second World War," Chuckles snorted derisively. "It didn't wash with the International Criminal tribunal, and it doesn't wash with me. Mr. Potts, you have a submission, no doubt?"

Toby didn't. "Do I, your Honour?"

"You do indeed, and quite right too. Members of the jury, Mr. Potts having submitted there is no case to answer on the count of common assault, I agree, and direct you to find the defendant not guilty. It simply beggars belief, does it not?" In fact, it didn't, as most of the jury had kids at St. Jude's, and if any teacher gave their kid a good clip round the ear, there'd be hell to pay. Discipline and GBH were the sole preserve of Mum and Dad, no matter what some toffy-nosed judge had to say on the matter. Still, it was his court, and who were they to argue? The not guilty verdict was duly entered.

"Now let us proceed to the gravamen of this case, namely the indecent assault."

As a child witness, and with Vicky qualifying as a child, just, she had been video-interviewed in a purpose-built suite, surrounded by cuddly toys, empty crisp packets, coca cola bottles and damp nappies, slumped down in a ghastly magenta coloured sofa, looking for all the world as if she were in the back row of Jack's class, bored and resentful. It was not a pretty sight. The police interviewer, bringing with him all the gravitas of a five-day course in child protection techniques, and assisted by the resident social worker, struggled to retain her interest, as he gently teased from her the complaint that gave rise to the charge of indecent assault. As the groping of the left breast, according to Vicky, had happened when the two of them were alone in the corridor, it was her word against Jack's.

Toby started softly. As Nick was fond of saying, keep the witness on side for as long as possible before putting the boot in.

"Now Nicky," he began, smiling in his most engaging manner, "why did you wait two days before telling your Mum what Mr. Masters had done to you?"

"Yer mean Jack?"

"Yes, Jack."

"'Cos I woz embarrassed."

"But from what I've been told, Vicky, you're not a girl who's easily embarrassed about these sort of things, are you?" There was a resentful silence. "Are you?"

"Wadda yer mean?"

"Well, you told the police Jack squeezed your left breast after he put you out of his class on the Monday morning. You didn't come into school the next day, Tuesday, and you told your Mum on the Tuesday evening, that's right, isn't it?"

"So wot?"

"Young lady," Chuckles interrupted, "Counsel has to ask these questions, and we'd get on much faster if you simply answered them, do you understand?" Another resentful silence. "Try again, Mr. Potts."

"So what did you do on the Monday after school?"

"Same as always."

"Which was what?"

"'ad me tea, then went down the Community Centre."

"And what did you do down the Community Centre?"

"Same as always."

Chuckles was getting fidgety. "The question is simple enough, young lady," he snapped, "what did you do on the Monday evening?"

"I've already told yer," she snapped back. A wellspring of sympathy for Jack was beginning to wash over Chuckles as he pictured the Herculean task of trying to communicate with the odious girl on even the most basic level. As Chuckles was about to wade in again, Vicky let out a long, bored, sigh. "We listen to music and 'ang around." At last, ignition, and lift off.

"And who do you hang around with?" asked Toby.

"Me friends, 'oo do yer think?"

"Girls and boys?"

"Yeah."

"And are you popular with the boys?"

"None of yer bizness."

174

"Yes, it is, Vicky, so answer the question." Toby was surprised by his own firmness, but it seemed to work.

"Yeah."

"Yeah what? Are you popular with the boys?"

"Yeah."

"And do you have a boyfriend?"

"I've got loads," she shot back. Wrong answer. Suddenly her defences were down.

"Do you have a special boyfriend?"

"Yeah." Her eyes lit up. "Darren." Lucky Darren, thought Toby.

"And do you have a kiss and a cuddle with Darren round the back of the Centre?"

"Yeah, sometimes." Now she was on her guard, the defences back up again.

"And did you let Darren give you a kiss and a cuddle that Monday night?"

"Can't remember."

"Yes you can, Vicky. And did you let Darren fondle your breasts?"

"No I did not." The reply was too quick.

Toby had done enough. He'd sown the seeds of doubt, time to call it a day. "No further questions, your Honour."

Chuckles was impressed, and it showed.

The next witness was Dr. Priscilla Goodbody, the police surgeon who'd examined Vicky and found the incriminating finger marks around her left breast. She was clinically efficient, and her findings were potentially damning.

Toby started tentatively. "Vicky is a well developed young lady for her age, is she not?"

"I don't know what you mean," she replied unhelpfully. She knew exactly what Toby meant, but the extra income she earned as a police surgeon was not to be lightly thrown away by agreeing with defence counsel.

"It's a simple enough question, doctor," said Chuckles irritably. "The jury and I have spent the best part of an hour watching a video taped recording of a very well developed fifteen year old girl, so what do you mean when you say 'I don't know what you mean'?"

Goodbody was taken aback. She wasn't used to being handled quite so roughly, but the judge was the judge, so better dance to his tune.

"Yes, your Honour."

"Yes what?"

"Yes, Vicky is a very well developed girl for her age."

"And may I add, a very well developed girl for any age, is she not?"

Goodbody paused. This was not how it should be going. "Yes, your Honour, you could say that."

"I could say almost anything in my court, but for the time being, the jury are more interested in what **you** say."

Another pause. "I agree," she said at last.

"Good, so let's not be coy. After all, you're a doctor, are you not? And you must have examined many females brought to you claiming sexual misconduct? Am I right? And some are more richly endowed than others, are they not?"

176

Goodbody was beginning to feel uncomfortable. Was it her imagination, or was Chuckles undressing her with his eyes? It wasn't her fault she was as flat as an ironing board in that department. It was getting very personal. "Yes, your Honour," was all she could think of saying.

Chuckles was on a roll. "When Vicky presented herself for examination, did you ask if she was sexually active?"

"Not specifically, but I got that impression from her language and demeanour."

"And was she wearing a brassiere?"

Goodbody coloured visibly, and looked over to prosecution counsel for help. Sensible man as he was, he averted his gaze and buried his head in Archbold. There was no way he was going to object to Chuckles doing anything. After all, he had a living to make, and a wife and family to support. She was on her own, sink or swim.

"Er, yes, your Honour."

"So give the jury some idea of its size."

"I can't be precise," she replied, her voice trembling under the strain, "but I would say it was a thirty six Double D."

"And is that big?"

"It falls within the top ten percentile of all females, your Honour."

"Really?" His eyebrows shot up. "That big? The sort of garment Nietzsche might describe as ***ein grosser bustenhalter***," and he exchanged knowing glances with Jack. The sort of garment, Toby thought, that David would have given his eye teeth to possess when going into battle against Goliath and the Philistine hordes.

"I'm sorry, your Honour, I don't understand." Goodbody was totally confused. She wasn't alone. Toby had absolutely no idea where

Chuckles was heading, only that he was batting for the defence, so let him get on with it.

"No matter. And did you examine it?"

"No, why should I?" Wrong answer.

"To see if there was any evidence to support your findings, why else?" Chuckles snapped back. "I should have thought that obvious." He looked over to Toby. "I'm sorry, Mr. Potts, I interrupted your cross-examination. Please continue."

"Thank you, your Honour." Toby was grateful for the chance to get a word in edgeways. "From your examination, and I am referring to your clinical notes…"

"Clinical notes?" Chuckles interrupted yet again, "what clinical notes?"

"The doctor's clinical notes disclosed to the defence as part of the unused material, your Honour," replied Toby. He had learned much from Sir James in the trial of Stubbs, and where medical issues are raised, always study the clinical notes.

"If they are part of the unused material, Mr. Potts," Chuckles retorted, "then I do not have them, as well you should know."

"I apologise, your Honour. Perhaps my learned friend for the prosecution could oblige."

A set was duly passed up.

Chuckles flicked through them. "It all looks complete gibberish to me. Anyway, what did you want to ask the doctor?"

"Doctor, I am looking at page three of your notes, where you refer to a small livid mark around Vicky's left nipple, and faint marks on her right breast, and yet there is no mention of these in your witness statement. Why not?"

178

Goodbody felt trapped. "I...I...I was asked to examine Vicky to see if there was any medical evidence to support her complaint against the defendant that he had fondled her left breast. There was, and I wrote my statement accordingly."

"But, doctor," back came Chuckles at full gallop, "if Mr. Potts, learned counsel for the defence, had not bothered to decipher your clinical notes, and had relied solely on your witness statement, he could have been seriously misled?"

"I wouldn't put it like that."

"Wouldn't you indeed!" Chuckles pushed back from the Bench and glowered at Goodbody.

"Your findings, I suggest," Toby continued, "are more consistent with the groping of both breasts and a possible love bite around the left nipple, would you not agree?"

"Possibly."

"Possibly?! At least I hope you'll agree that the livid mark around the left nipple and the faint finger marks on the right breast were not caused by the defendant?"

"I agree Vicky made no such complaint against the defendant," she replied lamely.

After the verdict, Jack was gracious enough to thank Toby for all he had done.

HT came over to offer his congratulations. "I never doubted you for a moment, Jack," he burbled, sounding less than convincing. "You've earned a well-deserved rest, so take time off, and we'll see you back after half term."

"I'm sorry, HT, but I don't think Nietzsche and I are ready for St. Jude's. No offence, but you'll get my letter of resignation in the post tomorrow morning."

"I can understand how you're feeling, but at least sleep on it. Act in haste, Jack, and repent at leisure," HT replied. "I wonder who said that?" he mused. "It wasn't Neetsher, was it?"

In the fullness of time, Jack got a job teaching English at Highgate, with polite, well-mannered children calling him 'Sir', listening attentively in class, doing their homework on time and moving effortlessly towards good grades in their exams. Every October, home or away, Chuckles appeared on the touchline for the Salopian soccer fixture, where he and Jack enjoyed many a happy hour discussing Nietzsche, morality, ethics, and the rich vein of German literature. Chuckles may have been a ghost from the past, but a very welcome one for all that.

As for Toby, there was so much to learn, and so little time. Now who said that?

CHAPTER FOURTEEN

TOBY GOES FOR GOAL

We woz robbed. I'm as sick as a parrot.
It was a game of two halves,
The lads are gutted.

[Anon]

Toby was not a soccer fan. He'd played rugby and cricket at school, and the occasional game of squash. Soccer was not on the sports curriculum at Rougemont College, as the Headmaster and Governors considered it too rough for the sons and daughters of gentlefolk, and more a game for the lower orders. But Toby had to learn the noble art of the national game, and learn it fast, if he were to do justice to Nutter Nugent, the star of Alchester Town Football Club.

It all started with the draw for the FA Cup, one of the premier tournaments of the football calendar, and involving the great, the good, and the downright awful of the English clubs. Minnows and sharks together, all names went into the hat for a chance of Cup glory and a memorable win against all the odds. And so it was when the draw for the third round was made by Sir Malcolm Sweet, the Chairman of the FA, and known to one and all as Sweet FA.

It was the match of the century, between Alchester Town FC and the all-conquering, all mighty Manchester United. It was the stuff of dreams, and almost too good to be true. Alchester Town had been languishing at the foot of the third division for as long as anybody could remember, and on any view, they were a naff team. The first eleven, or twelve when Nobby Fowler could be bothered to turn up, was a team of honest journeymen more interested in the day job than international fame and stardom. It was a chance for a bit of exercise on a Saturday afternoon, a hot bath and a few bevvies at the Three Horseshoes before trudging home to 'er indoors and the screaming kids. It was marginally better than self-abuse, but not much.

Then along came Jarvinder Patel, the Midas of Alchester. He took over the corner shop, which, like the team, was dead on its feet, and transformed it overnight into a veritable pleasure dome. Somewhat predictably, he called it Xanadu. He sold everything from newspapers to magazines of dubious provenance for which top shelves were invented, sweets, alcopops, fruit and veg, soft and hard drinks and greetings cards with smutty messages. He knew what the English liked, and if you can't beat them, join them, was his mantra.

Next came the take away curry shop, which, according to some locals, was the best thing you could do with the stuff, but, again, it flourished and profits soared. Finally, there was the cash and carry outlet, selling to local tradesmen at heavily discounted prices and open all hours. Everything he touched turned to gold, except Alchester Town FC.

It was Fred Basset, the outgoing chairman, who persuaded Jarvinder to pick up the torch and run with it. After twenty years of keeping the flickering flame alight, Fred had had enough and was ready to move on to a comfortable and well-earned retirement.

To Jarvinder, Fred was the key to the door. He was a past president of the Rotary Club, a past captain of Alcester Golf Club, and a past mayor. If it was there, Fred had been past it. Jarvinder's money and brand new Mercedes didn't of themselves bring him the social status he craved in his adopted town, so he jumped at the chance of taking over the football club. Not that he knew anything about football, except that it used to be a gentleman's game now played by hooligans, but it was a showcase where he could expose himself to the townsfolk. In return for Fred's controlling shares and the promise of a substantial injection of cash, Jarvinder secured pole position in the directors' box, a dubious honour, where he could freeze his gonads every other weekend and try and look interested.

182

The local press made it headline news, which was good for business, with lots of photos of the 'new saviour' of the club, standing in the water logged centre circle, holding a ball and surrounded by most of the team. Nobby Fowler, as usual, had forgotten to turn up.

Alchester Town's stadium was built, or more precisely, put up, in 1912, in the days when every town had to have their own club. Few improvements had been made over the decades, but at least Fred Basset had done his bit. A new team kit, new goalposts, and upholstered, water resistant, seats for the directors. Nobody could accuse Fred of being tight with his money.

Jarvinder, however, was more ambitious, reasoning that if the team did well, it was good for business. In his first two years at the helm, the club shop was given a facelift, and new ablutions, affectionately christened the Jarvinderloos. As in the way of these things, the team was known as the Gollies, but nobody knew why. One seasoned wag suggested it was a reference to those rare occasions when the team scored a goal: "Golly, they've scored a goal," but that was generally discounted. If their nickname had anything to do with their goal scoring prowess, they'd be known as the "F***ing Adas."

Jarvinder did what he could, and even named a curry the Golly Good Curry, special offer, Saturdays only, but, like the team, it was hardly a runaway success. His suggestion that it be served to the lads as a half-time snack was firmly vetoed. Whilst it might have kept the opposition at arm's length, the sight of eleven players running around aimlessly and not necessarily in the right direction, was hardly going to improve performance.

In spite of his best efforts, the team remained firmly rooted in the bottom half of the division, lurching from one crisis to another, and the average weekly attendance was disappointing. Something had to be done, so Jarvinder summoned Dapper Dave Johnson, the team coach, to a meeting.

Dapper Dave, so called because of his penchant for wearing cheap gold jewellery, sharp suits, a permatan from the bottle, and his habit of chomping on gut-wrenching cigars, was in the twilight of his career, but he was all the club could afford, so he was tolerated more than loved by the board and fans alike.

"What we need, Guv, is a new striker of proven quality to bang the ball into the back of the net, not just twice a season, but week after week."

"Looking at the results, what we are wanting is somebody to stop the ball going into the back of our net, not just twice a season, but week after week." Jarvinder had done his homework.

"True enough, Guv, but success breeds success. The lads need to know that if they boot the ball up field, there'll be somebody to take it on, you know what I mean?"

"So what are you suggesting?"

Dave was excited. "I've heard on the grapevine that Nutter Nugent may be available. He's a household name."

"Not in my household, Mr. Johnson," replied Jarvinder, unimpressed.

Bloody foreigner, thought Dave, but he pressed on. "Nutter's got the pedigree, he used to play in the second division for Notts County, he was their top scorer for three years running, and he's now being offered on a free transfer, so no money up front, that's the good news."

"And what's the bad news?"

"Well, we'll have to help him relocate and pay his wages."

Jarvinder heard alarm bells ringing. "How much?"

"He wants a thousand a week," the thud was Jarvinder's jaw hitting the desk, "but I reckon we can get him for seven fifty. After all, if you pay peanuts, you get monkeys, and we've got enough of them already to open our own menagerie. He's not exactly inundated with offers," Jarvinder was doing mental arithmetic as Dave continued, "so we could offer him a twelve month rolling contract, and I reckon it could make all the difference."

184

Jarvinder was in reflective mood, not saying yes, and not saying no. It could be a real coup for the club and, more to the point, his popularity in the community would soar, but this was not a decision to be taken lightly.

"And what's more, Guv, with a player like Nutter, we'd double gate receipts overnight."

That was music to Jarvinder's ears, and the clincher. "Alright," he replied, "I am leaving you to make contact, but not a penny more than seven fifty a week, and I hope he is worth it. By the way," he added, "why is this gentleman calling himself Nutter?"

"Well, it's a measure of his standing in the sport," Dave lied, "he does things with his head other players only dream about."

At least that part was true. Nutter Nugent was infamous for launching himself headlong at the opposition with a ferocity second to none, and if the ball happened to get in the way, it was a bonus.

Nutter's arrival was certainly the publicity coup Jarvinder had hoped for, plenty of photo opportunities, and a small but welcome run on 'Nutter' replica shirts. Even better news on the pitch, as Nutter crashed in the goals, whilst crashing into the goalie, the goalposts, the back netting and anything else that stood in his way. For those of a delicate disposition, it was a sickening sight, but sales of the Golly Good Curry rocketed. After all, if you could stomach a Golly Good Curry, you could stomach Nutter's antics. Results improved, and for the first time in living memory, Alchester Town climbed into the top half of the division. And even Dapper Dave got it right, as gate receipts doubled. At last Alchester had a team worth shouting about.

Alchester had progressed steadily through the first two rounds of the Cup. Their first scalp were lowly Bathpool Rovers, seen off comprehensively at home after their goalkeeper was carried off unconscious in the third minute following a goalmouth incident with Nutter. The linesman thought about flagging for a foul, but when he saw Nutter advancing towards him, thought better of it, and his flag stayed down. The away team surrounded and jostled the referee, screaming for justice, but as he was adjusting his bootlaces at the time, he saw nothing amiss. As Bathpool didn't boast a reserve goalie, the team physiotherapist was dragooned into action, against his better judgment, and after that it was like shooting fish in a barrel. Five nil.

Next came Coleswell Wanderers, away, a needle match if ever there was. Nil all until the last five minutes when Nutter launched himself at their centre half like an Exocet missile. Fortunately he saw Nutter coming, and took life saving evasive action. Nobby Fowler, who'd turned up for such an important fixture, had just punted the ball hopefully into the centre as Nutter was in full flight. More by luck than good judgment, his head contacted with the ball, which fizzed into the back of the net, closely followed by Nutter. It was a moment to savour. So much for the minnows, now for the big boys.

And so to the dream draw, and at home to boot. Jarvinder, embracing the football ethic, was over the moon, as was the whole town. Excitement reached fever pitch as the great day loomed. Volunteers with garden forks were conscripted into improving the drainage, but with only limited success. The directors' box was given a fresh lick of paint, supplied at special discount rates by Jarvinder's cash and carry, and new seat covers were installed. The thought of sitting between Sir Bobby Charlton and that strange American with a face like a ferret was almost too good to believe, and Jarvinder was determined to make the most of it. Copious quantities of Golly Good Curry were laid on for the half time bash, together with a full bodied Rioja for the men folk and a cheeky little Chardonnay for the ladies, again supplied at special discount rates by Xanadu. And as if that were not enough, Sky Sports and BBC Television were to film the match, Sky broadcasting it live, and the BBC showing highlights at three the following morning.

The great day dawned, and the ground was packed to overflowing. Sadly for Jarvinder, Bobby and Ferret Face failed to show, so he found himself wedged between two complete nonentities, men in suits with calculators and mobile phones that rang all afternoon. A sizeable contingent of Man U supporters helped to swell the numbers, and they were carefully condoned off in their own enclosure like a contagious disease. Man U had elected to field their reserve team, collectively worth in excess of ten million, but there was a sense of disappointment in the home crowd, who had paid to see the real stars. Still, their team was captained by Scholesy, with Giggsy, Smithy and Butty on the bench. Hang on a minute, hadn't Butty been transferred? Must be a look alike.

Finally, after what seemed like an eternity, the whistle blew, and they were off. The Gollies, having won the toss, elected to kick off. Dapper Dave's tactics, explained in words of one syllable, were crude but effective. Don't let them settle on the ball, keep harrying them, run them off their stride. For once in their lives, the team responded, and for a while, the tactics worked. Man U's reserves, used to playing quality football, with skilful one twos, close control and intricate step overs, found themselves flattened, with or without the ball, as the Galloping Gollies clattered into them. It was like lambs to the slaughter, and by the tenth minutes, the pea in the referee's whistle was burning red hot. And then it came.

Twelve minutes precisely, and the stuff of legends. A clearance down field from Man U's goalkeeper fell into the centre circle, where it stopped dead in the mud. Nobby pounced on it like a dog on a rat, and without a moment's hesitation, punted it back up field. He was good at that. It was his party piece. Nutter set off like a steam train, taking no prisoners on the way, and as he thundered into the penalty area, the ball hit him on the back of the head and looped majestically over the advancing goalie and into the net.

The crowd erupted. Nutter set off on his victory lap, pursued by the rest of the team, and slithered ten yards into the corner post, which snapped like a rotten twig. The Man U supporters were stunned into silence, but, as Dapper Dave was fond of saying, football's a game of two halves.

And so it proved to be, with Man U scoring four goals in the second half as the Gollies began to tire. Nutter's frustration turned ugly. There was an off-the-ball incident where a Man U player received an elbow in the face, fracturing his nose, and all hell broke loose. This time there was no reprieve, and Nutter got the red card. Red was also the colour of the mist before his eyes as he sloped off to an early bath, but not before gobbing at the linesman.

The FA took disciplinary proceedings, and banned Nutter for three matches. But there was worse to come. Having viewed the tape of the incident, the Crown Prosecution Service initiated a criminal investigation, and Nutter was charged with assault occasioning actual bodily harm, and common assault on the linesman. At a preliminary hearing, Nutter pleaded not guilty to both charges, and elected trial by jury at Croydon Crown Court. The good news was that Toby, by the usual circuitous route, and finding himself 'unexpectedly ' available for the trial, was briefed to represent him.

Croydon Crown Court, another purpose built Palais de Justice, was about as attractive as Croydon itself. It was a dormitory town, full of banks, building societies, egg box hotels and multinational conglomerates, attracted by the lower ground rents and overheads, but within easy striking distance of the City. That said, it had absolutely nothing else to commend it. Restaurants offering antiseptic food, and the occasional theme pub, but nothing to compare with a Golly Good Curry. It was totally anonymous, the sort of place you drive through without stopping to get somewhere else, and to add insult to injury, not even a football team worth spit.

Nutter's defence to the charges was blunt and to the point, rather like his football. The elbow in the face was accidental. He was back peddling, anticipating another Nobby belter up field, when he stumbled into the Man U player, lost his balance and put his elbow out to steady himself. It happens all the time, mate, know what I mean? As for gobbing at the linesman, every player gobs, on average once a minute, it goes with the territory. In fact, there was a television programme not so long ago called 'Gob of the Month', featuring the various techniques employed by players as they gobbed their way through ninety minutes, ranging from the short, staccato gob to the full blown, back of the throat, roll it round the tongue, gob, and several other permutations in between. Nutter went for distance, which was why his gob hit the linesman square amidships from ten paces. It wasn't Nutter's fault the daft bugger got in the way.

The trial was to be presided over by Mr. Recorder Sheldon, a local man with his own chambers in Croydon. He'd levelled out early in his career, and with a combination of age and mediocrity now rooting him firmly in the third division, he was ideally suited to the task at hand. By reputation, he was fair, if somewhat pedestrian in his approach, a bit like Nobby Fowler. The prosecutor, Harold Trumper, came from the same chambers, so was part of the home team.

Trumper met Toby in the robing room. "What we need here is a jury well versed in the niceties of the game, I'm sure you agree. With your client's defence of accident, they'll need to decide if the elbow in the face was part and parcel of the run of the game, or a deliberate and malicious act."

"I agree wholeheartedly," replied Toby. "No point having twelve housewives who go shopping as soon as football comes on the television. A joint approach to the judge, perhaps?"

"Leave it to me," said Trumper confidently, "Sheldon will do as he's told."

"And does he follow the game?"

"Oh yes, been a Southampton supporter all his life, poor chap. No wonder he's aged before his time."

With Sheldon's agreement, the jury panel was duly vetted, in spite of some mutterings of discontent from the ladies about sexual discrimination. Not one of those selected declared support for either team. Some had never even heard of the Gollies, which was hardly surprising, but all followed the game to a greater or lesser extent. No one, however, understood the new offside rule, but they were not alone. It was all in the eye of the beholder, which meant it was a good goal if you were supporting the team that scored, and a bad one if you didn't.

After his opening speech, Trumper addressed the judge. "Your Honour, it is my intention to show the televised match to the jury in its entirety."

"Really, Mr. Trumper? Is that necessary? After all, the jury are only being asked to decide what happened on two isolated incidents."

"Yes and no, your Honour. That is correct regarding the allegation of ABH. However, regarding the allegation of common assault, Mr. Nutter, in his defence statement, claims that when he expectorated at the linesman, it was one of many during the match…"

"Just pause there, Mr. Trumper, whilst Mr. Potts takes further instructions."

Toby was beckoned over to the dock by an agitated Nutter. "What's all this expecting stuff he's on about? It's a stitch up if you ask me. I want a retrial."

"Calm down, Mr. Nugent, it's just a pompous word for spitting. Leave it to me." Toby turned back to the judge. "The defendant is confused by my learned friend's use of the word 'expectorated', your Honour."

"I agree with him, Mr. Potts. Mr. Trumper, this is the third division, not the Chancery Division. Let's keep it simple."

"As your Honour pleases. It is the Crown's case that the offending evacuation of spittle," not much better, thought Toby, "was deliberately aimed at the linesman who had flagged for the foul and, in the eyes of the defendant, was directly responsible for his dismissal. By comparing that evacuation with others during the match, the jury can make up their own minds."

"Very well. Members of the jury, you have heard what is proposed. I shall therefore adjourn now until two fifteen this afternoon, when we shall all watch the match here in court."

At two fifteen precisely, the jury filed back into court. Toby wondered whether he should insist on the commentary being turned off in case it influenced the jury, but as the commentator hailed from the dark side of the Gorbals and was totally incomprehensible, the risk was minimal. He also noticed that, to a man, they were all carrying bags with them from the local Spar store. As soon as the lights went down, there was an audible rustling, and the distinct sound of cans of lager and packets of crisps being opened. As they settled down to enjoy the match, the smell of salt and vinegar was almost overpowering.

It was strange but true that, with the obvious exceptions of Old Trafford in Manchester and the entire Far East, Manchester United Football Club was disliked with an abiding passion. It may have had something to do with the fact that they were the biggest, and sometimes the best, club in the world, conquering all before them until that Ruski bloke with the stubble chin bought the title for Chelsea. So it was clear, from the opening minutes, where the jury's sympathies lay. It was not just the Englishman's love of the underdog, it was their dislike of mighty Man U.

Then came the goal, with several replays, that had the entire jury and Nutter on their feet, whooping with delight, and it was all Nutter could do not to embark on a victory lap around the court. Sheldon thought about trying to restore some order in the court, but thought better of it. He didn't want cans of lager being lobbed at him from the direction of the jury box. The match continued, and as Scholsy did one of his trademark double-footed tackles, there was a roar of outrage and a chant of "Off! Off! Off!"

There was an audible groan when the first of Man U's goals went in, and a plaintive shout of "Offside ref!" from the back row. Then came the elbow incident. It looked pretty deliberate to Toby. Nutter was backing into the Man U player, as he claimed, but the ball was nowhere to be seen. Out went the elbow, down went the player like a pole axed heifer, clutching his face and streaming blood. It was not a pretty sight. The jury fell silent, absorbing the enormity of the assault and Nutter's flying elbow.

Finally, the gobbing incident. As lawyers were fond of saying, the defendant was in evidential difficulties. Instead of making his way to the tunnel and the Jarvinderloos, Nutter seemed to walk deliberately towards the linesman before 'evacuating his spittle' at him. Toby was not hopeful.

"Pausing there," came Trumper's voice out of the darkness, "Sky Sports have a tracking device that enables the viewer to track one particular player regardless of what else is happening on the pitch. Using that device, I shall now invite the jury to watch the defendant being tracked, to determine whether or not the spitting incident was deliberate or accidental."

Toby had to hand it to Nutter. He had the full repertoire, which he used to maximum effect. As an added bonus, he also indulged in bouts of free-range snotting, one finger either side of the nose, and then wiping his hand on his shorts. Handkerchiefs were for girlies.

Toby called Nutter to give evidence, and he was true to form, taking the jury through the match, using the highlights and replay buttons to make his point. Some of the fouls were pretty horrendous, and together they demonstrated the very physical nature of the game. In the early part of the match, before the Gollies tired, the Man U players were going down like ten pins.

Then came the foul that led to the charge of ABH.

"Right, your Honour and members of the jury," he continued, clearly excited, "I've got Ramondo, their flanker, crowding me, and I'm backing into 'im, to give meself room to break, know what I mean? A player of my calibre needs to be ready for anything. And as I'm backing into 'im, 'ees pushing into me, and I lose me balance. Now, what would you do?" he asked. "Do you mind if I demonstrate, your Honour?"

"If you think it will help, by all means do so," replied Sheldon, ever anxious to please the crowd.

Nutter stepped out of the witness box and beckoned the usher. "'ere, mate, come and stand behind me." The usher reluctantly complied. "Now, you start pushing into me, know what I mean, and I'm backing into you, see? Then I'm about to wheel away, right, you're right up close, I lose me balance, out comes me elbow, and pow!"

Fortunately for Nutter, the usher declined to press charges for a chipped tooth and a badly swollen cheek, which, in the circumstances, was very decent of him.

The jury were out for over two hours before acquitting Nutter of ABH, reasoning, as they must have done, that if you play for Man U, you deserve everything you get, and more. But they convicted him of common assault. After all, the linesman was only doing his job.

Sheldon fined Nutter a week's wages, and another week's wages in compensation. Toby was bemused, but Nutter was well pleased with the result. A definite score draw, with the moral advantage to the home team.

Nutter lasted another two seasons with the Gollies before hanging up his boots. He bought a small pub, where the picture of his victory lap was prominently displayed, and at the drop of a beer mat, he'd regale his long-suffering customers with a blow-by-blow account of his finest hour and twenty minutes.

CHAPTER FIFTEEN

TOBY TAKES TIME OUT

Take time to play,
It is the secret of perpetual youth,
Take time to laugh,
It is the music of the soul.

[Anon]

All work and no play makes Jack a dull boy. Quite who this Jack was, nobody seemed to know, but it was good advice, and advice Toby was determined to follow. Since being taken on as a tenant at Brick Court, he'd worked non-stop. Still, he wasn't complaining, at least there was work to be had, but with his nose buried in Archbold and the daily cut and thrust of the courtroom drama, he'd neglected the lighter side of life. Time to smell the roses and feel the grass beneath his feet. It was also time to play Bar politics. He was constantly reminded that, in his climb up the greasy pole, it was as much who you know as what you know, and at the Bar, he was spoiled for choice.

Gray's Inn, Toby's Inn of Court, was a good starting point. Each year, in July, the Inn hosted a Reception, followed by a Ball, and by all accounts, it was spectacular. The ball, that is. It boasted an ox roast, with a complimentary glass of vin ordinaire, a live band only the likes of the late and lamented John Peel had ever heard of, a disco and fireworks for the grand finale.

The Reception, in contrast, was a pretty turgid affair, but the setting was quintessentially English. The green sward of The Walks stretched right up to Theobalds Road, and was planted with enormous lime and

194

plane trees, together with an ancient catalpa tree which, according to legend, was either planted, or sat on, or played under, by the equally legendary Sir Francis Bacon, the darling of sixteenth century philosophy and the favourite of King James the First. By all accounts, he was a formidable advocate and latterly Lord Chancellor who dabbled in the natural sciences and Aristotelian polemics, and for which he was generally rubbished. Proof, if proof were needed, that you should stick to what you do best, but at least he died in his own bed. Those who, from time to time, visited the catalpa, walked around it in a reverential hush, like some holy shrine. They'd heard of him, of course, but they weren't quite sure why. Americans from Baconsville Nantucket were regular pilgrims to the site.

After touching base with the Under-Treasurer's office, and upon payment of the princely sum of twenty five pounds, Toby eventually received his embossed invitation to the Master Treasurer's reception, and immediately set about his plan of action. There was no published guest list, and worse still, no lapel badges in the best traditions of the American convention circuit, so he would have to feel his way.

Dress code was the first priority. A sober suit, white shirt and sober tie, and black, highly polished brogues. Best to blend in and then, with luck, stand out, than stand out for all the wrong reasons and be the object of ridicule. Convention played an important part in these events. As his mother was fond of saying, you can always dress down after you've arrived, but you can never dress up. A woman wise beyond her years.

Toby's plan of action was simple. He had two hours to put himself about, to get noticed and known in equal measure by the great and the good whilst avoiding the boring old farts. The third hour was the social graveyard, as those still there would be far too inebriated to remember the time of day, or Bacon and his poxy tree, let alone Toby's name or anything else about him.

The problem about distinguishing between the great and the good and the boring old farts was they all looked the same. How was Toby to tell the difference between the Lord Chief Justice of England and Wales and some old buffer from the Outer Hebrides? It was a nightmare scenario.

He consulted his slim volume of 'Social Etiquette - How to get there and stay there', given to him by his mother after he'd passed his Bar finals. Somewhat of a back handed compliment, he thought at the time, as he felt his social graces were up to speed, but his mother was leaving nothing to chance. It was written by a titled lady, or so she claimed, powdered down and touched up and looking like a younger version of Barbara Cartland, all crêpe de chine and clutching a lap dog. Mark you, everybody looked younger than Barbara Cartland, whatever their age.

He was advised to arrive between fifteen and twenty minutes after kick off to make the maximum impact on arrival. Unfortunately, all the other guests must have read the same book, as he joined the long queue snaking through the enormous wrought-iron gates and up to the reception line. Toby spotted none of his contemporaries, and must have been the youngest there by at least forty years. No matter, at least he would have the field to himself, to exploit and explore at his leisure.

From his place in the queue, it was also a good vantage point to sort the wheat from the chaff. The reception welcoming party consisted of the Master Treasurer, Lord Justice Maurice Oldland, the Presiding Judge of the Admiralty Division, and his fragrant wife Madge, looking for all the world like a younger version of Barbara Cartland. To Toby's untutored mind, the Admiralty Division was all about slapping speeding tickets on ocean-going tankers, with the occasional high seas collision to leaven the bread, lots of oil sludging on to pristine white sandy shores, and flapping cormorants being hosed down by local worthies from the RSPCA. All very commendable, but not exactly Toby's idea of a good day out. The outgoing and incoming Master Treasurers were also there to greet the guests, and bringing up the rear was Rear-Admiral 'Salty' Matravers, retired seadog and now the Under-Treasurer. From seadoggy to dogsbody, all in one effortless stride. As Toby watched, those who were passed along the reception line like hot potatoes, with barely a nod of recognition, could be firmly placed in the boring old farts category. Those who lingered, and who were treated to a few words and a welcoming smile, were prime targets for Toby's plan of action. He tried to memorise as many faces as he could before he too, was passed down the line in record time and out the other side.

Armed with a luke warm glass of South African Chardonnay and a bonne bouche of some description, Toby set off in search of his first target. As luck would have it, a distinguished looking man, dressed in pinstripe trousers and a lightweight summer jacket, had just detached himself from a group of acquaintances and was making his way to the marquee for a refill. Time to pounce.

"Good afternoon, sir," said Toby respectfully, "may I introduce myself?"

"Good Lord, boy, whatever for?" he replied without breaking his stride.

Pompous jackass, thought Toby, as he stared at his retreating back. Undaunted, he pressed on, and spotted a splendid old buffer sporting a Panama hat, sitting alone in the shade. Perhaps it was Lord Denning, the retired Master of the Rolls. One way to find out.

"Good afternoon, sir. May I introduce myself?"

"No need, my boy," replied the splendid old buffer, peering at Toby from beneath the brim of his hat, "I know you well. Now don't tell me, let me guess," he continued, looking Toby up and down, "it's Paul Featherstone. Haven't seen you in a while. What are you up to?"

"Well, actually, sir, it's Toby Potts."

"Can't say I know the chap," replied the splendid old buffer, looking around him, "which one is he? Still, there are so many coming to the Bar these days, it's difficult to keep track of them all." Why bother, thought Toby, but how to slip away graciously? Too late. "Sit down, Paul, and tell me all the latest gossip."

"I'm in Gazzard's chambers, sir, and greatly enjoying it."

"Ah yes, Gazzard," he mused, "Palmer and Camley Borough Council. You know it, of course?"

"Indeed I do, a landmark case in public negligence…"

"Yes, yes, as Gazzard was fond of reminding us at every opportunity." He paused. "Is the old fool still alive?"

"Still alive and still head of chambers," replied Toby.

"Can't think why on either score. Should have punted off years ago. Peaked after the Palmer case, don't you know, and has never looked back, or forward, for that matter, ever since. Couldn't abide the chap at any price. Waiter!" he bellowed at the Master Treasurer, "another bottle of that revolting Chardonnay, chop, chop. You'll join me of course?" he added, smiling indulgently at Toby.

This was the encounter from hell, and not in Toby's plan of action at all. "That's very kind of you." What else could he say?

"Those were the days. Gazzard took over his father's set, and I opted for service overseas. You know, of course, I was Chief Magistrate of the Solomon Islands for twenty glorious years." His eyes misted over. "Service over and beyond the call of duty, but somebody had to do it. Did I tell you, Paul, when I arrived, a bevy of bare-breasted maidens, every one a virgin, or so they claimed, swam out to meet me and carry me aloft on a bed of palm tree matting." He was off, and there was no stopping him. "Damned decent of them. The whole island turned out to greet me. The King was particularly solicitous, and offered me three of his wives. Such a generous man."

"And did you accept?"

"That, Paul, is between me and my Maker," and he chuckled. "We had the death penalty in those days, and public flogging, so the responsibility was considerable."

"Good Lord," Toby was horrified, "you didn't condemn anybody to death, did you, sir?"

"Heavens, no," he laughed, "they were such a gentle people. Generally speaking, it was unpaid work for the community, that sort of thing. If you stole from your neighbour, you had to work for him until you'd paid off the debt. It was all very civilised."

"And what about Old Blighty?" Toby asked, "didn't you miss it?"

Good Lord, no. Would you?" He had a point.

Just then there was a stir in the Walks and a frisson of excitement ran through the assembled guests. The Master Treasurer, on his way over with another bottle of wine, stopped in mid stride.

"Go and grab that bottle from the idiot waiter, there's a good chap, Paul. Looks like he's distracted. So difficult to get good servants these days."

Toby got up, relieved the Master Treasurer of the wine, and returned. He half thought of making a run for it, but that would be rude, and besides, the splendid old buffer was far more interesting than listening to the usual shop talk. As he poured another glass for the two of them, he spotted two familiar figures out of the corner of his eye, and his heart began to pound. Up the Walks strode Jumbo Bingham and Archie Scott-Malden, larger than life in every sense of the word. Judging from the Master Treasurer's reaction, it was as if royalty had arrived. The other guests were spellbound.

"Mo!" bellowed Jumbo, "hope we're not too late."

"Not at all, Jumbo, a delight to see you both. How are you, Archie?"

"Passably well, thanks, Mo. Picked a good day for it," he continued, looking up at the cloudless sky, "but then, God always smiles on the Admiralty Division."

"So they say, Archie, but I couldn't possibly comment. Now, a glass of wine," and he beckoned over a waiter.

Jumbo inspected the contents as if he were being offered a poisoned chalice. "You're not seriously expecting us to drink this, are you Mo?" He took his arm conspiratorially. "What's the point of being Master Treasurer if you can't enjoy the perks from time to time? Now," he continued, lowering his voice, "I happen to know you have a particularly fine '71 Veugeot laid down in the cellars waiting for a moment such as this. Six bottles should suffice. And we need some crusty French bread and a slab of mature cheddar, and thee and Madge beside us. What more fitting way to end the term, don't you agree, Archie?"

"I agree," laughed Archie, "and have nothing further to add."

"Good man, Archie, and breaking the habit of a lifetime. Now go to it, Mo, and with any luck, by the time the wine has caught its breath, all these ghastly people you've invited will have drifted off."

"Please, Jumbo," Mo whispered, "keep your voice down, or you'll get me sacked."

Jumbo bellowed with laughter, and with the Head Butler duly dispatched on his errand, Mo began to lead them to his table.

"If it's alright with you, Mo," said Jumbo, taking his arm, "I'm not in the mood to socialise. Besides, your guests look a very dreary lot. Archie and I need gaiety and laughter to do justice to your magnificent wine."

"Give me ten minutes and I'll join you."

Jumbo looked around and spotted Toby. "Aha, I see a young friend of mine. Come on, Archie," and to Toby's trepidation, they bore down on him, with the remaining guests open-mouthed in astonishment.

"Archie, this is Toby Potts, a splendid lad and my saviour in Wood Green. By the way, I received a delightful letter from Mario after the trial, accompanied by a very drinkable bottle of wine, very thoughtful of the chap."

"Hello, Toby," said Archie, "do you mind if we join you?"

"A great honour, but this isn't my table. This kind gentleman invited me to join him."

200

"This kind gentleman, as you delicately put it, is Mungo Fitzgerald, the toast of the Pacific."

Mungo rose slowly from his chair and lifted his hat in salutation. "Jumbo, dear boy, and Archie, what a pleasure. Now, if you will excuse me, the heat and this atrocious wine have had a debilitating effect upon my sang froid, so I shall leave you in the company of my charming friend Paul Featherstone. Until the next time."

"Dear old fellow," said Jumbo, as Mungo tottered off, "and the last of a dying breed. Mark you, they say that about me," and he roared with laughter. "Now, to the business in hand, where's that wine?"

As if on cue, the Head Butler approached, bearing the fruits of his search, and carrying the bottles of vintage Clos de Veugeot with much the same care as Mungo had been carried ashore by that bevy of bare-breasted maidens, and closely followed by the crusty bread and cheese. Mo, not wishing to miss out on a drop of this liquid nectar, quickly made his excuses and joined them, with Madge in tow.

"Come on, Madge, plant those firm, tight, buttocks on this old man's lap," boomed Jumbo.

"I shall do no such thing, Jumbo," she replied, colouring visibly.

"That's not what you said when we were students together," he quipped.

"That was light years ago," she smiled, "and a lot of water has gone under the bridge since then, so behave yourself."

"I have my orders," he laughed, "so I shall do my best. Now, Toby, do the honours, there's a good chap. Mo, have you met?" and he waved his hand in Toby's direction.

"Only briefly. A pleasure, young man." The Master Treasurer extended his hand as Toby rose from his seat.

He was in the presence of greatness, and totally overwhelmed.

"It's been a great privilege meeting you again, Sir James," said Toby, not wishing to intrude, "but I think I should be going."

"Nonsense, dear boy. Yours is the spirit of perpetual youth and the future of this God-benighted profession. Without you, we are nothing, so stay, and let us old fogies enjoy a few moments in your company. You shall be our Peter Pan, our Dorian Gray."

And so the wine flowed, the most exquisite Toby had ever tasted. Far from the dry old stick Toby had imaged, Sir Maurice was the soul of wit, giving as good as he got from Jumbo, and loving every minute. Sir James had that rare gift, an infectious sense of humour and a love of life, which was irresistible.

As the third bottle was poured, Sir Harry Hogswell loomed out of the gathering gloom. "Just popped over to thank you, Master, for such an enjoyable day." He eyed the bottle of Veugeot enviously.

"Ah," boomed Sir James, "Mr. Justice Hogswell, as I live and breathe. Still putting the world to rights, I hope?"

"One does what one can, Sir James," he replied tartly.

"With your lordship on the Bench, there is no safer pair of hands." He grinned mischievously. "Let me introduce you to my friend Toby Potts, that is, unless you've met already?"

Toby stood up and immediately recognised the pompous jackass who'd cut him dead. It was a moment to savour. "No, I don't think we've met, unless we spoke earlier." Toby's eyes held Sir John's for just long enough, " a great pleasure, my lord."

"Please, Toby," he replied, obviously embarrassed, "no formalities here. After all, we're all equal on these occasions."

"Primus inter partes, is the expression I was clumsily groping for." Jumbo was unstoppable. Hogswell turned on his heel and marched off. "There goes Mr. Justice Hogswill, a man who was never born, but simply dug up at the age of fifty five, a fully formed high court judge.

Pompous jackass, could never abide the man! Now, dear hearts," Jumbo was back to his most expansive, "a toast, to good friends, good wine, the exuberance of youth, and the loveliest woman I never made mine." There was a glint in his eye as he gazed affectionately at Madge. "Still, my sweetheart, if you had to settle for second best, you couldn't have chosen a finer man than Mo." Mo laughed. "To the victor, the spoils! To Mo and Madge!"

The Gray's Inn Ball the following night was bound to be an anti-climax, but with Susie at his side, it was to be a memorable weekend, and one Toby would never forget.

By prior arrangement, Toby met Susie at the Savoy, where they had a dry Martini in the American Bar before a short taxi ride to the Inn. George Sandwell was a stickler for convention, and besides, the thought of his beautiful daughter spending the night in some impoverished barrister's grotty little flat off the Earls Court Road was more than a father could bear. The fact that his beautiful daughter had spent the best part of a year sleeping under the stars in Botswana simply didn't enter into his calculations.

Susie looked stunning, and he was not the only one to think so, judging from all the envious glances he received throughout the night. They formed a table of eight, gorged themselves on ox roast and salad, and danced the night away. John Peel's rock band was nothing if not loud, and it gave Toby the chance to show off his 'solid gone' act as he gyrated round the floor. After a good workout, they made their way back to the marquee, where the lights were now dimmed as the DJ played a succession of slow, romantic, numbers. Toby was lost in a world of his own, holding Susie tight, just happy to have her and to hold her.

Back at their table, chatting easily about nothing in particular, they were interrupted by the arrival of the Head Butler.

"With the compliments of the Master Treasurer," he announced gravely, placing an ice-cold bottle of champagne in front of them. Reverentially, he opened the bottle, poured two glasses, bowed gravely, and withdrew.

Toby was astonished and delighted, and looking round the marquee, spotted the Master Treasurer in the corner. He made his way over.

"It's exceedingly generous of you, Master. Will you and Lady Oldland care to join us?"

"A kind thought, Toby," he smiled, "but the night belongs to the young, and besides," he added, looking at his watch, "it's past our bedtime."

"It may be past your bedtime," Madge retorted, "but Toby is about to ask me to dance, and I suggest you do the same with his absolutely divine girlfriend."

Mo needed no second invitation, and after two numbers, they exchanged partners and danced, cheek to cheek, until the lights went up. After the fireworks, the four of them finished the champagne, and then it was time to go. Madge had taken Susie by the arm and was chatting to her as if they'd been friends for life. Toby and Mo followed a few paces behind.

Mo smiled, and turned to Toby. "Madge and I have had a gloriously happy life together, but there are times, when she's with Jumbo, she wonders what might have been. They were very much in love in those early days, but for one reason or another, it never happened, and I think they both regret it more than they can say. So if you'll take the advice of an older but well-meaning man, don't make the same mistake, my boy. Susie's adorable. If you love her, as you obviously do, don't let her get away."

Back at the Savoy, Toby gave Susie a long, lingering, kiss. "It's been a wonderful evening, my darling, and I don't want it to end, but I suppose I should be getting back home. How about a late breakfast?"

"Toby, you're very sweet, but if you think I'm going to sleep alone in an enormous double bed in the best hotel in town, then think again."

They showered, and then made love, hot and passionately to begin with, and then slowly, intimately, sensuously, not wanting the moment to end. Finally, holding each other in their arms, they fell into a deep, contented sleep.

After a late breakfast and more champagne, Toby put his arms around Susie and gazed adoringly into her eyes. "I can't think of one reason why you would want to…I mean, I'm an impoverished barrister and likely to remain one…so I can't promise you much…in fact…"

Susie put her finger to his lips. "Yes, Toby darling, the answer is yes."

CHAPTER SIXTEEN

TOBY AND THE WEASEL

Up and down the Walworth Road,
In and out the Eagle,
That's the way the money goes,
Pop goes the Weasel

[After W.R. Mandale]

It was the ambition of all aspiring barristers to cultivate a stable of solicitors to call their own, who would love, honour and cherish them till death, or retirement, did them part, and Toby was no exception. After all, solicitors were his lifeblood, and without them he simply couldn't function.

According to his lectures on the History of the English Legal System, it all went back to the days of the blessed St. Thomas à Becket, before his untimely martyrdom at the hands of King Henry and his merry men. There's nothing quite like a gory slaying in the House of God to move you rapidly up the beatification ladder, and St. Thomas was no exception.

But before his elevation to heavenly grace, he was the king's favourite, and as such, enjoyed rapid promotion. After a few non-descript jobs to whet the appetite, he was appointed Lord Chancellor. Not that he knew anything about the law, a precedent set for generations to come, and it wasn't until the nineteenth century that judges were expected to be learned in the law and not simply make it up as they went along.

But his heart was in the right place, and feeling the urge, as is the way of saints, to do something for the Great Unwashed, Thomas started his own court, which he named the Court of Chancery. It was an overnight success, and everybody with a gripe, real or imagined, trundled off to the Court to argue the toss and await the Lord Chancellor's judgment.

The Court became a victim of its own success, with litigants jostling and pushing and shouting the odds. It was a complete shambles, so Thomas was forced to introduce a few simple rules to restore some semblance of order. To keep the disgruntled litigants out of his face, with abusive shouts of "Do you want some!?" and "What's your f***ing problem!?" hurled at him from close proximity, he erected a stout wooden barrier, or bar, between himself and the rabble. Those with an eye on the main chance and who claimed a familiarity with the law, offered their services as advocates and pleaders, for a modest fee, of course. When called upon by the Lord Chancellor to address him, they had to do so at the Bar.

It soon became bruited abroad that the chances of successful litigation were greatly enhanced by employing this new breed of barristers, as they had the ear of the Court and were reasonably literate, an irresistible combination. But as the litigants far outnumbered barristers, and as barristers could only plead one case at a time, it was the devil's own job to get the right man at the right price, and successful barristers found themselves very much in demand. How times have changed.

Something had to give, and it did. Enterprising touts began offering their services, introducing the favoured few to the barrister of their choice in return for a slice of the action. It was a cosy arrangement that suited both parties, and these touts became known as solicitors. And so grew the convention that barristers would only accept work through solicitors. Nine hundred years later, the convention persisted, but with the tail now firmly wagging the dog.

Toby could boast only one solicitor who favoured him above all others, but he had to start somewhere. Derek Finnan was a sole practitioner, operating out of his own kitchen in Camberwell Green, and relying on day-to-day support from the likes of Bootsy Farmer. But Del had an eye for the well-turned heel, so he engaged the services of Jane Hodges, known affectionately as Breezy for her purposeful and business-like manner and her magnificent hairdos, a triumph of lacquer over gravity.

Toby's professional relationship with Del began when he was instructed to represent a wide boy clocked at over a hundred and twenty miles an hour on the M1 motorway in his Porsche Boxter sports car. Appearing at St.Alban's Magistrates Court, Toby put in a compelling plea in mitigation, lots of guff about the breadwinner with a young family, needs the car to sell insurance to the world and his dog, will lose his home and his job if he can't drive. To his amazement, it worked, the wide boy kept his licence and paid Toby's fee of £50, there and then, in cash from the back pocket. Within the hour, the grateful client, hammering up the M1, phoned Del on his mobile phone to sing Toby's praises, and from that moment on, the dye was cast.

As the clerks were fond of saying, if you provide a service, sooner or later, a plum will fall into your lap. Put another way, better to be working on crap than be sitting in chambers chewing the fat. No doubt about it, the clerks had a way with words, so Toby, whilst waiting for the plum, obliged with endless applications, more applications, the occasional summary trial and pleas in mitigation.

Del didn't like clients who wanted to plead not guilty. It was time consuming, with forms to be filled out, statements to be taken and some sort of defence to be cobbled together on the kitchen table. A plea of guilty was far neater, almost clinical in its simplicity, go to court, take your medicine and move on. Del was in it for the quantity, not quality. If it couldn't be turned round and the taxed bill submitted to the Legal Services Commission in seven days flat, Del didn't want to know. That is, until Danny 'The Enforcer' Bloom came into his life. Although he didn't know it at the time, Danny was about to provide Toby with that long-awaited plum. Problem was, by the time it fell into his lap, it was putrid and rotten to the core.

Danny was the product of his time. Born and raised in Camberwell, with little or no formal education, he couldn't see the point, all that crap about Neetsher, and the bloke didn't even speak English, and who was he to tell the likes of Danny about the infinite chaos underlying primitive life? Danny knew about primitive life. After all, he lived in Camberwell.

Del knew all about Danny, and in the normal course of events, avoided him like the plague. After leaving school with no qualifications, Danny joined the Green Youth Club and excelled at boxing. He wasn't big, but he was very stocky, all muscle from the tips of his toes to the space between his ears. He even thought at one stage of turning professional, until he met The Weasel, or, more to the point, The Weasel arranged a meeting with him.

The Weasel was a small time hoodlum and infamous on the Green. Protection, prostitution, gambling and drugs were controlled with ruthless efficiency from his club, fetchingly named the Copa Cabana. The Weasel was a fan of Barry Manilow, and what was good enough for Barry was good enough for him, know what I mean?

He modelled himself on Al Pacino in the Godfather Parts One, Two and Three, even down to the brilliantine hair, the loud, pinstripe suits, and the two-tone shoes. The videos had pride of place in his penthouse suite above the Weasel and Trouserleg Public House, one of his many haunts. It was also the origin of his nickname, but those who used it in his presence did so at their peril. 'Boss' was a safer bet, or better still, Don Cornyony, although that could have been a misspelling. Nobody saw fit to ask.

The Weasel was always on the lookout for enforcers, and Danny fitted the bill. He was duly summoned into the presence and made an offer he couldn't refuse. On the down side, it was unsocial hours, no sickness benefits and the pension plan was dead in the water, like those who crossed his path. But the money was good, all cash in hand with no deductions, two free drinks a night with nosh at the Copa Cabana, selected dishes only, and the occasional torrid tumble with a girl of The Weasel's choice, at special knock up rates.

To oil the wheels, The Weasel also had a handful of bent coppers on the payroll, and in return for party favours, he was left very much to his own devices. Then, one day, somebody stood up to be counted.

Yu Flung Dung, which meant something else in Cantonese, ran a dry cleaning business just off Walworth Road, on the edge of The Weasel's patch. For the first two years he'd been willing to pay a modest sum to keep the peace, but when the rate doubled overnight, Mr. Dung drew a line in the sand and refused to pay. Billy 'Fingers' Malloy, one of The Weasel's collectors, got two fingers back when he called, and a good spanking into the bargain. Time for the Enforcer.

Danny and three mates, all chiselled from the same block of granite, paid Mr. Dung a visit, put him in hospital and firebombed his premises. No half measures when the Enforcer came to call.

As luck would have it, a new superintendent had been appointed to the Green barely six weeks earlier, and he had The Weasel firmly in his sights. He'd obviously been speaking to 'Hot Hands' Spinks, just down the road in Hackney, and was damned if he was going to let 'Hot Hands' steal all the headlines. Besides which, the thought of 'Hot Hands' getting promoted over his head was more than a body could bear. Time to clean up the cesspool and all that, and grab a share of the limelight.

Mr. Dung knew The Weasel and his gang well. Most of them brought in their sharp suits to be dry cleaned, six for the price of five, and The Weasel's Fedora hat was a regular visitor. Mr. Dung, a brave if foolhardy man, was willing to give evidence, so in a blaze of publicity, The Weasel, the Enforcer, his three mates and Fingers Malloy were all arrested. As Del was duty solicitor that day, he represented the five foot soldiers and sat in on the interviews with the police, where they all went 'no comment'. The Weasel had his own brief, 'up west', who danced to his tune, know what I mean?

Toby was instructed to make a bail application on behalf of Danny. The others had been scattered round the Manor to other lucky solicitors, as Del couldn't cope with more than one client at a time. The crush round the kitchen table would have been unbearable, not to mention the run on the coffee and the chocolate digestive biscuits.

The application was an unmitigated disaster, and refused in short order. The CPS had thrown the book at him, conspiracy to commit

GBH with intent, GBH with intent, blackmail, intimidation, threats to kill and arson. It was the full Monty, short only of compassing the death of the Sovereign, and the CPS were working on that. Still, Danny could draw comfort from the fact he was not alone, as the remaining foot soldiers were similarly charged, and even The Weasel was in the frame, but not for long.

The Weasel's brief from 'up west' had instructed the oleaginous Noël Cantwell, he of Snaresbrook fame, to represent him at the preliminary hearing. With no evidence that the Danny and his mates were acting on his orders, and the only evidence connecting The Weasel with Mr. Dung's business was a Fedora, the occasional sharp suit and several pairs of over starched boxer shorts, the CPS were onto a hiding to nothing, and, gritting their teeth, withdrew all charges. Whatever else, Cantwell was good, even if he practised on the dark side of the street. To many in the profession, he was riding for a fall, and it was only a matter of time.

That left the foot soldiers, and a round kitchen table conference was called by The Weasel to review progress and determine the way forward. After all, languishing in prison as they were, the boys needed to know their defence, and once decided, to begin singing from the same song sheet. Toby didn't like the idea of a conference in Del's kitchen, but as the clerks wryly observed, in this day and age, when solicitors call, counsel come running.

Del's kitchen was situated in a small terrace off Bethwin Road, and a stone's throw from the Green. Outside No. 27 was a small brass plate announcing "Derek Finnan - Solicitor" and a phone number. Toby arrived promptly at two and was met at the door by Breezy. He duly complimented her on her statuesque hairdo, reminiscent of an inverted pyramid, everything thrusting upwards and not a hair out of place. What does she do with it when she goes to bed, and what does she do with it in the morning? These and other questions would have to wait another day as Del came out to meet him.

"So good of you to come to my humble abode, Tobes," he enthused, leading the way into the kitchen, "coffee?"

"Yes please."

Ignoring Toby's request, Del motioned him to a chair and sat down opposite, looking agitated. "I hope you don't mind, but The Weasel has invited himself to sit in on our little discussion. As you know, Danny and the boys work for him, and he wants to see them right." Del hurried on before Toby could reply. "You've read the committal bundle, no doubt?"

"Yes, thanks, Del, but I'm missing Danny's proof of evidence. I don't know how to advise him, or how to prepare the case properly, until I know that."

"You've wisdom beyond your years, Tobes, but all in good time. That's where The Weasel can help, put flesh on the bones so to speak. Oh, and before he arrives, a word to the wise, don't call him Weasel, know what I mean? Best stick to the formalities. He likes to be called Don Cornyony."

"You must be joking," Toby laughed.

"With The Weasel, you don't joke unless he jokes first." Del was deadly serious. "It's not easy for either of us, Tobes, I know that, but this is my living, and The Weasel's a part of it."

Just then, the doorbell rang, and Del jumped up like a startled rabbit. "That'll be The Weasel now, so better leave the talking to me," and with that, he hurried out.

Toby could hear Del greeting The Weasel effusively, and a few snatched words of conversation.

"He's young, but bright, and a fast learner..."

"So long as he learns to jump through my 'oops, Del, that's all that matters. Danny's one of my best boys, and 'ee deserves the best."

"And he'll get the best, you've my word on it."

"You givin' that girl of yours a portion, Del?" he asked, as Breezy walked past the open door and out of sight.

"No way, Don, why do you ask?"

"She wants to let 'er 'air down a bit, thought that might do the trick."

Del laughed nervously. "Now what about Spud? He can wait in the front room if you like, there might be some boxing on Sky Sports."

Spud, one of a rapidly dwindling band of faithful retainers, was so called because of his uncanny resemblance to a large potato.

"Nar, Spud can stay outside and swat any tosspot warden what tries to slap a ticket on the motor."

The kitchen door opened and in walked The Weasel. It was like something from a time warp. In his late forties, he was short and wiry, with jet-black, brilliantined hair and a thin, cruel, face. He was wearing Aviator sunglasses, which he removed slowly and put into the top pocket of his sharp, pinstriped suit jacket. Across his scrawny shoulders was draped a yellow, cashmere, coat, which Del offered to hang up.

"Yeh, but be careful. That cost more than you make in a month."

Again, Del's nervous laugh. "Let me introduce you to Danny's counsel, Toby Potts. Toby, this is Mr. Don Cornyony."

Toby extended his hand, which The Weasel ignored. "A pleasure," he lied, "and such an unusual name." Del shot Toby a glance.

"Yeh, it means 'eart of a lion in Eyetalian," Toby didn't have the 'eart to disabuse him, "but you can call me Don." He turned to Del. "You were right, Del, 'ees young alright, but does 'ee know 'is arse from 'is elbow?" he quipped, as if Toby wasn't there.

"Sit down, Don," said Del, fussing around him like a mother hen. "How about a coffee?"

He could have mine, thought Toby.

"I'd rather 'ave a vodka on the rocks."

"Sorry, Don, fresh out, but I can get Breezy to run down the off-licence if you want."

"Nar, next time perhaps," he added ominously. "Right, let's get down to business," he continued, fixing Toby with his beady eyes, "so, what's the score, sunshine?"

"Toby's read all the papers, Don, and is well up to speed..."

"Shut it, Del," snapped The Weasel, "I want to 'ear it from the boy."

Toby smiled through gritted teeth. He'd taken an instant dislike to The Weasel, and it could only get worse. But one look at Del's pleading expression persuaded him to tread lightly. "Well," he began cautiously, "if Mr. Dung gives evidence and comes up to proof..."

"Wadya mean, sunshine, come up to proof?"

"It's an expression we use," said Toby pompously, "meaning if he says in court what he says in his witness statement..."

"'ees got all the lingo, Del, I'll give 'im that. Yeah, go on."

"Then Danny is almost certain to be convicted, and the same goes for the others."

There was a long silence, with The Weasel deep in thought. "So," he said finally, "the cheeky little Chink is an important witness?"

"Crucial."

Another long silence. "So what if we whack 'im? Are the boys home and dry?"

Toby was horrified. "Good God, you can't be serious, Mr. Cornyony! I think I should remind you this conference is not privileged, as you

214

are not my client, so if anything happened to Mr. Dung, I'd be obliged to inform the authorities."

"Calm down, sunshine," The Weasel replied, but there was a cold edge to his voice, "just testing the water." Toby was far from convinced. "But watch my lips. Don't threaten me, it could damage your health."

Del, as ever the peacemaker, turned to Toby. "I'm sure Don was only speaking hypothetically, weren't you, Don?" As The Weasel had never knowingly spoken hypothetically, whatever that meant, he hadn't the first idea what Del was on about, "so let's move on, shall we, and discuss the case like mature human beings." That would be a first for The Weasel, but there was a first time for everything.

Toby felt he was in the conference from Hell, and was getting badly out of his depth. He didn't like The Weasel dictating the terms, or threatening him, but he had no choice. He was treading a fine line between humouring Del and keeping The Weasel off his back. Best to press on. "I haven't viewed it yet, but there's CCTV footage, or so I'm told, showing Danny and the boys arriving at Mr. Dung's premises shortly before the incident."

"No there ain't," The Weasel interrupted.

"Well, according to the witness statements and the list of exhibits, there is."

"Take my word for it, sunshine, there ain't." The Weasel's expression spoke volumes. "So, what's the bottom line?"

Again, that uneasy feeling, as Toby continued. "Well, I can't rule out a cut-throat defence."

"I like the sound of that, meaning?"

"How sure are we that all four will stick together? After all, they have different solicitors and different counsel, and if one or other decides to do a deal to save his own neck and blame the others, or worse still, give evidence for the prosecution, it's a whole new ball game. It could put you in the frame." Time to stir the pot.

"That won't 'appen," replied The Weasel.

"Why not?" Toby asked naïvely.

"'Cos it's more than their lives are worth," said The Weasel, and he meant it.

There was a long pause. "Alright then," said Toby, breaking the silence, "Danny has two choices. He pleads guilty to something acceptable to the prosecution and gets credit for an early plea of guilty, or he takes his chances with Mr. Dung."

"And if he goes down?"

"He's looking at double figures."

Another long pause. "Right then, so what's Danny's defence?"

"I don't understand." Things were turning nasty again.

"It's a simple question, and Del tells me you're a fast learner, so let me spell it out to you in words of one syllable." The Weasel's favourite form of communication. "If the Chink comes up to proof, as you call it, 'ow does Danny talk 'is way out of it, or, more to the point, 'ow do **you** talk Danny out of it? After all, you're 'is brief, and you're there for the money, that's right, ain't it?"

"Somewhat crudely put, Mr. Cornyony, and here's me thinking I've been working for the love of it these past two years. However, if I were Danny, I'd have two choices. Either I wasn't there, so Mr. Dung is mistaken, or I was there with three other thugs, and in the course of assaulting Mr. Dung so severely I put him in hospital for four weeks and emerged without a scratch on me, I was acting in lawful self-defence. Now, Mr. Cornyony, you're an intelligent man, which defence would **you** choose?"

The Weasel didn't like multiple-choice questions, he usually got them wrong. He liked things in black and white. He was watching a travel programme on afternoon television the other day, and to win an all-

216

expenses paid holiday, he had to answer a simple question, or so the presenter said: "In which Eyetalian city is the leaning Tower of Pisa? Is it: (a) Rome? (b) Venice? (c) Pisa, or (d) Naples?" Alright, so how was he to know it wasn't a trick question? And besides, Naples is full of towers, some straight, some leaning.

Del, sensing The Weasel's unease, and knowing him a whole lot better, rode to the rescue. "Well, it's obvious, Tobes, Danny goes for mistaken identity, isn't that right, Don?"

"Yeah, Del, stands to reason," The Weasel replied, nodding vigorously in agreement, "and without the CCTV," why was he so sure, Toby wondered, "it's the Chink's word against ours, and we outnumber 'im four to one."

"Probably not our best point, Mr. Cornyony, but no matter." Toby had had enough, and wanted to end the conference on a high note. "Of course, all this is hypothetical," there goes that word again, "and until Del and I go and see Danny in Brixton, we don't know what his defence will be."

"Yes, we do," replied The Weasel, and on that, he was as firm as the Rock of Gibraltar. "Right, Del, my time's valuable and I've got calls to make." He turned to Toby. "Don't screw it up, sunshine," he added ominously, "I've got a lot riding on this result, and I don't like disappointments."

After The Weasel had gone, Del flopped back into his chair and mopped his brow. "I need a drink," and pouring himself a large scotch, pushed the bottle towards Toby. "I wouldn't want to go through that again." He paused, and looked intently at Toby. "Question is, Tobes, are we up for it?"

Toby poured for both of them. "Whatever else, Del, I'm keeping a packed suitcase under the bed, ready for a quick getaway," and they both laughed. "But seriously, if I think I'm being manipulated, I shall have to return the brief. I hope not, as we've worked so well together, but I'm not prepared to compromise my standards. Of course Danny is entitled to put the prosecution to proof, that's his right, and if they can't prove their case, he walks, and I'm absolutely comfortable with that. It's the system, warts and all. But there I draw the line. My reputation is too important to me."

Del looked reflectively into the bottom of his glass, and then looked up. "Yeah, I know what you mean, but don't worry. If it goes pear shaped, we'll both bail out."

Toby didn't see The Weasel again until the day of the trial. In Toby's case, absence did not make the heart grow fonder.

Surprise, surprise. When Del and Toby went to visit Danny on remand, his instructions were clear and unequivocal. He wasn't there, and it's a case of mistaken identity, and he was gutted to find himself in the frame. And surprise, surprise, the other three were saying exactly the same thing.

The trial was listed before His Honour Judge Huw Goldsmith at the Old Bailey. According to robing room gossip on the first morning, Goldsmith was very popular with the Bar. Polite, unfailingly courteous, patient beyond measure, and above all, fair, a judge unique in the annals of the Old Bailey.

The three other defendants were separately represented by Cantwell and two others from his chambers, known to one and all as the Twilight Chambers. As Danny was first on the indictment, this meant Toby had to cross-examine the witnesses first, an awesome responsibility, and one he was dreading. He should have followed his instincts and returned the brief, but too late now for regrets.

With the jury empanelled, the case for the prosecution was opened by Brendan O'Hara, the darling of the CPS with his beguiling Irish lilt and in line for promotion to junior Treasury Counsel. This was the 'A' list for prosecutors at the Old Bailey, elevating those selected to the Pantheon, and handling all the most serious cases. If he succeeded, this would mean an unremitting diet of prosecution work, a fate worse than death in Toby's book. All those reviews by the likes of Paul Newman, and 'Advocate Evaluation' forms by the score, but then, as Churchill once quipped, s**t happens, and somebody has to clean it

218

up. Or was that Ronald Reagan in one of his more lucid moments? And did it matter?

And then, the moment they had all been waiting for, as Mr. Dung was called to the witness box. You could cut the atmosphere with a knife, something The Weasel was working on.

Mr. Dung was a small dapper man, in his late fifties. He walked across court with a pronounced limp, but had otherwise full recovered from his injuries. The usher thrust the Bible into his hand and instructed him to read the words from the card.

Mr. Dung, slowly and deliberately, took out his reading spectacles, and then looked up. "I no berieve in God," he announced, "I berieve in Shinto."

Goldsmith, smiling indulgently, looked over to Brendan. "Do we have an oath in Shinto, Mr. O'Hara?" he asked, translating as he went along.

"I'm afraid not, my lord."

"Such a pity the witness wasn't asked in advance to state his religious beliefs, but no matter." He turned back to Mr. Dung. "I apologise for the discourtesy, but I wonder if you would be willing to affirm, Mr. Dung?"

"Velly well." The affirmation card was thrust into his hand. "I do soromry, sincery, and tlury affirm that the evidence I give shar be the tluth, thc whore tluth and nothing but the tluth."

"Well," observed the judge, "there we are. At least we've made a start. Pray begin, Mr. O'Hara."

"Thank you, my lord." Turning to the witness, he asked, "Is your full name Yu Flung Dung?"

"It is, but it means something erse in Chinese, so no sirry jokes, if you preeze."

Cantwell oozed to his feet. "My lord, my learned friend begins his examination-in-chief with a leading question."

"He does indeed, Mr. Cantwell, but if I may venture an opinion, a relatively uncontentious one. However," he continued, before Cantwell could reply, "you and I will remain vigilant to ensure the rules of evidence are strictly applied. Pray continue, Mr. O'Hara."

"Thank you, my lord. Mr. Dung, before your premises were destroyed by fire…"

Cantwell oozed to his feet again, but Goldsmith was equal to the task. "I feel, Mr. O'Hara, you had better proceed on the assumption that everything is in issue, that way we'll get on faster. Let me see if I can help. Mr. Dung, what do you do for a living?"

"Raundly," replied Mr. Dung helpfully.

"Is that what we Occidentals call laundry?"

"That's what I say, Raundly."

"Well, there you have it, Mr. O'Hara, Mr. Dung does Raundly for a living."

"I am obliged, my lord. And what do you do now for a living?"

"Nothing." Progress at last.

"Why not?"

"Business burn down." Almost too good to be true.

"Tell the jury about that, will you?"

"Terr the july what?"

"How did your business burn down?"

"I no know. I in hospritar at time."

"And why were you in hospital?"

"Getting tleatment for injulies."

"Getting treatment for your injuries," repeated O'Hara.

Up oozed Cantwell again. "My lord, I am concerned about the attempts by your lordship and in particular, my learned friend, to translate the witness's answers as he gives his evidence. Whilst they are laudable and well motivated, it may be that some of the answers are being inadvertently mistranslated, thus denying my client a fair trial. I am sure your lordship is familiar with Article Six of the European Convention on Human Rights?"

"I read nothing else, Mr. Cantwell," quipped Goldsmith, "but leaving that on one side for the moment, it doesn't take rocket science to work out that the last answer should read: 'getting treatment for injuries', or do you seek to persuade me to the contrary?"

"That's what I said," Mr. Dung added helpfully, "getting tleatment for injulies."

"Just a moment, Mr. Dung."

"No, my lord," continued Cantwell, "at this stage of the evidence, the witness's answers are uncontroversial, but that might change. Certainly my learned friend Mr. O'Hara hopes so, otherwise he doesn't have much of a case."

"Pausing there, Mr. Cantwell," Goldsmith turned to O'Hara. "Mr. O'Hara, I imply no criticism of Mr. Dung, but the defence may well have a point, and I am anxious above all else to ensure a fair trial. In the circumstances, therefore, I am going to adjourn until tomorrow morning. Will you please arrange for an interpreter?" The judge turned to Mr. Dung. "We're having a little difficulty understanding you, Mr. Dung, and as your evidence is very important, it is vital we understand everything you say."

Mr. Dung was not amused. "My Engrish velly good," he retorted.

"Then the fault is entirely ours. May I enquire, do you prefer Cantonese or Mandarin?"

"Cantonese," he snapped, "Mandalin sirry language."

Promptly at ten thirty the next morning, and with Mr. Dung and the interpreter side by side in the witness box, the trial resumed.

"You were telling the jury you were in hospital, getting treatment for your injuries. Can you tell us why you were in hospital?"

"I was assrorted."

"No, no, Mr. Dung," said Goldsmith, "please wait for the interpreter, and he will give your answer."

There followed a few minutes of animated conversation in Cantonese, or so it was assumed. Finally, the interpreter turned to the judge. "The witness says he was assrorted, my rord."

"That's what I said, assrorted," echoed Mr. Dung triumphantly.

Goldsmith raised his eyes to the heavens. "Let's press on, Mr. O'Hara."

"And who assaulted you, Mr. Dung?" There was an audible hush in the court.

"Those men there," he replied, pointing to the four defendants in the dock.

This time, even Toby joined the mass uprising.

"Yes, yes, gentlemen," Goldsmith's patience was being pushed to the limit, "I am aware of the rule against dock identification, and I shall direct the jury to disregard the witness's last answer." He turned to the jury. "Members of the jury, wc have strict rules of evidence, and one of them forbids a dock identification. It is nobody's fault, but the identity of those responsible for assrorting, I mean assaulting, Mr.

Dung, must be proved by admissible evidence and by no other means. I hope that is clear. Mr. O'Hara?"

"Can you describe the men who assaulted you?"

"No need, they're sitting over there."

This was going from bad to worse, and Goldsmith's patience was reaching breaking point. "Please just answer the question Mr. Dung."

"I have…."

"And please wait for the interpretator…."

"Ok, but I need no interpleter."

"Let me be the judge of that Mr. Dung."

"OK, Jo, you judge."

"Thank you," Goldsmith sighed, "now let's begin by describing the colour of their skin, and please don't say, no need, they're sitting over there, otherwise I will have to stop the trial. Alright?"

The interpretator jabbered away. "The witness say, ok, Jo, you judge."

"Good, now what's the answer to my question?"

More jabbering. "The witness ask, what question?"

"Can he describe the colour of their skin?" Goldsmith snapped.

More jabbering. "The witness say, yes."

"So what was the colour of their skin?" Goldsmith repeated through clenched teeth.

"White," replied Mr. Dung.

"Please wait for the question to be interpreted, Mr. Dung!" The veins on Goldsmith's forehead were beginning to stand out.

"I no need, my Engrish velly good."

The judge's pencil snapped in his hand as they jabbered away. "The witness says, no need, his Engrish velly good."

Goldsmith took a deep breath, counted to ten, composed himself, and then turned to O'Hara. "I'm sorry, Mr. O'Hara, I interrupted you. Pray continue."

"Thank you, my lord. So how many of the men who assaulted you were white?"

This time, Mr. Dung waited for the interpreter. "All four."

"Excellent."

"That's a comment, my lord," interrupted Cantwell.

"You have been warned, Mr. O'Hara," replied the judge wearily.

"And what else can you tell us about the four white men?"

More jabbering. "The witness says, all white men look same to Chinese, but," the interpreter added, "the witness say, look at men in dock, the four men who assrorted him were their spitting image, if not men in dock, then their twin blothers, right down to their sirry sriped suits."

"And how many times had you seen these men before the night you were assaulted?"

"Many times," replied the interpreter, "the witness say men bling in sirry stliped suits once a month, legurar as crockwork, six for plice of five, special offer."

Goldsmith was curious. "You say six, Mr. Dung? To whom did the other suits belong?"

"Witness say, Fingers Marroy and The Weasel."

"The Weasel?"

"The witness say, boss of gang, sirring in pubric garrely," and Mr. Dung pointed him out. This was The Weasel's worst nightmare, public exposure in a court of law, as he rose and left with as much dignity as he could muster, all eyes following his bright yellow cashmere coat slung casually across his scrawny shoulders. Cheeky little Chink, he should have whacked him months ago when he had the chance. Too late now for regrets.

O'Hara felt he was on a roll at last. "And can you tell the jury why the four white men, who looked the spitting image of the four defendants, right down to their silly striped suits, assaulted you?" He was suddenly enjoying every moment at the sight of clear blue water. Cantwell squirmed, but there was nothing he could do.

Mr. Dung waited for the interpreter. "The witness say plotection, my rord."

"Protection from what, Mr. Dung?"

"The witness say," the interpreter continued, "if no pay plotection money, they burn down shop."

"And did you pay protection money, Mr. Dung?"

"No."

Game, set and match. "No further questions."

"Before you call your next witness, Mr. O'Hara," said the judge, "Mr. Dung has referred to the men who attacked him wearing silly striped suits. Do you have any evidence to support him?"

"I do, my lord. Following the assault on Mr. Dung, all six, who included Mr. Malloy and the man known as The Weasel, were arrested, and six striped suits were seized. I have them in court."

"Pass them up."

After a lot of pulling and tearing at the tamper proof bags, the suits were revealed in all their glory, and duly passed on to Mr. Dung, who immediately identified them from his own dry cleaning marks inside.

They were passed back to the judge, who held one aloft. "Very striking, Mr. O'Hara. I wonder if they glow in the dark?"

Cantwell rose to his feet. "That is a comment, my lord, and wholly inappropriate."

Goldsmith had had enough of Cantwell and his oily ways. "It is indeed a comment, Mr. Cantwell, and as I am the judge, I shall feel free to comment as I see fit. I shall be directing the jury in due course that they are free to accept or reject my comments, as they are the judges of the facts. Now, unless you have any further submissions," he turned to the usher, "pass the suits to the jury for their closer inspection."

That done, Goldsmith turned back to O'Hara. "What other evidence do you call?"

Brendan stood up. "There was to be CCTV footage of the defendants, or their twin brothers, entering Mr. Dung's laundry at the time of the assault, my lord, but when the master tape was removed from the police property store for copying, it had been taped over. I am still waiting for an explanation. Needless to say, there will have to be a full investigation."

Better ask The Weasel, muttered Toby.

"Very well. Is that your case?"

"It is, my lord."

Toby's prediction was right on both counts, as he reminded himself of the advice given to The Weasel round Del's kitchen table. If Mr.

Dung came up to proof, they'd all be convicted, and they'd get double figures. He did, and they did, twelve years imprisonment.

Cantwell oozed back to Twlight Chambers, muttering darkly about the Court of Appeal, but it was an empty gesture. With his foot soldiers out of the way, The Weasel's empire crumbled. Three detective constables resigned, and their resignations were accepted with immediate effect. Mr. Dung became a hero on the Green. His Raundly was rebuilt, and business was better than ever.

Danny Bloom, taking advantage of his enforced leisure time, retrained as a plumber. After all, he was good with his hands, and according to word on the street, a good plumber could earn more than a criminal barrister. What's more, it was daylight robbery and legit. What more could he want?

Six months later, The Weasel was found dead in an alley behind the Copa Cabana, knifed through the heart following a turf war with local drug dealers. With no enforcer to protect him, he was easy meat. By a strange twist of fate, Mr. Dung bought the club and turned it into the finest Chinese restaurant south of the river, rubbery chicken, bean splouts and flied lice the specialities of the house.

As for Toby, he went back to the day job to await the next plum to fall into his lap. He and Del remained good friends and colleagues, with Toby getting the lion's share of applications, mentions and the occasional plea in mitigation. Breezy let her hair down, became pregnant, and joined Del's practice as his sleeping partner. An irresistible combination.

CHAPTER SEVENTEEN

TOBY AND THE GALLOPING GOURMET

There is nothing under the sun better for man
Than to eat, drink and be merry.
Go therefore eat the chef's special with joy
And drink his overpriced wine with cheer.

[After Ecclesiastes 8:15]

It was one of those days when Gazzard, the Head of Chambers, chose to put in an appearance, and such days were not entirely popular with chambers. For a start, he occupied the only parking space, much coveted by the senior members, he occupied the best room used to impress privately paying clients in conference, and as a man with nothing else to do, he sat at his desk with the door open and collared anybody and everybody who happened to cross his line of sight and chat away endlessly about this and that and, inevitably, about Palmer v. Camley Borough Council.

On this particular day, it was Toby's turn, as he tried to sneak past on his way to lunch.

"Come in, dear boy," Gazzard beckoned, "are you a chambers solicitor?"

"Er, no, I'm a tenant," replied Toby.

"Are you indeed? And in whose chambers?"

"Yours, Gazzard. You were kind enough to take me on."

"Was I indeed? So you'll be…?"

"Potts, Toby Potts."

"Can't say I remember the name," Gazzard was really losing it, thought Toby, "so how are you enjoying life as a tenant? Keeping busy?"

"Fairly busy, thank you, highs and lows, but mustn't complain."

"Nobody complains in **my** chambers, boy, the best set in the Temple. If you can't make it here, then you shouldn't be in the profession."

"Quite so."

Gazzard studied this youth with suspicion. "So, what did you want to talk to me about?"

This was going nowhere. "Well, actually, I was on my way out to lunch."

"Lunch? Can't be doing with it! Besides, rich food gives me dyspepsia. There's too much self-indulgence in these chambers if you ask me, with long lunches and wine, some even taking a small glass of sherry at midday. I won't be having it in my chambers, do you hear?!" He glared at Toby.

"Well, as they say, Gazzard, good food is like music to the soul."

"Poppycock!" snapped Gazzard, as he leaned down and retrieved a tin from under his chair. "A heavy lunch with wine dulls the senses, and in this profession, and particularly as a tenant in **my** chambers, there's no room for dull senses."

"A sobering thought indeed, Gazzard," replied Toby mischievously, "but according to Henry Fielding, 'it is widely conceived that too much wine will dull a man's senses, and that is indeed true, in a dull man'."

Gazzard didn't appreciate the humour or the wit of this upstart youth, and it showed. "A word of advice, young man," he said gravely, "you'll get nowhere espousing such flippancies. I didn't get where I am today by worshipping at the shrine of Bacchus. Be in no doubt, you must remain active and alert throughout the day, as I was when I appeared in the House of Lords in the case of Palmer v Camley Borough Council. You know it of course?"

"I do indeed, and the leading case on public negligence."

"Quite so," Gazzard looked pleased with the boy's response as he wandered down memory lane. "For as long as I can remember, I've got by with a cheese and onion sandwich and a piece of fruitcake. My wife Mildred makes them for me, don't you know?" Lucky Mildred, thought Toby, but at least it gets him out of the house and from under her feet, "I used to have an apple, but the teeth can't cope any more, keep coming out with every bite," he chuckled. "Here, boy," he said, pushing the tin towards Toby, "help yourself, but not the fruitcake."

For the next ten minutes, they sat together, munching Mildred's sandwiches, and saying nothing. Meanwhile, in another part of town, food of a different variety was being contemplated, under the close supervision of Jock Romsey.

Jock Romsey, he of Milli Pini fame, had decided long ago that his future lay elsewhere, so he'd been saving his pennies in pursuit of his dream, to open his own restaurant and join the big hitters in the culinary world. Once established, that same world would be his oyster, or lobster, or whatever, with the rich and the famous beating a path to his door, and bookings being taken two years in advance. Then the TV series, which he thought of calling 'Jock's Spot', but on mature reflection, that sounded too much like an athletic support, so he'd come back to that one. With the series a runaway success, the companion cookbook would follow, brim full of delicious recipes lovingly photographed in colour by Patrick Lichfield, together with a cover photograph of Jock himself, displaying a few tufts of electric red chest hair over his apron, to give the recipes that 'Man Appeal'. He could see it all, and it was only a matter of time.

As luck would have it, The Greasy Spoon was up for sale, and affordable. Just off the Portobello Road in Notting Hill, it was an ideal location, and with a complete hose down and some remodelling, it could be up and running in no time. Contracts were exchanged, and Jock and his nervous 'small business' bank manager set about the transformation. What he needed was a theme, perhaps with a Scottish flavour, which was more than you could say for the food, but the bank manager quickly vetoed that idea. Being a Sassenach who'd never ventured north of the border, Scottish food was all about glutinous bowls of porridge oats, haggis, and Arbroath Smokies, and great slabs of venison and mounds of neaps and suet, which might be alright for those hairy Scots in skirts with nae knickers, but not for the rich and famous, so keep it simple, and keep it international. The bank manager gave way on tartan-covered chairs, but that was as far as he was willing to go, and Scottish piped pipe music was definitely taboo.

The choice of name became a nightmare, as various permutations were tried and rejected. Le Gavroche; good name, but the Roux brothers might have something to say on the matter, Jock on the Square; same problem with Gary Rhodes, and besides, there wasn't a square for miles around, so confusing for the punters. Brazz; 'fraid not, some bloke in manure and green wellie country down Somerset way had got his handle on that, Brown's; which the bank manager Mr. Brown particularly liked, had been taken, the eponymous Jock's; too Scottish, and anyway, they'd been through that before, Smith's; wasn't there some lass who cooked a bit and owned a football team, possibly the Gollies? They were getting nowhere fast.

How about the Aurora, suggested Mr. Brown, who'd just watched a television programme on the National Geographic channel. Jock was sceptical, as he didn't know his aurora from his borealis, but Mr. Brown was enthusiastic, and he who pays the piper plays the tune, although Mr. Brown remained adamant, no piped music. The Aurora was a spectacular light sensation seen in both hemispheres at night, and, as he explained, Jock's restaurant would be a culinary night time sensation, or so he hoped. Yeah, muttered Jock, but what about lunch time? There was no pleasing some people!

And so the Aurora opened its doors to a blaze of publicity, as Jock stepped onto the first rung of the ladder to fame and fortune. Acting on Mr. Brown's advice, the opening night was to be a celebrity affair, with specially invited guests and a handful of food critics to write pages of wonderful reviews and fill the tables for months to come. A publicity agent was engaged to ring round the usual celebrities, those who wouldn't turn down the chance of free scoff and their photos in the tabloids.

The celebrities weren't exactly 'A' list, in fact Jock didn't recognise any of them. A few television presenters, a chat show host or two and that twerp from the National Lottery. There were also some freeloading politicians, either yesterday's men on the way down, or tomorrow's men on the way up, or so they hoped, with dolly birds in tow and definitely not their wives. Even 'Hot Hands' Spinks made it, way off his patch, but free publicity was better than no publicity, and he was still working to his agenda. Sadly, Mrs. Spinks couldn't make it, yet again. Mr. Brown, with his good lady wife, the incredibly dull Mrs. Brown, occupied a corner table, where he spent the night picking nervously at his food and drinking mineral water, all the while number-crunching into his personal organiser.

Of greater interest to Jock were the food critics, and two put in an appearance. There was Michael Windbag, more a self-professed gourmet, who insisted on having his photo taken with Jock and his staff, Windbag to the fore. Jock could handle him, give him double portions of everything and keep the wine flowing, and Windbag would come up trumps. The chances of him remembering what he'd eaten the next morning were remote in the extreme.

The critic Jock and his fellow chefs feared the most was BB Fish, presumably a *nom de plume,* otherwise it was a very silly name, who wrote a syndicated column for most of the Sunday broadsheets. The tabloids were for intellectual pigmies. It was common knowledge he could make or break a restaurant, such was the power of his pen. Jock half hoped he wouldn't turn up, but he did, accompanied by a very attractive girl he called The Blonde. Fair enough, as that was obviously her colour for the night, and certainly better than calling her The Weasel. His table had been carefully selected, not too bright to draw attention to himself, and not too dark to avoid the originally presented dishes as they exploded in a symphony of mouth watering succulence. He looked tired, almost liverish, perhaps The Blonde had something to do with that, and worse still, obviously sober. Windbag hooted at him from across the room, BB Fish studiously ignored him.

With the benefit of hindsight, it would have been better if BB had come once the teething troubles had been ironed out, but too late for regrets. The Head Waiter, Gaston from Belgium, was good, but the others were on a sharp upward learning curve, and good staff were hard to come by. Gaston's English was not conversationally fluent, and when taking the order, referred to The Blonde as The Blob, which BB Fish found singularly unamusing. Not an auspicious start.

Jock rated the evening a success, with his guests singing his praises and making the usual complimentary noises as they stumbled out into the cold night air. Jock stood at the door, beaming effusively and thanking them for eating and drinking him out of house and home. Windbag, the last to leave, approached him for the photo call, and Jock looked round for BB Fish and The Blonde to join them for a real moment to savour, but to his horror, they were nowhere to be seen. S**t! They'd left early, and nobody had bothered to tell him.

The following Sunday, Jock bought all the broadsheets and, pouring himself a strong black coffee, sat down to know his fate. It was not good, but worse still, it was not fair. Still, as they say, one man's meat is another man's poison, but it was no consolation. BB Fish's remarks about the service were not too wide of the mark, but his niggling complaints about Jock's food were nothing short of outrageous, with gratuitous comments like stodgy, insipid and uninspiring, peppering his column. Worse still, he claimed a stomach upset the next morning from the medley of seafood on cracked ice, briefly earning him the epithet of the Galloping Gourmet. Not all the comments were negative, and he was nothing short of effusive about Jock's fruits of the forest Pavlova drizzled with a raspberry coulis and a splash of Grand Marnier, but overall, it was damning with faint praise.

It was not all doom and gloom, as Windbag gave him a good write up, and the photo call was welcome publicity, but the epicureans would go with BB Fish. Jock had half a mind to phone and give him a piece of his mind, but he didn't have his number, and anyway, it would do more harm than good.

As Jock sat fulminating, the phone rang. It was the publicity agent. "Thought you might like to know," he said, "I've had great feedback, if you'll forgive the pun, on your big night. I rang round the celebs we invited, and to a man and woman, very positive and very upbeat. Looks like you've got a winner."

"Then you haven't read BB Fish's column about me in the Sunday broadsheets?"

"Er…yes, but it's not the end of the world, Jock, and Windbag had some nice things to say about you, so cheer up. After all, hardly anybody reads these critical broadsides, and fewer still take them seriously, and it'll soon be forgotten. If you want my opinion, the likes of BB Fish would find something negative to say about the Garden of Eden, it goes with the territory."

He was half right, as bookings remained strong, but with no sign of the TV series on the horizon, BB's column continued to rankle with Jock. He was like a dog with a bone, lightly seasoned with garlic, no doubt, and cooked slowly in a casserole. The bone, that is.

Mr. Brown, ever the efficient 'small business' bank manager, had kept all the bills and costed them down to the last penny. The total outlay for Jock's big night was just in excess of seven thousand pounds. Let's hope it was worth it.

Six weeks later, Jock was taking the night off, and had accepted an invitation to join his friend and fellow chef Alphonse for dinner at Chez Alphonse, a fashionable bistro in unfashionable Battersea. Like Nico before him, and that bloke who opened a grotty little restaurant with his mother called the Three Nines, or was it the Three Sixes, and served roast-suckling pig to royalty, Alphonse was trying to civilise the natives and was failing miserably, but his bistro attracted the 'A' list in their droves, and he was minting it.

As luck would have it for Toby, Del and Breezy were also dining there that night, celebrating Crispin's first birthday. Del was like a fine wine, he didn't travel well, so Battersea was as far as he was prepared to go for overpriced nosh. Good God! Del kept saying, have you seen these prices, and even the house wine was off the Richter Scale. Breezy told him to belt up, called him a tight-fisted bastard, and proceeded to order the most expensive dishes on the menu. To rub salt into the wound, she also ordered a bottle of '82 Puligny-Montrachet, because she liked the name, modestly priced at a hundred and thirty pounds. After all, it wasn't every day Crispin celebrated his first birthday. If egg and chips and a pint of bitter had been on the menu, Del would have gone for it. Such a peasant!

Jock and Alphonse were enjoying the warm foie gras with crispy bacon in a rich, wine sauce, with a very drinkable bottle of St. Emilion, cheeky yet delicate, with just a hint of fresh gooseberries, when Alphonse looked up and nodded across the room. "I see a friend of yours is dining with us tonight."

Jock turned round to see his Nemesis, seated with the same attractive girl, this time calling her the Redhead, and just about to order. It was a red rag to a bull, as Jock got up.

"Leave it, Jock, he's not worth it, my friend."

"Don't worry, Alphonse, I'll just go over and introduce myself," he lied, and with that, he marched over and stood, arms folded, smouldering with pent up anger, just waiting for the fuse to be lit.

"As I live and breathe," he snarled, "the great food critic himself, the high and mighty BB Fish, or is it Haddock?!"

BB Fish looked up, taken by surprise. "Have we met?"

"Have we met?! Oh, yes, my friend, we have! I'm Jock Romsey, the owner of the Aurora, and you wrote a column about my restaurant a few weeks ago. Remember?"

"Actually, no, but so what?"

The other diners were beginning to feel uncomfortable as the temperature began to rise.

"So what?! You called my food stodgy, insipid and uninspiring, that's what!"

"Then it must have been." Wrong answer.

"I'll show you stodgy, you big p***k!" and with that, Jock grabbed a roll and stuffed it into BB's face. The Redhead screamed hysterically and fell backwards off her chair. BB, who used to be a prop forward for London Irish before he took to food, leapt to his feet and aimed a hard punch at Jock, catching him right between the eyes. But Jock was made of sterner stuff, as he came back, crashing over the table, fur and feathers and skin and hair flying in every direction. The diners ran for cover as Alphonse, shouting Gallic obscenities, and his waiters, tried to prise them apart. Eventually they were bundled outside, the police were called, and Jock was charged with assault with a bread roll, freshly baked that morning as Alphonse was keen to point out, and affray.

Jock's fortunes were at an all time low. He was just beginning to break even after the seven thousand pound opening night, but his antics in Chez Alphonse cost him dear. With the damage caused during the affray, and refunds to the terrified diners, he was faced with another unwelcome bill, this time in the region of three thousand pounds. At least Del was well pleased, as there was no charge for the meal or the bottle of Puligny-Montrachet.

Del also banked with Mr. Brown, and used his 'small business' expertise from time to time, so he wasn't surprised when asked to represent Jock, best rates for miles around. Sadly, Del couldn't oblige, as he might be called as a witness, but recommended a colleague, who in turn, and at Del's insistence, briefed Toby, young and inexperienced, but best rates for miles around.

Jock didn't have much of a defence, in fact, if the truth be known, he didn't have any defence at all, and the damage to his reputation was already there to be seen, or read, on the inside pages of the tabloids.

236

Headlines such as 'Jock's away' and 'Fishy business at the Bistro' had done the rounds.

Toby met Jock in conference at his chambers, and it was not a happy encounter. Toby explained, as gently as he could, that stuffing a bread roll, even a freshly baked one, in BB Fish's face, was unlawful, whereas BB's response in hitting Jock was lawful self-defence. The affray, by using unlawful violence and putting the diners in fear of their personal safety, was also made out, and there was no choice but to plead guilty and throw himself on the mercy of the court. It was a case of confession and avoidance, an expression Toby had read somewhere in Archbold, it sounded rather grand and gave him the air of a man with wisdom beyond his ears, or rather, beyond his years.

As for Jock, he wanted to put the whole sorry mess behind him as quickly as possible, and pick up the pieces of his ruined life, or what was left of it.

"You know what rankles most of all," he sighed, "is this bastard Fish claiming in his column I gave him food poisoning from my seafood platter."

"Yes, I read that. He got the trots, and called himself the Galloping Gourmet. Not helpful. So what about it?"

"Well, my bank manager retained all the bills from the opening night, for tax purposes he said, and I've got BB Fish's bill here." He pushed it across for Toby's inspection. Thanks to Mr. Brown and his meticulous accounting, starter, main course, the Pavlova, coffee, wine and the ubiquitous mineral water were all itemised. At first glance, Toby didn't get it, but then, on closer inspection, it was as plain as a pikestaff.

"He didn't have the seafood," Toby exclaimed, "he had the wild duck terrine with a cherry confit." Looking at the bill carefully, in case he'd missed something, he looked up at Jock. "I can see why you were so angry. And that's why you confronted him?"

There was a long pause. "Er…actually, no, I hadn't seen the bill until the other day,

"Oh dear." That was the confession, so where was the avoidance?

"But it's still f***ing slanderous!" Jock's notorious short temper was beginning to surface. He'd make a terrible witness. "He shouldn't be allowed to get away with it!" he ranted, slamming his fist on the desk.

Toby thought for a while, then came up with an idea. "From what I've heard, BB Fish is a fair man," Jock snorted in derision, "no, please listen to what I have to say."

"Alright, but it better be good."

"His column is intended to be controversial, I have his last six here, and that's why he's paid a shed load of money," Toby added enviously, "but I doubt if he's deliberately malicious."

"Don't you believe it! He's a…."

"Hold on a moment, Mr. Romsey, please let me finish. At least he should be given the chance to put the record straight, and who knows, he may wish to reconsider his position. After all, a conviction for assault and affray, in a restaurant, could cause all sorts of problems with your licence, to say the least, as well as the damage to the future success of your business."

"You're right there, laddie. So what do you suggest?"

"I'd like to contact BB Fish, through your solicitor, of course, and see if we can reason with him. I suggest, initially, Mr. Romsey, that you keep well away. We certainly don't want another incident, and you have a notorious short temper."

"What me!" he exploded, "I'm a f***ing pussycat, laddie!"

Toby looked hard at Jock, and then they both started laughing.

"OK, do what you think best," and with that, Jock stood up, gave Toby a bone crunching handshake, and got up to leave.

"Just one final question, Mr. Romsey, and it's not intended to be impertinent."

"Aye?"

"How good a chef are you?"

For a moment, Jock bristled, but it was a fleeting moment. "The best, laddie. Does that answer your question?"

A week later, Toby and his solicitor duly presented themselves at Pennington Street and shown into an enormous conference room, where BB Fish was waiting to meet them, together with a very smart corporate lawyer. Not an auspicious start. BB was not as Toby had imagined, tall, broad shouldered, with a rugged, rather knocked about face and an easy smile.

After the introductions, Toby came straight to the point, and produced the offending bill.

BB was mortified, and checked his diary for the day in question. He was aghast. "You're quite right." He paused, studying the diary intently. "How could I have made such a mistake?" The corporate lawyer shifted nervously in his seat at the thought of a writ for slander thudding onto his desk. "I have it," he continued, "lunch at Longmeads, a rather pretentious place just behind the Ritz, you may know it?" he looked up. Don't be so ridiculous, muttered Toby, on my income?! "Yes, I see it now. I had the seafood platter at Longmeads, absolutely ghastly, so bad in fact, I decided not to review it. No wonder poor Jock Romsey was so angry." Toby was conspicuous by his silence, as he and his solicitor exchanged knowing glances. "I've done him a great injustice."

The corporate lawyer shifted even more nervously in his seat. This wasn't even confession and avoidance, and to make matters worse, it was in front of Romsey's barrister and solicitor.

It was damage limitation time. "I wonder if I might make a suggestion?" he began tentatively.

"I have a suggestion of my own," Toby interrupted, "which I hope will meet the justice of the case."

"Which is?"

"You, Mr. Fish…"

"Please call me Harry. BB Fish is my ***nom de plume.*** Silly really, but I'm stuck with it," and he laughed.

"Thank you," Toby smiled, "now what Mr. Romsey deserves is to put the record straight, so I suggest as follows. He tells me he's the best, so let him prove it, to you of all people. I read your column regularly," he lied, but time for some ego massaging, "and I know you're a hard hitting man but also a fair man." Keep it coming, Toby, keep it coming. "Let him cook you the meal of your choice, and then write it up in your column, no punches pulled, no favours asked, just fair." BB nodded. So far, so good, now for the hard part. "I also ask you in your column to set the record straight about the seafood, and," Toby gulped, "to drop the charges against him."

Harry looked intently at Toby, then laughed out loud. "You're on."

"Just a minute, Harry," said the corporate lawyer, "shouldn't we discuss it first?"

"Nothing to discuss. It's a brilliant idea, so long as we both understand, no punches pulled, if you'll forgive the expression, and no favours asked. I'd better bring Doom and Gloom here," he nodded towards the corporate lawyer, "to see fair play, and of course, you'll be there as well."

Toby laughed. "Not on my income, Harry, and besides, I'm saving my pennies to get married."

"Then you and your fiancée will come as the Paper's guests, I insist on it. It's the least I can do, and we need some female company to lighten the mood. It promises to be a memorable evening."

And so it was. Jock was as good as his word, he was the best. The finest food, the finest wines, Jock on his best behaviour, and Susie captivating one and all. It was the mother of all meals, and to cap it all, BB had arranged for a photographer to capture it all for posterity.

The following Sunday, and with trembling hands, Jock read BB's column. He couldn't have written it better himself, and on the back page of the main section, a photograph of BB and Jock, shaking hands and smiling broadly.

True to his word, BB dropped all charges, and Jock's reputation was restored. With BB's column up in lights of Aurora proportions, bookings were being taken two years in advance, and a television series in the pipeline.

Some months later, a package arrived for Toby in Chambers. It was a case of Veuve Clicquot champagne and a book of Jock's favourite recipes, lovingly photographed in glorious colour, with Jock beaming out from the front cover. Inside, Jock had scribbled:

"To Toby Potts, my very good and learned friend. Nothing stodgy, insipid or uninspiring about you, laddie! Five stars in anybody's book, and mine in particular. Every future success, you deserve it!"

CHAPTER EIGHTEEN

TOBY AHOY THERE ME HEARTIES

Once more upon the waters! Yet once more!
And the waves bound beneath me as a steed
That knows its rider.

[Lord Byron]

August was a quiet time for the profession. The High Court had closed for the summer, with only a Vacation Judge holding the fort for emergency applications, and a skeleton staff drifting around aimlessly and wishing they were somewhere else. The Crown Courts ticked over, but as most of the villains were on holiday in Spain, it was plain fare, with applications, mentions and the occasional review hearing under drug treatment and testing orders. This involved former drug addicts, high on life or whatever, turning up with their urine test certificates and either being congratulated for keeping to the straight and narrow, or reprimanded for returning to their nasty habits. Toby did a couple, but he was there for window dressing, as the probation service made all the running. The excitement was almost too much to bear, and he was back in Chambers by midday, hoping the next day would bring riches beyond measure.

He enjoyed, or rather endured, long lunches in Middle Temple or Gray's Inn Hall with chums who'd also succumbed to the siren call of their senior clerks, and then it was back to Chambers to reread those two briefs adjourned from yesteryear and never destined to see the light of day. He'd browse through the occasional dusty law book, chosen at random, or the latest supplement of Archbold, brim full of new Acts of Parliament and helpful comments from the editor, but it was hard work, and his heart wasn't in it.

This was his first summer as a full tenant, and unlike his senior colleagues washing around Tuscany, braying a few words of pigeon Italian, pestering the peasants and drinking overpriced espressos in Sienna town square, Toby had elected to remain at the masthead, a steady hand on the tiller, and wait for all those returns to come flooding in, or so the clerks reasoned in that rather skewed way of theirs. The sort of returns being returned to Toby were the sort of returns he'd like to return somewhere else, but he persevered.

"Take my advice, Mr. Potts," said Fred, "with the competition out the way, there'll be rich pickings to be had, and by the time term starts again, you'll have stolen a march on them." He couldn't have been more wrong, but Toby wasn't about to tell him that. You argue with the senior clerk at your peril. Fred, needless to say, spent the whole month of August in his villa just north of Torremolinas, which left Mike, the first junior clerk, and Paul, the monosyllabic grunter, in charge of the shop.

By the end of the second week, and the diary for the third looking as blank as the expression on Paul's face, time for Toby to make a stand.

"I'm thinking of taking next week off, Mike," he ventured tentatively, "with not much going on, I thought I'd spend a few days in Cornwall."

Mike drew in his breath sharply. "You're the governor, Mr. Potts," he lied, "and you're at liberty to take as much time off as you wish. But," he warned, "you can bet your bottom dollar something juicy will come in for trial Monday, and you'll be kicking yourself for months to come."

"Something juicy, you say? Such as what?"

"Too early to say, Mr. Potts," Mike replied in a matter of fact sort of way, "if I had a crystal ball, I wouldn't be doing this job now, would I?"

"Can't argue with that, Mike, and neither would I. Ok, then," said Toby, with as much spine as a jellyfish, "let's see how next week pans out."

On Friday evening, the phone on Toby's desk rang. It was Mike. "Got two cases for you on Monday, Mr. Potts," and, for no obvious reason, he sounded well pleased with himself. "Breach of probation, Snaresbrook, first on at ten, then not before two, Croydon, committal for sentence, prosecution. That's a hundred and thirty five quid for a day's work. Not bad if you can get it. I told you it'd be worth your while staying on."

Toby didn't know what to say, so he didn't, but by Tuesday he'd had enough.

"If you can spare me for the rest of the week, Mike, I'm going to spend a few days with my fiancée in Cornwall. I've been neglecting her, and we've got a wedding to plan, so I'll phone in on Friday, if that's alright?"

Mike was not amused. "Paul, fetch the diary." Paul brought over a large book and set it down in front of him. "Right," he continued with thinly disguised contempt, "Mr. Potts of Counsel, Wednesday AWAY," he wrote in large capital letters, "Thursday AWAY, Friday AWAY." He looked up and smiled, or what passed as a smile. "Have a good time, of course this means I'll have to return your work at very short notice, but I'll do my best. After all, that's what clerks are for."

Toby felt like that bloke with the four feathers, but he wasn't going to be bullied, well, not all the time.

Happily, Susie was up for it. "I know a divine little hotel in St. Mawes," she said excitedly, "Mummy and Daddy used to stay there years ago. They may have a room, so leave it to me, and see you later."

"We're in luck," Susie told him delightedly when she picked Toby up from the station. "Apparently the best room in the hotel was booked for the week by some hugely important barrister who stays there regularly when he's in court at Truro. His trial had to be adjourned, as the defendant was on holiday in Spain, so the room is ours. It's going to be such fun."

244

They set off the next morning after an early breakfast, Toby guiding his top of the range Ford Focus down towards the M4 motorway. "I reckon we should be in St. Mawes by mid afternoon, then a Cornish cream tea and a stroll through the village. What could be better?"

It turned out that several million other motorists had decided to take a short break in Cornwall at the same time, so the journey was long and tortuous, and they eventually pulled into the Rising Sun car park just before seven. After a shower together, their spirits soon revived, and they went down for a stroll along the seafront before dinner.

They found St. Mawes enchanting. It was a delightful fishing village where nobody fished any more, and was now a tourist resort, boasting the mightily expensive Tresanton Hotel on the road up to the castle, and a few more modestly priced hotels down on the front. Toby, feeling in holiday mood, took Susie into the Tresanton for a drink, and when he got the bill, rather wished he hadn't.

As they strolled back to their hotel, Toby noticed a large sixty-five foot ketch, named La Estella, a little distance from the shore, and just outside the harbour wall, listing over at an alarming angle. It was very much the talk of the bar as they sat down to peruse the menus. All the locals had an opinion to offer, rather like barristers, but from what Toby and Susie could glean, the ketch was loaded down to the gunnels and had run aground on a sandbank. Four men, obviously not locals, were huddled together in the corner, talking in whispers over pints of the local brew.

"It'll be ten in the morning, earliest, afore the tide's 'igh enough to free 'er, I reckon," ventured one ancient mariner.

"You be right, Bill," added another. Barnacle Bill be right most of the time when it come to boats. The others nodded knowingly.

"It's all so wonderfully quaint, darling," Susie whispered, squeezing Toby's hand. Bloody Townies, muttered the locals.

They went into dinner, to be met by La Patronne of the hotel, Annie Short. She was cook par excellence, bottle washer, car park attendant, front of house and, judging from her paintings on the walls, an accomplished artist. Shades of the Aurora, but without the histrionics. Susie let slip that Toby was a barrister. Mrs. Short pricked up her ears.

"So you'll know Mr. Harvey-Jones, a very eminent barrister who stays here all the time? So charming, and so witty, our favourite guest, and a very generous tipper."

"Er, no," replied Toby, "I don't practise in this area, I'm afraid. I'm from London," he added rather grandly.

"Yes," said Mrs. Short loftily, "we have heard of it. Now, if you'll follow me, I'll show you to your table."

In spite of the initial froideur, the meal was excellent, and the house wine from somewhere east of the Andes was very drinkable. The waitress, a rather gawky girl plucked at random from the local stock, was very pleasant and attentive, and by the time pudding was served, Mrs. Short was doing her rounds.

"An excellent meal, Mrs. Short," said Toby, anxious to make amends, "absolutely delicious." Mrs. Short was not the sort of woman you addressed in the vernacular unless specifically invited to do so.

"I'm so glad you enjoyed it. Now, coffee and brandy in the lounge? Mr. Harvey-Jones always has coffee, a large espresso, brandy and his favourite Havana cigar in the lounge, and he always brings his own supply of Bendicks chocolate mints. I don't suppose he'll mind me offering you one."

"That's very kind of you, Mrs. Short," said Susie, ever the diplomat, "such a treat."

This Harvey-Jones chap, thought Toby, sounded like a complete pain in the arse, but when in Rome and all that. Just to be awkward, he helped himself to three mints, under the watchful and disapproving eye of Mrs. Short and the gawky waitress. As they were leaving, Mrs. Short, as ever in close attendance, mentioned breakfast.

"Mr. Harvey-Jones takes his breakfast promptly at eight, full English with fried bread, to give himself plenty of time to get to court. Shall I expect you at the same time?"

"Oh, no thank you," replied Susie, smiling, "we're on holiday."

"Are you indeed?" she said somewhat sniffily, as if eminent and hugely important barristers ever took a holiday, "Mr. Harvey-Jones is such a workaholic, but then, he is exceptional. We finish serving breakfast promptly at nine thirty."

"If she mentions Harvey-Jones once more, I'm going to throttle her," muttered Toby on the way out.

There wasn't much to do in St. Mawes of a night. They could return to the bar and listen to tales of derring-do on the high seas from Barnacle Bill and his motley crew, or they could join the queue at the Fish and Chip Bar opposite the hotel. The Ship and Castle Hotel round the corner was running Bingo, but last 'eyes down' was at nine. It was the sort of hotel where all the inmates were in bed by nine thirty, doors locked promptly at ten, and no room service. There was nothing for it but to retire to bed and make hot, passionate love to Susie, Toby's preferred option, as it had been since the moment they arrived.

Toby sat bolt upright. It was either a cat being neutered, or an infant child in the next room screaming for its early morning feed. He glanced at the bedside clock. Four thirty. Another screech. Toby put his head out of the window, and staring at him on the ledge, barely three feet away, was a seagull the size of a top of the range Ford Focus, eyeing him malevolently. Toby tried to shoo it away. The gull stared back, with one of those 'Bloody Townie' looks, gave another ear piercing screech, and lifted off, defying all the natural laws of gravity, winging slowly out to sea. .

That bird should not be flying, thought Toby, watching its progress, it was positively dangerous for its health. But there was progress of another sort that caught his eye. Down below, and pulling gently away from the quayside, were three of the men he'd seen in the bar the night before, rowing a small dinghy out towards La Estella, which was still listing, and still stuck on the sandbank.

Toby and Susie came down for breakfast at nine fifteen, well within Mrs. Short's deadline, and ordered the full English with fried bread. That went down well with all three of them. The morning was fine, warm and sunny, so they took their coffee out onto the terrace and drank in the invigorating sea air. Just as they were contemplating a walk up to the castle, giving the Tresanton a wide berth, the harbour side suddenly erupted into a picture of frenzied activity.

First on the scene was a Customs launch, rounding the head and making straight for La Estella, which was beginning to right itself but was still stuck on the sandbank. Then three police cars, blue lights flashing and sirens blaring, and containing probably the entire Cornish Constabulary, shot past them and slammed to a halt at the end of the quay. All eyes now turned to La Estella, where, after much heaving and ho-ing, the three men were taken from the boat and into the waiting arms of the Constabulary. It was tremendously exciting.

Over the next four hours, a total of eight tons of cannabis resin, all neatly baled and stamped 'Produce of Morocco - Enjoy', and with a street value of sixteen million pounds, was unloaded from La Estella.

In the bar that night, the hubbub of excitement reached fever pitch. One of the Customs officers who'd raided the boat was a local, Ronnie Pike by name, so he was holding forth in a most knowledgeable way, to the rapt attention of the assembled multitude.

"Afore they set sail from Morocco," he was saying, puffing on an ancient pipe, "we 'ad a tip off they'd be putting into Plymouth for victuals and refuelling, and then on to Tilbury, where the drugs were to be unloaded. As 'apchance would 'ave it, there was a freak storm in the Bay of Biscay, and La Estella 'ad to make for the nearest port. That's why she ended up 'ere in St. Mawes."

"Stands to reason," growled Bill, and the others growled in unison.

"But I'm 'ere to tell you," Ronnie dropped his voice in conspiratorial fashion as the assembled multitude leaned forward, "the CIS…"

"'oo be the CIS, Ronnie?" asked Bill.

"They be the Criminal Investigation Service, Bill, very 'ush, 'ush," and he tapped the side of his nose, "you never see 'em, you never know they're there till they pounce, you know what I'm saying 'ere? They're like James Bond, licence to kill."

"'ooh, arr," muttered the assembled multitude.

"They're masters of disguise, blendin' in. They 'ave eyes everywhere. For all we know, they could be sitting in 'ere, even as I speak."

All eyes turned to Toby, seated with Susie at a corner table by the door, and the assembled multitude shifted uneasily.

"So the CIS 'ave been tracking the boat from the moment she left Morocco," Ronnie downed his pint of bitter and looked expectantly at the barman, "and them what masterminded the venture are being watched, even as I speak. They call 'em barons, you know what I'm saying 'ere?"

"ooh, arr," muttered the assembled multitude.

"So what'll 'appen now, Ronnie?" asked Bill, "and what about the crew?"

"Can't say for sure yet, but the crew to a man are denying all knowledge of the drugs, claim they must've been loaded on board overnight when they were fast asleep. I say, pull the other one, that's what I say."

"Don't be too 'asty," counselled Bill, playing the devil's advocate, "me and the lads saw the four of 'em, sitting over there, larger than life, without a care in the world. They'll get some expensive barrister to defend 'em, I shouldn't doubt."

"Four, you say, Bill? But there were only three on board when we arrived." Ronnie emptied the cremated contents of his pipe into the ashtray. "Sounds like one's got away."

Once again, all eyes turned to Toby, 'ee being a stranger in these parts.

Ronnie downed the rest of his pint in one. "You and the lads could be witnesses, Bill," he replied, "might even be on telly."

"ooh, arr," chorused the assembled multitude.

"Now I must be going," he said, giving Toby one last look. "There's work to be done," and with that, he hurried out.

For the remainder of their stay, Toby and Susie were treated with exceptional deference and free drinks in the bar, lots of forelock tugging from the locals as they moved quickly to one side. Opinion was divided. There were mutterings from some about 007 and Miss Moneypenny, and Toby's licence to kill, although he didn't look like a natural born killer, not with them ears. Still, all the better for listening with, quipped a local wag. One even claimed to have seen a suspicious bulge inside Toby's jacket, where his Walther PK handgun was kept. Others reckoned that if he wasn't 007, maybe he was the fourth man, brazening it out and reporting back to the barons. It was the most exciting thing that ever happened in St. Mawes since the great storm of '63.

Come Friday evening, Toby phoned Chambers.

"Sorry, Mr. Potts," said Mike, without a hint of sincerity, "but you're out of court on Monday. It's very quiet at the moment."

"ooh, arr," muttered Toby, feeling duly chastened.

After breakfast on Sunday morning, it was time to head for home. As a memento of their stay, Toby bought one of Mrs. Short's paintings as a present for Susie. Mrs. Short was delighted. Apparently, in all the years Harvey-Jones had been staying, he'd never once expressed an interest in her paintings. Too busy expressing an interest in himself, no doubt. One up to Toby.

"All being well, we should be home by tea time," said Toby, washing off several leaving presents from the enormous gull and his fellow travellers. Wrong again, and it was just before ten when they finally drove into Prestwood.

The following Wednesday, as Toby walked into Chambers after an exciting afternoon at Bromley Magistrates Court, Mike looked up. That was promising, thought Toby.

"There's a message for you, Mr. Potts. Somebody called Mr. Tomkins phoned, said it was urgent, wouldn't say what it was about, but asked you to ring back as soon as you came in." He paused. "Nothing for me to worry about, I hope?" he asked, his curiosity getting the better of him, "you've paid your annual subscription to the Bar Council, haven't you?"

"Oh, yes, Mike, a long time ago." The name Tomkins meant nothing. "Perhaps it's a solicitor wanting to instruct me in a murder most foul, you never know."

Mike was unimpressed. "Quite so, Mr. Potts, you never know," and he returned to his work.

"Mr. Tomkins? Toby Potts."

"Thank you for returning my call, Mr. Potts," replied the disembodied voice on the other end of the phone, "I work for the CIS," Toby's throat went dry and his ears turned red, "and we're investigating the seizure of a large quantity of cannabis resin in St. Mawes last week." There was a pause. "We understand you were staying at the Rising Sun for a few days when the seizure was made, so if you could spare me the time to come in and make a statement, I'd be greatly obliged." Another pause.

"Yes, of course."

"Thank you. Shall we say six o'clock tomorrow evening? I wouldn't want to interfere with your busy practice. You know where we are, just the other side of Westminster Bridge from the Houses of Parliament. Come to Reception and ask for me by name, and by the way," he added, "congratulations on a good result at Bromley," and with that, the line went dead.

Toby began to perspire, for no reason at all. The building referred to by Tomkins was the Headquarters of MI6, or was it 5, and did it matter, as everybody knew it, or they certainly did after the outgoing Director-General, or M, as she was known, broke cover and lined her pockets with a turgid book about it. And how did Tomkins know about Bromley, where he'd saved some ghastly yob from a richly deserved spell in detention for breaching an Anti-Social Behaviour Order? Were they following him, and if so, why?

He'd done nothing wrong, he kept telling himself, and had nothing to hide, and all that nonsense about a licence to kill was just nonsense, wasn't it? Perhaps the CIS had been tipped off about him being a natural born killer. Worse still, what if they thought he was somehow involved, perhaps one of the barons Ronnie was talking about, down there to oversee the operation? Should he have a solicitor present, just in case? Should he speak to Gazzard? Probably not, as Gazzard would ask him to resign from Chambers on the spot. Nick Ridley was his obvious choice, but like all senior members of Chambers, he was on holiday abroad. And what about Susie? Would she ever speak to him again? And more to the point, would she come and visit him in Belmarsh prison, reserved for Category 'A' prisoners and those deemed a threat to national security?

Toby spent a restless night, tossing and turning, as he considered his options and his future. He hadn't the courage to phone Susie, at least not until his meeting with Tomkins, when things would become clearer. The poor girl, as he pictured the ordeal ahead. It was Senator McCarthy and the fifties all over again.

"Is your fiancé, or has your fiancé ever been, a member of the Communist Party?"

He'd just returned from a committal for sentence at Southwark Crown Court, a bundle of nerves, when the phone rang. It was Del.

"Tobes," he asked excitedly, "are you sitting down?"

"I always stand to attention when you phone, Del."

"Always the wag," he laughed, "but seriously, I've got some good news. There was a drugs bust down in Cornwall last week," Toby froze to the spot, his worst nightmare coming back to haunt him, "the bust of the century. Over eight tons of cannabis resin recovered from a boat marooned in some poxy little harbour, I forget the name..."

"With a street value of sixteen million pounds."

"Yeah, that's the one, so you read about it?"

"I didn't have to, Del, I was there."

"Lord love us, Tobes, whatever for?"

"It was quite by chance, but that's another story. The CIS want to interview me about it this evening."

There was a long pause. "Is there something you're not telling me, Tobes? You're not involved, are you, or perhaps you'd rather not say."

"Of course I'm not, Del. You sound like a solicitor."

"It has been said. So what's the score?" Toby explained his predicament. "Then you'll have to cancel your appointment, and now!"

"Why?"

"'Cos I've been retained by the London end of the conspiracy, and I'm instructing you, that's why."

It took a moment to sink in. "My saviour, my knight in shining armour, Del, you're the best!" Now Tomkins could go whistle. "Tell me more."

"Well, as you may know, the drugs were due for Tilbury when they were intercepted in Cornwall. Customs and the CIS had arrest warrants for two men here in London who they say were the brains behind the importation, and we're representing one of them."

"That's brilliant, Del," Toby was very excited for a number of reasons, "so who's representing the other?"

"Nobody at the moment. They'd had the house under observation for days, but when they went in, Mr. Big was nowhere to be found, vanished into the night. Probably in Spain by now, sunning himself on the Costalot."

"So what's our man's role in all this, where does he fit in?"

"They're saying he's the banker, sorted out the purchase of the drugs and the boat and arranged all the finances. I'm glad he's not my banker, strikes me as a complete dipstick, but you know what they say, still waters run deep and all that."

"What's his name?"

"Terry Knowles."

"And what's his defence?"

"I Knowles nothing," and Del laughed. "Anyway, brief on its way for a preliminary hearing at Camberwell Green Magistrates Court next Tuesday, so see you then, and ring Tomkins now before you forget."

Not something Toby was likely to forget.

Mr. Tomkins was not amused. "You are, of course, a barrister, albeit according to my records, young and inexperienced, so far be it for me to offer you legal advice, but have you considered your position?

After all, you are very close to this case, perhaps closer than you imagine."

Again the dry throat. Why did Toby feel so guilty when talking to this man? "Thank you for your concern, Mr. Tomkins," he tried to sound calm and in control, "and, needless to say, if at any time I feel professionally embarrassed, then of course I shall withdraw. At the moment, I don't see a problem. After all, I was there quite by chance, and simply witnessed the arrest of the crew."

"Yes, I was meaning to ask you about that." There was an ominous pause. "Had you ever visited St. Mawes before?"

"Well no, it was a spur of the moment thing…"

"Quite so." Again the ominous pause. "According to my information, you were booked to work all last week, but then suddenly decided to take a few days off, on the spur of the moment as you put it, and just happened to be in St. Mawes when the crew of La Estella and their cargo of drugs put into port."

"They deny all knowledge, I suppose you know that?" As soon as he'd said it, Toby wished he hadn't.

There was another long pause. "Yes, I do," replied Tomkins, "question is though, Mr. Potts, how do you know? That information is not yet a matter of public record."

This was going from bad to worse, time to shut up and bale out. "I'm sorry I can't help you, Mr. Tomkins, but in the circumstances I can't discuss the matter further. I'm sure you understand. Now I've detained you long enough. Goodbye," and Toby put down the phone. He was perspiring heavily and feeling sick. He'd done nothing wrong, so why was he shaking like a leaf? He was being treated like a criminal, or certainly a suspect. He immediately phoned Susie and told her the whole story.

"They might contact you for a statement, so I thought I'd warn you."

"It's too awful for words, darling, no wonder you're upset. They think you're a drugs baron, how ridiculous!" She paused. "You're not, are you?" she asked, giggling.

"Very funny, Susie, but we must be careful what we say to each other. Our phones might be tapped."

"Now you're just being melodramatic, Toby, and anyway, it's against the law."

"And so is importing eight tons of cannabis resin, but it happens." He took a deep breath. "I'm just asking you to be careful, that's all."

"Of course I will, darling, now will I see you at the weekend?"

"Unless I've been arrested and held incommunicado, in which case, bring a fruit cake with a file inside," and they both laughed nervously.

To Toby's great relief, Mr. Tomkins and his conspiracy theories were never heard of again, but for a while, Toby kept looking over his shoulder:
Still as they run they look behind,
They hear a voice in every wind,
And snatch a fearful dread.

It was as if they had never been, but there was a respectful gait to Mike's tread Toby had never seen before, and all the more welcome for that. 007 was alive and well and swaggering around the Middle Temple.

Eventually, with Del surprisingly proactive and Toby following in his wake, the dipstick cut a deal with the prosecution. Knowles, who'd been laundering drugs money through offshore accounts for years, agreed to plead guilty to the single charge of being concerned in the importation of the cannabis resin in return for a half hearted promise to give evidence for the Crown if Mr. Big were ever arrested. As that was remote in the extreme, it was a calculated risk and an offer too good to refuse. He got a remarkably light sentence, and was well pleased.

Aided and abetted by their barrister, too clever by half in Toby's opinion, the crew abandoned the defence that some unknown party had loaded eight tons of cannabis resin onto their boat without their knowledge whilst they were having supper and a well-earned kip at the Rising Sun, and instead put forward the defence of necessity. They claimed the drugs were destined for a country beyond the jurisdiction, and they were forced by the storm to seek shelter in St. Mawes to avoid death or serious injury. Whilst superficially attractive, their defence was immediately holed below the Plimsoll line when the prosecution recharged them all with trafficking on the high seas, under some obscure International Co-operation Act Toby had never heard of, but then, as it was none of his business, it didn't matter. Just as well, really. To put it bluntly, they were dead in the water, so to speak, and had no option but to plead guilty.

As for Mr. Big, he remained as elusive as ever, just like the Scarlet Pimpernel and that bloke in The French Connection.

Now who said crime doesn't pay?

CHAPTER NINETEEN

TOBY AND THE PORN KING

Thank Heaven for little girls,
For little girls get bigger every day,
Thank Heaven for little girls,
They grow up in the most delightful way.

[Gigi]

Toby was in good spirits. After the long summer vacation, the courts were busy again and work was picking up. He and Susie had decided on a Spring wedding and a date had been set. This was the signal for both sets of parents to rush around like wet hens in a thunderstorm and in a heightened state of panic. After all, there were only eight months until the big day and so much to be done. It was also an excellent opportunity to touch base with long forgotten relatives, dead or alive.

Fortunately for Toby, he had other more pressing matters to attend to, like earning a living and keeping his intended in the manner to which she was accustomed. On that front, the work was getting better, with more solicitors briefing him, and some even sending him work in his own name. His overdraft remained perilously close to the maximum agreed, with no sign of a significant move in the right direction, so it was very much 'hand to mouth', but he was not alone. Somehow, that was little comfort to him or his bank manager, and with a Lord Chancellor, on a salary of two hundred thousand pounds a year, with pension, benefits and expenses, implacably opposed to any increases in the legal aid fund, the prospects looked bleak. Still, he had been warned, and had nobody to blame but himself. There was an air of militancy at the Criminal Bar, with the great and the good of the profession rattling their cages and crying foul, but with the government as the monopoly provider, they were voices crying in the wilderness.

Fred had returned from Torremolinas, looking like an overcooked lobster, and with the reins of power firmly back in his grasp, Mike returned to what he did best, a hive of activity and little to show for it. Paul was Paul, as predictable as summer rain, grunting away and waiting interminably for a shot at the big time. In that regard, he and Toby were kindred spirits.

Peter Rolls, of Rolls Royce & Co, Solicitors to the Gentry and anybody else with cash up front, had briefed chambers over the years with a variety of work, some civil, some matrimonial, and occasionally, very occasionally, crime. Peter didn't want his firm associated with the riff raff, and the criminal elements were usually moved on as quickly as possible, for an introduction fee of course, to the likes of Del and that lot. After all, Peter hadn't spent his early years in practice, searching the length and breadth of the land for a partner with the name Royce, for no good reason. Rolls Royce by name, and Rolls Royce by reputation, that was his motto, and although Gerald Royce lacked Peter's dynamism and his great vision, he was competent enough without being spectacular. He left that to Peter.

Their offices were just north of Cambridge Circus in Charing Cross Road, a stone's throw away from Shaftesbury Avenue and luvvieland. They picked up some contract work when the luvvies fell out of luv and started bickering, as well as the occasional breach of copyright, and personal injury, when one of the luvvies fell down an open trap door. That would have been right up Gazzard's street, were he still practising; House of Lords, here we come! The firm also specialised in Wills, Gerald Royce's department, advising luvvies who wanted to give their wealth, or lack of it, to some obscure dogs' home or retired donkeys' sanctuary. It was all too divine, my dear.

Larry King provided entertainment of another sort, far removed from the smell of the greasepaint and the roar of the crowd, in his outlet in Meard Street in the heart of Soho. Larry catered for the grubby raincoat variety of life, something for every taste and prurient pleasure in his video shop, fetchingly named King's Video Shop. A lot of thought went into choosing that name.

When Larry wandered in off the street one afternoon, Peter Rolls's first reaction was to show him the door. But Larry was a cash buyer, bundles of it in his hot, sweaty fist, so against his better judgment, Peter took him in.

When Peter contacted Chambers, it was Mike who recommended Toby, perhaps still wary of his 007 label and his close encounter with the CIS, and besides, with Rolls Royce & Co not wishing to be publicly associated with crime, and definitely not this sort of crime, Peter wanted to keep it low profile. Poor Toby, forever destined to be low profile.

The brief was duly delivered to chambers, and it made for interesting reading. Larry's shop had been raided by the boys from the Obscene Publications Unit at Scotland Yard, following an anonymous tip off from a killjoy calling himself 'Deep Throat'. Quite what he was doing in Larry's shop in the first place was never explained, perhaps the video jammed just as it was reaching its climax, and the anonymous punter had been denied a refund. Larry had four invariable rules. No kids, no animals, no cheques, and no refunds, a simple and effective business policy, with no exceptions.

During the raid, over three hundred videos and DVDs had been seized, and Larry was arrested and charged with publishing obscene articles for gain. The prosecution had chosen five videos as a representative sample, ranging in their titles from Babes in the Wood, What the Butler Sore, and Nymphs and Shepherds come again and again, through to Life on the Ocean Rave with Captain Horny Blow Job and Erection Night Special, presented by David Dimpleby. Surely not?

Larry King's video shop had everything the lusting heart desired, and more. On public display in the main shop were magazines of every size and description, in full colour and leaving nothing to the imagination. After a period of idle browsing, the favoured few, about two thousand at the last count, were admitted to the inner sanctum, the Holy Grail, where, for a modest subscription, explicit videos were available, for purchase or hire, to suit every perversion. Viewing booths were set aside for previews, maximum two minutes, with a maximum of five videos per session, after which, the selections were made and carried from the shop in a plain, brown paper bag. It was all very discreet.

Peter Rolls arrived early for the conference, and without Larry, who was left to make his own way to Chambers. Peter may be willing to represent him, but he was certainly not going to be seen with him. Rolls looked like a cross between John Gielgud and Noël Coward, a felt trilby hat with an enormous brim, a startling lemon yellow suit with pink shirt and matching socks, suede shoes, and a silk scarf knotted lightly around his neck, which fluttered provocatively in the breeze as he walked, and every movement accompanied by extravagant theatrical gestures.

Peter sat down, crossed his legs in an extravagant, theatrical gesture and engaged Toby with a troubled expression. "Now, Mr. Potts," he began, "I've brought the offending articles with me for your perusal," and, dipping into his briefcase, he removed the five videos with all the care of a surgeon removing a malignant growth. "You'll need to view them in due course, you poor lamb," he continued.

"I suppose you've watched them already, Mr. Rolls?" Toby asked.

"Absolutely not, young man! What do you take me for?!" A competent solicitor preparing his client's defence might be a good starting point, thought Toby, but he wasn't about to make an issue of it. "I mean, it's all too, too, distressing. I wonder if I've done the right thing, after all, this is not the sort of work Rolls Royce cares to be associated with," and he threw back his head in another extravagant theatrical gesture.

"I'm sure Mr. King is in excellent hands, Mr. Rolls," replied Toby, anxious to ingratiate himself.

"I have no doubt of that. We are not called Rolls Royce for nothing, you know."

"Absolutely."

"Now, I have here a transcript of each video, lovingly prepared by the prosecution," he continued, dipping back into the briefcase and removing a large bundle of papers. "I have skim-read some of them, and I have to warn you, Mr. Potts, they are filthy, yes, there's no shying away from the word, filthy!" he added for emphasis, and back went the head again. "Absolutely disgusting!"

"Well," said Toby, trying to put a positive gloss on the matter before Larry King's arrival, "I suppose beauty is in the eye of the beholder, and each man to his own."

"Very droll, I'm sure, but I beg to differ…"

Just as Rolls was about to launch into a diatribe on the concept of absolute morality, Paul knocked and entered. "Mr. King has arrived," he grunted, "shall I show him in?"

Toby looked enquiringly at Rolls. "Shall we get under way, Mr. Rolls?"

"I suppose so," he sniffed, "the sooner we start, the sooner we can get this whole unfortunate business behind us." Not quite how Toby would have put it.

Larry King was a showman of sorts, but not in Peter's class. A short, fat man, almost round, with thinning hair combed across his head to hide his balding pate and meeting in a small widow's peak somewhere off centre. He sported a loud, multi-coloured waistcoat with gold buttons, and his remarkably small feet were encased in black, patent leather shoes, with gold buckles. A jovial man with a moist handshake, he acknowledged Rolls and sat down.

"This is Mr. Potts, Larry, your barrister," said Rolls, making the introductions.

"A pleasure, Squire." Larry paused. "You're very young, are you sure you're up for it?" Again, not quite how Toby would have put it.

"I haven't had any complaints so far," Toby lied, "but if, after the conference, you have any doubts about my ability to represent you, please say so."

262

"I will, Squire, I will. After all, Pete," he turned to Rolls, "this is my livelihood we're talking about here."

Peter Rolls winced. To address him by his Christian name was a privilege for the favoured few, but to address him as 'Pete' was unforgivable. What an absolutely ghastly little man.

"I fully understand, Mr. King," said Toby. Hardly a vote of confidence, so it was time to impress with his grasp of the law. "Now," Toby continued, "turning to the allegations, you're charged with offences under the Obscene Publications Act…"

"I know that."

"Yes, of course." This was not going well, time to assert himself, "but I need to know you understand all the relevant implications, so if you'll bear with me?"

"Fair enough, you're the boss." That's better.

"Now the prosecution have to prove that you had these videos to sell or rent for gain," Toby looked up, "I don't suppose they'll have any difficulty there, and secondly, they have to prove that the videos tend to deprave or corrupt persons who watch them. Presumably, you say they don't?"

"I haven't a clue, Squire," replied Larry, somewhat disarmingly, "you don't think I watch this crap, do you? I mean, it's complete garbage but I provide a sort of social service, for all the inadequates out there, and what they do in the privacy of their own attic is up to them. I should add," and he did, "I have a lot of self-satisfied customers."

"With the obvious exception of one," Toby quipped, "otherwise known as Deep Throat."

"Yeah, slimy bastard, spoiling everybody's fun. If I get my hands on him…"

"Now," Toby hurried on, "I think we might watch excerpts from the videos, to get a flavour of what we're up against, if you'll forgive the pun." Larry did, as he hadn't spotted it. "According to the transcripts, each video runs for approximately sixty minutes, so if we were to watch them all from beginning to end, it might be emotionally draining for all of us."

"Amen to that," said Rolls, already feeling faint.

"Fair enough, Squire, you're the boss."

Word that the videos were to be played spread like wildfire to the clerks' room, and Toby lost count of the number of cups of tea and plates full of digestive biscuits brought into the conference room over the next hour, service over and above the call of duty.

They started with Babes in the Wood, which, according to the transcript, was a tale of four lesbians and a dildo romping in the wood. There was very little plot, in fact, there was no plot at all. As soon as the girls reached the woodland glade, they got their kit off in record time, and set about enjoying each other's company. The dildo was passed around like a joint of cannabis, and much fun, accompanied by moaning and groaning and lots of passionate embraces, was had by all.

Toby, no prude he, was amazed by the sheer size of them all. "Do you think they're digitally enhanced?" he asked, in between mouthfuls of tea and digestive biscuits.

Peter Rolls spent most of the time, feigning utter disgust, throwing his head back theatrically, whilst keeping his eye on the action. Such a dutiful solicitor.

Captain Horny Blow Job was one more for the boys, with Seaman Stains and Roger the Cabin Boy performing unnatural acts to the accompaniment of jolly nautical ditties. But the *piéce de resistance* was undoubtedly Erection Night Special. Toby considered himself reasonably broad minded, but this explored the very limits of human proclivity and beyond. His eyes began to water, Peter Rolls was uncharacteristically silent, and even Larry let out a low whistle, as yet another tray of tea and biscuits came winging, unannounced, into the room.

"Well," said Toby, as the curtain came down and the lights went up, "that's the knob, I mean the nub, of it, Mr. King." He paused. "I don't believe we can avail ourselves of the statutory defence, so we'll have to go with deprave and corrupt. We say they don't, the prosecution say they do, and it's for the jury to decide."

"Yeah." Larry was deep in thought, or so it appeared. "So what's this statutory defence?" he asked at last.

"As I say, I don't believe it's available, unless we've missed something in all the excitement, but," and Toby opened Archbold at the relevant section and began to read, "if we can show that the videos are for the public good on the ground that they are in the interests of drama, opera, ballet or any other art, or of literature or learning, the person publishing the articles for gain, that being your good self, shall not be convicted."

"So why not?" Larry was excited. "I mean, there's drama aplenty, will he stick it to her or won't he? And in Babes in the Wood, the girls are up on their toes from time to time, great little movers, if you want my opinion," Toby didn't, "then you've got opera, well, in Life on the Ocean Rave, there's singing of sorts, all those sea shanties, as they shag to the sound of music, and as for Erection Night Special, that's got to be educational. Am I right, Pete, or am I right?"

Pete was having a fit of the vapours, and well out of it, as he dabbed his forehead with an enormous silk handkerchief.

"It's an interesting argument, Mr. King," said Toby, not wishing to crush him, "let me think about it, and I suggest we discuss it again nearer the time."

The trial was listed at Middlesex Crown Court, a fitting venue for such a case. The court was built at about the same time as the Houses of Parliament, in whose shadow it now reposed, and as such, retained all the grace and charm of Victorian High Gothic. The judge was His

Honour George 'The Glums' Clutterbuck, so named because of his perpetual morose mood and gloomy expression. The prosecutor, Bernie Bernstein, was home grown, a CPS Higher Courts Advocate, self-selected on the basis that not even he could cock it up, if you'll forgive the expression. All he had to do was press the start button on the video recorder, sit back and enjoy himself, then stand up and tell the jury that the videos are filthy, disgusting, tending to deprave and corrupt, and sit back down again. Not even he could get that wrong, and besides, he'd written it down, word for word, and rehearsed it several times in front of the bathroom mirror.

Peter Rolls, determined to distance himself from the sordid mess, had instructed an agent who, in turn, had delegated Bootsy Farmer to come and sit behind Toby. It was just like old times, which Toby had tried to forget. No question of copping a plea on this one, Bootsy was well up for it, and raring to go.

With Larry firmly planted in the dock, the judge addressed counsel's bench, where, to Toby's surprise, Bernie had taken up residence. Shouldn't he be sitting one row behind, reserved for solicitors and other lesser mortals? The cheek of the man.

"Gentlemen," he droned, "I propose asking the jury panel if they feel able to discharge their duty, especially the ladies, in this distasteful matter. I had a similar case recently where three lady members of the jury asked to stand down half way through the first video, for obvious reasons. These cases can be very distressing, the more so for those of a delicate disposition."

Enquiries were made, and eventually eight robust blokes and four women, game for anything, were selected. The videos were played, with appropriate breaks in between for all parties to compose themselves. Then it was Toby's turn to open the defence.

"I am going to ask your Honour to take a view," he began pompously.

"I thought that's what I'd been doing for the past five hours, Mr. Potts." It was not intended to be funny.

"I'm sorry, your Honour, that's not what I meant. I invite your Honour to turn to Chapter thirty one, paragraph sixty three, in the current edition of Archbold." Toby waited whilst the Glums found the page. "I submit that these videos, taken as a whole, are not such as to tend to deprave and corrupt persons who see them."

"But isn't that a matter for the jury?"

"I submit that your Honour is a person…"

"That is not an assumption you should make lightly, Mr. Potts." That, too, was not intended to be funny. "I take the view that the persons referred to in the section are represented by the twelve members of the jury, and it is for them to decide. Now if we were discussing a film like Polyanna," his all-time favourite, and he always cried at the end, "then your submission would have obvious merit, but that is not the case here. Let's hear what Mr. Bernstein has to say."

Bernie got to his feet, a mounting sense of panic seizing him. This wasn't in the script, so he hadn't rehearsed it. "Er…Um…Er, your Honour…."

"Yes, thank you, Mr. Bernstein. I am afraid I am against you, Mr. Potts. Now shall we get on?"

Toby was down, but not out. "Before we do so, your Honour, may I enquire if you propose leaving the statutory defence to the jury, in any event?"

The Glums was taken aback. "How so, Mr. Potts?"

"Well," Toby continued, doing his best to humour Larry, " the Babes in the Wood had a certain balletic quality, I'm sure you agree…"

"What?! Are you referring to the four maidens prancing around in the buff and waving a long, cylindrical, rubber object about the place?"

"That was obviously a stage prop, your Honour, to enhance the action…"

"It certainly did that, Mr. Potts, but what do you say about Life on the Ocean Rave? Where is the defence there?"

"Opera, your Honour," replied Toby, keeping a straight face, "and I refer to the excellent and melodic singing in a nautical vein running like a golden thread throughout the video."

"As far as I could make out, Mr. Potts, the excellent and melodic singing in a nautical vein, as you describe it, began with the lyrics:

"T'was on the good ship Venus,
By George, you should have seen us,
The figurehead was a whore in bed,
And the mast a rampant penis."

"Any further submissions, Mr. Potts?"

"Finally, your Honour, Erection Night Special, I suggest, has a strong, educational quality to it."

"It was certainly an eye opener, Mr. Potts, but its educational merits are highly dubious. However, in fairness to the defendant, and in the light of Article 10 of the European Convention on Human Rights being engaged by section 2(1) of the 1959 Act, I shall direct the jury on the statutory defence, and leave it to them to decide."

Damn, thought Toby, had he missed a trick? Too late to bone it up now.

The jury were out for most of the next day, and at three o'clock, sent a note to the judge. The Glums read it out: "We are hopelessly divided eight to four, and no chance of reaching a verdict. Can we go home?"

He addressed counsel's bench. "I have no option but to discharge the jury from returning a verdict. Mr. Bernstein, I take the view there is no point having a retrial; it's a waste of public time and money. Whilst the videos are undeniably explicit, I've seen much worse in my time, in my professional capacity, of course," he added, almost too quickly. "I doubt if any jury, properly directed, would consider them tending to deprave and corrupt. Mr. King, stand up. I am entering verdicts of not guilty on each charge, and you are free to go. The five videos and the remainder seized by the police will be returned to you. Good Day."

"I'm well pleased with the result, Squire," said Larry outside court, pumping Toby's hand warmly, "and I loved all that crap about ballet and opera. I must remember that for future reference. Now, to show my appreciation," for a moment, Toby was half hoping for a wodge of sweaty money, to help with the wedding and all that, "I'm going to give you the five videos as a present. Watch them at your leisure, and think of me affectionately."

Toby was underwhelmed, and speechless, and thinking of Larry affectionately was the last thing on his mind. Once Larry had waddled off, Bootsy, ever attentive, volunteered to take charge of the offending articles, and was last seen hurrying home.

Larry's business went on as usual, and to his delight, eight new members signed up in very short order. They looked vaguely familiar, but where had he seen them before?

CHAPTER TWENTY

TOBY MEETS SANTA

So nigh is grandeur to our dust,
So near is God to man,
When duty whispers low, Thou must,
The youth replies, I can.

[Ralph Waldo Emerson]

It was that time of the year again, and how quickly it comes around. In fact, said Toby's mother, who had a knack of stating the obvious, it seems to come earlier and earlier each year, and this year in particular, with the wedding plans still in their infancy, it was most inconvenient.

It was early November, and the stores were already decked out in tinsel, with fairy lights, greeting cards, artificial trees, and presents to suit all the family, with nothing to pay for six months. It was Christmas, or so screamed Noddy whatsisname from that pop group back in the sixties, with the nation's yuletide favourite belting out from every retail outlet in the country. Another year of the great British public gearing themselves up, once more, to the dubious delights of over-indulgence in the name of our Saviour Jesus Christ. Who?

Toby's in-tray was not exactly groaning with work, and little on the horizon to meet the extra expenses of the festive season. Larry King's wodge of sweaty money never found its way into his back pocket, as Peter Rolls took the view that Toby's time and effort would be more than adequately compensated by Legal Aid. How wrong could he be!

It was a hard and unrewarding slog, as he travelled the length and breadth of the metropolis in search of an honest crust. Relaxing weekends were spent with Susie, at home in Prestwood, enjoying each other's company and keeping out of the way of the parents as much as possible.

Just as Toby was resigning himself to ending the term with a whimper, the case of George Albert Spencer unexpectedly landed on his desk. It was a moment of great excitement, not least because the brief was addressed to Toby in his name, with no also-rans to muddy the waters. His instructing solicitor was Duncan Campbell of Maltravers & Co, another one man band, who'd been in court at Middlesex during Toby's submissions on the artistic merits of Larry's videos, and was singularly impressed for all the wrong reasons. Whatever else, he'd liked Toby's style and delivery, the name stuck, and the rest, as they say, is history.

George Albert Spencer's whole life revolved around Christmas. In short, it was his reason for living. During eight memorable weeks of the year, George was Santa Claus personified, as he took on the look and persona of the ubiquitous fictional character. The remaining forty-four weeks were simply a precursor to the big event, a time to put his house in order, to get the elves motivated, the workshops in the North Pole igloo-shape and ready to roll, and Donner and Blitzen and Rudolf and the other reindeer fed and watered and ready for a hard day's night.

During those forty four weeks, he jealously guarded his weight to just the right Ho! Ho! Ho! proportions, his Santa suit was kept in mothballs and a protective covering, lovingly taken out each week to be brushed and aired, and his beard kept long and bushy and white and as clean as possible under sometimes difficult circumstances. Bread and soup, kindly supplied by the Salvation Army, were his particular bugbears in that department, and once, awakening from a deep sleep on a park bench one warm Spring day, he found a mating pair of wrens nesting in his luxuriant growth.

But these were no more than distractions, which he tolerated with good humour, until on the twenty third of October each year, he reported for duty at Racey's department store on Regent Street, ready to bounce little children on his knee, under the watchful eye of Santa's beefy helper, otherwise known as Mel from the store security, and to weave his magic for the endless queues of snot gobbling kids who pulled his

beard, poked his stomach, made indelicate remarks about his breath
and the all-pervading smell of mothballs, and asked for ludicrously
expensive presents such as PlayStations, DVD players, computers and
season tickets to watch Chelsea beat all comers. George went Ho! Ho!
Ho! at each and every request, and promised to do his best if they'd
been good children. That was the ultimate cop out, and with Santa
safely back in the North Pole for a well-earned rest, there was no come
back.

It was a cold, wet, November night, and a few minutes to ten, and Sam
Wellard was about to close his corner shop, when in walked Santa
Claus. Without hesitating, Santa walked straight up to Sam behind the
counter, and pointing to a large protuberance bulging inside his trouser
pocket, growled: "This isn't a joke, I've got a gun, so empty the till,
now!"

Sam was having none of it. He'd spent the whole of the day working
his butt off, and he wasn't about to hand over the fruits of his labours
to some beery Bozo from Neverland. Reaching under the counter, he
produced a baseball bat, special offer £9.99, and swung it, catching
Santa a glancing blow on the forearm. This was not in the script, so
Santa, taking fright, scampered off empty handed, down the street and
around the corner. Sam immediately called the police and set off in
pursuit.

As luck would have it, there was a patrol car in the immediate vicinity,
and Santa was soon spotted nearby, running at a lively pace for such a
big man. One of the officers gave chase, felled Santa with a rugby
tackle, and arrested him. Sam arrived a minute or so later, and
immediately identified George Albert Spencer as the man who'd tried
to rob him. After caution, Santa replied: "Ho! Ho! Ho!"

When interviewed by DC. 'Five' Watts, so called because he was
incredibly dim, George denied any involvement, claiming it was a case
of mistaken identity, and besides, he was the real Santa, and Santa
didn't behave like a common criminal. To prove his point, George
offered to bounce DC. Watts on his knee, an offer the constable
declined. As far as Watts was concerned, Santa was a sandwich short
of a picnic.

272

"So you're saying you're the real Santa Claus?" asked the sceptical DC. Watts.

"I most certainly am," replied George.

"That's a lie. Everybody knows it's Richard Attenborough, and he lives on Thirty Fourth Street in New York." DC. Watts, besides being incredibly dim, was also an impressionable lad.

"An impostor!" trumpeted George, "and a charlatan!"

"Alright then, if you're the real Santa, ask me what I want for Christmas, and if I get it, I'll personally apologise."

"Ok, so what do you want for Christmas?"

"Something about five foot four, big up front, playful and easy over will do nicely."

"That's disgusting!" retorted George.

"If you think that's disgusting, mate, just wait till I unwrap her," replied Watts, leering.

"And are you going to be a good boy?" asked Santa.

"Course not, that'd spoil the fun."

George was charged with attempted robbery and remanded in custody, to await his trial at the Old Bailey.

Toby and Duncan Campbell went to see George in conference, and in spite of his predicament, he was in remarkably good spirits. They found a man in his middle fifties and surprisingly cultivated for somebody in his straightened circumstances.

"So, Mr. Potts," said George after the introductions, "you are to defend me. You look very young, if I may say so," he added.

"It has been said before, Mr. Spencer, " replied Toby somewhat wearily, "but Alexander the Great conquered most of Asia Minor before his eighteenth birthday, so youth is not necessarily an obstacle to success."

"Well said, Mr. Potts," George laughed heartily. "I feel we shall get on splendidly."

"Thank you for the vote of confidence, which I hope isn't misplaced. Needless to say," Toby continued, "the circumstantial evidence is quite strong, so I cannot guarantee an acquittal. Let's consider the case against you together." Toby flicked through his notes. "You were arrested, only minutes after the attempted robbery, running away from the shop…"

"Pause there, if you will, Mr. Potts," George interrupted, "I was not running away from the shop, rather I was running towards a Number Nine bus, which was about to pull away from the bus stop. That would have taken me to the Salvation Army Hostel in Bermondsey where I was staying at the time. Such kind people," he added reflectively.

"Not exactly five star de luxe," quipped Campbell, smirking.

"May I remind you, Mr. Campbell," George chided, "that Jesus Christ was born in a stable." Campbell, duly chastened, shut up.

Toby continued with his review of the evidence. "Next we have the large salami found in your trouser pocket when you were arrested, which the police say was an imitation firearm."

"Quite so, Mr. Potts, and positively ridiculous. I had bought it that very night, to leaven the bread when I returned to the Hostel and the banquet awaiting me."

"And finally, a mark on your right forearm, which the police say was caused by a blow from the baseball bat."

"I was rugby tackled to the ground, Mr. Potts. That was not my only injury, you know."

274

Toby didn't, and made a note to examine the doctor's attendance record whilst George was in police custody.

"That's very helpful, Mr. Spencer," said Toby, "and Mr. Campbell and I will follow up the matters you've raised. Now, looking ahead, I doubt very much if your trial will be listed before the New Year. There's a considerable backlog of cases at the Bailey waiting to be tried, and we must take our turn."

"Fear not, Mr. Potts," George replied, "I am confident I shall be tried before Christmas, and in your young but capable hands, I shall be acquitted. After all, I am innocent. Thereafter, I have pressing business to attend to, with not a moment to lose."

"Barking mad, if you ask me," muttered Campbell on the way out.

"Possibly," replied Toby, "but they said that about Jesus Christ when he claimed to be the Son of God, and who are we, mere mortals, to unfold the mysteries of the Almighty?" There was no answer to that.

To Toby's amazement, Spencer's trial, as he had foretold, was listed at short notice in the last week of sitting before the Christmas recess. A window of opportunity had appeared following the collapse of a terrorist trial, when one of the defendants had slipped through the net, travelled unchallenged on false documents through Dover and Calais, courtesy of Eurostar, and was last seen heading for ports of call east of Suez. It was late on Friday evening when Mike informed Toby of the Monday listing, guaranteeing a stomach-churning weekend as Toby went over the case line by line, rehearsing each and every point, covering every angle.

Monday morning dawned grey and bleak, the pavements washed with rain, and a cold, biting wind, as Toby walked the short distance from Chambers to the Bailey. As he robed, he espied a familiar face, grinning inanely at him across the room.

"Hello, Tony," whined Lionel Berger, his former pupil master, "what brings you here?"

"It's Toby actually, Leonard," replied Toby, giving him a wintry smile, "and I'm here to represent George Spencer."

"Are you, by Jove? Then we have the pleasure of doing business together, as I prosecute. It's going to be interesting, to see if the pupil can teach his master a few tricks."

"Quite so, and I shall listen in awe as you open the case and call your evidence, whilst the jury and I will remain ever vigilant."

Berger smiled. "Well put, I can see I'm in for a rough ride," he added flippantly. "We're before Mr. Justice Boniface, you probably don't know him," he continued, trying to faze Toby, "but I know him well of old. Off the Bench we're good friends, but on the Bench, he shows no favouritism, and rightly so. Firm but fair, they say, so don't let him intimidate you. You'll need to be at your sharpest if you're to get anywhere with him. Open and shut case, but you don't need me to tell you that."

"Ah, yes, old Sourpuss," replied Toby. "My first case with you in pupillage, when you prosecuted Sir Adrian Browne. I remember it as if it were yesterday."

Berger's inane grin vanished in a trice. "See you in court," he whined, before trotting off. First blood to Toby, and a moment to savour.

It was all frighteningly déja vu, Berger locking antlers with Sourpuss all over again, and Toby thrown in at the deep end. It was as if everything he'd done before had been a rehearsal for this defining moment in his career. It was to be Toby's ultimate trial of strength, but was it to be his ***tour de force*** or his ***tour de farce***? Suddenly he felt desperately inadequate for the task that lay ahead. Steadying himself, he determined to see it through.

Promptly at ten thirty, Court One assembled, as Boniface sloped into court and slumped down in the judicial throne, glaring at one and all, and decidedly irritated at the thought of trying an attempted robbery with a salami. This was not why High Court Judges were appointed, and the blithering idiot responsible should be strung up. Did he have the power to so order, he wondered, or had the law changed? Parliament in its wisdom set too heady a pace for the Honourable Mr. Justice Boniface. Just when he'd mastered some new piece of legislation, along came another to trouble him and interfere with a good round of golf, or gofe, as he preferred to call it. The whole game had gone to the dogs, with absolutely ghastly commercial traveller Johnnies clogging the course and braying like asses in the clubhouse. And the clothes they wore, tartan bobble caps with matching tartan trews, and absurd, furry like creatures in brushed nylon, covering their woods, it was an utter disgrace, not to mention their vulgar BMW sports coupés with simulated leather and wrap around stereo systems. A damned good thrashing was too good for them.

The court clerk rose. "Are you George Albert Spencer?" he asked in a spirit of enquiry.

The defendant rose. "I prefer to be known as Santa Claus, as that is my real name," replied Santa.

"Your preferences are of no interest to this court," snapped Sourpuss, setting the mood, "so unless and until the contrary is proved, you shall be known as George Albert Spencer, and," he added menacingly, "if you know what's good for you, I advise you to proceed on that basis. Do I make myself clear?"

"Crystal clear, my lord," Santa smiled back soothingly. For the love of God, George, muttered Toby to himself, don't offer to bounce him on your knee, and don't ask him what he wants for Christmas.

"Mr. Potts," Toby shot to his feet, "are you satisfied that the defendant is fit to plead and stand trial?"

"Absolutely, my lord."

"Then let him be arraigned."

George duly pleaded not guilty, and sat back down.

"Now," continued Sourpuss, in much the same vein, "who prosecutes?"

Berger rose to his feet. "I do, my lord."

"Mr…er…McDonald," Sourpuss, failing to recognise his good friend, glanced down at the slip of paper in front of him, "are you ready to proceed?"

"Berger, my lord," bleated Berger.

"Moderate your language, Mr. McDonald, or I shall hold you in contempt." An unfortunate turn of phrase. "Kindly remember you're in a court of law, and what's more, **my** court of law!"

"No, no," Berger added hastily, "your lordship misunderstands me. My name is Berger, Lionel Berger, and I prosecute."

"Then why does it plainly say McDonald here on the slip of paper handed to me by the usher? It reads Mr. L. McDonald for the prosecution, and Mr. T. Potts for the defence." Sourpuss allowed himself a little chuckle. "I suspect you've been the butt of a few jokes about that over the years, Mr. Potts," he chortled.

"I think I can explain the misunderstanding, my lord," whined Berger. "The usher, surprisingly, did not immediately recognise me, despite the fact that I am routinely instructed for the prosecution at this court," Berger allowed his chest to swell with his own sense of self-importance, "so when he asked my name, I told him it was Berger, as in McDonald's. They're a fast food outlet selling burgers," he added helpfully.

"I'm aware of that, Mr. Burger. After all, I do have grandchildren." This statement was greeted with an audible gasp of disbelief. "In future," Sourpuss continued, "best to leave the funnies to me." He scribbled heavily on the slip. "I am now writing B..U..R..G..E..R." Ham was about to say something, but thought better of it. "In future, it would help all of us if you provided your correct details." He turned to the long-suffering usher. "Empanel the jury, we've wasted enough time as it is."

Toby couldn't help himself, as he stifled a smirk at Berger's expense. Berger noticed, and was not amused.

It took a good ten minutes for the jury panel to file into court and sit at the back, waiting to be called.

The court clerk rose. "Let the defendant be upstanding." George duly obliged. "Prisoner at the Bar, the names I am about to call are the names of the jury who will try you. If you object to them, or any one of them, you should make your objection known before they come to the Book to be sworn, and your objection shall be heard." The clerk then turned to the jury panel. "Members of the Jury in waiting, answer to your name as it is called, and take your seat in the jury box as directed by the usher."

Damn, Toby kicked himself, he'd forgotten to tell Santa about his right of challenge. He rose swiftly from his seat, bowed to Sourpuss, and made his way hurriedly to the back of the court and the dock.

Sourpuss, predictably, was not amused. "What on earth are you doing, Mr. Potts? Leaving us already?"

"I'm sorry, my lord, but I omitted to advise the defendant on his right of challenge."

"Really, this is intolerable. Do get on, and let's have no further interruptions."

Now it was Berger's turn to smirk at Toby's discomfort.

Santa leant over the medieval spiked surround of the dock as Toby approached. "Calm down, Mr. Potts," he said soothingly, "his bark is worse than his bite. Underneath the gruff exterior is a pussycat."

"I wish I could agree, Mr. Spencer," he couldn't, "but this isn't the time for pleasantries. Now, if you recognise any juror who is called to try you, for whatever reason, let me know before he takes the oath. Is that clear?"

"Crystal," replied Santa.

Toby made his way back to Counsel's bench, bowed and sat down as the court clerk rose and called out the names of twelve jurors. They were a mixed bunch. From their appearance and demeanour, four were clearly from Middle England, Telegraph readers and pillars of their community. As arbiters of law and order, they would lean towards the prosecution. The next four looked as if they'd wandered in from the day job, greasing nipples and clogging up the M4 with forty-four ton juggernauts, honest horny-handed sons of toil, wishing they were somewhere else and likely to go with the defence. Finally, four floating voters, an open-toed libero-pinko with a pony tail and a corduroy jacket, an earth mother with a dress made from recycled waste, a young and attractive polytechnic student with an earnest expression and spectacles with varifocal lenses, and a transvestite who could swing either way. He, or she, sporting a two day stubble, looked particularly fetching in a two-piece outfit with matching handbag and accessories.

It was Toby's task, on instructions, to challenge three of the jurors. Had they ever visited Racey's department store during the Christmas season, and if so, had they ever bounced on Santa's knee? Santa thought they looked familiar. Each challenge was met with a flat denial. Santa may be able to swing the lead in Neverland, but at the Old Bailey, he was good old George Albert Spencer.

Once empanelled, the jury settled down to listen to Berger's opening.

"Mem' jury," he began, as if addressing the wife of some Middle Eastern potentate, "I appear on behalf of the prosecution, and my learned friend Mr. T. Potts appears for the defence," the penny having finally dropped, Berger thought he'd break the habit of a life time and try to be witty. Wrong move.

"I'll do the funnies in my court, thank you, Mr. Berger," snapped Sourpuss, singularly unamused, "now do get on."

280

Berger, duly chastened, did as he was told, and whined on about the strength of the case against the accused, adding, as an aside, that the prosecution must prove the case, but in all the circumstances, it was a mere formality. He then called his first witness.

Sam Wellard took the oath, and promptly sat down. As somebody who spent the whole of his working life on his feet, it was a welcome relief. But Sourpuss was not in the business of bringing relief to those who came before him, and he scowled down.

"Do you suffer from an infirmity, Mr…er…Wellard?" he asked testily. Sam, not immediately conversant with the word, stared back, grinning foolishly. "You're sitting down, Mr. Wellard, so I ask again, do you have an infirmity?"

Time for Berger to intervene. "It's usual for witnesses to give their evidence standing up, Mr. Wellard, so his lordship is wondering why you're sitting down?" he whined.

"Well," said Sam, not one to mince his words, "there's a chair right be'ind me, plain for all to see, mate, so if you don't want me to sit down, what's it doing 'ere?"

"Why are you calling Mr. Berger 'mate', Mr. Wellard? Do you know him?"

Sam peered long and hard at Berger, obviously thinking this had something to do with the evidence he was about to give, perhaps a sort of courtroom identification, so he took his time, much to Sourpuss's irritation.

"Well, Mr. Wellard, do you know Mr. Berger or not?"

"Face looks familiar, mate, but the man I remember was taller…"

"This is intolerable, and I am certainly not your mate, and never likely to be. You will address me as 'my lord' or 'your lordship', and when answering questions from Mr. Berger, best say nothing at all. Now let's get on."

"Are you Samuel Frederick Wellard?" Berger began uncontroversially. Silence. "Please answer the question."

"I'm sorry, mate," replied Sam, "but my lordship told me to say nothing to you."

Sourpuss threw down his pen. "That's not what I meant at all. Are you deliberately trying to obfuscate the issue, Mr. Wellard?"

Sam couldn't remember the last time he tried to obfuscate anything, and was beginning to feel hard done by. Here he was, as a public minded citizen, doing his bit for law and order, and all he was getting was verbal flak from some overdressed old codger wearing a ridiculous ill-fitting toupée who couldn't even speak the Queen's English, what with infirmity this and obf***ing that and the like. He had half a mind to jack it in and go back to the shop for some peace and quiet. And besides, he'd left his missus in charge, wrestling with the complexities of the new electronic till he'd installed for the Christmas rush, and who was going to cook his dinner?

Sourpuss, determined to move things forward, decided on a different tack. "Let me see if I can help, Mr. Wellard," he said through gritted teeth, "I hope we can all agree your name is Samuel Frederick Wellard, agreed?"

"Yeah, my lordship."

"Good," progress at last, "and you are here to tell us that on the thirteenth of November last, a man dressed as Santa Claus tried to rob your shop, that's right, isn't it?"

"Yeah, my lordship, got it in one."

Toby, alarmed at the way things were going, felt he should say something, so taking his courage in both hands, rose from his seat. "My lord, I am somewhat concerned that your lordship is leading the witness."

"Somebody has to lead the witness, Mr. Potts, otherwise we shall be here until the New Year. Correct me if I am wrong," he continued icily, "but the defence here is one of mistaken identity?"

"That is correct, my lord…"

"Good, then resume your seat, and let's have no further unnecessary interruptions. Now, Mr. Wellard, in your own time and words, tell the jury what happened."

At last, English that Sam could understand, and he was off like a long dog. With any luck, he'd be back at the shop by twelve. A vain hope, as it transpired.

"Not so fast, Mr. Wellard," snapped Sourpuss, "I have to take a careful note of what you're saying."

Sam, aware the proceedings were being tape-recorded, was about to say something, but thought better of it, as he waited for the judge to catch up. At a snail's pace, Sourpuss and Berger, when he could get a word in edgeways, took Sam through the events of that night. Then it came to the concealed weapon.

"I'm going to show you an exhibit, Mr. Wellard…"

Toby was up on his feet in a flash. "I object, my lord. That would be leading the witness."

Sourpuss agreed. "You must first lay the ground, Mr. Berger, as well you should know."

Berger grinned inanely. "Can you describe the protuberance in the man's pocket?"

"Yer what?" asked Sam.

Sourpuss took over. "You saw something sticking out from inside his pocket. Can you describe it?"

"Oh, right, I follow. There was something sticking out from inside his pocket. He said it was a gun."

"And what was it?" asked Berger.

"How do I know? He never took it out. It could've been a gun, or his finger, or Santa's big dick for all I know."

"Or a salami!" trumpeted Berger.

Toby was back on his feet.

"Point taken, Mr. Potts," said Sourpuss, glaring at Berger. "Mr. Berger, that is a wholly improper suggestion, assuming it is your intention to invite the witness to compare a salami with Santa's big dick, and I shall direct the jury to disregard it."

After a few more questions, it was Toby's turn to cross-examine.

"Mr. Wellard," he began soothingly, "you run a busy corner shop selling a variety of goods, assisted only by your good lady wife, is that correct?"

Before Sam could reply, Sourpuss intervened. "Really, Mr. Potts, you must adopt the basic principles of cross-examination in my court, assuming of course, that you are familiar with them," he added acidly. "You have just put three questions to the witness. Which one do you wish him to answer first?"

Oh dear, thought Toby, public humiliation, and so soon. Silly old fool, but he must play the game by the rules. "I'm sorry, my lord," he turned to Sam, "you run a corner shop, is that correct?"

"Yeah, mate." Sourpuss glared, and was about to say something.

"My lord, I have no objection to Mr. Wellard calling me 'mate', if that puts him at his ease. After all, it can be quite an ordeal giving evidence in your lordship's court."

"Yeah, too right, mate," agreed Sam, "good on yer."

It was an inspired move by Toby, as he now had Sam on his side, and hopefully, Sourpuss back in his box.

"And at this time of year, when the attempted robbery took place, the shop was busy?"

"Yeah, mate, too right. Rushed off me feet."

So far, so good. "And when the attempted robbery took place, it was at the end of a tiring day?"

"Yeah, too right, mate, I was absolutely knackered!"

"And when this man came in, dressed as Santa Claus, he came straight up to the till?"

"Yeah, too right, mate."

"And before you could draw breath, he was demanding money from you?"

"Yeah, that's right."

"And almost immediately, you grabbed a baseball bat and swung it at him?"

"Yeah."

"And then he ran off?"

"Yeah."

"So you had the man in your sights for no more than a few seconds?"

Sam's eyes narrowed. He may be a fool, but he wasn't a complete fool, and he could see what was coming. "Long enough to recognise him if I saw him again, mate."

Damn, thought Toby, wrong answer, but he shouldn't expect everything to go his way. Time to try a different approach. "As a rough estimate, how many men dressed as Santa Claus were operating in your area that night?"

"Can't say for sure, a dozen or more, maybe, but I know most of them by sight. They're always hanging around, day and night, and," he added gratuitously, "the robber wasn't one of them."

Use that to your advantage, muttered Toby. "So you'd never seen the robber before, is that what you're saying?"

Sam realised, too late, that he'd walked into that one, but had to agree.

"And the complete stranger who attempted to rob you was dressed in a traditional Santa outfit?"

"Yeah, but…"

"So the only part of his face you could see were his eyes?"

"Yeah, and they were evil, know what I mean? I'm not likely to forget them in a hurry."

"Can you remember anything else about the man?"

"Yeah, his breath smelled of alcohol. He looked drunk to me."

"Finally, Mr. Wellard, were you ever asked to see if you could pick out the man on an identification parade?"

"No need to, mate, the police nicked him within minutes. They asked me if that was the man, and I identified him there and then"

"So you did, Mr. Wellard, but you identified the wrong man."

"No I didn't, mate, as God is my witness."

"Are you suggesting, Mr. Potts," Sourpuss interposed, "there should have been a formal identification parade, with ten or more Santas lined up, all dressed identically?"

"I am, my lord. Where identity is in issue, it is the defendant's right."

"That's a bit far fetched, isn't it, if they all look the same?"

"With respect, my lord, no. All high court judges dress identically, but they don't all look the same."

That remark could have gone either way, as Sourpuss glared at Toby. Then he smiled. "Point taken, Mr. Potts," and nodded encouragingly. "Do you have any further questions of the witness?"

"No thank you, my lord."

After lunch, Berger called the doctor to give evidence about the mark on the defendant's forearm. In his opinion, it was consistent with a glancing blow from a blunt weapon such as a baseball bat.

"And equally consistent with the sort of injury sustained from a heavy fall onto a hard surface," suggested Toby.

"I wouldn't say 'equally consistent', but I certainly couldn't rule it out." Fair enough.

"And when you examined the defendant, you found other marks and abrasions consistent with a fall onto the ground."

"That is correct, but the mark on the forearm stood out."

"Pause there," said Sourpuss, making a careful note.

Finally, 'Five' Watts was called to deal with the interview. His Christmas wish list had been edited out to avoid unnecessary embarrassment, otherwise the interview was uncontroversial. At last, and to Berger's evident satisfaction, the salami was produced and became Exhibit One.

"A few questions, Constable Watts," Toby began. "Can you confirm that, when arrested, there was no trace of alcohol on the defendant's breath?"

"As far as I'm aware, that's correct."

"So he was as sober as a....." Toby paused.

"As sober as a judge, is the expression you're looking for, Mr. Potts," Sourpuss interjected, "and as drunk as a lord."

"As your lordship pleases," replied Toby without the trace of a smile. Touché, as Sourpuss allowed himself a chuckle.

"Finally, please confirm that close to where the defendant was arrested, is a bus stop with services to Bermondsey."

"There's certainly a bus stop. I can't say if they go to Bermondsey."

"Thank you, no further questions."

"Very well. Members of the jury, we will now adjourn until ten thirty tomorrow," and so saying, Sourpuss rose and swept majestically from the court.

After a courtesy visit to George in the cells, Toby and Campbell went their separate ways. George had been decidedly upbeat, and well pleased with the way the case was going. Campbell added his vote of confidence, but there was still a long way to go.

Back in chambers, Toby reviewed his notes, and prepared for the next day. He'd call the defendant, of course, and hoped George would keep it simple. Sourpuss was the sort of judge who could turn nasty if rubbed up the wrong way, and Toby felt he'd managed to hold the line. He didn't want George undoing all his hard work. He made a mental note to speak to him in the morning and school him on content and presentation.

Toby also had witnesses up his sleeve, a doctor to say that the mark on George's forearm was consistent with a heavy fall against the kerb, and a ranking member of London Transport to deal with the Number Nine bus. Finally, the Adjutant-General of the Salvation Army Hostel in Bermondsey, to speak of George's gentle character and mild manner. That should be enough, God willing, but nothing was certain in trial by jury.

And what of the jury, and what were they making of the case? Toby had kept half an eye on them during the day, and following Nick Ridley's advice, had tried to identify the foreman, the man or woman to whom he should pitch his closing submissions. The four from Middle England were giving nothing away, and nobody had broken ranks. They smiled appropriately, nodded together, and made the occasional note as they exchanged glances together. Of the others, Toby noticed the polytechnic student making copious notes yet keeping her own counsel. At first blush, a rank outsider, but coming up fast on the rail. One to watch, and not just a pretty face.

He slept badly, awoke early, and arrived at court by nine. Avoiding Berger and the robing room, Toby made his way upstairs to the Bar Mess for a coffee and Danish pastry from last week's batch. He glanced fitfully through the latest edition of Counsel magazine, the in-house journal, with articles of doom and gloom from the front. Another coffee to steady his nerves, and then down to robe. Fortunately, Berger was nowhere to be seen, probably down in the CPS office receiving last minute instructions and a copy of his Advocate's Evaluation form.

It was now ten, Campbell had arrived, and together they went down to see George and give him his little pep talk. It was what Nick called the 'Punter Patrol', keeping the lay client happy and informed. George was up for it, and surprisingly calm.

Sourpuss had two applications, listed at the last minute, so instead of starting promptly at ten thirty, they were kept waiting until nearly eleven, which did nothing for Toby's nerves. Berger kept his distance, whining away to the CPS representative and 'Five' Watts, glancing occasionally in Toby's direction and grinning inanely.

At last, the usher called them into court, and the trial resumed.

"May it please your lordship," said Toby, opening the batting for the defence, "I shall now call the defendant to give evidence."

By Toby's standards at least, George performed well, and was as good as gold. He stuck to the script, answered Toby's questions, and gave a very good account of himself. He came over as the innocent victim of mistaken identification, and a decent, caring man. The jury seemed impressed, and even Sourpuss managed to control himself for the best part of an hour. Toby sat down, exhausted. Then it was Berger's turn.

"So as I understand your evidence," he began querulously, "you're the real Santa Claus, and the real Santa Claus doesn't go around robbing corner shops. Have I got it right?"

"Your perspicacity is a marvel to behold, Mr. Berger," replied George without a hint of sarcasm.

"Never mind the clever talk, what proof do you have?"

"Let me ask you a question, Mr. Berger. Christians and Jews alike believe in Almighty God, and after a blameless life, they will go to Heaven, correct?" Berger stood in a sullen silence. "The jury and I will take your silence as acquiescence. Now, I ask you, have you ever seen God? Have you ever seen Heaven? Do you know where it is? Do you believe in celestial bodies with wings?"

"What has this got to do with anything?" snapped Berger, losing patience and the argument.

"So why not a real Santa Claus, who lives in the North Pole, and who delivers presents to good children with the help of flying reindeer? Just because you never see them, doesn't mean they don't exist. Was it not our Saviour who said to Doubting Thomas, because thou hast seen me, thou hast believed: blessed are they that have not seen, and yet have believed?"

"Fascinating though this ecumenical discussion may be," interrupted Sourpuss, "I wonder where this is getting us, Mr. Berger, and does it really matter? The jury will have to decide whether the defendant attempted to rob Samuel Wellard of a sum of money, regardless of his beliefs or otherwise. Isn't that right?"

Berger was like a dog with a bone. "The defendant claims to be the real Santa Claus, my lord, and therefore not capable of a criminal act. I'm suggesting he's not what he claims to be."

"Quite so, I follow that, but your line of questioning is only relevant if you've inviting the jury to accept there is a real Santa Claus, and the defendant is an impostor. Is that what you're suggesting?"

"Absolutely not, my lord. Santa Claus is a figment of the imagination, nothing more."

There was an audible gasp from the jury, as Berger set about shattering all their illusions. This was not playing well.

"So I come back to my question, Mr. Berger," persisted Sourpuss. "If, according to you, there is no Santa, real or imagined, does it matter what the defendant believes?"

"Very well, my lord," he turned back to George, "let me ask you about the attempted robbery. The man was dressed as Santa Claus, and so were you, correct?"

"Correct."

"Still dressed as Santa Claus, you were arrested close to the scene, correct?"

"So it would appear."

"You had a salami in your pocket, which you used as an imitation firearm."

"If you'll forgive the pun, Mr. Berger, that's a load of baloney."

The pun went right over Berger's head, a case of one flew over the cuckoo's nest, as he whined on. "And minutes later, Mr. Wellard identified you as the robber."

"He did indeed, but the jury know that already."

"And he identified you as the robber because you **were** the robber."

"Wrong, and a clear case of mistaken identification."

"He was right, wasn't he?"

"No he wasn't."

"Yes he was, so why not admit it?"

"You and I both know he was wrong, Mr. Berger, so why should I admit to something I haven't done, just to please you?"

Berger sat down, looking decidedly miffed. Toby glanced over at the jury. On balance, he felt George had done well, but only time would tell.

The defence doctor and the ranking member of London Transport did their bit. Berger went through the motions, but there was little he could say.

The Adjutant-General ended on a high note, describing George in fulsome terms, a generous and noble man, and an example to one and all. Berger trotted out the 'real Santa' bit again, but the A-G was having none of it. Putting Berger firmly in his place, he quoted from the Book of Psalms: 'eyes have they, and see not, they have ears, and hear not'. In that respect, Berger had the hide of a rhinoceros and half the intelligence.

After lunch, Berger made his closing address, heavily laced with 'mem jury' this and 'mem jury' that, and then sat down.

Now it was Toby's turn to dazzle, cajole, charm, and persuade. Many a case was won or lost on final speeches, and Toby was determined to make this a memorable one for all the right reasons. He'd learned a number of basic principles listening to others more experienced. Never be flippant, as the jury, for the most part, took their public duty very seriously, so opening his speech by telling the one about the judge and the usher was doomed to failure. Never be boring, as it insults the jury's intelligence and risks losing their sympathy and goodwill. Always engage eye-to-eye contact, and make each and every juror feel important. Never read from a prepared text, as the jury expect counsel to have all the facts at his fingertips. And most important of all, never go on too long. Make the speech brief, to the point, leave them wanting more, and leave them with something ringing in their ears.

Making sure the jury were settled down and attentive before rising to his feet, Toby began with a review of the evidence, bringing the judge into the frame as much as possible. He reminded them of the obvious dangers of mistaken identification, and the failure of the police to conduct a parade. He praised Sam Wellard, as he'd gone down well with the jury in his down-to-earth, no nonsense approach. But he reminded them that a mistaken witness can nonetheless be an honest and convincing one, and his lordship would be giving them a careful direction.

"Finally, Ladies and Gentlemen," he concluded, in marked contrast to Berger's Mem jury approach, "you have heard much during the trial about the defendant's beliefs, and a lively discussion initiated by my learned friend Mr. Berger, for reasons best known to him." Nice little dig without being disrespectful. A number of the jury nodded in agreement. "Perhaps, in the context of this trial, it doesn't really matter, but there must be millions of children, of all ages, who, even as I speak, would be mortified to learn of Mr. Berger's dismissive attitude." More nodding, as Berger looked down at his papers. "As some of you will know, the Royal Mail handles over eight million letters every year addressed to Santa Claus, and it is a hard-nosed and insensitive man who lightly dismisses Santa as a figment of the imagination. Of course I adopt his lordship's remark, and it would be foolhardy of me not to do so," a few sympathetic smiles, "that we are here to decide if the defendant attempted to rob Mr. Wellard's corner shop, and not to decide if there really is a Santa Claus, and if this defendant really is Santa Claus." Toby paused for effect. "But in one respect I beg to differ with his lordship, and for this reason. You have heard much about the defendant, especially from the Adjutant-General of the Salvation Army, one of the finest charities in the country." Nice touch, as everybody loved the Salvation Army at Christmas time. "You have heard that for eight weeks of the year, the defendant is Santa Claus personified. He bounces children on his knee, listens patiently to their hopes and fears whilst they pull his beard and poke his stomach and make outrageous demands of him. You have heard that after a long day at Racey's department store, he makes his way home, or what he calls home, and after expenses, donates his entire salary to the Hostel." Another pause and a sip of water. "So if the prosecution be right, this good, virtuous and noble man, in a moment of total madness, abandons all the principles he holds so dear, and for what? A wodge of sweaty money!"

Nearly there. "If there is a real Santa Claus, holding dear all that we hold dear, and bringing happiness and laughter into our lives, then he is here with us today, sitting in the dock. Thank you for the care and attention you have brought to this case, and I invite you to find him not guilty as charged."

Toby sat down, drained of all emotion, but hoping he'd done enough.

"Thank you, Mr. Potts," said Sourpuss. "Members of the jury, the hour is upon us, and I will not tax your patience any longer. I shall sum up tomorrow morning at ten thirty."

"Court rise," intoned the usher. Tomorrow would be another day.

And so it was, and one that would remain with Toby for the rest of his professional life.

Sourpuss summed up fairly, directing the jury on the law and making the obvious points for the prosecution and defence. True to form, he warned them of the dangers of mistaken identification in difficult circumstances, late at night, with only a fleeting glimpse of the robber. It was, he observed, and Toby had to agree, a classic case for a jury to decide. It was eleven thirty three by the court clock when the jury retired to consider their verdict.

Now came the worst part, the interminable waiting, endless cups of coffee, pacing up and down outside court, wondering what the jury were discussing, how long would they be out, the dry throat, the clammy hands, and the churning in the stomach.

Toby and Campbell went down to the cells to see George, who was the calmest of them all.

"Whatever the verdict, Mr. Potts," he said softly, "I couldn't have asked for a better advocate, and I am most grateful to you, and Mr. Campbell, for all you've done."

"You're very kind, Mr. Spencer," replied Toby, "whilst there's life, there's hope."

"Spoken like a real Santa Claus," he beamed back.

"Now to more pressing matters. You appreciate that, in the event of a conviction, the judge has no option but to send you to prison. Of course I hope and pray it won't come to that, but you must be prepared for the worst."

"I appreciate what you're saying, and I hope I am strong enough to bear what the Almighty, in His infinite wisdom, has in store for me."

Toby smiled. Brave words. "Now I gather from the prison staff that your good friend the Adjutant-General has come to visit you, so we'll leave now, and see you back in court."

It was just after one when the tannoy crackled into life.

"No verdict will be taken in the case of Spencer until two fifteen."

Chance for a breath of fresh air as Toby and Campbell repaired to the Tyburn Tavern on Ludgate Hill for a pie and a pint. Toby prodded listlessly at his *plat du jour* and stuck to mineral water. He needed a clear head, whatever the outcome, but not so Campbell, who set about demolishing an enormous Guinness steak and kidney pudding, with chips, and a pint of the landlord's Old Peculier. How could he eat at a time like this, thought Toby, but kept his thoughts to himself. After all, Campbell may have earmarked Toby for his next big case, so best to keep in favour and smile ingratiatingly. Fortunately, with Campbell's mouth full most of the time, intelligent conversation was at a premium, and Toby preferred it that way.

They got back to court at ten past two, and Toby hurried to Court One for an update. He found the usher, deep in the sports section of his favourite tabloid.

"Any news?" Toby asked, trying to stay calm.

"As quiet as the grave, Mr. Potts," he replied, sucking his teeth, "I'll tannoy you when you're needed."

Toby's first instinct was to retire to the Bar Mess, slump into a chair and be alone with his thoughts, but that might appear rude, so he joined Campbell in the public cafeteria, bought them each a stewed coffee, and for the next hour, listened without hearing, to Campbell's life story. On any view, it was catatonically boring, and to make matters worse, the pie was beginning to repeat on him. On he droned, in between thinly disguised burps, about the wife and kids, and life in the fast lane with his new Vauxhall Vectra, which, on a long run, topped thirty six miles to the gallon. If it hadn't been for the incessant churning in his stomach, Toby would've dozed off well before the tannoy called them back to court. It was twenty past three.

As Toby walked into court, barely able to control his emotions, he spoke to the usher. "Verdict?"

"I 'aven't a clue, guv," he replied unhelpfully, "I simply do what I'm told." A rare breed indeed.

The jury filed back into court. Toby studied their faces for any indication, but there was none.

"All rise," intoned the ever-obedient usher, as Sourpuss entered, a tad flushed around the gills after an expansive lunch chased down with two or three glasses of medicinal port.

The court clerk rose and addressed him. "My lord, the jury have been deliberating for three hours and fifty seven minutes," Sourpuss nodded, feigning interest. "Let the defendant be upstanding." Then, turning to the jury, he continued, "will the foreman please stand." It was one of the honest, horny-handed sons of toil who rose, not Toby's first, second or third choice, but no matter. What counted was the verdict, not who delivered it.

"Mr. Foreman, please confine yourself to answering my next question either yes or no. Have the jury reached a verdict on which you are all agreed?"

"Yus." Toby's heart started pounding. "Well," he added, clearly overwhelmed by the ordeal, "eleven of us are all agreed, and one disagrees." The eleven all glared at the transvestite, sitting prominently in the front row, resolute of countenance and clutching his or her handbag for moral support.

"Pause there if you will, Mr. Foreman," snapped Sourpuss, shaking himself out of his post-prandial torpor. He was obviously dealing with the biggest idiot on the planet, so, speaking slowly and deliberately, he continued as if addressing a five year old at the back of the class. "I must assume from what you say that you are not all agreed. That being so, the law now permits me to accept a verdict on which at least ten of you are agreed. Is that clear, or do you wish me to repeat it?" There was an irritable note to his voice, as he smiled through gritted teeth.

After a moment's reflection, enlightenment broke across the foreman's countenance like a shaft of sunlight behind a bank of dark clouds. "No thank you, my lord," he replied confidently, "so can we now return our verdict?"

"No, you cannot!" Sourpuss's patience was being sorely taxed. "You must retire again and see if you can reach a unanimous verdict, that is," he added with emphasis, "a verdict on which all twelve of you are agreed. If that is not possible, then I can accept a verdict on which at least ten of you are agreed. Do I make myself clear? You can't sit in court and jabber away like a cartload of monkeys, you need to reach your verdict in the privacy of your retiring room."

The foreman reflected on the enormity of this statement, and was far from convinced. "As I see it, and from what your lordship is saying," he blundered on at his peril, "you want us to retire, then come back into court and return a verdict what eleven of us already agree, when we could do that now, so I don't see the point."

"Yeah," muttered somebody from the back row, keen to get back to the day job.

There were rumblings of discontent at the palace gates. Time to placate the mob with a few well-chosen words. Sourpuss rose to the occasion, or so he hoped.

"Members of the jury," he was at his most urbane, "the law is the law, however ridiculous it may seem to you, so you must retire, as directed, and when you have reached a verdict, let me know."

The jury retired, somewhat truculently, as directed, and before Toby had the chance to draw breath and calm his nerves, there was a loud knock. Reprising their role of a few minutes earlier, the jury filed back, and the court reconvened.

The clerk went into his routine again. "Members of the jury, have you reached a verdict on which at least ten of you are agreed?"

"Yus," replied the foreman, "we reached our verdict three hours ago."

"On the charge of attempted robbery, do you find the defendant guilty or not guilty?"

"Not guilty, my lord. In our hunanimous opinion, Santa is as innocent as the driven snow, and all eleven of us 'ave written letters to 'im, 'oping it's not too late, if you'll forgive the inconvenience," he added, turning to George and smiling.

"The sooner I leave, Mr. Foreman, the sooner I can attend to your each and every wish," replied Santa. "After all, there are only five days left before Christmas."

Sourpuss interrupted this mutual admiration society. "Mr. Spencer," he looked over to the dock, "It gives me great pleasure to inform you that you are free to go, and without a blemish on your impeccable character. I shall rise."

Just before he left court, the Honourable Mr. Justice Boniface handed an envelope to the usher, and nodded in the direction of the dock. "From the grandchildren," he whispered. Toby was just able to make out the writing: 'To Santa'.

As soon as Sourpuss had left, the court erupted, with the jury to a man applauding wildly and crowding round the dock, such was their delight. Even Berger managed a wintry smile. The only thing missing was Tiny Tim bleating: 'God bless us all, every one'.

For Toby, it was a moment to treasure, as George approached and gave him a big, warm, hug. Not a dry eye in court, and then it was time to go.

"My dear Mr. Potts," said George, "I must now take my leave, as there is work to be done. I would like to promise you something special for Christmas, but you have gifts beyond measure that even Santa cannot match. You have the love of a good woman," curious, thought Toby, as he'd never mentioned Susie, "and a warm and loving family. But above all, you also have the gifts of compassion, of caring for your fellow human beings, and real humanity. And fortunately for me," he added with a chuckle, "you also have the gift of the gab." Shaking Toby firmly by the hand, he continued, "lay to rest the demons of your self doubts, as many great triumphs lie ahead of you, and without you, justice and the search for truth will be the poorer for it. So fight on, we need you, we all need you."

A few well chosen words for Campbell, and then George took his leave.

Christmas Day dawned wet and windy, one of those days when the clouds scudded across the sky, threatening rain, as Toby awoke and made his way downstairs. It was a tradition in the Potts household, to hang stockings above the fireplace, together with a mince pie and brandy for Santa, and a carrot for Rudolf. Toby had hung up his stocking for as long as he could remember, marvelling at the goodies Santa had purchased for him at Marks and Spencer and other high street chain stores, the pack of three linen handkerchiefs, the socks, sweets, puzzles, games, fruit and nuts, all were part of the magic, and for him, the best part.

On this particular Christmas Day, Toby emptied the goodies from his stocking onto the carpet whilst his father poured Bucks Fizz, thrilling over the pack of three linen handkerchiefs, and as his mother was fond of saying, you can never have too many handkerchiefs. Then socks, sweets, and one of those puzzles where you move the pieces around to form a picture. Right at the bottom, and almost overlooked, was a small glass globe containing Santa on his sleigh, loaded with toys for all good children, and being pulled by Donner and Blitzen, and Dancer and Prancer, and Rudolf and the one whose name nobody could remember. When shaken, it snowed.

"How very thoughtful of you, mother," said Toby, kissing her on the forehead.

"How curious," she replied, taking it in her hand. "I wonder where that came from?"

After Evensong, the two families assembled for Christmas dinner. Susie was looking radiant, all were perfectly relaxed in each other's company, although much of the conversation was dominated by the forthcoming wedding and the heightened state of panic as each day succeeded the next. Toby and Susie took it all in their stride, simply happy to be together. The turkey was brought in with great ceremony, the lights dimmed and the candles lit, Toby said grace and the feast began.

They all heard it. It was after pudding, as they were settling back, congratulating the ladies on the magnificent dinner, and ready for family charades. It was a quiet, yet incessant, tapping on the dining room window.

"I wonder what that could be?" asked Molly Sandwell.

"Probably the copper beech," replied Toby's mother, "I've asked you more than once, George, to cut back the branches."

"You have indeed, my dear," replied George, "but as the copper beech is a good twenty feet from the house, I think it unlikely in the extreme. Perhaps learned counsel could take a view?" he added, nodding towards Toby.

Toby, rising from his seat, peered behind the curtains, just as the full moon appeared through a bank of clouds, and for a moment, he could have sworn he saw a familiar figure at the bottom of the drive, smiling and waving and calling out 'Ho! Ho! Ho!' It couldn't be, thought Toby to himself, it must be a figment of his imagination.

"Anything out there, Toby?" asked his father.

"Not that I could see. It must be the wind," and so saying, he raised his glass in a silent toast to Santa Claus.

Toby would never forget George Albert Spencer, his greatest triumph. Whatever life might throw at him, whatever the future might hold, for three days he strode a small corner on the stage of life, and strode it like a Colossus.

THE END

Or is it?

As Bootsy Farmer might well say, quoting Churchill:

This is not the end,
It is not even the beginning of the end,
But it is, perhaps, the end of the beginning.

Printed in the United Kingdom
by Lightning Source UK Ltd.
116314UKS00001B/307-348